Be Ready!

Acclaim for
Be Ready!

"The Spirit of God is moving throughout the world today in preparation for what God is going to do. Diane Frost has caught the vision of this in her book, Be Ready, *and I believe it will be of great interest to many people."*

—Evangelist Charles Thompson
Jesus Is Lord Ministries

"This book is put together with much prayer and heart-searching—with encouragement that many may come to know God. There is no question in my mind that if the thousands that read this book have an open heart, another great revival could start in this country."

—Pastor Billy C. Irions Jr.
Walk on Faith Ministries
pastor, Eagleville Baptist Church, Eagleville, Tennessee

"An entertaining read that will inspire you to share your faith and challenge you to grow in God."

—Reverend Casey Dunn
It Is Done Ministries

"Such joy and comfort abound from these pages. Rivers of abundant life and inspiration pour through Be Ready *and will fill your heart to overflowing. Diane's down-home style is truly like a breath of fresh air in these days.* Be Ready *is an oasis for weary travelers—you—to spare some time and drink of the refreshing rivers of life coming from Diane's pen."*

—Susan Dunn
It Is Done Ministries

"Right on target. This book will awaken the Christian to prepare, be alert, and lead the lost to salvation. The time is now! "Be Ready!"*

—Pastor Darrel Whaley
Kingdom Ministries Worship Center

Be Ready!

Diane Goodfellow Frost

PROVIDENCE HOUSE PUBLISHERS
Franklin, Tennessee

04   03   02   01   00   1   2   3   4   5

Library of Congress Catalog Card Number: 00-103837

ISBN: 1-57736-189-X

Cover design by Gary Bozeman

Cover photo by Diane Goodfellow Frost
Photo of author by Glenn Frost

PROVIDENCE HOUSE PUBLISHERS
238 Seaboard Lane • Franklin, Tennessee 37067
800-321-5692
www.providencehouse.com

Then we who are alive and remain shall be caught up together with them in the clouds to meet the Lord in the air. And thus we shall always be with the Lord.

1 Thessalonians 4:17 (NKJV)

I dedicate this to the *Father*, who created me

The *Son*, who saved me

And the *Holy Ghost*, who comforts me

CONTENTS

PREFACE

IN 1996 I SAW TWO VISIONS. ONE WAS KIMBERLY CLEANING THE Manhattan office building after working hours and the other was my country cousins visiting me in Manhattan. I knew by those two visions how the book was to evolve around them to bring the novel to life. God wanted it to take place in the present time, be a witnessing tool, and end with the rapture.

I kept trying to figure out how I would write a novel with a full-time job, which, counting travel time, took almost twelve hours out of my day. Not to mention I helped my husband with his business and we had five children at home. Then one morning about 2:30 A.M. I heard as clear as can be in that gentle voice, "Do what I told you to do." I knew what I had to do! I kept trying to figure out how I would have time and then I put paper in the typewriter and turned it on . . . there came *Be Ready*! The story poured from my fingertips and onto the paper. I learned that when God tells you to do something, He has already prepared the way! You must go ahead and get into your place, which for me was putting my fingers on the keyboard, and He led me to accomplish the task He asked me to do. I will never question or try to figure out God again. Just do what He asks you to do and know He will open all the doors and make ways where there are no ways!

> Behold, I do a new thing, now it shall spring forth; shall you not know it? I will even make a road in the wilderness and rivers in the desert (Isa. 43:19 NKJV).

There were times I felt I had failed Him by procrastination and other obstacles along the way. I knew there was an anointing on the book and even though I got rejection slip after rejection slip for about one year, I knew it would be published. None of them even bothered to read my manuscript. Several of my prayer partners would prophesy to me about the book and that it would all come to pass and be a great witness to many. I had written the book in my daughter's room while she was away at college. One morning at about 5:30 A.M. I walked past her room and I couldn't believe my eyes when I noticed the doorpost to her room was lit up with a bright whitish blue light. I blinked my eyes several times, but it was real. Another sign to me that God's hand was on the book. I felt peace and knew I must persevere.

> Therefore, since we are surrounded by such a great cloud of witnesses, let us throw off everything that hinders and the sin that so easily entangles, and Let us run with perseverance the race marked out for us (Heb. 12:1 NIV).

I knew God didn't create the book for it to just sit in my home. One day I turned on the TV and I heard a preacher say, "He is not only the author, He is the finisher" (Heb. 12:2). A short time later I carried it to Providence House Publishers and it was read for the first time and I was sent a contract.

The walk with God in completing the mission He gave me to do has been an awesome experience and a growing experience. I have learned that I need to depend totally on Him and keep my opinions out of it. I am telling you this so that you will know to go ahead with what God has told you to do. He has something for every one of us to do! If he hasn't told you what to do, seek Him and ask Him. What a blessing it is to do His work. It is the feeling of complete fulfillment! Remember you must walk in faith and not by sight. You must do what God tells you and not what everyone else tells you or thinks about it. After all He told you, not them! God has given you the strength, talent, and ability to finish what He has set before you. You must be patient and trust in Him. There is no greater joy than finishing what God had given you to do! My utmost desire is to hear these words when I appear before God . . .

> Well done, thou good and faithful servant: thou hast been faithful over a few things, I will make thee ruler over many things: enter thou into the joy of the Lord (Matt. 25:21 KJV).

ACKNOWLEDGMENTS

I WOULD LIKE TO THANK ALL THOSE WHO PRAYED FOR ME AND encouraged me to follow through with the vision God gave me in writing this book. Especially to my husband, Carl, who proofed *Be Ready!* over and over, never tiring from correcting and referencing the Scriptures. Also to our daughter, April Frost Bunn, who spent many hours reading and editing. Many of the characters in the book are real people in my life and they are the ones who prayed and cheered me on to the finish line. A special thank-you goes to Mary Bray Wheeler at Providence House who was the one who believed in this novel and knew it needed to be published. I want to thank It Is Done Ministry, Your Loss Is His Gain Ministry, and Jesus Is Lord Ministry for granting permission to use their names and ministries in this book. I extend my thanks to the Frost Brothers Quartet for granting permission to use their name in this book.

Above all, I want to thank God for choosing me and giving me the vision for *Be Ready!* and for all the signs and wonders along the way. Thank you God for guiding me to accomplish the task you gave me to glorify your Kingdom!

Be Ready!

Country Cousins
Visit New York City

LIGHTNING CRACKING ALL AROUND US AND THOUSANDS OF cars bumper to bumper. Ribbons of red lights from the heart of New York City flowing through a hundred arteries bound for a thousand destinations.

"I'm late!" I muttered frantically to myself, "I'm late for the arrival of my cousin, Jan, and her two daughters. Their plane arrived thirty minutes ago! They are probably frantic by now, especially in this city! Landing in this storm and thinking they are stranded, and of all places, New York City! They probably wish they were back in Rockvale, Tennessee, already! A place where there are no traffic lights, no traffic jams . . . just peace and quiet, except during the Fourth of July celebration or a ball game. Peace and quiet, boy, does that sound good—unbelievable really!"

Finally! The exit to the airport was in sight. So much for my mental visit to quaint little Rockvale. We were back to big city reality here. Oh no, all this traffic! "Get over Jack, I'm coming through," I yelled as I swerved in and out of traffic, as if they could hear me anyway. Oh, I was almost there! Boy, would it be good to get a touch of the past through Jan. I was so anxious to hear what was going on in that little village and see if it has changed or remained the same. It made me feel rather peaceful inside already just remembering what it was like back there all those years ago . . . Thank God, the storm was clearing!

"Hey, cuz!" I yelled. Jan turned and a beaming smile of relief and happiness rushed over her face. We hugged and laughed, yet I knew both of us were on the brink of tears. I backed up quickly and grabbed her arms and said, "Well, look at you! Rockvale must definitely be agreeing with you!" She laughed and said, "It sure looks like the big city life is for you."

I saw two beaming young faces and said, "Oh, my goodness, look at these two beautiful young ladies!"

"This is Amanda and this is Linda," Jan said as she put her arm around each one of her daughters. I gave both of them a big hug and they were almost as tall as me and only fourteen and fifteen!

"I just cannot believe both of you. We have waited too long for a visit!" I exclaimed. "The last time I saw you was twelve years ago when I flew in for a class reunion. My, how time flies and things change!" I avowed. "I should have known both of you wouldn't be little girls anymore! The last time I saw you Linda, you were real proud you could go to the bathroom by yourself. Amanda, you were sitting on the couch with your doll watching Sesame Street." They looked at each other and giggled.

"Well, we can visit at home. Let's get going! I want to apologize for being so late. I didn't mean to worry you. I guess you were already scared to death flying here in that terrible storm!" I exclaimed.

"Oh, it was horrible! We were saying our prayers," Jan stated. Her eyes were as big as half-dollars just telling me about it.

"We asked our angels to carry us in safely and they did!" Linda said.

"Mama, Linda and I had joined hands and had our heads bowed praying out loud. When we finished and looked up a stewardess was staring at us and she sort of smiled and walked on to the back. Then we noticed the people sitting around us were looking at us. They all quickly went back to what they were doing, reading their newspapers or books, or working on their laptops," Amanda explained.

"One man drank a mixed drink all down in one gulp and sighed! I don't know if they were glad someone was praying or thought we were weird!" declared Amanda. We were all laughing at this point.

"It doesn't make any difference. Our angels delivered us safely and I hope all those people knew that it was God's angels who brought us in!" professed Linda. "Sounds like a whole lot of religion was flying around up there too!" I remarked as I laughed. They gently smiled, but I laughed by myself.

"Mama, I forgot to tell you, the man sitting behind us, you know, the one in that really nice suit with the red tie?" questioned Amanda.

"Oh yeah, I know who you mean. He looked like a successful businessman to me," Jan said.

"Yeah, that's him. Well, when we were getting our luggage he came by me and said, 'Thanks for praying. I knew we were in trouble up there, but I didn't know what to do and I should have known! Thanks for not being ashamed to pray in public. I'm the one who should be ashamed. Your prayers, I believe, saved us and the three of you taught me a valuable lesson. I feel refreshed, I believe would be the word!' Mama, he had such a soft smile and tender look in his eyes. I believe it really touched him," admitted Linda.

Jan softly said, "Oh-h-h . . . see ya'll, some good came out of that storm after all!"

I looked at Jan's face and saw a fulfillment that I couldn't really explain. How do you have to feel inside to look like that on the outside? Well, it must have something to do with religion, I guess. Seems like they are happy about it. I never got that excited about it myself. . . . Is there something I missed?

"Stay here and I will get the car. By the way, always be aware of who is near you and what is going on around you," I instructed.

"Are you serious?" questioned Jan.

"Afraid so," I said. I walked to the parking lot and turned to observe them. Their heads were shifting about watching everyone close to them and what they were doing. It was rather amusing.

I got the car and pulled up to them, but they kept looking at the car instead of moving. "Wow! Mama, look at her car!" announced Linda.

"Golly!" laughed Jan.

"Man, a gold Jag!" squealed Amanda.

I got out and grabbed a bag and said, "Let's load up ladies, it is time to head to Manhattan." Off we went into the evening sun, streets still wet, but the sky clear and fresh. We were jabbering a mile a minute heading for the heart of the city. I yelled, "Quiet a minute!" as we began to cross the Queensboro Bridge. They all laughed and looked at me and I announced, "Welcome to New York City!" as they looked across the bridge at all the skyscrapers of Manhattan silhouetted in a golden sunset. That was a picture in itself! They were intrigued with the trillions of lights coming on everywhere and the excitement on every corner. They were like little kids in a candy store, except louder!

"Look at that man with the green spiked hair. It must be ten inches high!" yelled Amanda.

"That's nothing, look at all those store windows over there. What a huge store! Oh-h-h, would I love to shop there all day!" Linda sighed. I was really enjoying this! They could not stop staring and telling each other to look at what they were looking at and right now too! Yes, it is a city of constant motion, no matter what time of day or night!

We pulled into the parking garage of my apartment building, got the luggage, and caught an elevator. We stepped out on my floor and they loved the decorated hallways and beautiful pictures. "This way girls . . . we will look at the pictures when we are not carrying luggage," I sighed, rather short-winded, as they snickered.

"I feel like I am sinking down in this carpet," whispered Amanda.

I unlocked my door, turned and looked at them and announced, "Ladies, here is your home away from home this week," and slung the door open.

"Wow, look at this!" squealed Linda.

"Man oh man, this is fantastic!" exclaimed Amanda.

"Oh . . . golly!" laughed Jan.

The girls scurried in the door, sat their luggage down and ran over to the windows. I didn't want to miss one second of their excitement and the look on all their faces. "This is too much," Jan implied as she walked in and sat her bags down. I was chuckling at their reactions as I closed and locked the door behind us.

"Mama, look out the windows! Look at all the buildings and look, there are lights everywhere!" Linda said in amazement.

"Mama, look at the sky with all the purple and orange colors. It looks just like the poster of New York City at dusk," Amanda said.

All of a sudden all three of them got quiet and the wonderment of the skyline at dusk just overtook them. I could understand that. I had been looking out those windows for twenty years now, and it was still breathtaking.

"I ain't believing this!" whispered Jan.

"It is always clear and beautiful after a storm moves out this time of summer. You enjoy the view and I bet, I just bet you would like some cappuccino," I offered.

"Yes! The last few shopping trips to the mall Mom treated us to cappuccino. We love it!" said Amanda. "I bet you have one of those fancy machines too," she said as she and Linda dashed to the kitchen.

"What flavors do you have?" she asked.

"Well, I have French Vanilla, Swiss Mocha, Irish Creme, and . . . "

"Never mind, stop right there! Amanda and I want Swiss Mocha and Mama loves Irish Creme," Linda confirmed.

"Well then, we are in business," I stated. I was happy I had something they liked. Preparing for their visit, I had to kind of guess what the girls would like. I didn't want to ask Jan because she would have told me not to bother.

"Come on girls, sit over here on the sofas where we can view the city and enjoy our cappuccino," I said, carrying our drinks out on a serving tray.

"Oh, look at the cups. These are neat!" squealed Linda. They started commenting on their cups and looking them over so carefully, as not to dare spill one drop.

"I have collected cups from different places here in the city and thought you would enjoy looking at them," I said.

"Golly girls, don't you dare spill anything on these white sofas. It would never come out!" Jan stammered. "Diane, these sofas are beautiful! What color do you call this?" Jan asked as she smoothed her hand up and down the cushions.

"It is antique ivory. I love them and have had them forever," I answered. "I remember years ago when the furniture company sent the movers up here with them. That was a story in itself! They were so heavy and I was worried they would hit the door getting them in here. They finally got them in and set up and I was so proud of them. Do you know that I have never moved them?"

"Well, this is perfect the way they are. In this big U-shape you can sit to watch TV or see into the kitchen, but mainly you can view the city wherever you sit," Jan said.

I told her I had already bought pictures, pillows, and plants to set them off before they arrived. "I was so pleased when I finally got them and it all came together just like I planned," I smiled.

"I couldn't wait for Carl to come over to see them. He came in the door, looked at them, and told me he sure would not have picked that color. I couldn't believe it! After a couple of months he told me they looked pretty sharp after all. He said at first he couldn't get over anyone wanting huge white sofas taking up the whole center of a room," I laughed.

"You're still seeing Carl, aren't you?" Jan asked.

"Of course! We have grown old together. We can't throw each other out now!" I laughed.

"Well, I couldn't imagine you and Carl not together anyway," Jan stated.

"Are you ever going to marry him?" asked Amanda.

"Amanda!" Jan scolded.

Linda chimed in, "Why don't you marry him! Ya'll been seeing each other forever!"

"Good grief girls, you need to mind your own business!" Jan exclaimed. I was amused as well as taken back by the honesty of the girls. I couldn't blame them, after all how many people date for twenty years!

Jan was bracing her forehead with her hand and sheepishly looked over at me and whispered, "I'm so embarrassed."

"Oh, Jan! They just spoke what they thought," I said, trying to calm her.

"Well," stated Linda, "Are you ever going to marry him?" Amanda got tickled over her boldness.

"Girls, I ain't believing ya'll!" screamed Jan, still holding her forehead.

"Girls, I'll tell you what. He'll be here any minute. Why don't you two ask him!" I insisted, laughing inside at the look on their faces.

Jan laughed and gasped, "Don't you dare!"

The girls looked at Jan and I, back at each other with a mischievous grin, and shook their heads up and down. "Oh yeah, we are going to ask him," they reassured us.

"Now girls, just calm down," I instructed. "Don't ask him unless I can see the look on his face," I said. They smiled at each other and Jan had her head buried in her hands, shaking it back and forth. There was a knock at the door. The girls jumped and covered their mouths with their hands so Carl would not hear their laughter. "Ssshhhhh!" Jan and I both demanded, although we were tickled ourselves.

I tried to compose myself before I got to the door, but none of us could stop laughing. I looked out the peephole and saw Carl and began to unlock the door. In a feeble effort to regain some seriousness, I told them never to unlock the door unless they knew the person on the other side.

It wasn't helping, and I burst out laughing while I was talking to them. I had to wait a minute to calm down, then I turned and looked at them real serious as if to say, "OK! This is it! Get a grip!"

I opened the door and saw Carl's warm smile. He lightly kissed me on the lips as I stroked his face with my hand. "Come on in, sweetie. I have some ladies anxious to see you," I informed him. I heard the girls giggle lightly.

Jan was the first one he saw and he went over and hugged her, chuckled, and said, "How many years has it been, girl?"

Jan laughed and said, "Well, it's been about twelve years. Diane and I were talking about that a little while ago. You both flew in for Diane's class reunion and rented a car and came over."

"Carl, remember these two little girls?" Jan laughed as she pointed to Amanda and Linda. They stood closely together, still giggling.

Carl said, "Goodness sake, don't tell me they are the two little girls!" He put his arms around them, asked them how old they were, and told them how pretty they were.

"What do you two think of this big city anyway?" Carl asked.

"We love it!" the girls answered.

Jan said, "I love it so far and can't wait to see it, but whoo whee, I don't think this big city life would be for me!"

"Well, I can understand that! When I go to Amber Lake on the weekend I can hardly stand coming back to the city . . . I'm anxious to see Diane, but that is all," he corrected himself.

"Where is Amber Lake?" asked the girls.

"That is where my country house is. Well, I might as well just say my home. It is a good two-hour drive from here, but I'll be leaving the city in a matter of months anyway," Carl told them.

"What?" asked Jan. "What do you mean you are leaving the city?"

"I'm retiring. I've been around this city a bunch of years. I'm ready to go to Amber Lake and let my dog run around the lake and woods, fish, and watch the sun set over the lake. By the way, that is how it got its name. The whole lake is amber at sunset and it is a sight to behold! I will never tire from looking at it."

"Sounds beautiful!" exclaimed Jan.

"Wow! How much land do you have there?" asked Amanda.

"About ten acres," Carl replied.

"Do you have a cabin out there or a house?" asked Linda.

"I have a four bedroom home that sits near the lake," Carl answered.

"Oh, it must be wonderful out there!" Linda imagined.

"You all are more than welcome to come out this weekend. That is, if you have had your fill of the city," smirked Carl. "Diane is out there almost every weekend anyway, unless of course, she feels the urge to climb another step in that corporate ladder. That is when she works in that big old office building all weekend for weeks on end," he said boldly.

"What do you think of seeing the city tomorrow and Friday and then we could leave Saturday morning and mosey through the country-side to Amber Lake? We would be at Carl's by late afternoon Saturday and we could have dinner at sunset. He can grill us some steaks out by the lake and cook a big country breakfast Sunday morning for us," I suggested.

"Yes!" the girls quickly agreed to.

"You sure that isn't too much on you, Carl?" asked Jan.

"Are you kidding! If I can put up with Diane on the weekends, anything else is a cinch!" he kidded.

"Gee thanks!" I said as we all laughed. "Is late afternoon Saturday OK with you, Carl?"

"As far as I know now, but we will all talk about it Friday night over dinner," Carl said.

I grinned and asked, "Where are we going Friday night?"

Jan said, "Now Carl, you are doing too much! Saturday and Sunday is enough."

Carl said, "Let's go to Tavern on the Green. I have to work late Friday, so I'll meet you over there at eight o'clock. I have already made reservations."

"Well, I guess that is settled!" I confirmed, knowing he had made a great choice.

I put my arm around his shoulder and said, "A man of action, that's my Carl. I just want a big juicy steak Saturday and one of your fantastic omelets Sunday morning."

Carl looked at them and said, "I guess you know she is not bashful."

Jan laughed and said, "I knew that a long time ago!"

"Well, what is on the agenda the rest of this week?" Carl asked.

"I'm going to surprise them tomorrow, but we are definitely going to see the Statue of Liberty, the Empire State Building, and the Twin Towers this week," I answered. "Next time you see the movie *King Kong* you will recognize more things," I kidded.

"This city is fun and exciting, but watch your every move and be careful. This isn't Country Village USA," Carl declared to our guests.

"I'll teach them the ropes tomorrow," I quickly replied to him.

"You are going to teach them that in one day, huh?" he shot back.

"They'll learn fast," I piped up as all three of them looked back and forth at one another. "After all, remember all those many years ago? I know there was a country girl who hit the Big Apple and she survived . . . and rather well I would say," I affirmed. Carl and I looked each other over. Jan and the girls watched our every move.

"Of course she had an old country boy showing her the ropes," I said, grinning and pointing back at Carl. "Us country people are fast learners, right, girls?" I snapped.

"It's a different world out there now though!" Carl replied, as he smiled at Jan and the girls.

"So tomorrow is a surprise?" he asked, changing the subject.

"Yep, and we are very lucky because we are supposed to have very nice weather the rest of the week," I said.

"After that frightful plane ride, we deserve it," said Linda.

"We are still blessed, we could have had that all week!" piped Amanda.

"You all look so cozy. Let me bring out some refreshments, something light since it is so late," I said. I brought out a pitcher of iced tea I had bought, and a platter of light cheeses and wafers. We visited and talked about what we wanted to see and do. The girls kept looking out the windows, the city lights still enthralling them. I pointed out the window and said, "We'll be out there in the midst of it tomorrow. We better turn in soon. Tomorrow is a big day!" I chuckled.

Carl leaned over and kissed me goodnight. He told Jan and the girls he would see them Friday and to have fun. He looked at me and said he would call me in the morning. I walked him to the door and mused, "Be careful big man, it's a different world out there now!"

"You're the one who better be careful," he instructed, pointing his finger at me.

I locked the door behind him and looked at Linda and Amanda and said, "Gee, I think we would make a wonderful married couple! Why didn't you ask him when we were getting married?" They all laughed and Linda exclaimed, "Just you wait!" Amanda said, "When the time is right, we'll hit him with that question!"

We put the food up and they put all their things in the guest bedroom. They loved that room. I decorated it in Americana since I

11

wanted something to remind me of the countryside where I grew up. I had all my pictures on the wall of years gone by and wall shelves loaded with past memories.

The room was furnished with heavy oak furniture and a big country blue comforter lay on the bed with pillow shams and a dust ruffle to match. The head of the bed was loaded with needlepoint pillows of the American flag, kids fishing in a pond, country fields and all. It always took me back when I stepped in this room, and sometimes that was kind of fun, just reminiscing.

Amanda and Linda asked me if they could spend the night out on the big sofas because they wanted to fall asleep looking out over the skyline. "Jan, you got that big old bed all to yourself. Let them sleep out here. You know twenty years ago when I first got this place I slept on the floor the first month until I could buy these huge sofas. I still remember falling asleep looking out over the skyline. It was so beautiful and even though the bustle on the streets never stopped, it was serene up here. My, how the years have flown," I said rather melancholy.

"The closet has room and the bureau drawers are empty. Go ahead and put your things on the shelves in the bathroom too. We'll get up and get a fairly early start. I want to take you someplace for breakfast and we'll be gone the whole day," I told them.

"What's early?" they asked.

"We need to be out of here by eight o'clock," I said.

"Oh, that is not bad," they all agreed.

"Well, considering it is already midnight, it might be," I replied, grinning at them.

I laid sheets and pillows on the sofas and they got their gowns on. The girls came back out and Jan wanted all of us to say a prayer together.

"Well, sure," I said as we all formed a circle and joined hands.

As we bowed our heads, Jan softly spoke, "Dear Lord, thank you for getting us through that horrible storm. I praise you for the people who you touched and that they knew it was you that brought our plane in safely. I thank you for Diane and this trip. Keep your angels around us this week in all that we do and everywhere we go. Lord, lead us so we may be a testimony to glorify your name. In Jesus' name we pray, Amen."

We all hugged and turned in. I laid in my bed thinking how sweet it was of them to want to pray about everything. They all seemed so grateful. I don't know, they were just so serious about being thankful. I guess humble would be the word. Then the angels . . . I mean they really have no doubt angels will protect us! I've always heard that, but just took it with a grain of salt like most people. When they prayed they meant it.

I'd seen a lot of people pray and it was just like part of the program. It was either a short, "Dear Lord, thank you for . . . Amen," or a prayer by someone who was just trying to impress us with all of his many eloquent words. It sure wasn't that way with them! They acted like they were speaking to God and not like, "OK, let's say our bedtime prayers." Maybe I'd just seen the wrong way of praying all these years. Jan and the girls truly believed God would answer their prayers and their angels would actually protect them . . . interesting! Oh well, enough of that!

I began thinking about what all we would do this week. I had been all over the city a thousand times and couldn't wait to take them around tomorrow, like it was my first day here. I heard the girls whispering to each other. I couldn't wait to see their faces when I took them in Macy's. I wondered what it would have been like if I had had children?

The last time I saw them, they were so cute and into everything! I remember Jan looked so worn out! She was barefoot and wore jeans, an old T-shirt, no makeup, and had her hair pulled back, except for a few straggling strands. She couldn't go anywhere because she didn't have a sitter and Ray was working overtime. As if that wasn't enough, both of the girls had diarrhea too! I left there thinking this was not for me!

Now, it seems like I just turned around and they were young ladies and Jan's best friends! She brought those girls into the world and they would always be her children and she their mother . . . part of her. Things in life come and go, but being a mother and having a child never changes, no matter where they are or who they are. Looks like she sacrificed for a few years to have great treasures later. I wished I could call Carl, but it was too late now. I guess it's too late for a lot of things . . . I drifted off to sleep.

"Get up and get rolling!" I announced to Amanda and Linda. They were buried in those big sofas, hair tuffs sticking out here and there.

"Oh! Time to get up already!" they groaned.

"Girls, look out there. The morning sun is shining over the city. Isn't it beautiful? I see the sun set behind the city at evening and then see it cast its radiance over the city in the morning. You ought to see the lightning and storm clouds from up here!" I told them.

"You're not afraid of a storm?" questioned Amanda.

"Well, not really," I answered.

"What about the elevators going out? That would scare me to death!" exclaimed Linda.

"Yeah, would it fall to the bottom, or would you be stuck in there or what?" asked Amanda.

"You know, I never thought about it," I admitted, rather puzzled that I hadn't. "Girls, come on in here and get some good cold orange juice," I suggested. They came in the kitchen and drank their juice. "I have some bran muffins you can heat up in the microwave if you would like. I want you to save your appetites since I am taking you someplace special," I explained.

"Where are we going?" they asked with a note of enthusiasm.

"Diane, we could have just as well eaten right here," said Jan as she turned the corner in her robe with her hair all tied up in a huge terry towel.

I looked at her and snickered, "Jan, what happened? You couldn't find a towel big enough?"

The girls started giggling and Amanda said, "Mama, it looks like you have a bedspread around your head!"

"Is it a beach blanket?" asked Linda.

"Well, this is what I found in the closet," answered Jan.

"That was when I had a whim to buy those huge luxury towels. Now I could use them for a throw. Well, at least your hair should be fairly dry! Come on, Jan, get a cup of coffee," I offered. She sat down at the kitchen bar. "Don't lean forward or look down, the weight on your head will slam your face onto the countertop!" I kidded as we all laughed.

"Girls, get in the shower and get ready," she instructed as she sipped her coffee.

They finished their muffins and juice and both headed for the bedroom. I looked at Jan and said, "Jan, you must be proud of them. It must be wonderful to have two special daughters. You all seem like best friends!"

"Well, thank you," she smiled. "They are really good kids and we are together all the time. It isn't easy raising kids, especially this day and age. If it had not been for the Lord answering my prayers and giving me guidance, I don't even want to think what it would have been like!" she confirmed as she drank her coffee.

"Well, are you talking about it being so expensive to raise children nowadays?" I asked.

"No, there are so many drugs and evil things going on that you wouldn't believe it!" Jan informed me.

"Out in Rockvale?" I shrieked.

"It is not just Rockvale, it is everywhere. I don't care where you are! It is just the day and age we are living in," Jan acknowledged.

"That must be a nightmare! What do you do to protect them from all this?" I asked.

"You ask their guardian angels to watch over them and protect them" (Ps. 34:7). "We all have a guardian angel," stated Jan (Ps. 91:11–12).

"Mine is probably asking for overtime rates," I whispered to myself.

"Jan, whatever you are doing is working. I admire you for that," I told her as I walked over to the window, thinking about what she said about angels. "Look at the morning sun shining across the city," I said as I nodded my head to the grandeur of it all.

"Oh, that is awesome!" she whispered as she looked over the rows of skyscrapers welcoming the light of a new day.

"It is hard to imagine that all those skyscrapers have every floor loaded with people. It's unbelievable really! I should be used to it by now. This city still amazes me!" I admitted, shaking my head. "When you think about it, how does Manhattan hold up all those trillions of pounds of buildings? It is just sitting out here in the middle of the water. Can you imagine how much water New York City uses in just one day and we take it for granted. Think of how many toilets are flushed a day!" I stated.

Right at that moment we heard the toilet flush in the guest bath.

Jan and I burst out laughing. "Well, there is one for the count," Jan chuckled.

"And many more to follow with us drinking all this coffee and juice! Jan, help yourself to the muffins, just save your appetite for a big breakfast," I suggested. "I am going in there to call Carl. All I have to do is shower, slip on my clothes, and I will be ready," I said.

"What time does Carl go to work?" Jan asked.

"Well, he calls his own shots pretty well, but he likes to be there by eight o'clock. He is going in a little later this morning. Let me catch him because right now he is reading the morning paper and sitting by the phone," I said.

"OK, I'll get ready," Jan replied.

"Wear something comfortable, Jan. We'll be running all over the place," I said leaving the room.

"All right," Jan replied.

I went into my room and closed the door, sat my coffee on my desk and called Carl.

"Hello," answered Carl.

"How you doing, sweetie?" I asked.

"Pretty good. How are all of you doing today?" he asked.

"Well, we are all doing fine. We're getting ready for a big day in the city," I answered.

"I thought you had that every day," he joked.

"Well, this will be a fun day, not a stress day!" I exclaimed.

"Are you sure?" Carl kidded, knowing shopping for hours would be a nightmare for him.

"It will be great! Jan and the girls wanted to pray last night and we all gathered in a circle and prayed for our angels to be around us in all we do and everywhere we go. Now, you know everything will be just perfect and nothing can happen to us," I kidded with a smirk of sarcasm.

Carl paused and then quietly said, "Well, there is surely nothing wrong with praying for something."

"Well, I know that, but I don't understand praying for everything (1 Thess. 5:17–18). After all, I made it all these years by my own strength and determination and you know I haven't done bad at all!" I professed with emphasis on "at all."

Carl replied back quickly but softly, "Yes, but who knows what your life would be like now if you had been praying about it" (Phil. 4:6).

I sat there, rather uncomfortable, and snapped back, "Well, there is nothing I could do to change it if I wanted to."

"Well, today is a new day and one you are blessed to have in case you didn't know," he informed me.

"Don't you start getting religious on me too," I instructed him. "And another thing, you never talked to me like this before. Have you been going to church or something and haven't told me? Is it a guilt complex or what?" I questioned.

"No, none of that. You better get on with your day. They are probably ready," he softly said, disregarding my harsh words (Prov. 15:1).

Calming my tone, I replied back, "I'll call you tonight. I'm excited about taking them shopping. I can hardly wait to see their faces when they go in Macy's!" I told him.

"I'm glad it is you going, and not me!" he stated.

"I know that! Good grief, I wonder who buys your underwear the way you hate to shop! By the way, who does buy your underwear, Carl? It certainly isn't me!" I mischievously asked, wishing I could see his reaction.

"Goodbye!" he announced and hung up. I chuckled as I put the phone down.

I walked out in the living room and Jan was sitting in the recliner in front of the TV, which was Carl's spot when he was here. I noticed she was reading her Bible. I quietly walked over to her and she didn't even look up. She just kept reading.

"What are you doing, Jan?" I asked.

She smiled. "Now seems like a good devotion time."

"Do you read the Bible everyday?" I asked.

"Yes! The Word is a lamp to my feet and a light for my path and I need that everyday" (Ps. 119:105). "By the way, the girls and I are ready and they got the bed made and the room all straightened up. They're in there looking at your yearbooks. They found a picture of me when I was in the first grade with my hair in pigtails and my two front teeth missing," she laughed.

I chuckled and said, "I would have been in about the seventh grade then." I paused and whispered, "Golly, Jan, do you know that was thirty-nine years ago! Over half a lifetime ago! I guess we are pretty lucky, Jan. We are in great health and still absolutely beautiful!" I emphasized, closing my eyes, strutting about and stroking my hair.

Jan laughed and said, "Yes, we are both blessed in many ways" (John 1:16).

"Jan, Carl just told me I was 'blessed' a few minutes ago," I said as I put my hands in the air and curled my fingers as if to put "blessed" in quotes.

"Well, you are!" exclaimed Jan. "Just look how healthy you are, not to mention successful! You feel like going and doing anything and have the money to do it. You have been doing that for years and years and are fortunate enough to still be able to. If nothing else, Carl is a blessing. He is a wonderful man! He loves you and would do anything for you," she stated with great emphasize on "anything." "You should be praising God everyday for everything!" she professed.

"Well, thank you, Jan. You saying that makes me realize how much I have taken for granted. I guess that is what Carl was trying to tell me this morning," I said, while reflecting on how "blessed" I really was. "Well, what about you! You are healthy, happy and have a devoted husband and wonderful children! I haven't seen Ray for years and have never seen Michael. Michael looks like a doll by his pictures. You are at peace and most people don't have that. You are definitely 'blessed' (Ps. 32:1–2). Now you have me saying that word!" I joked as Jan chuckled.

"When I call Carl tonight, I'm going to tell him how blessed our day was. There is one thing though. I need a facelift and then everything would be perfect!" I said, pulling my face and neck back, as I looked in the mirror, joking around.

"Good grief! OK then! I want to get in shape and loose some weight!" Jan admitted as she got up out of the chair and started hitting her back end and thighs. I started laughing at her.

"What in the world is going on in here?" Amanda asked in amazement as her and Linda walked around the corner.

"Golly, mama is beating her hind end and legs and Diane is pulling her face and neck back. Do we have to keep an eye on you two all the time?" Linda questioned, her eyes as big as half-dollars.

We all were tickled by then, and the girls were shaking their heads at us. Jan and I told the girls what we had been talking about and how we had a few things we would like to change about our looks. We all agreed that we needed to do the best we could to look nice and stay healthy. Jan said our bodies are temples of God and we must care for it in all ways (1 Cor. 6:19–20). We also agreed we need to be content with what we have (Phil. 4:11–13). Then we got our fanny packs on and I opened the door and announced, "We're off to the big bad city, ladies," and out we went.

"Good morning, Miss Danay. Taxi?" asked Gilbert, our doorman and security guard.

"Please. How are you today, Gilbert?" I asked.

"Just fine, Miss Danay. Who are these lovely ladies with you today?" asked Gilbert, with his usual big smile.

"Well, this is my cousin Jan and her two daughters Amanda and Linda. We haven't seen each other for twelve years," I told him.

"It is good to see you out having a day of fun," he informed me as he kept looking down the street for a taxi. He pointed to me and told them,

"I've known this lady a long time and she leaves for that big office building over there, the one with all that silver glass, early in the morning and stays until dark. Now is that any kind of life for a beautiful lady?" he laughed.

"No, she needs to relax and enjoy life a little," teased Jan.

Gilbert hailed a taxi and as it was pulling over he informed them, "Now every once in a while, this tall, handsome businessman by the name of Carl will come here and whisk her away." He just chuckled as we all got in and he closed the door and waved bye as we sped off.

"The Ritz hotel," I instructed the driver.

"The Ritz hotel!" the girls whispered to each other with excitement. "Golly, who knows!" Jan said, as she laughed and shook her head. We drove down the street and Jan and the girls were looking everywhere, taking in the sights on the streets. They were commenting on all the tall buildings and how wide the sidewalks were, so on and so forth. It made me realize I had become so used to everything, I didn't even notice the things they noticed anymore. It tickled me to hear them comment on things. They were all talking a mile a minute. "Look at all these skyscrapers," squealed Linda.

"Our motto is 'Ever Upward' and now you can truly believe it!" I professed.

We pulled in front of the Ritz hotel and a doorman opened the door for them while I paid the taxi driver. Then I got out and we walked inside and they loved it. They were telling each other to look at this and that as we walked around. We went into one of my favorite restaurants and the maitre d' asked how many there were in our party. "Four, and we would like a window seat please," I answered.

Our waitress gave us our menus and I said, "The omelets here are great, if you like omelets. You all get whatever you want."

"Boy, you would sure have to have a lot of money to live here!" Amanda declared.

"I can't even imagine! I wouldn't even get to eat breakfast!" Linda said, never taking here eyes off the menu.

"At home, all of us could eat breakfast for what this one item costs! Imagine what dinner would cost if these are the breakfast prices!" Jan shrieked. We all giggled to ourselves.

"They have every kind of breakfast drink and cappuccino," I told them.

"We had that at your place. I will just settle for water," Jan said.

We ordered omelets and drank water. They got a big kick out of the people who came in. The gentleman who sat near us ordered gourmet coffee, a two-minute egg, and an exquisite French pastry.

"We need a place like this in Rockvale," Amanda suggested. We all chuckled.

"Yeah, right! No one would go to it. Who could afford it?" questioned Jan.

"And do away with country ham, redeye gravy, eggs and biscuits? Boy, I remember that! We didn't have country ham all the time, but we always did on special occasions and during our Christmas break," I said.

We finished eating breakfast and then we looked around the hotel. "I haven't been down here for a while. Carl and I used to come here at least once a month for brunch. He is out at the lake almost every weekend now. He is ready to leave the city," I said, looking around the fabulous hotel, remembering all the times we used to come here. "We were out on the town constantly, especially on the weekends and then we would be out from dusk 'til dawn," I said, fondly reminiscing.

"Do you miss going all the time now?" asked Linda.

"You know, I really don't miss running everywhere. I look back and I love all the times we went and wouldn't give it up for anything, but I wouldn't want to do it again either!" I smiled. "I am very happy when I am out at the lake with Carl. I have to work some weekends and when I do, I put in at least twelve hour days. He just stays cooped up in his apartment all day until we eat a late dinner. I would much rather he be at the lake enjoying the outdoors."

"Let's go girls!" I instructed. "Day one—en route to stop two." We piled into another taxi and went on to the next place.

"Stop one was wonderful! Where are we going next?" asked Amanda. We all laughed.

"I think you will like this next stop!" I stressed. They looked at each other, giggling. We pulled up in front of Macy's Department Store. "Time to go shopping, girls!" I announced. I paid the taxi and we all bailed out and into Macy's we went.

We decided to stop and look on every floor. Absolutely beautiful furniture, sports equipment galore, jewelry, and the latest clothing by the acres, literally. We all flipped over the bedding and bath departments. There were room displays in every style and color imaginable.

"Mama, Amanda and I can get you this whole bedding set with curtains and pillows to match for only $1,200," Linda said as they both stood in amazement.

"Go for it girls! That fantastic sale will go off tomorrow," I kidded, looking serious.

"This is on sale?" yelled Jan, her eyes bulging and her lip curled. "I wouldn't sleep on it if I ever paid that much for something!"

"Every time the sun came out, you would be a nervous wreck thinking it was fading your curtains," I joked. We all agreed. We were having a ball looking at everything and especially the prices, which were very reasonable to extravagant. The furniture section was tremendous.

"This store is bigger than our farm!" squealed Amanda. We all broke up over that comment.

They sat in living room displays and imagined how they would look in their own living room. Amanda and Linda found one black leather sectional which would fit in only a one thousand square foot living room—minimum. "Mama, this is as much as some people pay for a new car!" gasped Amanda.

Jan had to run over and look for herself. She stared back at me in amazement and shouted, "I don't believe this!"

"Well, it's all leather and it is black leather . . . jazzy, jazzy, jazzy!" I whispered.

"Diane, you're crazy!" said Amanda as we all giggled again.

"I wonder how many cowhides it took to make this sectional alone?" questioned Linda.

"I don't know, but I think the State of Texas supplied it," I added.

We moved to dinnerware. There had to be every pattern that anyone could imagine and some prices they couldn't imagine! The glassware was beautiful! "If I had money I would go crazy!" insinuated Linda.

"If all these beautiful things are here, can you imagine what heaven is like!" Jan smiled (Rev. 21:9–27).

Linda put her arm around Jan and Amanda and said, "One day we'll know, and we'll all enjoy it together forever and ever" (Rom. 6:20–23).

"Mama, I want to show you the pattern I want you and Daddy to buy for me when I get married," Amanda said as she pointed to a beautiful pattern. It was covered with rose and cream peonies edged in gold and was set with crystal stemware in rose.

We looked at the price and Linda said, "Mama, start saving your paychecks now!"

"I never would want to pay this much for something I could drop and break!" I said shaking my head. "Matter of fact, I'm getting nervous in here. I feel a sneeze coming on. I want to take you girls somewhere you would really like!" I grinned.

We took the elevator to the junior department and the door opened and I said, "Go git 'em, girls. Let's look and try on something." They looked back at their mother and didn't know if they should, but they were dying to. "Come on, let's see how this stuff looks off the hanger and on you," I encouraged. Jan and I sat on an overstuffed couch made out of heavy denim with pockets, silver studs and all. It was really neat and comfortable. "Jan, do you think we have walked nine miles or ten?" I asked her, looking rather serious.

"I would say eleven!" she sighed and we both chuckled.

About that time Linda came around the corner sporting a denim jacket with "New York City" embroidered across the back and all kinds of silver studs and unique trimming. "Oh, Linda, that is so cute on you!" whispered Jan.

"Mama, I love this!" Linda whispered back, turning and looking in the mirror at herself.

"Don't sit down on this couch, we will never find you," I laughed.

"How much is it?" Jan questioned.

"Don't worry about it, Linda. Do you like it?" I asked with my head resting on the back of the couch.

"I love it!" shouted Linda.

"Does it have a hat that goes with it?" I asked. Jan sighed, shook her head and chuckled.

"Well, yeah, but I didn't try it on," Linda said softly.

"Go get it and let's see how it looks with that jacket," I instructed. She turned as not to let me see her grinning.

Amanda popped in front of us decked out in a navy silk jacket and ball cap that matched with "New York City" embroidered on both in pale burgundy. "Oh, wow, does that look sharp on you!" I professed. Linda joined her in her denim hat and both of them stood there like fashion plates looking for our approval.

"You both look so cute!" Jan announced proudly.

"Are you sure that is what you both want?" I asked, still laid back on the couch. They meekly said, "Yeah, we love these, but . . ."

"I wanted to get you something. Let's go to the counter." The girls ran over and hugged me and thanked me. I paid for the merchandise and told the girls, "Gee, I'm proud of you. I thought you might have to try on fifty-seven things to find what you wanted."

"Now let's go to the women's department and see what damage your mama and I can do!" I asserted as I raced to that department.

"Diane, this is too much," Jan declared.

"That is exactly where I like to cruise, in the 'too much' lane! Let's go!" I announced.

The elevator doors opened to women's casuals. "Look out girls, your mama and I are hitting the racks!" I shouted as I grabbed Amanda and Linda's shoulders and parted a path for Jan and me.

"You two are worse than teenagers!" shrieked Linda.

"I want you to pick out a nice outfit or something, Jan," I told her.

"Now, Diane . . . ," she uttered.

"Jan, I want you to know this is a real pleasure for me. I rarely get to take any of my family shopping and I'm having a ball!" I stated, hoping she would understand how much I was enjoying myself. "Jan, look at this," I said, holding up a two-piece black slack outfit.

Jan and the girls came over and Amanda said, "Mama, go try it on. That would look good on you."

"You have been needing something like this," Linda said. Jan tried it on and came out and it looked great on her. Jan looked at herself in the mirror admiring the outfit.

"Do you like it, Jan?" I asked.

"Do I like it, I love it!" smiled Jan. "It is perfect for me. I either have church clothes or jeans and stuff like that."

"Is that what you want, or do you want to look around some more?" I asked.

"No, I love this and it is washable too," smiled Jan.

"Let's get it then," I said. We paid for it and looked around some more.

"Are you going to look at anything?" Linda asked me.

"No, I don't need anything, except lunch. How about all of you?" I asked. The vote was unanimous. Everybody was starving!

"Golly, it is two o'clock! No wonder we are starved to death!" Jan gasped.

"You won't be much longer. Not where we are going next," I informed them as we left the store. "Oh, I almost forgot. Let me get a picture of you holding up your shopping bags with the Macy's name on it," I suggested. We got the picture and I hailed a taxi. We all jumped in, ready to go to lunch!

I turned and said, "Do you all like Italian food?"

"Do we ever!" . . . "I love it!" . . . "Let's go now!" hailed a chorus from the back of the taxi.

"Angelo's, please," I told the driver.

"Oh boy, real Italian food ya'll!" squealed Amanda.

"I can hardly wait!" announced Jan and Linda. We wheeled through the city to Little Italy, gawking and taking in every sight. We got out at Angelo's and already the aroma oozing from every restaurant on Mulberry Street was fantastic! We were seated and they brought us a loaf of delicious bread, hot out of the oven. The first loaf was practically gone by the time it hit the table!

We all ordered something different so we could divide our order and each one of us could sample four different entrees. The atmosphere was inviting and the food was delicious. Halfway through our meal I leaned back and sighed, "The Italians would want us to sit back, relax, and thoroughly enjoy our meal. I would say that is exactly what we are doing!" and we all agreed.

We left there and walked through Little Italy for several hours. I bought some bread, salami, mozzarella, pepperoni . . . you name it.

"Girls, when we get home tonight, we'll have Little Italy with us, and we can eat and snack to our hearts delight!"

"That's fine with us!" they proclaimed. We found an interesting cafe and got some cappuccino and it was wonderful. We all agreed our feet were throbbing and it was time to head back.

"Amanda, hail us a taxi," I instructed, as we all stood on the sidewalk, bogged down with all our packages. She hailed a taxi immediately.

"They are going to stop real quick when they see a pretty young lady out there," I teased her. "Girls, we are going to take a longer way home. There is something I want to show you," I said.

"What is it?" Amanda said.

Jan chuckled and said, "I don't think I can walk another step."

"We are not even getting out of the taxi. You'll be able to see the sights from your window," I informed them.

"I just love looking around this city" sighed Linda.

"You may not love what you are going to see next," I said, on a serious note, shaking my head.

"Why not," inquired Jan. "Well, in this city you either make it or you don't. As you have already seen, it is about people and money. This country was built on people who came here determined to make it. Many of them did make it and built this country into what it is today—the greatest country in the world. I want to show you how far you can sink when you are not so lucky. It will make you realize how fortunate you are!" I said soberly, "Sometimes we all need a reality check—even me!"

We rambled through the city until we came to the Bowery. I asked the taxi driver to meander through the streets. "Make sure the doors are locked!" Amanda instructed once she saw this area.

"The greatest country in the world and we still have this! Some of these people were probably successful at one time. Who can imagine the stories they could tell you if they were able," I said with empathy.

"Oh, this is awful!" squealed Amanda.

"Wonder if they have any family?" asked Linda.

"I'm sure they do. Who knows what happened! Maybe their families don't even know where they are or if they are even alive," I sadly replied.

"What do they do in the winter?" asked Jan.

"Well, there are people who freeze to death on doorsteps and in the streets every year," I replied.

Gasps of disbelief wailed from their lips. The taxi driver never wavered in his emotions for he knew it was a fact as much as I did. "Somebody, a church or a mission needs to be helping these people!" Jan exclaimed.

"Jan, would you want to get out and go over in the middle of those people and be with them for the day?" I asked.

"No, but we are not supposed to be that way. All people are precious to God (Heb. 13:1–3). Christ was not afraid to touch anybody, even lepers (Matt. 8:1–3). That is what the meaning of love is all about, having love for your brother or sister, no matter who they are. God will surely bless those who do that. In the Bible, Jesus says 'when you have helped the least of these, you have helped Me'," Jan told all of us (Matt. 25:37–40).

"Even to have the desire in your heart to tackle a situation like that . . . well, that would have to be from God. Like myself, I pity them and would love to see them get help, but I don't want to do it," I truthfully admitted.

"Would you mind donating money to a cause that helps people like them?" asked Amanda.

"No, I would be willing to do that. I don't know who I would give it to, but I would be glad to give," I said.

"Everyone plays a different part and some play several, but every part is very important," Jan avowed.

"That is what the church is supposed to be all about, witnessing and helping people so they can help themselves (Matt. 28:19–20). If every church did what the word said, we wouldn't have this. It is easy to get love and kindness when you are a big shot and rich. When these people get love and kindness they know it is from the heart," confirmed Amanda.

"Some of them are so bitter I bet they would resent it. Look how young so many of them are! It is so sad! It would be interesting to see what could happen to these people if they were truly cared for and loved," I affirmed.

"All things are possible with God—all things!" said Jan (Matt. 19:26).

I said, "All things, that sure covers a lot of ground, like in 'all' the ground!"

The taxi driver, who had been eavesdropping, said, "Whew, it sure does at that, ma'am. Just think about it! It is hard to believe!"

"If God said it, that is exactly what He meant. That is why we don't see many miracles today. Most people don't take God at His Word. When He said all things, He meant all things are possible to him that believeth!" testified Jan (Mark 9:23).

"All right lady, I believe you!" the taxi driver assured her.

After a pause, Amanda asked him, "Do you really believe it?"

The taxi driver shrugged his shoulders and tossed his head and reluctantly said, "Well sure. I mean well, if the Bible says it and all. It's just gotta be true, yeah yeah . . . sure why not! We would all be better off to listen to Him. I know I would. I just hadn't thought about it for a long time to be honest with you. Maybe that is why things hadn't been going so good in my own life."

He thought for a moment and we were all studying him. Then he said, "You know, my mother has been wanting me to come to church with her for years." He shook his head in regret and said, "I mean I'm talking years now!" he informed us, his voice cracking a little.

He regained his composure and put on a new face and announced, "I'm going to surprise her! She tells me all the time she is praying for me to come to church with her." He slapped the steering wheel with his hand and announced, "Well, she is going to see all things are possible this Sunday!"

We all applauded immediately. I turned and saw the girls smiling and they both screamed, "All right!" and reached up and patted him on the shoulder. Jan laughed and shrieked, "Praise God!" I turned and saw her brush a tear away. I patted him on the shoulder and commended him for the decision he had made.

As we left the Bowery and headed home, he continued to talk. "My mother is eighty-three years old and has been praying for me since the day I was born. I always wanted her to be proud of me and I haven't done such a good job of that either," he said with sadness.

"She just wants you to be a loving son. She loves you whoever you are and whatever you are doing!" I told him. I couldn't believe the words that came from my mouth! I never even had children, how did I know her love for him? I somehow just felt it—and strongly!

"What she wants more than absolutely anything is for you to show her how much you love her! I know your mother's prayers have been answered," Jan stressed. "Do not let Satan put anything in your way of going to church with her this Sunday," Jan instructed, smiling, yet pointing a shaking finger at him (James 4:7).

He shook his head again, and whispered, "All the years I have wasted! All the times I didn't show up for her birthday and sometimes I didn't even stop by on Christmas because I didn't have the money for a gift."

"She didn't care about a gift! Her gift was seeing you," I told him.

"My father died when I was fourteen and she worked two jobs to keep us three kids fed," he told us.

"Do you have brothers and sisters?" I asked him.

"A brother and a sister," he answered.

"Where are they now?" I asked, my curiosity aroused.

"My sister married a stockbroker and they have two great kids. My brother is the oldest and when my father died from a heart attack he had the gumption to keep my father's dry cleaning business going."

"It stayed in the red for months, but he finally got a handle on it and made it a success. It was really a challenge, but he did it and then paid for my mother and father's house within five years. Mother still lives there with my brother, his wife, and three children," he informed us.

"Then there is me, a taxi driver. I don't even make enough to take out a lady, much less get married!" he wailed.

"So what! You are you and you have a steady job and you are healthy and well and it sounds like you have a wonderful family," I snapped. "Don't you remember what we just saw back there?" I questioned, hoping would realize how fortunate he was.

"I know, I know," he agreed. "You know I never get sick and I don't smoke or drink. I can't afford it!" he laughed. Then his face saddened and he remorsefully said, "You know, I can't believe I treated my mother the way I have. How can I ever make up for all my mistakes" (Ps. 34:14)?

"By starting today! Call her and tell her you are sorry and that you love her," Jan proposed.

"You can't erase the past, none of us can. Today is a new day, so make the most of it!" I told him.

He perked up and said, "The minute I get off my shift I'm going to call her, apologize and ask her to please forgive me (Prov. 28:13). Something could happen to her or to me, and those words would never be spoken!"

"You need to call her today, we never know what tomorrow may bring forth," Jan stressed (Prov. 27:1).

I could see that something had touched this man. Was I beginning to see God at work right in front of my eyes?

"Ladies, you are here!" the driver announced. We all were shocked.

"Good grief, I didn't even realize it!" I gasped. I looked up and saw his name and said, "Mike, it has been a great and eventful trip across town. One I will never forget. I'm going to call you in a few weeks and see how you and your mother are doing, if that is all right?" I asked, and to my own surprise. I very seldom talked to cab drivers!

"Oh sure thing! That would be great to hear from you guys again!" he quickly answered.

"My name is Diane Danay and these are my cousins, Jan, Amanda, and Linda. They are visiting here from Tennessee," I said as I shook his hand.

We all said bye and Jan and the girls said they would remember him and his mother in their prayers. I reached in and handed him a tip and told him to carry his mother a bouquet of fresh flowers Sunday. "Oh, thank you, Miss Danay! Thank all of you for everything!"

We all waved bye and Gilbert was still there and he opened the door for us and said, "Well, did you all buy the town out, ladies?" he laughed, as he shook his head. We told him we did and had sore feet to prove it!

We got on the elevator and Amanda said, "I guess Mike's mother's prayers all these years have suddenly been answered" (Acts 16:25–26).

"Well, if his mother has been praying for him for years, I'm sure it doesn't seem like suddenly!" I insinuated.

"Her faith is strong and she believed God would answer her prayers (Mark 11:24). She must be a wonderful woman," Jan proclaimed.

"Boy, she will be thrilled to see her son at church, won't she?" I responded as I looked at Jan and the girls.

"I would love to see the look on her face!" Linda confessed.

"Yeah, me too!" Amanda added.

We got off the elevator and went down the hall, hauling all the new clothes and Italian food. "I bet the neighbors wonder what all the rustling of paper is," I whispered. We chuckled at all the sacks we were carrying . . . crinkle, crackle, crinkle.

I unlocked my door and we all sighed and I uttered, "Whew! There is no place like home! Let's get all the food to the kitchen and I'll put it up, unless you are hungry."

Three wailing voices of, "No way!" . . . "Are you kidding?" . . . "Maybe in three hours!" replied back.

I laughed to myself and suggested, "Kick your shoes off, get comfortable and relax!" I put all the meat and cheese up and figured it would make an excellent snack later. I felt so good about Mike, the taxi driver! I had to admit, I couldn't wait to call him in a couple of weeks to see how everything went. I hoped he would follow through with his plans! With Jan, Amanda, and Linda faithfully praying for him, he would go to church. I knew it would come to pass!

I fixed a cup of coffee and walked over to the windows. It was so beautiful out! It would be a beautiful sunset tonight and we had time to enjoy it from beginning to end. I heard them in there chatting about the day and their new outfits with excitement in their voices. It made me happy they had enjoyed themselves so much.

I looked over the city and sipped my coffee. I thought this sure did beat being in the office in endless meetings and staring into a computer for hours on end. Talking to Mike and experiencing that was worth missing a day's work! That is something you cannot pay money to receive . . . I felt good down deep inside.

I looked down on the city streets and saw several taxis and wondered how many "Mikes" there were out there . . . how many needed an encouraging word (Heb. 6:10). I wondered if Jan and the girls were praying for him as he was telling his story . . . I wondered.

"Oh, it feels so-o-o-o good to kick off my shoes and put on shorts and a T-shirt!" Jan sighed as she entered the living room, looking like she was ready to lay back and relax. The girls were behind her, dressed the same and barefoot.

"Go get whatever you want to drink. We have plenty of time to enjoy the sunset tonight. As clear as it is, the melons and purples will be dramatic as they start to melt behind all those tall buildings. You only caught the tail end of it last night," I said. "Amanda, get your camera ready." We all sat down and as we relaxed and talked the sun began to settle in for the night. Amanda took several pictures of the sunset. All the lights of the city picked up the grandeur as dusk handed night the stage and stepped gracefully behind the closing curtain.

"Well, what was your favorite part of the day?" I asked, as we all laid back with our feet up, sipping our drinks. We all agreed we liked everything. It was all different and it was all "favorite." We also all agreed that the Bowery touched us and Mike made us realize how each of us can give encouragement and how it changes lives . . . and in turn how it blesses us (Matt. 5:3–12)!

Jan and I started reminiscing about days gone by. The girls were getting a kick out of us telling on one another. We would get to laughing and they couldn't help but laugh. I guess the laughing was contagious! "Girls, we have had some good times and it is scary to realize how fast the years have gone by. Make the most of your life. It goes awfully fast!" I informed them.

"Matter of fact, what is the most important thing you want to accomplish in your life?" I asked them on a serious note.

"The most important thing to do in life we have already done," Amanda said and Linda shook her head in agreement.

Immediately I was curious and said, "Well, you both seem to know the answer to that beyond a shadow of a doubt. What is it you have both done to accomplish life's most important thing at your age?"

I couldn't wait to hear their answer! "Accepting Jesus as our personal Lord and Saviour," Amanda stated (Mark 8:36).

Linda nodded her head and replied, "That's right!"

Jan looked at them and was pleased. You could see it on her face. I sat there and didn't quite understand this. They were definitely sold hook, line, and sinker in what they were saying.

Jan broke the long silence by meekly saying, "Diane, let me ask you something. Have you asked Jesus to come into your heart and be your Lord and Saviour?"

I looked at her and said, "Jan, when we went to church together we read our book about being called to be a Christian and then we were all confirmed. I know that Jesus died for us, paying the price for our sins, so that we may have life." Jan and the girls sat and looked at me, rather concerned.

"This is true, but when you were confirmed, did you ask Jesus into your heart? If you just took it as a study program and never made a decision or commitment for Jesus then all you accomplished was hanging a certificate on your wall," Jan informed me. We both looked at each other and she softly said, "I'm not trying to step on your toes, but remember, the truth will set you free" (John 8:32, 36). Her boldness had an impact on me. The girls were smiling as they listened to their mother, yet they had a seriousness about them.

"I found out there is more to it than just knowing who He is and what He came to do," Jan stated.

"You need to tell me then, because you lost me," I said, wondering what I had missed.

"Amanda, go get my Bible. It is sitting on the dresser," Jan instructed. "I had someone show me Scriptures and explain them to me and was lead to Christ about nine years ago. I was just like you and must have had that same look on my face. I couldn't understand what I had missed and felt like I was fine all those years, trying to live to be a good person," Jan confided (Eph. 2:8–9). Amanda handed Jan the Bible. "Let me show you the Scriptures I am talking about. Diane, do you have a Bible here?" she asked.

"No, I don't," I answered rather sheepishly.

"Girls, did either one of you bring your Bible?" Jan asked.

"I have mine," Amanda answered.

"Go get it, please, and give it to Diane so she can read along with me," said Jan, as she looked through her Bible. Amanda came back in the room with her Bible and gave it to me.

"Diane, look up John 14:6 and read what Jesus said," Jan instructed.

"'Jesus answered, "I am the way and the truth and the life. No one comes to the Father except through Me",'" I quoted.

"Now, we know that no one goes to the Father except through Him. Why would anyone not want to be able to come to God? That is why we need to know Jesus, to know Him in our heart! Without Him we are nothing and have nothing!" Jan taught.

"When we pray to God asking Him to forgive us of our sins and accept Jesus, He forgives us and we spend eternity in heaven with Jesus (1 John 1:9). Remember all those songs we used to sing in church. 'Nothing but the Blood,' . . . 'can wash away my sins, nothing but the blood of Jesus.' Then there was 'Power in the Blood,' . . . 'there is power, power, wonder working power in the precious blood of the Lamb',*" she sang.

We both smiled at each other, remembering those songs we used to sing back in the little country church ages ago. Now all of a sudden they were beginning to take on a new meaning after all these many years.

"God hates sin and all of us are sinners, all of us! Look in Romans 3:23. It says, 'For all have sinned and fall short of the glory of God'. Now look also in Romans 3:10. It says, 'As it is written: There is no one righteous, not even one.' So He is telling us in another verse that you cannot get to heaven by your good works because all have sinned. If we could have been good enough to get to heaven, Christ would have died in vain. He came to save every single person in the world, and He would have died just to save one single person. He is not waiting for you to do better today to make up for a sin committed yesterday, wear yourself out and fret and worry. There is no tally sheet. Satan just wants to make you think there is. Remember John 8:44, where Jesus tells us that Satan is a liar, and the father of it," Jan taught as I listened intently.

"You are a sinner, period. Christ is your only salvation and He has already paid the price. He is waiting on you to come to Him, because He loves you so much that He shed His blood and died for you (Rom. 5:8). Not one person has to go to hell. He loves every single person no matter how big his or her sin is. Remember, sin is sin. There is no little or big sin to Him," Jan confessed.

"Diane read Revelation 3:20," she instructed, whipping through the pages. I could only remember where Genesis and Revelation were.

I finally found it and quoted, "Here I am! I stand at the door and knock. If anyone hears my voice and opens the door, I will come in and eat with him, and he with me."

"See," said Jan, "it is our decision to come to Him. The gift of salvation through Jesus is for all people, any one of us! The most wonderful gift ever given! He not only gives us peace and promise here on earth, He is forever (Heb. 7:24–25). He will not push Himself on us, or punish us. We punish ourselves and send ourselves to hell. We do it ourselves!"

"You hear people say, 'God is a good God, he wouldn't send people to burn in hell forever.' They don't know the Bible! He has already provided the way to heaven," Jan preached to me. "Let's turn to Matthew 7:13–14," Jan directed, as we both flipped through the pages of our Bibles. "Diane, go ahead and read that one too," Jan said.

"Mama is going to have you read the whole Bible tonight," Amanda giggled.

"Yeah, one verse at a time," Linda insinuated, grinning at me.

"I found it. 'Enter through the narrow gate. For wide is the gate and broad is the road that leads to destruction, and many enter through it. But small is the gate and narrow the road that leads to life, and only a few find it.' Well, if it sounds so easy, why is it so difficult?" I asked.

"For the same reason I hadn't thought about it and you probably haven't . . . We think we are OK the way we are going. We think we are decent people, not paying any mind to whether we are saved or not! Think about it!" she paused.

"How many people of all the people you know have ever confessed to you that they were saved? How many have tried to lead you to Christ and talked to you like we are talking right now?" Jan asked me as I looked at her, studying her question in my own heart. "Now, how many talk about the stock market, the home they are buying or remodeling, their retirement, gossip, dirty jokes, you name it? People are too bound up in the worldly things and all their dreams and desires!" (1 John 2:15–17).

"Diane turn to John 3:16. You probably know that one by heart anyway," Jan said, flipping pages.

"Well, I remember the Sunday school teacher would always have us recite it in front of the church when we were little. I hate to tell you that I do not remember it," I sadly admitted.

"Go ahead and read it. It will come back to you," Jan said looking down and holding her finger on the verse.

I found it and quoted, "For God so loved the world that he gave His one and only Son, that whoever believes in Him shall not perish but have eternal life." This time it touched me like it never did before. I sat there and read it over to myself again. "I believe in Christ. I know He lived and He died for my sins," I professed.

"Satan knows that too," Jan immediately acclaimed. The girls giggled, as they were taking in every word. Jan chuckled and said, "Well, that is a fact! Just knowing about Him and making a decision for Him to come and live in your heart are two totally different things. Satan knows all about Christ and he knows the Bible. He knows exactly what to do to try to keep us from being saved. Satan tricks people into thinking they are not worthy of salvation. He lies, telling them they are sinners and that they are already condemned," Jan attested. "Christ came to save the world, not to condemn it (John 3:17–18). They are dumb enough to believe Satan because they do not know God's word!" she said (Hos. 4:6).

"Look up John 10:10," Jan advised. We each flipped through our Bibles. She waited until I found it. "Read that verse and see what Jesus said," Jan instructed.

I quoted, "'The thief comes only to steal and to kill and to destroy.'"

"Stop right there," Jan directed, raising up her hand. "See, that is exactly what he does. You won't realize to what extent until you really think about it. Most people don't. They just know that Satan is really bad news. He kills you by getting you sidetracked into aiming for all the things of the world instead of Jesus. Then if he can get you out of here without accepting Christ, he has you in hell forever!" testified Jan (Matt. 16:26).

"He destroys you with war, depression, confusion, horrible diseases, unforgiveness, debt, you name it!" Jan added.

"People say, 'Why did God let this happen' or 'I am mad at God!' In other words, they want to blame God when things don't go right," I said, surprising myself.

"Exactly right! Now read the rest of the verse," Jan exclaimed.

"'I have come that they may have life, and have it to the full,'" I quoted and looked at Jan. .

"Now, we see we can never blame God!" Jan proclaimed. "For instance, just look at one of the ten commandments. 'You shall have no other gods before me' (Exod. 20:3). Diane, think about some of the people you know. How many of them put their career, sports, material possessions, or their desires before God. They make their own gods and put all these types of things in front of Him. There is nothing wrong with these things I just mentioned, until you put them before God or make a god of them."

"Satan has put blinders on many people's eyes and he is laughing his head off. If you follow God, He will give you guidance, peace, joy, everything that is important and supply your needs! It is our choice who we follow, our choice!" she declared. "Let's look up James 1:17," Jan said.

"I'll read it!" I quickly offered. "You don't have to hit me over the head with your Bible. Well . . . maybe you do," I kidded and we all chuckled. "'Every good and perfect gift is from above, coming down from the Father of the heavenly lights, who does not change like shifting shadows,'" I quoted.

"Amen," Amanda and Linda both whispered.

"Whew, hallelujah," Jan said with excitement, raising her hand in the air and we laughed with joy over her exuberance.

"Girls, why don't you fix all of us a platter of those Italian cuts and bread we got today, if you don't mind. You can get one of my serving platters over there in the bottom of the hutch. Everything is already sliced," I said.

"Bring us two more big glasses of iced tea first," Jan said, laughing at her orders.

"Yes ma'am," saluted Linda as Amanda and her went into the kitchen. Jan and I were so excited about looking verses up and reading that we became absorbed by it. I had to admit I was really enjoying this.

I could see and feel Jan's sincere belief in what she was reading. I wondered how you got to that point. I had never felt what I saw her feel. What was it like to feel like that? It must be terrific! She always seemed so peaceful. Man, I didn't see that very often, except maybe at happy hour!

I knew now I had to put Him in front of everything else I always thought was so important (Matt. 6:33). I wondered if I was headed for hell. Well, I was not any different than most of the people I knew. Matter of fact, a kinder person in most aspects. Surely, not ALL the people I was thinking of were going to hell! Surely not!

"Remember Matthew 7:13–14, Diane. 'Enter through the narrow gate. For wide is the gate and broad is the road that leads to destruction, and many enter through it. But small is the gate and narrow the road that leads to life, and only a few find it'," she said, never changing her calm tone and never looking up from her Bible. Linda handed me my tea and I thanked her.

Was that God that gave her that verse, knowing what I was thinking? Maybe what I heard that preacher say on TV last Sunday is true. "We serve an awesome God," he said, as I flipped through the channels. Maybe I should have listened to that sermon!

Linda brought Jan her tea and Amanda brought the food. It looked great and smelled wonderful. Linda brought us dishes, each one a different festive color. "I enjoyed that when you gave us all different mugs last night, so I thought I would do this so it wouldn't be, you know, boring," she said, so serious.

I started giggling and said, "Heaven forbid, we don't want to be bored, especially with plates. You could have bought me some of those fifty dollar plates today so I wouldn't be bored."

"We wouldn't be bored, we would be too busy working the rest of our lives to pay for them!" proclaimed Amanda. We all chatted and kidded while we stuffed our faces.

The night drifted on, and I asked many questions and Jan and the girls would find me the Scripture to back the answers. It was refreshing to me and I was so curious. It was exciting and uplifting to learn about God's Word! I was amazed at how much they knew about the Bible!

"Golly, it is already midnight!" squealed Jan.

"Are you serious?" I asked.

"I was thinking it would be about ten o'clock or so. It doesn't make any difference, this is way more important!" she greatly emphasized.

"I have a lot of soul searching, funny I should use that phrase," I whispered to myself. Then I told Jan and the girls, "There is a lot I need to absorb from tonight. This has been so enlightening and important to me. I know that what we have talked about tonight has truly come from your heart. I want to feel what I see in all your faces, but I am not there yet. It will take me some time. Thanks for caring about me and sharing all this with me."

"We love you," whispered Jan as she reached over and hugged me, her voice cracking.

"I love all of you, too," I whispered.

We all got up from our comfy places on the sectional and the girls hugged me. Jan took a hold of my hand and said, "You need to know how important your decision for Christ is." She paused and bit her lip and took a deep breath. "You never know when your life will be over and we are not promised tomorrow. If you decide not to do anything, you have made a decision," Jan pleaded, looking me straight in the eye.

"I know," I confessed, understanding her intensity.

"We are cleaning up everything and putting the food away," Amanda informed us from the kitchen.

"Good girls!" I replied.

"What time should we be ready to go in the morning?" Jan asked.

"Oh, we need to go have coffee in the morning on Wall Street and see all the hustle and bustle over there," I suggested, rather nonchalant. The girls looked at each other and grinned.

"Wall Street!" Jan exclaimed, looking at the girls and smiling.

"Yeah, let's go see some more skyscrapers first. I want you to have a broad view of New York City, from the Bowery to Wall Street," I mused. "Girls, as soon as you roll out we are going to run around the corner to my favorite bakery, Peggy's, and load up on fresh bagels. How does that sound?" I asked.

"Great! We love bagels!" they both chirped.

"That will give your mom some quiet time to read her Bible," I said, smiling at Jan. "Well, let's turn in for the night and get some good sleep. I've had a great day and a great night!" I confessed. The girls and Jan all hugged me and thanked me for their clothes, the great food, and lots of fun. Jan and I walked to our rooms while the girls laid out on the couches to sleep, viewing the skyline again.

I laid in my bed, looking out over the city that never sleeps, and yet it was so quiet from up here. I felt safe, like nothing could touch me, but something had touched me deep inside my heart and soul. It stirred me, like something powerful, yet quiet, yearning, desiring peace. There was no peace in my soul. What is this restlessness in my being? Is it God? I did not understand this, yet I knew I must seek the answer (Jer. 29:13).

"I have been fine and satisfied with my life all these years . . . haven't I?" I thought. "Have I been running the race so long I only aimed at winning the prize at the finish line? What is the prize anyway, more money, more success, or what? The thought of that just left me cold all of a sudden. The real prize, the gift—it could only be eternity in heaven. I mean, that is the only thing that really counts when it is all said and done. I can't get caught up in this, it is time to go to sleep. I must get a hold on things, as I always have!"

I awoke, turned and looked out over the city. The morning sun was young and streaming across the buildings outside my window. Another beautiful day! I laid there and thought how fortunate I was to have good health, my career, my friends, my cousins who cared so much about me, and of course, Carl . . . "Great, I'll get to see him tonight!" I said to myself. "I better scoot out there and put some coffee on for Jan and I, then I'll get back in here and call Carl." I got up and fixed the coffee quietly, since the girls were still sound asleep. The smell of fresh brewed coffee would probably wake them. I fixed a cup, went to take my shower, hoping that by that time he would be up for sure. I really needed to talk to him!

"Carl, how you doing, sweetie?" I asked softly.
"OK," he said, on the tail end of a yawn.
"Reading your morning paper?" I asked.
"Yeah, seeing what's going on in the world," he said as if he were still browsing the pages.
"Carl, I need to ask you something."
"Yeah?"

"Religiously speaking, who do you consider as being someone who is 'lost' . . . not going to church or what?" I asked.

"No, if they are 'lost' they have never confessed Jesus Christ as their Lord and Saviour, and they don't believe in their heart that God raised Him from the dead," he said without hesitation (Rom. 10:9).

"Well, I was in church for years and took a complete study course about being called to be a Christian, was confirmed with a big church ceremony, received a beautiful certificate and all. Doesn't that mean the same thing?" I asked, needing reassurance.

"If you did not accept Jesus in your heart as your Lord and Saviour all you did was get a nice certificate to hang on your wall," he stated. This was sounding very familiar!

"Remember, knowing Him in your head gives you knowledge, knowing Him in your heart saves you! You could be a doctor of theology and still go to hell if you only let Jesus into your brain. Satan knows about God and Jesus for sure! Satan, who was named Lucifer, son of the morning, was cast out of heaven and into hell because of his pride and jealously of God (Isa. 14:12–15). Why do you think we must know the Word? Satan knows it so well he tricks us in our ignorance. God told His people that they are destroyed from lack of knowledge!" Carl informed me (Hos. 4:6). Wow! I was hearing a repeat of last night! God was trying to tell me something!

I sat there a minute, everything whirling in front of me and sighed, "Well, I guess I missed it somewhere! I have always tried to do as the church taught and I have tried to be a good person," I stammered. The minute I spoke those words I remembered the verses Jan quoted to me about how we think just being a good person will get us into heaven.

Carl continued, "Being a good person is all well and good, but you are not doing what the Word says to receive salvation. If you go to a church that does not preach exactly what the Word says, you need to hurry up and change churches! You have to do what Jesus told you to do. You had better start reading your Bible!" he prescribed.

"I don't have one," I admitted.

"Well then, you better get one," Carl instructed.

"I don't even know what kind to get. I was in a bookstore last week and for some strange reason I happened to go over to the Bible section. They had at least a hundred different sizes and kinds. I didn't know there were so many!" I declared.

"I'll go with you and help you pick one out," Carl said.

"Every one I read, I don't understand too well. You, Jan, and the girls don't seem to have any trouble understanding it or explaining it. Why is it so hard for me to understand?" I asked.

"I will pick out one you will understand. It is nice to have one with a concordance, but whatever kind of Bible you have, God will give you the spirit of wisdom, which will reveal things to you beyond your own understanding. He wants you to know Him (Eph. 1:17)! Just ask Him and you will receive wisdom. All you have to do is open your Bible, read and believe His Word and do not ever doubt it (James 1:5–7). Satan will try to discourage you and confuse you, but don't let him fool you. He does not want you learning about the gift of salvation and all the wonderful promises and blessings we have right here on earth," Carl avowed.

Still overwhelmed by the realization of an awakening of my spiritual life, I said, "All this time I thought being a good person made all the difference. Doesn't being a good person account for anything? I mean I'm not perfect, but I'm kind to people and giving and all that," I pleaded.

"You cannot get to heaven by your good works and Jesus said that 'no one comes to the Father except through Me'," Carl stated.

Defensively, I thought, "How do all of them know that, and I know nothing? It is my own fault! I never wanted to go to church or learn about God. They love going to church and enjoy studying their Bible. All I do is go to work, see Carl, and as they say, 'get caught up in the world'! Boy, do I ever!"

"'Put your good works or treasures in heaven, where they count for all eternity' (Matt. 6:20–21). We will be rewarded for what we have done (Rev. 22:12). If you never get saved, you can take all your good works to hell," Carl proclaimed.

"Boy, sounds like I am no different than all the murderers, thieves, liars, you name it! So much for trying to be a good person! I guess it doesn't make any difference," I stammered, my insides in knots.

"All people are sinners and only the blood of Jesus covers your sins. A little sin is no different in God's eyes than a huge sin. God cannot tolerate any sin, regardless of the size or amount," he acknowledged, pausing a moment.

"If a murderer asked for forgiveness and accepted Christ in his heart and you tried to be Miss Goody Two Shoes and never repented of your sins or accepted Jesus, he would go to heaven and you would go to hell," Carl confirmed.

"What! That isn't fair!" I shouted.

"He didn't say anything in the Bible about being fair, because His grace and mercy are sufficient, and believe me, that surpasses 'fair' by a long shot (Eph. 2:8). It is plain and simple. The greatest gift is free and readily available. Everyone is a sinner, everyone! It is so easy that we let Satan make it difficult. Satan wants us in hell, not heaven!" Carl exclaimed.

"Do you know how mad people get when you tell them in so many words they are going to hell?" I avenged.

"We are supposed to do what Jesus told us to do, and He told us to preach the good news," Carl pledged (Mark 16:15–16).

He stopped a minute as if to give me time for it to sink in. I took a deep breath and sighed. To confirm what he was saying, I said, "Living only by your good works doesn't send you to heaven. He has given each and every one the gift of salvation through His Son, Jesus Christ. All we have to do is accept it."

"Yes! Hold on a minute and let me look up something I said earlier."

He put the phone down and came back and said, "Here it is in Romans 10:9, 'That if you confess with your mouth, "Jesus is Lord," and believe in your heart that God raised him from the dead, you will be saved.' When you confess and believe in your heart, your name is written in the Lambs Book of Life and you will go to heaven," Carl informed me (Rev. 21:27).

I sat there shaking my head, silence on both ends of the phone. I remembered that verse from last night also. "So if I believe in God, live a wonderful life as a Christian and my name isn't in the book, I'll go to hell?" I asked, dismayed.

"Yes, you will, and another thing, you are not a Christian until you are born again," Carl said firmly (John 3:3).

I slammed my hand down on my desk in frustration and replied back, "Well, that is just great!" and I threw my head up to the heavens.

I finally stammered back, "All these years, Carl, and you are telling me this now," I declared. I paused to try to regain some composure, but the hurt didn't leave. "I guess you didn't care if I went to hell!" I blurted out with force, but not much volume. I sure didn't want Jan and the girls to hear me. They were busy taking their showers and getting ready, but this was quite a heated conversation!

I knew Carl was ashamed, but he came back with, "It is up to you to know God's word and find out what it says. You should know that!"

Something rose up inside of me and I pointed my finger up in the air and replied back to that remark with, "You know, as a kid in Sunday school, we used to quote a verse that said not to hide your light under a basket (Matt. 5:14–16). I'd say that you have definitely hid your light under a basket all these years!"

There was a pause and Carl meekly said, "You are right." Another long pause as I paced the room with the phone, walking off my anger, hurt, and disappointment in him and myself.

Finally I was able to say, "Well, I've got to go. I hope they haven't heard all this!" I stammered, and there was another pause.

"Are you going to the office today?" I asked, changing the subject.

"Yeah, I need to settle out some accounts, so I guess I will," he answered.

On a lighter note I said, "You might look out your window and see us running around down there on the streets."

"I'm sure I'll spot you right away," he joked back, happy I had gotten off of his case.

"Do we still have reservations for eight o'clock at Tavern on the Green?" I asked.

"Yes, we do," he answered.

"Oh, they'll love that. We will just meet you there. There is no need for you to pick us up. I'll take them through the park and yes, I know to be careful," I assured him. "After we eat, are you heading for the lake?" I asked.

"Yeah, I'm anxious to get out there, unpack and relax," he answered. I could tell he was looking forward to going to Amber Lake. "I'll go over to the Goodfellows and get Pepper and in the morning I'll let him run loose a while."

"It is nice you have good neighbors who watch him all week for you . . . of course, their name *is* Goodfellow," I snickered.

He never picked up on my little joke and replied, "Well, they enjoy him. Their grandsons stay out there with them since their daughter works in the city. She comes out and spends the weekends though," he stated.

"Now I'm beginning to see why you are going out there every weekend!" I stated, inquiringly so.

"No, that is not it at all!" he snapped back. "I like being away from this rat race and getting out in the woods and running with Pepper," he said.

"Gee, it's nice to know you have been replaced by a dog and hopefully, that is all!" I added, knowing I was aggravating him.

"You're getting way off track! You are the one who decides to work weekends. I would rather have you out there with me, but you call the shots," he implied.

I paused a minute, and said, "Sweetie, we'll see you tonight at eight o'clock. Be careful and I love you," I told him.

"I love you too," he said and then he hung up the phone. Boy, he must have really thought I was mad at him! He said "I love you too" instead of "me too." I couldn't remember when that had happened!

I slipped on my clothes and went out to see what they were all up to. Amanda and Linda were drinking some juice and looking out the windows. "Good morning, girls," I announced as I hugged each one of them. "I hope I haven't kept you waiting. I was in a long-winded conversation with Carl," I informed them.

"Oh, was he proposing?" mused Linda, looking out the corner of her eye, grinning, as Amanda giggled.

"Not exactly!" I muttered as I poured a cup of coffee. "Where is your mom?" I asked.

"She is getting ready," answered Amanda.

"Girls, let's run around the corner to Peggy's and load up on bagels! Go tell your mom where we are going and that we'll lock the door behind us," I said.

The girls and I went out and there was Gilbert. "Hey Gilbert, what kind of bagel do you want this morning?" I asked.

"Well, now that you mention it, I'm suddenly craving a big blueberry bagel," he answered through that delightful smile.

"Cream cheese?" I asked.

"Why not!" he answered back with a twist of his head.

"OK, you got it," I loudly affirmed.

The girls giggled. "You two are crazy," Amanda said as we quickly paced down the street and around the corner. I told them I had picked up blueberry bagels loaded with cream cheese for Gilbert ever since I lived here.

"Sometimes I just ask him what kind he wants to kid him, and he plays right along with the whole charade!" I laughed as I told them. "Oh, doesn't that smell wonderful," I sighed holding my nose up in the air sniffing.

"Boy, that would make you hungry if you weren't hungry," admitted Amanda.

"What a cute name, 'Peggy's Piddl'n!'" Linda announced, as we crossed the street to the bakery.

"A lady named Peggy owns it and runs it. She has opened at the crack of dawn for years on end," I informed them. We went in and there was Peggy bringing out another tray of freshly baked bagels. "Hey lady, how you doing today?" I asked vibrantly.

"Just wonderful! How are you do'n?" she beamed.

"Great," I said. I introduced Amanda and Linda to her.

She looked at them and said, "Diane and I have this meet'n about every morning. All these big business ladies around here are really good to me. Early Saturday and Sunday morning they run in here with no makeup and old jogg'n clothes. They are usually hid'n under a cap or hooded sweatshirt, and they don't want anybody to know who they are! Honey, I know them for who they really are, and they don't want me tell'n what they look like without all that paint'n and hair fix'n!" she told them. I started laughing at her and especially at the look on the girls' faces. Peggy started laughing at them too and winking at me.

I had known Peggy since I first moved here twenty years ago. She was always a bright spot in my morning. She would always make me laugh and I knew I could trust her if I needed someone to confide in. I never had, but I knew I could.

We had fun picking out goodies and I told the girls, "It's just simple things, like us just being together and picking out fresh bagels, that makes life fun." They were still staring at the glass case full of perfectly lined up bagels, but gave me a smiling glance, acknowledging my comment.

Peggy put all our bagels in a box for us and I said, "Peggy, give me a blueberry bagel packed full of cream cheese with two napkins in a little bag, please."

"I have Mr. Gilbert's little sack all ready," she teased, waving the bag in the air. "Girls," she whispered, "Mr. Gilbert needs two napkins because he gets that gushy cream cheese all over his face and those people who live in that highfalut'n apartment build'n don't like their doorman greet'n fancy friends and all with a cream cheese face. I've seen his cream cheese face and Jesus is the only one who wouldn't mind if He met him look'n like that. Do ya know what I mean?"

"So long, Peggy," I said, still laughing at her fanatics.

We walked back and gave Gilbert his little sack and went in the building. Amanda and Linda watched him through the door as he ate his first bite, and sure enough it gushed out on both sides of his face. He shook his head like he really enjoyed his first bite and grabbed for the next, still wearing the cream cheese. We jumped into the elevator, all of us laughing. "I hope he didn't see us! He does that every time he gets one of those bagels. I get him one just to watch the show out of the corner of my eye," I chuckled as I told the girls.

"Jan, it's us," I whispered as I unlocked the door so we wouldn't scare her to death. She was in the kitchen pouring herself a cup of coffee.

"I was hoping it was you! I didn't want to be startled and drop a whole pot of hot coffee on me or have to throw it on an intruder," she chuckled. We savored our way through those fresh bagels and drank some juice.

We got ready and out the door we went for the day, cameras loaded. Gilbert met us at the door and all the gushy evidence of cream cheese was wiped away. He hailed us a taxi and off we went. The girls were laughing, telling Jan about Gilbert. "Peggy has put a triple dose of cream cheese in his bagel for years just to keep the neighborhood in stitches," I told them, chuckling over the matter again.

Down Broadway, we scanned all the sights of the busy streets to Wall Street. We got out on Wall Street, found a restaurant, and grabbed a window seat. We all ordered cappuccino and enjoyed it as we watched the well-dressed business people scurry to and fro, briefcases in hand.

Jan and the girls were in awe of Wall Street, but as I looked at the fast pace outside the window, it reminded me of myself. I was just like them and that was OK, but I was beginning to realize I didn't want that anymore!

We left, hailed a taxi, and went to Battery Park. We got our tickets and caught the first ferry to see the Statue of Liberty. The breeze was up just enough, and it was enthralling to be out on the waters. It was magnificent to see her, our lady, holding the torch to light the way to freedom. We talked about how all the immigrants must have felt when they sailed past her, lighting the way to a new country, a new life. They were entering a harbor of dreams and great expectations.

We got off the ferry and began to tour the Statue of Liberty. We walked around her, looking up at the 305-foot structure. She was a sight to behold! We went inside and took an elevator to the crown. It still amazes me to look out over the harbor and the tip of Manhattan— breathtaking! Jan and the girls were in awe. We took pictures and spent at least thirty minutes looking at the grandeur of it all.

We finally left the crown and went down to the base to see the exhibition. There we saw how the sculptor Bartholdi, challenged financially and physically, saw his creation turn into reality. It made us realize all the great people who have come and gone through the centuries and what wondrous things they have left us. Just look at this city alone!

We took the ferry across the harbor to Ellis Island. We entered the main building's baggage room, just as twelve million newcomers did between 1892 and 1954. We climbed the stairs to the registry room where millions had waited for medical and legal processing. We looked at the exhibits of their voyages and the old photographs and commented on what it must have been like back then. It would have been difficult to come here without the promise of a job, not knowing anyone, and speaking a different language. How brave they were!

Yes, the land of the free and the home of the brave. I thought of how all these unsung heroes made America what it is today by leaving behind loved ones and their homelands to come to an unknown country. I pondered all they faced once they left Ellis Island.

"Treasures from Home" was an exhibit of old clothing, jewelry, and rare photos as well as family heirlooms and religious items donated by the immigrants' descendants. It was very touching. It made all of us realize what America was about and how fortunate we were . . . in many ways.

I looked at the pictures and wondered what happened to all of them. It would be very interesting to know who all their children were, as well as the generations that have followed and who and where they were today. When we left there our hearts were moved, and although we never knew them, we were very thankful for them. For what we have today, we realized that many people paid a great price . . . a great price.

We got back on the ferry and finished our roll of film by taking pictures of each other with the Statue of Liberty and Manhattan as our backdrops. It was a beautiful summer day to review our heritage and history, as well as a sentimental journey. As we sailed back to Manhattan, we noticed several American flags here and there against the massive city, gently waving, proud and grateful.

"Everyone that comes to New York City needs to go on a subway at least once," I said to Jan and the girls. We left Battery Park and took the subway to the World Trade Center. We took an elevator up to the 107th floor to Top of the World and went to the food court and ate lunch. The view was fantastic, standing against those windows, looking straight down. It took our breath away! We went up to the observation deck on the 110th floor, as if 107 wasn't enough, and looked around the city on the world's highest open-air observation deck.

Jan and the girls were ready to get back down on the ground! I think it was getting to them. Especially on the observation deck with the clouds moving by, it felt like you were going with them.

Amanda hailed us a taxi and we took off for the Empire State Building. "I figured it's tough to come down all at once, so we better just wean ourselves from it. We'll only go up one hundred and two floors this time. Besides, everyone that comes to New York City needs to go up in the Empire State Building," I explained. "You need to go to see how King Kong felt in his first movie. At least we will be on the inside hanging on!" We all laughed.

We viewed a different part of Manhattan from up here and spent about thirty minutes in the glass-enclosed observatory. We had almost gone through another roll of film since Ellis Island. We went to the eighty-sixth floor observatory and out on the terrace, where you get that feeling of height from the wind. It definitely dramatizes the height—a chilling 1,050 feet in the air above Manhattan.

We all enjoyed it but again, suddenly longed to get our feet back on the ground.

It was already four o'clock! We left the building and Linda hailed a taxi and we headed for my apartment. We took the taxi through some areas they had not seen before. I really was trying to give them a good general tour of the city. They had a good idea of what New York City looked like for only spending a couple of days here. Tonight, they would see Central Park and Tavern on the Green.

Gilbert opened the taxi door and Amanda and Linda sighed deeply, got out, and stretched. I stood up and sighed, "Whew! We have been on the waters, in the sky, and through the streets!"

He shook his head and said, "My, my! Children, you writing a tour book on New York City?"

Jan slowly straightened up and moaned like she was in agony and he started laughing all over again, still shaking his head. We slowly walked up to the door as he ran ahead and opened it, showing us he had a lot more energy than we did. It was probably all the calories still kicking in from that blueberry bagel with all the cream cheese!

We opened the door to my apartment and Jan and I went over and laid out on the couches. The girls went over by the windows with a throw pillow and laid out on the floor. "There's no place like home, there's no place like home," I whispered.

"Ain't that the truth!" "Boy, that is for sure!" "You are so-o-o right!" chimed exhausted voices.

I sighed, "It must have been the altitude that wore us out." There were faint giggles. We laid there and totally relaxed until we finally decided to get up and get something to drink.

"It is already five o'clock! We are supposed to meet Carl at eight o'clock. I'm glad we didn't make it any earlier!" I remarked. "I'm going to take a quick shower just to perk up and change clothes," I said as I got up and headed for my bedroom. "We'll all do the same thing. It'll liven us up for the next round if nothing else!" Jan grinned.

"What are you wearing?" Jan asked as if she might be getting a second wind.

"I'm going to wear a nice, but casual slack outfit and flats. We will take a taxi and walk around the park a bit, just a little bit!" I added quickly as they stared at me with exhausted faces. "Carl will be in a suit, I imagine. He probably will come there straight from the office," I said.

"Does he work that late?" Jan asked.

"No, but he wanted to tie up all loose ends before the weekend. He has played an important role in his corporation and his accounting skills are second to none. He is ready for his retirement and to let the younger guys take the reins. He is just staying around to train them," I replied.

We all got ready quickly and put a new roll of film in the cameras and took off. Amanda and Linda had us a taxi in nothing flat. It was a beautiful evening and people were out enjoying the beginning of the weekend. We had the taxi leave us near Tavern on the Green and began to walk around the area.

I began telling them about the park and all the times Carl and I used to come here on the weekends. I told them, "We used to come to Sheep Meadow because it was more laid back than some other areas of the park. On Sunday we would get the *New York Times* after a late breakfast, come down here and read the paper to see what was going on in the city."

I paused a moment while we walked, reminiscing and then said, "We lived for the big city life then and whatever was going on, we were there. There wasn't much we missed, I'll tell you!" We walked, taking in the sights of the park and I told them, "There are all kinds of people in this city! Just watching them is entertainment in itself!" They totally agreed with me on that comment. We wandered our way around to Tavern on the Green.

We went in and they were so impressed by it. It was a neat place and had always been one of my favorites. I felt a hand on my shoulder and turned quickly and there was Carl smiling at me. Jan and the girls turned and hugged him. I felt like I hadn't seen him for weeks!

I gave him a soft kiss and hugged him and said, "How you doing, sweetie?"

"Oh, just fine," he said, grinning, with a sparkle in his eye.

"Well, this is perfect timing," I said.

"I figured you girls had been resting all day, saving your energy for tonight," Carl mused.

"Oh, yeah, right!" laughed Jan.

The girls started telling him about everywhere they had been. Carl had reserved a table where we could look out over the park. It was dusk and twinkling lights on nearby trees began to come to life. We could not have had a more beautiful ending to an exhilarating, eventful day!

"You girls may be so hung up on the city, you may not want to come out to the lake," he kidded.

"Oh, we can't wait to go out there and see your home and the lake," Jan beamed.

"I have one of those paddleboats and plenty of life jackets. You girls can sail into the sunset while Jan and I walk around the lake," Carl told them.

"What am I going to be doing?" I mused, acting serious.

"You'll be grilling our steaks," Carl replied. Jan and the girls started laughing.

"This trip has been so wonderful and being out there at Amber Lake will really cap it off. It sounds just beautiful and so serene!" Jan commented.

"I'll have a big steak, baked potato, and salad for everyone, so you better bring your appetite! I'll have iced tea for you girls too. Jan, if you all like banana pudding or cobbler, I can fix that. I don't know too much about desserts other than those two," he confessed.

"You better have Diane stop at the store if you all want anything else. She'll stop and get coffee anyway. She would pass out if there was no coffee, sugar, or milk when she got up in the morning. Did you know she carries a coffee pot, water, coffee, sugar, and creamer in her trunk at all times!" Carl attested. I shook my head and rolled my eyes at Jan and the girls as they all giggled.

"I don't care for creamer, but in a pinch it will substitute for milk," I quietly responded.

48

"Carl, is there a church near you? If you have plans for us to do something Sunday morning, that is fine. If not, we would like to go to a church service Sunday morning," Jan indicated.

"I already had plans for us to go, so I'm glad you are in favor of that!" Carl said proudly.

"You had plans for us to go to church?" I asked, rather surprised to say the least. He was full of surprises lately!

"Yes, I have been going on Sunday when you're not there. You always have other plans if you are out there," he confessed. "I have really been enjoying it and realize how much I have missed it all these years. I have also gotten involved in the Sunday night service and we all have a big time," he joyfully revealed, as he took another swallow of iced tea.

Needless to say, I was a little embarrassed! Good grief, why didn't he ever tell me he wanted to go to church on Sunday morning!

"I'm anxious for all of you to meet the folks there at Lakeside," Carl smiled, delighted we were going. I stared at Carl, still astonished he had gotten that involved in church and I didn't know it!

"Carl, you never told me you were going on Sunday night," I said, rather dismayed he had never said anything to me about it.

"Well, when you do come out you always leave for the city about four o'clock. I figured I would go on over to the evening service since Sunday evenings were pretty lonesome. Now I really look forward to it! It would be nice if you went with me sometime. Of course, Sunday morning we all can go," he said, acting a little sheepish in that he had never asked me to go before now. I knew Jan and the girls could feel our sentiments about this subject, so I decided to change the mood before I got upset with him again.

"Well, I'm looking forward to going. I would love to meet the people over there at Lakeside. Jan, you and the girls will love that church! It is a beautiful white country church and it sits on the banks of Amber Lake. It looks like it should be on the front of a greeting card, it is so pretty and serene," I portrayed to them. "They even have the parking lot near the woods, as if to leave the church by itself for photos. By the way, make sure you have film left," I suggested.

I imagined what they were thinking by the look on their faces. . . . "Diane, wake up here! You are working all the time and Carl is lonesome. He is trying to tell you to stop taking him for granted! He wants you to be with him and start going to church for your own sake as well as his!"

49

Our dinner arrived and Carl said, "Jan, would you like to say the blessing?" I must have looked like I went into shock.

Jan said, "Sure Carl," and we all bowed our heads and Jan prayed, "Our heavenly father, thank you for dear family and friends. We are having such a wonderful visit and we look forward to the rest of the weekend. We praise you now for keeping us safe and enjoying our time together. Bless and protect Diane and Carl and thank you for guiding our way in all that we say and do. In Jesus' name we pray, Amen." Carl and the girls said, "Amen."

I raised my head and tried not to look around, but I happened to notice several people were staring at us, then they quickly returned to their dinner. Why did praying in public make me so nervous? I felt everyone was looking at us. Probably because they were!

The dinner was wonderful and we talked and laughed about all the things that had happened in the last two days, even about Gilbert and the blueberry bagel overfilled with cream cheese. Carl burst out laughing because he had seen that cream cheese face on many occasions! Carl and I told them about some of our crazy times in the city and some of the funny things that had happened to us. Of course, we couldn't tell them all, that would take days!

We ended our meal with a luscious dessert and I mused, "Carl, can you fix this dessert for us tomorrow night?"

"No, I already told you I only know how to fix cobbler or banana pudding and I would rather have it anyway," he shot back. Jan looked at me and tried not to laugh and the girls giggled to themselves. That was just Carl.

We left the restaurant and Carl got us a taxi and said, "I'll see you tomorrow. Bring your appetites and be careful." We hugged him and thanked him for the wonderful dinner. I kissed him and thanked him for taking us out as they got in the taxi.

"Are you going to the lake tonight?" I asked.

"As soon as I get back to my car. I'm already packed," he answered.

"You got your keys to the house?" I asked.

"I got my pants on, don't I?" he replied. Jan and the girls heard him from inside the taxi and broke up over that comment! They were trying to stifle their laughter so he wouldn't hear them.

"Well, I didn't know you carried the house keys with you all the time," I replied. Carl always carried his keys in his pants pocket and evidently all of them.

"Goodnight, see you tomorrow and be careful," I told him as I took my seat in the taxi. As he walked away, I watched from the taxi as he drifted into the night, until he was out of sight. Jan and the girls were still tickled over his comment and then I joined in on the laughter too.

We got back to my apartment, relaxed, and decided we would leave fairly early and take the scenic route up to Carl's. There were several quaint little towns I wanted to take them to see. We talked and laughed and I asked them if there was anything special they wanted to see before they left the city. "No," answered Jan, "We wanted to see the Empire State Building, the Statue of Liberty, and some of the other sights of the city. We got to see those and more!"

It was about midnight and we got up from our comfy spots on the couch, hugged each other and Jan and I headed for our rooms. The girls wanted to spend the last night looking over the city again. We all turned in, knowing we wouldn't have any trouble sleeping!

I stretched out in my bed, looking out over Manhattan, thinking about Carl. It wouldn't be long before he would be gone from here. I knew I could always go out to the lake on the weekends, but it was still a very long week without him . . . a very long week.

Of course, I could spend ten to fourteen hours a day working with my associates, but it wouldn't be the same. The firm had been a blast and very rewarding as well, but the work grind was getting a little old. "Boy," I thought, "the people who would love being a consultant for big corporations! Maybe I'm having second thoughts about my work just because Carl won't be here anymore."

I always knew Carl could meet me wherever I was in the city and he would always be available on short notice. We had some fantastic times here—the times of our life really! I felt that Jan and the girls would pray for me about the situation. Thank God I could count on them!

Carl had said, "Who knows what your life would be like now if you had been praying about it." I wondered, what would it be like? I wondered if Carl prayed for me? I wondered if he prayed for us?

I was kind of anxious to go to church Sunday. All these preachers and Christians say there is power in prayer. They say that prayer changes things . . . well, I feel a change coming on!

Amber Lake

I OPENED MY EYES TO ANOTHER BEAUTIFUL MORNING. THESE LAST few days with Jan and the girls had been too good to be true, in many ways! I walked out and put on the coffee. The girls were still asleep on the couches, but I heard Jan moving around. Next week it'll just be me, I thought, heading to the office.

"Good morning, Jan," I whispered.

"Hey," she whispered back with a smile, then she came over and gave me a hug. "I don't know why we're whispering, the girls have to get up anyway," she said, still at a low volume.

"Well, alright then!" I broadcasted. We both started giggling. The girls stirred and Jan and I went over to the table and chairs and sat down for a minute.

I told Jan I was so surprised about Carl going to church so much. She told me I needed to start going with him and she knew he wanted me to be out there, but that he was not going to push me. He knew too well I was my own person, but the door was open for me. I guess it always had been and I knew that, but now our lifestyles were starting to differ somewhat.

"Good morning, mama. Good morning, Diane," said Amanda. Linda stuck her head out from under the covers and whispered, "Morning." We laughed at her.

"It's time to pack, girls, and get ready. We are not coming back here. We will go straight to the airport when we leave Carl's home, so make sure you haven't left anything. Golly, I can't believe we are leaving tomorrow!" exclaimed Jan.

"Man, this has been a ball!" Amanda said to herself, staring out the window at another sunny morning.

"I can't wait to get our pictures back!" exclaimed Linda.

"I'm so glad you have had so much fun," I announced.

"Are you going to call Mike the cab driver next week?" asked Linda.

"Yep, I sure am. I'll have to tell him I went to church too, and with someone who has been wanting me to go for a long time," I said quietly. They all looked at me with soft smiles and no words were exchanged.

"I'm going to get ready and get packed too," I said as I got up and poured another cup of coffee to take back to my room.

"Girls, who wants in the shower first?" asked Jan.

Amanda said, "I will go first and yes, I will hurry up."

"Please do!" ordered Linda and Jan. We all proceeded to get ready and packed.

"We still have some wonderful bagels from Peggy's. Warm them up in the microwave and eat them. There is plenty of cream cheese. I always have that on hand. We will eat later on the way there. I know a place you will love. That will hold us until Carl flips a huge steak on our plate. Carl will be ready to start cooking no later than four o'clock, although he will wait until we get there. There is nothing he hates worse than to have a wonderful meal ready and no one is there that second to eat it. He does not like eating late either, although he does sometimes. When he retires to the country he will eat breakfast at eight, a light lunch at noon and a big dinner at five. He will be right on schedule when he can control his own hours," I told Jan and Linda, as I took another sip of coffee and headed for the shower.

We had all our bags in the center of the room and the girls had cleaned up the kitchen. We took some pictures in the apartment and then carried our bags out and locked up. We went down the elevator, to the garage and packed the car. Off we went and they enjoyed seeing another side of Manhattan as we headed for the countryside.

"Oh, I love this little town!" Jan said as we drove into Apple Valley. We passed a century-old church with two little barefoot girls sitting on the steps, licking ice cream cones. At that moment, Amanda and Linda fell in love with this quaint old town. I parked at the town square and we got out and stretched. "You want to look in some antique shops a few minutes?" I asked.

We all meandered down the sidewalk and the front of the old stores were picture postcards in themselves. We looked in a few stores and Jan found two small antique pictures of angels in flowing white gowns playing harps in the clouds. The frames were gold and rather ornate. She loved them and wanted to put one in Amanda's room and one in Linda's room. "That will be quite a keepsake for you girls," I said. They agreed and as we left the store with our purchase, they were talking among themselves as to where they were going to hang them.

There was a gazebo in a little park across the street, so we walked over there and took pictures in it. Flower baskets were hanging all around it and the old stores were in the background. We felt like we stepped back fifty years in just ninety minutes from Manhattan. We left and drove on through the quaint, rolling countryside.

Thirty minutes later we came upon one of my favorite little towns. "There it is!" I announced. Three "oh-h-hs" were exhaled. We looked over Silver Lake, nestled in a green valley with three church steeples rising above it. We passed two boys with fishing poles resting on their shoulders, heading for Silver Lake, which greeted you as you entered the town.

We drove around the little square, which had a huge Victorian gazebo in the center, adorned with rose bushes all around it. There was lush green grass and flower beds everywhere with brick walkways leading through the flower gardens to the gazebo. There were about twenty black wrought-iron park benches sitting along the brick walk-ways here and there. Some old gentlemen were sitting on one of them, whittling and laughing, telling stories of old. There was a young couple sitting in the grass on a quilt, under the shade of an oak tree. They had a small picnic basket between them, getting their lunch out. By the look on their faces, no one could have paid them enough to be anywhere else.

We walked inside the gazebo and looked out over the quiet town with all the flowers and old, unique buildings. There was a light breeze blowing, and you could see Old Glory lightly flapping in front of the stark white boards of the old post office, and smell the fragrance of all the roses. I heard some children laughing from a distance, while the old men kept whittling and telling stories, chuckling now and then.

"This is like heaven on earth, isn't it ladies?" I asked.

"Yes! It is so peaceful and beautiful," answered Jan.

"I would love to live in a town like this," whispered Amanda.

"Well, we just about do. There is no gazebo, but it is quiet and beautiful out where we are," Linda said quietly.

"You are all lucky to have that. Never take it for granted!" I stated. We took some more pictures and then drove back to the lake and turned on a side road and went down to Thornton's Bed and Breakfast.

"You ready for lunch, ladies?" I asked.

"Oh, Diane, this is gorgeous!" Jan exclaimed. I laughed and the girls said, "Let's go!" We walked up to the huge porch lined with weathered rockers, and a huge calico cat was curled up in one of them. The house was painted in midnight blue with pale yellow shutters and trim. Flower gardens graced the walkways and the lake's edge was at the backyard. There were ornamental grasses scattered throughout the yard, and midnight blue iron benches graced resting places around the large yard, usually near a unique birdhouse.

There was a weathered gazebo at the end of an inviting pier which jutted out into the lake. There were flower baskets brimming over with pink and red flowers, swaying in the breeze. Our flag was hung at the front of the gazebo, hanging out over the waters, as to greet those who sailed by. There were places on both sides of the pier to tie boats, and many did just that and came in and dined from early morning to late evening.

We entered the main foyer and were greeted by Charmaine, the lady who managed Thornton's. We gave each other a hug and I introduced her to Jan and the girls. She seated us in the Lakeside Room at my favorite booth, which gave me full view of the lake and the gazebo. There were several sailboats on the lake and with the ornamental grass waving back and forth in front of the lapping waters, it was quite picturesque. The huge dining room was paneled in old gray barn lumber and had different types and sizes of baskets hanging from ceiling rafters. There were huge ferns sitting here and there and quilt pieces framed and hung on all the walls with name plates on them.

"Charmaine told me one time that local residents handmade all these quilts and many were over one hundred years old," I told Jan and the girls. I took a picture of them in this unique room and then we went up to the buffet.

"Golly, I wasn't expecting a selection like this from a bed and breakfast!" exclaimed Jan.

"Why do you think I brought you here. Isn't this terrific!" I announced.

"I would come here just to sit and look outside," said Linda.

"I would come here just to walk around the yard!" chimed Amanda.

We all ate a terrific meal and were filled to the brim. We went out into the yard and took some pictures. It was so restful and every corner was a photographer's delight. One of my favorites during the summer was the huge arbor with clematis blooming all through it in purple, red, and white. We were finally able to pull ourselves away from this blissful haven and head for Carl's.

I stopped at the grocery before we got to Carl's and got coffee, milk, and a bag of sugar, just in case. We turned down the road to Carl's place, winding around the lake. The homes were far apart and private. Then we caught a glimpse of Lakeside Church through the woods, sitting on the other side of Amber Lake. So reverent, this place of praise and worship, stark white against the emerald woods and yard with her steeple piercing the royal blue sky.

"I have heard people say it stirs their soul to hear the church bells ring out over the waters on Sunday morning," I told them.

We drove down Carl's drive and there his home was, resting upon a manicured yard and about three hundred feet in front of the lake. His home sat at the edge of the woods and the sun lay dappled on the black roof as the tall maples played with the summer breeze. It was in cape style, built in Old Williamsburg red brick with black shutters and stark white trim. It had a large front porch, gracing six rockers and several huge ferns that I had given him for his birthday earlier in the summer. There was Pepper, his bluetick hound, sniffing all through the yard and woods, looking for something to tree.

Oh-h-hs and ah-h-hs exhaled from Jan and the girls as they looked around their weekend retreat. "Wow! This is beautiful!" announced Jan.

"It's definitely Carl," I laughed.

"I can't wait to go to the lake," squealed Linda.

"Yeah, and get in that paddleboat," added Amanda. We pulled up to the back and into the garage.

Carl was on the back patio and had the grill ready to go. "Hey, you got out of those antique stores after all!" he said as he hugged us and gave me a kiss.

"Carl, your home is beautiful and this whole area out here is awesome. New York City is a blast, but I sure see why you want to be here!" Jan said.

"Yeah, this is my type of living. Peace and quiet! I can let Pepper run through the woods and fish right in my own backyard!" Carl said, proud of his soon-to-be lifestyle. "Let me get these bags to your rooms," Carl said.

"We'll get our bags. You're too busy. Ladies, all the bedrooms are upstairs, except for Carl's. Where are you putting everyone?" I asked Carl.

"I'm putting the girls in the north bedroom and Jan in the bedroom next to them so they can share the same bath. I'm going to have you stay in the south . . ."

"Not the fishing room!"

"Well, I cleaned it up where you can get your bags in and get in the bathroom," he sheepishly said.

"Not the fishing room! I'll gladly claim the den, or scoot Pepper over. You got room in your doghouse, old buddy?" I asked Pepper and he perked up his ears and wagged his tail.

"Good grief, what is the fishing room?" Jan asked, her curiosity aroused.

Carl tried to be serious and told Jan, "It's the room I use to work on all my fishing gear and get my tackle boxes organized. That's all." I was standing in front of Jan and the girls, and as I rolled my eyes back, Amanda and Linda immediately left to keep from laughing. Amanda yelled back, "We're going to take our bags to our rooms," and I heard them giggling.

Jan couldn't help it, she just started laughing as she looked at me. She tried to straighten her face up and asked, "Does it have a bed in it, or is it just a room with fishing equipment, or what?"

Carl was so serious and exclaimed, "It has a nice bedroom suite and is right there on the southwest side of the house and has a great view," he said as he pointed up to the window of the room in question. "I spent almost all morning cleaning it up, so it is not as bad as you think it is," he scolded me.

"Thanks! That means I can stick my big toe in the door," I commented as I walked over to pick up my bag, winking at Jan. "Carl, I'll be down tonight if I don't get tangled up in a mass of fishing lines," I answered back to him as Jan and I carried our bags to the house. Jan and I started giggling as we turned the corner and headed down the sidewalk to the front door. "Jan, you will love his house, except for one room!" I teased.

"Mama, wait until you see our rooms!" announced Amanda from the front porch. Jan and I were almost out of breath as we came up the porch stairs with our bags.

"Boy, we need to get in shape, Jan!" I sighed. We set our bags inside the front door of the foyer, greeted by the beautiful wide stairway leading upstairs.

"Mama, how do you like this?" we heard Linda yell, but didn't see her. We followed her voice to the right end of the foyer and there she was, sitting in the huge den in an oversized red and green plaid sectional, facing a massive rock fireplace.

Amanda joined Linda on the sectional, sprawled out and laid back, then took a deep relaxing sigh. We started laughing at the expression on Jan's face as she looked around the room, amazed by the size of it. "Jan, do you think this place is big enough for Carl? I just hope he doesn't feel cramped," I said ironically.

Jan and I went over to the wall of north windows facing the woods where you could see part of the lake, too. The windows took up almost the entire wall and the dramatic fireplace was in the center of it, with gray rugged rock climbing the twenty-foot wall to the cathedral ceiling. You felt like you were standing at the edge of the woods instead of in the den and it was a refreshing, serene feeling.

The fireplace had a wide hand hewn stone slab for a mantle. A beautiful fern adorned the left edge of the mantle and her fronds stood very tall and cascaded, as if she knew she was responsible for setting off this work of art. At the right edge there was a clear cylindrical glass jar about seven inches high and just as wide. It was half full of the marbles that Carl had played with as a child.

Sometimes the child in me would step upon the hearth and get down that heavy jar, take off the cork stopper, and dump them all out on the red braided rug in front of the fireplace. I would scatter all of those marbles out and pick out the cat eyes I could find and hold them up to the sun and look through them. I can see why children are so attracted to them, they are such beautiful colors and each one is unique. Evidently, even grown-ups are entranced by them!

Sitting beside the marbles was an earthen brown jar, crude and rugged, laying on its side with arrowheads filling the inside until they trailed out onto the stone slab. There were about thirty or forty he had collected from the farm he grew up on as a child.

Below the earthen jar on the hearth was a huge antique fish bowl with very long, slender branches of red berries we had found in the woods. Their stems were braced in the jar among pretty rocks Carl and I had gathered from here and there through the years. At the other end of the hearth was a brass fireplace set and antique leather billows laid against the rock front.

The cathedral ceiling was finished in natural pine and all the floors on the first floor were oak, except Carl's bedroom. The unique chandelier that hung from the center of the room was made of dramatic elk horns and was the finishing touch to this room.

The sectional took up the whole center of the room with a very large coffee table that was a five-by-five foot piece of glass, supported by elk horns at each corner. There was a spectacular willow basket that adorned the center of the table. It was filled with hundreds of different types of nuts and pinecones that had spilled over and were scattered about the glass. The burly red pillows that sat around the sectional brought the natural effects to life.

On the west wall was a bay window with a window seat and a red cushion all the way across it. It was large enough to sit in, straighten your legs out, and totally relax. I would spend time there in the winter looking out over the lake and listening to the fire crackle in the fireplace.

Every once in a while I would see children skating and I could hear their laughter through the window. I loved March, when the wind would howl and the lake had waves trying to escape from under the ice, the madness breaking through here and there. It was like the waters were unleashing to tell Mother Earth, "Spring is almost here, we are coming out of our icy mask, slowly but surely!"

Bookcases covered the entire wall on each side of the bay window, holding hunting books, stories of war, atlases, corporate rules and laws old and new, and framed pictures of generations covering 143 years. There were pictures of us at my parents' farm, along with mom, dad, and my sister in the yard and on that big country porch. There were about ten pictures of us back in the fields and lanes of that dairy farm, where I used to walk with my dog and ride my horse.

Carl's family graced two whole shelves. He had hunting pictures with dogs that had come and gone and each one of them held fond memories and many a story! Two more shelves held pictures and albums of his brothers when they sang in the Frost Brothers Quartet for years. Pictures of all sizes held memories of Carl and me on the beaches, in the mountains, at Christmas time, and throughout the seasons. Celebrations, weddings, retirement parties, and holiday gatherings of all our families and friends were there too.

Oh, all the places and events in New York City we had been to! My, how the years had flown! There were two shelves in the center on each side he left bare, except the center shelf on the left side held a fat clear jar, full of milkweed, held in by a heavy glass lid with a ball on top. On the bottom of the jar it read, "Carl and Diane gathered near College Grove, Tennessee, 1979."

The wall behind the couch had two beautiful oak gun cases. One was an antique and the other was custom built to hold antique and unique guns. He had this wall paneled in white pine all the way up to the open ceiling and had shelves designed to hold special mounts that included many different types of fish and wildlife. It was quite impressive!

The east wall had two large windows that looked out over the front yard and porch. He had a long desk in front of these windows and this is where he did his paperwork. He was always a morning person and the sun gave him light and energy to work by, he would say. On the corner of the desk a two-foot glass bottle lay on its flat side filled with green leaves. They were pushing up against the inside of the terrarium and trailing out the mouth like wild bungee cords, dangling about one inch above the floor. They seemed frantic to jump out to freedom but knew just when to stop.

A huge green leather recliner sat on the other side, near the fireplace, with a bold oak end table holding only his Bible and a tall heavy lamp made from an old wagon wheel hub and spokes. The lampshade was covered in the same red material as the pillows and window seat.

"Diane, wonder why he left two shelves right in the center of the two bookcases bare?" Jan asked.

"I've been wondering that myself," I mentioned, glad I was not the only one who had noticed.

"He is waiting to put your wedding pictures there," Amanda seemed convinced.

"Yeah, you two hadn't figured that out?" questioned Linda.

Jan and I looked at each other and shouted, "Not this again!" Jan scolded, "Girls! Don't get started on this again." We all started laughing.

"What is so funny?" Carl asked as he entered the room, to our surprise. We all turned around and Jan and the girls looked at me, holding their breath. "W-e-l-l, Jan and I wondered why you left these shelves bare and the girls said you were saving this space for our wedding pictures," I stated looking at him closely to see the look on his face, yet I was a little embarrassed at the same time. Jan and the girls were frozen where they were.

"That's not a bad idea," Carl said, looking me in the eye.

"You ladies been upstairs yet?" Carl asked them, totally changing the subject. We were still stunned by his comment about the wedding pictures, but finally Amanda answered his question with, "Oh, yeah, we put our bags in our room already."

"Mama hasn't been up there yet," Linda said quickly, trying to add on to Amanda's sentence.

"I have to go to the store in a few minutes to get Pepper some dog food. Diane, you check and make sure there is nothing else we need and if there is, I'll get it while I'm out. I have to find the life jackets and get the paddleboat out now. As soon as you let me know, I'll go to the store," he said and turned and walked through the kitchen and out to the garage.

We all took a deep breath, then we all started laughing. The girls started giggling and whispering to me, "See, what did we tell you!" Jan and I just kept giggling . . . I guess it was the embarrassment of it all. We realized we had better check and see if we needed Carl to pick up anything. Heaven forbid he come back in and we are laughing again!

"Come on, Jan, let's look in the kitchen and see if we need anything. Girls, check the bedrooms and make sure there is soap, toilet paper, tissue, and shampoo," I instructed as the girls flew upstairs and Jan and I went towards the kitchen.

"Golly, we better watch what we say kidding around! How embarrassing!" Jan giggled.

"Oh, well! No use being embarrassed over something that is not a bad idea!" I confirmed. Then we both started laughing again.

We walked back through the foyer and into the dining and kitchen area. "Oh, what I wouldn't give for a kitchen this size and with a gorgeous view of the lake too!" she said as she walked over to the French doors that went out to the patio and overlooked the lake. We could see Carl out there getting the paddleboat tied to the dock.

As soon as you entered the dining room from the foyer there was a bold oak dining table with eight chairs and an enormous hutch against the south wall. The hutch had a big black iron kettle sitting on top filled with silk trailing ivy and stems of bright red berries. The center of the table was set with five vanilla candles of all sizes in antique wooden candle holders. The holders were unique, and each one was hand carved. They all were standing inside a red tin serving tray with raised reed handles. Carl had bought it years ago along the coastline of Massachusetts at an estate auction.

The east wall had two large windows just like the living room, so when you sat at the dining table you looked out over the front porch and yard. The dining room was open to the large kitchen and you could see the lake through the French doors.

There were many oak cabinets and a bay window above the sink with flourishing African violets sitting in the window. In the center of this room was a kitchen island with pots and pans hanging from a black wrought-iron rack. Behind this were the French doors that went out onto the patio. The patio floor was rock and there was a three-foot rock wall planter on the south side brimming over with cascading red and pink flowers—beautiful!

There was a black wrought-iron table with matching chairs and several lounges. The chair and lounges were set with inviting tufted pads in a rich burgundy, green, and blue flower design. A blue bowl filled with pink, burgundy, and ivory silk peonies sat in the middle of the table. Real ones were never in season long and I could enjoy these all summer. I had always told Carl that peonies were about my favorite. I still remember mom having a clear glass bowl full of them in our living room when they were in bloom.

Jan and I checked what we needed for dinner and breakfast and all we needed was a loaf of sourdough bread to bake. I loved that with my steak. Carl had milk, sugar, and my favorite coffee. We needed some more juice and we better get some popcorn for tonight. Carl came in and said the girls could put on their life jackets and get out in the boat as soon as he got back.

"I just absolutely love your home, Carl," Jan announced.

"Thank you! You need to thank Diane. We picked out the land and house plans together. She picked out everything else, except what I already had. All I did was write the checks," he laughed. He got my list and left for the store.

"Diane, mama, come on up. We got your luggage up here," yelled Amanda from the upstairs hallway.

Jan and I looked at each other. Jan said, "I guess they heard us gasping coming up the porch steps and thought we would never make it up these stairs."

"Golly, have we gotten in that bad a shape? I have to get back in shape! I may be facing a two-week honeymoon!" I stated and we both started laughing again.

Amanda greeted us at the top of the stairs. "This way is our room, mama," she said and we all walked down the hallway into the north bedroom. Linda was studying the pictures on the wall. I believe she was imagining she was one of those young ladies, sashaying about in long rustling skirts, with a lace parasol and derby to match.

"Oh girls, you're going to love staying up here!" Jan laughed. "Diane, you picked out everything in the house?" Jan asked.

"Just like Carl said, and believe me, I had a ball! I call this the Victorian Room," I told them. The bedroom suite was solid cherry with a soft pink comforter and deep burgundy ruffles for a skirt and burgundy ruffled pillows to match. The bed was high and four posted. The wallpaper was ivory with heart-shaped clusters of small pink and burgundy flowers throughout. The curtains were soft pink, ballooned twice, and draped onto the floor with a burgundy ruffled valance.

The carpet throughout the entire upstairs was ivory. There was a brass stand with a huge fern in front of both windows. The north window overlooked the woods and the west window looked over the lake. There were old-time Victorian pictures on the walls, all in ornate gold frames.

"This room makes me feel like I want to wear my hair up and put on a long Victorian gown with lace and covered buttons down the front," said Amanda.

"Don't forget your gloves and parasol," teased Linda.

"And maybe a gold locket on a fine chain around your neck," I added to their imagination.

There was a large birdcage in the corner with burgundy and pink silk rose bushes blooming out through the brass cage. About the room were flowered hatboxes, some on wall shelves, and three stacked on the floor beside the birdcage. All of them were different designs, but vibrant and ornate, completing the Victorian authenticity of this room.

On the dresser sat a gold mirrored tray with a matching gold handled mirror and brush. Resting to the side was a pair of ivory lace gloves and a lady's pink derby with an ivory ribbon tied about and bowed in the back, trailing down the side of the dresser. The girls wanted to try on the hat and gloves and look in the mirror. They were having a ball.

"Mama, are you ready to go to your room?" Amanda asked anxiously.

"Yeah!" Linda said as she gingerly removed the derby and laid it back exactly where it was. They walked her back out in the hall and down one bedroom, Amanda opened the door and Jan went, "Oh-h-h-h, what beautiful colors and what a view of the lake!"

The girls and I giggled and I told Jan, "I always wanted a peaches and cream room, so this is it!"

The bedroom suite was solid oak with an oak braid that went around the entire trim of the headboard, footboard and the oval mirror on the dresser. The dresser and chest of drawers were trimmed with the same rolled wood braid. The bedspread was cream satin with peach satin ruffles and pillows to match which complimented the peach wallpaper splashed with elegant magnolias. The huge heart-shaped bed pillows were Jan's favorite thing in this room.

There were cream wrought-iron parlor chairs and a glass-topped table to match. The seats were done in peach satin. They sat in a quiet corner of the room and a peach planter sat atop the table with rambling ivy trailing over the edge and down the sides.

Delicate teacups were hung on gold shelf hooks, and saucers to match in many styles and colors sat above them. There were seven shelves of these unique pieces, most of them brought back from our trips to Europe. All of them had peach or cream tones or a dash of those colors in them and they definitely livened up the room. There was a huge gold mirror above the chest and a magnolia vine laid over the top and down the sides, trailing onto the chest.

Over the bed was a huge picture of a maiden, sitting in a tea garden, as the sun drifted to colors of peach over a calm lake. It fit the room perfectly. Peach and cream material was loosely intertwined above the window, held at each side by large gold brackets and then flowing full and free to the floor.

The three of them shared a bath between the two rooms and it was painted in cream and had a hunter green marble countertop and oak cabinets. The towels and accessories were all in sea green. This bath was decorated in seashells Carl and I had gathered from everywhere. We had the unique ones mounted in deep frames with hunter green velvet backing. We had dates and places written on the back of each frame. There were green wrought-iron shelves holding all shapes of glass jars, full of shells. Sponges of all sizes dotted the shelves and countertops and each one was different. The tub was in cream and all the fixtures were in gold. Jan and the girls still had plenty of room and shelf space to lay out their toiletries and get ready. Their favorite thing about this bath was the large octagon window that was just high enough for privacy, but had a perfect view of the lake too.

"Well, now let's go see the fishing room," I sighed. We walked to the last bedroom and the door was closed. That was a sign right there! I slowly opened the door, all of them peeking around my shoulder to see what this infamous room looked like! I grabbed the door and flung it open to fishing poles stacked in corners and tackle boxes emptied on the tops of the chest and nightstands. The dresser contained five empty tackle boxes waiting to be filled. There were lures laid out in rows at different spots on the floor. The whole place was booby-trapped! "Good grief!" I yelled, "At least there is a pathway to the bed! I hope I don't get a stray hook in my foot!"

"Golly, I hope you don't sleepwalk, you won't live through it!" Jan gasped and then burst out laughing.

"There must be ten thousand dollars worth of fishing tackle in there!" exclaimed Amanda.

"If you would marry him, you wouldn't have to sleep up here," Linda informed me. We all started laughing then!

I looked at them and said, "That's not a bad idea! Maybe this is his way of 'luring' me into matrimony." We burst into another fit of laughter.

"What is so funny up there?" Carl yelled from the bottom of the stairs. We all clamed up and covered our mouths, trying to refrain from our mad laughter.

"We're looking at the fishing room," I yelled back as all of them walked in there so he couldn't hear them.

"Now that you're over that, how do you all like your steaks done?" he shouted. Jan and the girls sat on the floor at this point, they had laughed so hard.

I walked to the edge of the staircase and gave Carl our steak orders. He looked quite the waiter, writing our steak orders down on a small tablet. "Tell the girls to go to the lake if they want too. They can use the paddleboat and tell them to stay close to the shore since we will be eating soon. Don't forget the life jackets!" Carl stressed. "Go ahead, girls! Get out there and have some fun in the water. It is a beautiful time of the day," I said as they scampered down the stairs and out the French doors.

"Jan, let me show you Carl's room and then we'll go on out. It is so beautiful today."

"Diane, is there a bath off the fishing room for you to use?" Jan asked.

"Well, yes, there is one, but who could get to it anyway! Besides, he's probably got minnows in the tub!" I announced as both of us started laughing again.

We went down the stairs where Carl's room was in the back of the house on the first floor. I opened the door and Jan's mouth flew open and she exclaimed, "Golly, this is huge!"

"Well, he uses part of it for his office because it is so private. No one ever sees this like they do the rest of the house."

"How big is this room?" Jan asked, still amazed.

"It is thirty by eighteen." He had built a big bath and closet at one end of it. The room was all done in western cedar and it smelled good too.

The back wall had French doors where he could go directly onto the patio and bay windows on both sides of the doors. He did not want to miss looking over the entire lake and I didn't blame him.

He had a massive bedroom suite made of solid oak. The bed looked huge since it was king size with a very tall headboard and foot-board which were swirled and uniquely cut. The chest was as tall as I had ever seen one and the dresser was a triple with a mirror that covered the entire length. He had a rich carpet of heather berber with traces of navy and hunter green. The comforter was a green and navy paisley with a hunter duster.

On the other side of the room he had a huge oak rolltop desk with brass desk lamps and green shades. The desk had to weigh a ton! He had a navy leather recliner to the side of that with an oak nightstand and a tall lamp made from the hub of a wagon wheel, like the one in the den, with a matching paisley shade. There were two hat racks on the wall behind the desk that must have been holding at least sixty baseball, hunting, and fishing hats.

Several pictures hung on the walls and they were scenes of the countryside and old barns that were very unique and quaint. I think his favorite was the one of springtime in Tennessee with all the dogwoods blooming and the willow limbs bringing forth that color of green that only Mother Nature has claim too. I found him that picture years ago and he said it reminded him of spring when he was growing up in Tennessee.

His bath was done in antique white walls, oak cabinets, and all gold fixtures and had the only Jacuzzi in the house. In my antique ventures

I had found old shaving mugs and brushes and leather sharpening straps among other things. He had an oak shelf up to display them and it was very interesting to look at all the items.

"Jan, you haven't even seen the lake yet! Let's go out to the pier and see what the girls are doing," I suggested. We went through Carl's French doors and into the backyard.

Carl was in the process of building a walkway out to the pier. He already had it lined out and graveled in. He just had to get someone to lay the rock. It would lead from the patio to the pier and be the same rock as the patio. I helped with it in the spring and put a few interesting little turns here and there instead of a straight path. I had taken several days off work and came out here to try my hand at garden design and landscaping.

We had so much fun and it was so beautiful and fresh outdoors. I already had in my mind what flowers to plant along the walk, what benches to use and all. He would complain about the way I did some things, but I think he was always pleased with the final results.

"Golly, I wish Ray and Michael could see this. What they wouldn't give to be out there fishing right now!" Jan said.

"Well, come on out sometime. Carl will be able to tell Ray when the fishing is good. He doesn't have to bring any fishing stuff, I know where they can get plenty!" I chuckled. With that, we both started laughing again.

"Diane, this is so peaceful out here! I love where you live in the city, but isn't it hard to go back there after being out here?" Jan asked.

"It's as different as day and night, Jan, and yes, it is a rat race there and it has it's fun and excitement like no place else," I explained. "You know, I have had twenty grand years of living in one of the most exciting cities in the world. I love my job and have some great friends there, but I'm beginning to feel this life here is me. There are some other things I want to do with my life. The big thing is, Carl has always been there in the city and now things are going to be really different when he comes out here for good!" I told her.

"Do you think you are ready to give up your job, or can you retire yet?" Jan asked.

"If I wanted to leave, I can do it. I have enough in my 401K and I would get a retirement. Naturally, it wouldn't be as much as it would be if I worked ten more years, but that's a lot of years when you are ready for something else in your life! Plus, my apartment would bring a good amount of money. Remember, I bought it twenty years ago and

I have it paid off. I would still do some kind of work after retirement. I have always wanted to write short stories or maybe even a novel. That would give me time to do that," I told her.

"Diane, remember what we talked about several nights ago. There is something much more important than anything else in this world," she seriously told me.

"Knowing Jesus Christ as my personal Lord and Saviour," I said reassuring her I knew. "Jan, I know it, but I don't feel anything inside of me to move me to do it. I don't understand that," I confessed.

"You have closed the door on Him for so long and you are just now beginning to crack it open. You need to open your Bible and start going to church before it is too late. Satan doesn't want you saved. He'll trick you into keeping everything else more important! You must wake up and see what is going on, because that is what is going on!" Jan confirmed.

She looked out over the lake at the girls, then said, "Tomorrow morning will be a good start, provided you don't have something happen to you tonight," she said firmly. "The girls and I will be praying for you. You must seek Him. Only the Holy Spirit can move you to accept Jesus. You will know when He touches you and move then, and right then! Do not harden your heart and stiffen your neck when the Holy Spirit moves you to make a decision for Him. That feeling may never come again!" she persuaded.

The dinner bell rang and we turned and saw Carl motioning for us. "Come on girls, time to eat now!" Jan yelled. "Don't forget to tie the boat up real good," she instructed. Jan and I turned and walked back to the patio. "Is there another house over there? I thought I heard some kids through the woods," asked Jan.

"Yes, that is where the Goodfellows live. They're the ones that watch Pepper during the week when Carl is gone. Mary and Harold Goodfellow live there and their four grandsons live with them," I said.

"Four grandsons!" exclaimed Jan.

"Yes, their daughter works in the city and they wanted the boys to be out here where they weren't cramped up and could be outdoors. It is nice they have a big home because to find a nice place in the city for five people to live costs quite a bit! There is a great school here for them and they are on the lake boating and fishing a lot," I informed Jan.

"Carl leaves Pepper over there on Monday morning and picks him up Friday night or early Saturday morning. They all love Pepper and he loves playing with the boys. Their daughter, Trish, comes in on the weekends and visits her family then. If I'm not mistaken, they go to church at Lakeside too," I added.

"What does Trish do?" asked Jan.

"She is a makeup consultant with a leading cosmetic company, so she travels during the week a lot. I know she really misses being with her boys from what Carl said, but we all have to make a living. She is very fortunate that her parents have this place on the lake where they all can live," I answered.

"She must be single," commented Jan.

"Yes, she is divorced. Carl said she told him she was looking for a man who would take care of her in the lifestyle she wanted to become accustomed to and who wanted to move out here on Amber Lake," I laughed.

Jan looked at me and said, "You better watch out, she may be looking at Carl!"

"I never thought about that. I guess I'm naive. I met her once in the spring when I was helping Carl with the walkway. She was jogging and stopped by. She is very attractive and she sure loves it out here!" I confessed.

"Diane, you have some serious decisions in your life to make! You are easygoing and you don't like confrontations, so to speak, but there are some things you better start paying attention to before it is to late!" she warned me.

The girls ran up behind us and Carl had just put the steaks on our plates and had our places set. We got our salad, baked potatoes, and the iced tea that he fixed especially for us.

"I'm going to start fixing iced tea for myself," Carl said. "It sure is good. I was just about raised on it and realize how much I have missed it after all these years. I went over to get Pepper a couple of weeks ago and Mary, Harold, and Trish were sitting out watching the boys swim. They offered me a seat as well as a glass of iced tea. I ended up drinking two large glasses and told them that it tasted better than anything I had drank in a long time. Next thing I knew, Trish walked over here carrying a gallon of tea she had made. Boy, it was good too!" he laughed, pouring himself another glass.

Jan glared at me across the table like she was saying, "See, what did I just tell you!"

"Who are they?" asked Linda.

"Mary and Harold Goodfellow are my neighbors and Trish is their daughter. She works in the city, but she stays at the lake every weekend," Carl informed them.

"Where is her husband?" asked Amanda.

"She is divorced," Carl answered, taking another bite of steak, never looking up.

Amanda and Linda glared at me with that, "Ya better pay attention!" look and Jan saw it and started giggling and I did too. Gee, I must be stupid, I thought. Even teenagers catch on to these things. What is my problem!

"You girls gonna start laughing again? I didn't say anything funny. Must not need to. I think you all got the giggle bug," he stated, still looking at his plate, scooping another bite of baked potato.

"Isn't that sourdough bread delicious!" I announced. They all commented how good it was.

Carl laughed and said, "I'll say one thing about Diane's cooking, she sure knows how to buy good bread."

Amanda looked at me and said, "Ya better learn how to fix stuff!"

"It would be a good idea," Jan said as she looked at me and raised her eyebrows.

"Especially iced tea," I said and looked back at her.

"Especially that," Linda said, nonchalantly, never looking up from her plate. Amanda, Jan, and I started laughing again. Carl just shook his head this time and said, "Pass me the iced tea, please," and we all started laughing at that. "Whew! You girls got it bad," he informed us and went on about his eating.

The sun sat over the lake and we all walked down to the pier. It was so beautiful and then to hear the water lapping onto the shoreline, how peaceful! "You need a gazebo at the end of the pier, Carl. We saw one at a bed and breakfast Diane took us to today. It was beautiful and it would be perfect out here," Jan said.

"Oh, that had to be Thornton's. Diane takes me there for lunch when she comes out and that is exactly what she keeps saying."

"Why don't you build one then?" asked Amanda.

"If I had an occasion for one, I might be tempted to build one. Besides, just me out here, I wouldn't use one much. Pepper and I usually just sit over there on that bench, watch the sunset, then go back in and turn in for the night," he admitted.

We stood by the shoreline and the girls commented on the small branches and limbs that drifted by us like they were on their way to some unknown destination, which in reality, they were. "I bet they were knocked off the trees during that storm we had the night all of you flew in. The Goodfellows told Carl it was really a bad storm here," I told them.

The sun was finally gone and we all turned to walk back to the house. Carl was chatting to the girls and asking them about their paddleboat ride. Jan and I were walking in front of them and she whispered, "All he needs is an occasion to build the gazebo on the lake," with great emphasis on "occasion."

"Great place for the bride and groom to eat their first piece of wedding cake, don't you think?" I whispered back.

"Yeah, if you are the bride," she whispered back, looking me in the eye.

"I get your 'drift'," I whispered back. She looked at me and I whispered, "No pun intended of course." She shook her head and we started laughing.

We heard Carl behind us tell the girls, "Uh-oh, there they go again!"

We returned to that fabulous den, and we got down some of the photo albums. It was fun looking back at those old pictures. We finally put them up and were talking about everything, still trying to catch up on all the years gone by. Carl invited all of them to visit and stay at his home when the fishing really got good. He had a beautiful bass boat in the garage and he loved to have company share in his fishing ventures. He would carry Trish's boys in the evening when he was here during the week. He looked forward to that and they did too.

Carl got us some drinks and then brought us a tray of assorted crackers and cheeses. It was right tasty! Carl loved the different types of cheeses and the older the better. There was a little town that he would stop at between here and the city and they had a store called the Country Creamery. That was his version of shopping entertainment, to see what type of cheeses were out and the age they were. He would delight in having some samples of each ready for me when I would come out on the weekends. He was telling Jan and the girls about the Country Creamery and how he enjoyed shopping there.

I said, "One time I pulled in the driveway early Saturday morning and Carl came out carrying a tray of different cheeses he had just sliced. I was still in the car sipping a cup of coffee and he is wanting me to try them right then! I felt like I was at a cheese drive-thru, whatever one of them would be like. I guess they would be cheesy," I kidded. Jan and the girls started laughing.

Carl was not too amused and shook his head and said, "Oh, well!" and grabbed another cracker and slice of cheese. "After that comment, we better turn in, it could get worse," Carl suggested.

We all giggled and Jan looked over at the clock and squealed, "Golly, it's after midnight!" None of us could believe it was that late.

"We need to leave here in the morning around nine, because Sunday school starts at nine thirty," Carl stated.

"You want us to go to Sunday school too?" I asked.

"Well, I don't think it will kill you to go," Carl informed me.

Jan and the girls giggled and I said, "Well, that is fine. I didn't know you were planning on going to Sunday school, but we will be ready," I informed Carl. "Jan, we will need to leave here by three o'clock. That will give us plenty of time to get to the airport, but it is better to be early than late," I said.

"I can't believe it is time for all of you to go back! Girls, don't forget to take your camera with you in the morning. You will definitely want one of the church and some of Carl's place too," I suggested.

"Do you care if we take pictures inside the house, Carl?" asked Amanda.

"No, you take pictures of whatever you want! Help yourself, girl," Carl insisted as he put his arm around her and hugged her.

He went over and put his arm around Linda and Jan and said, "Now all you girls are early risers I hope. I don't have to beat the door down to get you up in the morning, do I?"

They laughed and said, "Don't worry, we'll be up and ready!"

"No one has to worry, I'll be up before anyone is anyway," I informed them. "Yeah, the coffee pot calls her out of bed about daybreak, if not sooner," Carl said, shaking his head. Jan and the girls looked at me and snickered.

"Goodnight, ladies," Carl said as he walked around the corner to put the empty glasses and cheese tray in the sink, and then he went to bed. Jan, the girls, and I walked up the stairs and as we topped the stairs, I looked at them and said, "I'm going on to my room, but when you all pray together tonight, please pray for me," I requested.

"We are praying for you and we will continue," Jan said without a doubt in her voice. I felt reassured. "We love you," all of them whispered as they hugged me and said goodnight. I was moved as I walked to the fishing room, entered, and closed the door behind me. Even that mess couldn't change what was going on inside of me, whatever it was. Matter of fact, I found the room rather amusing.

I changed and put on my nightshirt and laid in the bed and looked out over that gorgeous lake. The moon was shining on it and it looked like a million diamonds shining. I was sure Jan and the girls were standing there getting ready to pray and looking out over it too. It was so majestic and peaceful.

I wonder what church will be like tomorrow? I hadn't been for so long, I was really looking forward to it. I was feeling that I would be . . . refreshed, yes, that is the word, refreshed. Carl told us that his Sunday school teacher was a very good teacher and Jan and I would certainly enjoy the class. Well, I guess I'll find out for myself in the morning.

Carl had also bragged on the preacher and his wife. I was anxious to meet them. I couldn't remember the last time I was in church, at least for a worship service. Maybe tomorrow would be a new start for getting back in church. If nothing else, I'd go because Carl wanted me to. Maybe tomorrow would be a new start for a lot of things I didn't see before.

I woke up and looked out over the lake. The early morning sun was shining across the yard and onto the lake—so beautiful! I thought I better plan to get to the bathroom now. It may take a few minutes to figure out the best path to avoid any loose hooks. I made it to the bathroom and back without any injury and laid back down and looked out over the lake again.

Now that it was still, I found myself reflecting on all God had done for me (Ps. 46:10). As I looked outside, I realized everyone needs to give thanks for what He has so graciously given all of us! "God," I prayed, "don't let me take anything for granted anymore."

I turned and looked at the clock, six o'clock. Well, time to start the coffee pot! I quietly tiptoed downstairs and into the kitchen and started the coffee pot. I walked into the den and looked out over the woods, so green and lush. I sighed as I caught sight of bluebirds darting about the woods. They were so beautiful and such a brilliant blue.

A lady from the Lakeside Church makes houses for bluebirds. She gave Carl several, hoping they would start nesting here at the edge of the woods. Carl told me she and her husband lived about two miles from him. She was making these bluebird houses and giving them to people at church.

Carl said one of her dreams was to see bluebirds become a common sight around Amber Lake. What a wonderful idea! Jan and Carl would say, "You know God made all the animals when you see a beautiful bird like that."

I watched them play and then, a-h-h-h, the smell of fresh brewed coffee. I poured my first cup and then quietly peeked in on Carl. He was buried in his comforter and I saw a tuft of gray hair sticking up. Kind of funny really. I was tempted to go in there and pull the drapes all the way back, but that wouldn't be too nice this early. I quietly closed the door and opened the French doors off the kitchen, went out to the patio and drank my coffee as I walked down to the pier.

I stood in the early morning breeze and listened to the water lap upon the shore and the trees rustle all their lush greenery. Then I heard loons on the north side of the lake. How heavenly I thought, realizing I very seldom take the time to capture moments like these. About then, another pair of bluebirds darted by me and to a birdhouse Carl had put up on a tree by the edge of the woods. I guess that lady's dream is coming to pass.

I walked back to the house, into the kitchen and poured another cup of coffee. No one was even stirring and I tiptoed back upstairs and into the fishing room. I looked around and realized what a beautiful room this could be if it was cleaned up. A good idea would be to use the big storage room across the hallway. It had a south window in it and after all, it was a thirteen by seventeen foot room. He could make this into the new fishing room.

Carl could build shelves and worktables right into the wall. He had a table saw and all. Then he could work up there any time of the year on all his fishing gear. Heaven knows he would need weeks to get it all organized! No need to throw it all in the garage for the winter. What a great idea! He would enjoy having a room just for that!

I made up the bed. Even though I picked out everything for this room, I decorated it for an outdoorsman, and that was Carl! He didn't want all the upstairs rooms to be feminine. Of course, I can see why. I mean, it is his house. Now that I think about it, he sure gave me a free hand at doing my thing—just like it was both of ours!

The furniture in the fishing room was northern white pine and it was handcrafted, very woodsy, and unique. The walls were painted in a light coffee and of course, that would be a color I would love. This room had a border with wildlife, such as ducks, fish, deer, and so forth. It was very artistic though. I had found various old and new fishing bags that were woven and unique and I had them hanging on different shelf pegs on the wall.

The bedroom suite consisted of a huge chest, a dresser, and a queen-size bed. I had bought a very large oblong mirror to go over the dresser and had glued long twigs and branches all around the frame and let the edges always have twigs that jaunted out with delicate branches that sprawled out of control. I had hung fishing lures here and there in the twigs and over the edges.

I told Carl I did that because it reminded me of him. Some of his lures ended up just like that—caught in branches underwater and sorry to say, a few overhead. We both found out the hard way we didn't need to get to carried away with our casting near low hanging branches. One day I treed more things than I fished out.

The huge chest had a heavy chocolate vase full of pheasant feathers, probably at least eighty, and they were dramatic. The comforter was chocolate, sand, burgundy, and forest green. It brought all the border, lures, and leather strapping on the fishing bags to life. There were canvas pillows of green and burgundy at the head of the bed. A large burgundy wool throw rested over the back of the northern pine rocker. It sat in front of the window looking over the lake, as if waiting for an occupant to cover up on a winter day and rock—looking out over winter waters. Maybe they would catch a glimpse of ice skaters skim across the frozen lake or catch a flight of geese overhead.

I had collected wooden ducks from everywhere and had them placed throughout the room. The bathroom had a large shelf with pegs across the bottom that held fishing bags with burgundy and green towels hanging out of them. The shelf racks were filled with antique wooden ducks, some very old and well worn, but definitely full of character. The bathroom was painted in a sandtone with the same border as the bedroom and had a dark sandtone tub and countertops.

There was a large octagonal window, just like the bathroom at the other end. The floor was vinyl and looked like real pebble stones. The fixtures were gold, as usual, and the cabinets were in natural white pine. The mirror had all the glued twigs and branches again. I had so much fun with the first one, I did the bath mirror too. I had unique fishing and hunting pictures hanging in the bedroom and bath. All of them were matted in burgundy and green, and needless to say, they added the final, dramatic touch to this outdoorsman's room and bath.

I drank my last sip of coffee and took my shower and washed my hair. I got ready and put on everything and slipped on a day dress. I walked down to Jan's bedroom and knocked on the door. I heard the hair dryer going and then, "Hey, good morning!" I didn't say anything since I wanted her to wonder if it was Carl or not and laughed to myself. I went down and knocked on the girls' door and said, "Hello, it's me. Good morning!"

"Just a minute," I heard one of them say. The door opened and they were fixing their hair, running around in their slips. "We'll be ready in about fifteen minutes." They already had their bags fairly well packed. Amanda said, "We can hardly get ready for looking out the windows."

"It is something out here isn't it," I said, totally understanding. "I still have that problem, and I have been here many, many times!" I told them.

"Time for breakfast!" yelled Carl from the bottom of the stairs.

"Come on, he doesn't like anyone to be late!" I reminded them. "Good thing he doesn't have close neighbors. They would all be walking over here after hearing that announcement," I mentioned. We all chuckled on our way downstairs.

We sat at the kitchen bar and Carl gave us a hot plate of sausage, pancakes, sunnyside-up eggs, hot biscuits, butter, and jelly. We had orange juice, coffee, and milk. Carl automatically returned thanks and we all ate heartily. "All of you finish getting ready and I will clean up the kitchen. I have been up forever and have everything done that needs to be done before we leave today," I said. Jan and the girls wanted to help, but I scurried them upstairs.

Carl got up to finish getting ready and turned to me and said, "I want to leave in time to introduce all of you to some people before Sunday school and show you the church."

"OK, honey, go ahead, you have been waiting on me all weekend. The least I can do is clean up the kitchen. Thanks for everything. We have really enjoyed ourselves and you went all out, as usual!" I told him. He smiled back, enjoying every word, knowing I appreciated him . . . and that, I certainly did!

We all met in the den and went out and got in Carl's Jeep. "Boy, you can tell when someone is getting ready to leave New York City—when they buy a Jeep!" I stated and all of us laughed. Jan and the girls commented on how nice Carl looked in his snazzy suit and red tie. He looked good in whatever he wore, being six-foot four and slim, never gaining a pound.

Fifteen minutes later we were at church. We could see the steeple across the lake, but we had to drive halfway around the lake to get there. "Hi there, neighbor!" Carl yelled. The Goodfellows had pulled up and they got out of their car as we were getting out. Carl introduced Jan and the girls to Harold, Mary, and Trish. I had met them before, but only once.

Carl started to introduce the grandsons to all of us. "Amanda and Linda, these two boys are your age, or close to it. This is David and he is sixteen and Glenn just turned fourteen. Now this rascal here is Calvin and he is ten. And Nathan is the baby, but not a baby anymore, and he is nine. This is my girlfriend, Diane. This is Diane's cousin, Jan, and Jan's two daughters, Amanda and Linda," Carl said.

We all talked back and forth and they had lived on a dairy farm in Ohio most of their lives, so I could relate to that. The cold winters here didn't bother them, since they were used to it. Besides, the boys loved winter sports anyway. They came to Amber Lake several years ago, when Trish got a large promotion and had to move to New York City. They all wanted to keep the four boys in a small town atmosphere, yet as close to their mother as possible. They seemed very content with Amber Lake and it was a great place for kids to grow up. Well, it was just a great place for anyone to live!

I was proud Carl introduced me as his girlfriend instead of a friend. I don't know why I thought he wouldn't call me his girlfriend, we had only been dating for twenty years! Jan had looked at me with a gentle smile after that introduction. I knew through that smile she was telling me many things. I was blessed, and Carl was definitely one of those blessings, and I should not take him for granted!

We went on in the church and Carl showed us all around and it was a beautiful old church. Deep red carpet, oak pews, and an open ceiling with beautiful wood beams and three chandeliers that were made to look like large candles in clear glass chimneys. Each chandelier had five candles that sat on top of a large brass ring, which hung from the center rafter by a gold chain. They were so dramatic! Carl said during evening weddings, they would dim them all the way down, and it looked just like real candles gracing that huge open ceiling.

More people started coming in and we went on to our classes. Carl introduced me to Carolyn, our Sunday school teacher. David and Glenn took Amanda and Linda to the Youth Class. Carl, Jan, and I went to the Adult Class. Carolyn had a wonderful lesson and it was on what God's word was for husbands and wives, how they should love and respect one another and the part they play in the household (Eph. 5:22–33). Jan had brought her Bible and I looked on with Carl. I was so surprised how marked his Bible was with verses he had underlined, dates he had written out to the side, notes, etc.! I was really getting an awakening this weekend! The class was over before I knew it and I had thoroughly enjoyed it.

Amanda and Linda met us in the hallway and Carl wanted to introduce us to the pastor and his wife. Brother Darrel, as they all called him, came up and Carl introduced us to him and his wife, Judy. We chatted a minute and Carl invited them to go to lunch with us over at Grinder's Mill. It was about fifteen minutes away and served a fantastic buffet. It was an old mill that had been done over with antiques throughout. It had a quaint, relaxing atmosphere—not to mention the river and the dam right outside. This time of year we could sit out on the patio which overlooked the river.

We went out in the auditorium and were introduced to many people that came up to meet us and talk with Carl. We sat in about the fifth pew back. I was used to sitting in the very back when I went to church as a teenager. I looked in the very back just for curiosity and it was full of teenagers. Well, that part hadn't changed much! The choir sang and then they made announcements. Brother Darrel came to the podium and said April was going to sing a special. This young lady, tall, slim with beautiful dark hair and eyes came up to sing. She looked so pretty and fair. She looked like the lady in one of the pictures in the Victorian Room. She fit that image perfectly!

Without any music, she began to sing "Amazing Grace" and there was no sound other than her sweet voice, yet something else filled the air. It was like heavy air was falling on me and going through me in a mysterious, wonderful way. I could feel Carl's reaction without looking at him and knew he was moved. I heard Jan sigh, but didn't look at her.

Brother Darrel took the podium back and praised the Lord for moving in April's life and the gift of singing He had given her. He gave the verses he was going to preach on and it was about Lazarus and the rich man, Luke 16:19–31. "Lazarus, a poor beggar, died and went to heaven, and a very rich man died and went to hell. The rich man was tormented in hell and looked up and saw Lazarus in Abraham's bosom in heaven. He asked the Father to have mercy on him and send Lazarus that he might dip the tip of his finger in water and cool the rich man's tongue, for he was tormented in the flame. Abraham told the rich man that in his lifetime he received good things and now he was tormented, and that Lazarus received evil things and Lazarus was comforted. Abraham told him that there was a great chasm fixed and no one could pass through it," Brother Darrel said.

"The rich man begged Abraham to send Lazarus to his father's house to testify to his five brothers because he did not want them to come to this place of torment. The rich man told Abraham that if one goes to them from the dead, they would repent. Abraham told him if they do not hear Moses and the prophets, neither will they be persuaded by one who has risen from the dead," he finished.

Brother Darrel pointed out that being rich or poor does not have anything to do with whether you go to heaven or hell. One's destiny depends totally on one's decision to accept or not to accept Jesus.

He told us that this shows us that heaven and hell are real. Heaven is comfort and hell is torment and they are eternal and you can never pass from one to the other. We are to believe the word and the prophets who preach the word. God is not going to send someone back from the dead to tell us. God's people who are preaching the word are telling us right now.

He looked at the audience and pointed his finger throughout the congregation and with his Bible in the other hand he said, "If there is anyone here who has not accepted Jesus Christ as their personal Lord and Saviour, you need to come forth and repent of your sins and He will forgive you. You need to confess with your mouth that Jesus is your Lord and Saviour and He will come into your heart and live. He will wash your sins away and you will be saved from damnation."

"Let me warn you, hell is real . . . hell is real! The minute your heart stops, you are either going to be in heaven or hell. The choice is yours. Tomorrow may be too late. You are not promised tomorrow. Salvation is now . . . right now, right now!" he proclaimed.

The soft music started to play and he stood up front holding his Bible, looking, hoping for one unsaved soul to come forth and be saved. I felt like I had a weight on me, heavy and awful. Why didn't I move, I knew I needed to! Did I really not want to? It was like a fight inside of me!

Brother Darrel stepped forward and above the music he said, "God is working on your heart. Listen to him. If I could walk down this aisle for you, I would. You have to make the decision. No one can do it for you. He is waiting. Is he knocking on your heart? Let Him come in today . . . don't wait . . . don't wait," he pleaded.

Why didn't I move? I knew he was talking to me. He had to know, the power was so great. I needed to go. I really needed to go! He looked dismayed and slowly turned and nodded at the piano player. The music stopped.

Church was dismissed with a prayer. We all turned to leave and met some more people whom we missed earlier. I got to meet Ann, the lady that made the bluebird houses. She had such a sweet spirit about her, as did her husband. I told her about seeing several pairs of bluebirds just that morning. That thrilled her and she was in the process of making more houses for a children's class at Vacation Bible School. The children would be able to paint them, take them home and put them up somewhere in their yards. What a great idea! It would be something special for the children, not to mention the bluebirds having a home.

"Diane and Jan, I want you to meet Sharon. She is leading a seminar here at church about taking care of your body and how to feel better and lose weight the right way," Carl announced.

We shook hands and Jan said, "I would love to go to a program like that! I wish we had something like that at my church. I need encouragement to eat the right food and exercise."

"Well, this lady is the one you need to have come to your church, Jan. She has lost 182 pounds," Carl said, bragging on her.

"Wow wee!" I exclaimed.

"182 pounds!" Jan squealed, her eyes as big as half-dollars.

Jan and I were so interested we talked with her about fifteen minutes. She gave Jan and me her card. Sharon said her body was a temple of God and with His strength and guidance she was able to overcome being overweight, as well as other serious problems in her life. The Lord led her through them all!

"Only the strength of the Lord could have brought me to where I am today. He is leading me to help other people and I started with a program right here in my own church. Now I'm visiting churches all over the state, and getting more phone calls every day! I have quite a testimony and the Lord is using it to help others and to bless me beyond belief!" she said.

"Anyone who has lost 182 pounds and looks as good as you do is quite a testimony!" I confirmed.

"I can see joy and strength in your spirit. It is inside of you shining out like a bright light," Jan told her.

Sharon shook her head and said, "Ain't God good!" and gave both of us a loving hug. This lady had real peace and unwavering strength about her. I longed to hear her testimony and attend her seminar. I needed to lose at least twelve pounds and learn how to take better care of myself too. We said bye to her and Jan was excited about getting in touch with her to learn about her program.

Brother Darrel and Judy were still visiting and they had to close the church up. The girls were outside taking pictures of the church and lake. Carl told Brother Darrel he would drive on over and get a table for us. There wasn't any room in Carl's Jeep anyway. The drive to the mill was beautiful. There were farms nestled here and there with ponds reflecting the clouds and cows grazing on the rich fields. We pulled up to Grinder's Mill and Jan and the girls loved it already. "Get your camera back out girls," I laughed. Carl went in and requested a table on the patio, overlooking the mill dam.

We walked down to the river's edge and the river was so clear, brushing over rocks and curves en route to another destination. It was like the river was saying, "I'm passing through, enjoy me as I do!" and that we did. Brother Darrel and Judy waved at us from the mill's front porch and we walked back up to join them. In the front yard was an old green wagon and the entire bed was brimming over with flowers of all kinds. Brother Darrel and Judy were sitting in rockers on the porch where there were half barrels running over with flowers and enormous ferns hanging all across the front of the porch.

We walked inside and the large dining room with the buffet had a spectacular white stone fireplace at the far end. There were antiques everywhere. Lanterns were hanging from ceiling rafters and there were old black and white pictures throughout the mill of days gone by. They had framed some remaining, unused meal and flour bags from the flourishing mill days and had them hung on the walls.

We went on out to the back porch, which jaunted out to the river's edge and we looked over the mill dam. It was not only serene to look over, it was very peaceful to listen to. All of us were at a huge, black wrought-iron table with matching chairs and there were baskets of flowers hanging and sitting all around. They were mostly in pink and red, and accented the green woods and sparkling water perfectly.

We had a wonderful dinner and visit. I told Brother Darrel and Judy I enjoyed their church and service. I kidded them, saying I didn't know people could go there and receive bluebird houses, go to weight seminars, and receive the plan of salvation too. We all laughed and Brother Darrel said that they had a very well-rounded church and their members had many different talents and the diversity worked for everyone's needs. I told him it wouldn't be well-rounded long with Sharon leading that weight seminar. We laughed and chatted more about the church and its members. Brother Darrel said that the Holy Spirit had sent people there to give as well as receive.

"We aim to draw all ages and types of people here at Lakeside. Everyone needs to enjoy coming to church and everyone needs to know how crucial being saved is. It is the only important decision anyone ever makes, because you live with it throughout all eternity," he stated.

Carl, Jan, and the girls said a loud "Amen" to that. I just listened.

"All of us are going to die someday and we don't know when. After all, that is the only way we can get out of here," he said smiling. We all chuckled. "Unless of course, you are living when the rapture occurs," he acknowledged, taking another bite of baked beans. All of them started talking about how close it was, what prophecy had already been fulfilled, and that it could happen anytime now. They said everyone better be ready and that the Christians needed to be busy witnessing and leading as many people to Christ as they could. They talked about how awful it would be to be left behind and how wonderful it would be to be raptured, and caught up in the clouds with Jesus (1 Thess. 4:17).

I listened to all this intently and wondered what on earth the rapture was, but was far too embarrassed to ask. I was really hoping they didn't ask me my thoughts or opinions. I was totally lost! Now that I think about it, I really was lost . . . seriously lost!

We finished our meal and were walking to our vehicles and Judy was talking to Carl, Jan, and the girls. Brother Darrel was walking beside me and I told how much I enjoyed April the young lady that sang and how good his sermon was. He thanked me and looked me straight in the eye and as he had my undivided attention, he calmly said, "We will be praying for you."

I could see the concern in his eyes and I knew he was most sincere and I meekly whispered, "Thank you." It was all I could muster. His sincerity touched me and brought tears to my eyes.

He quietly turned and reached out and shook Carl's hand as all of them had caught up with us. I turned quickly and blinked my eyes, hoping none of them would notice. Then Jan, the girls, and I hugged both of them. Brother Darrel and Judy told Jan and the girls to come back up here and bring Ray and Michael. They told me to get back up here next Sunday. They said Carl had been wanting me to come to church with him for a long time. I could tell Carl had enjoyed all of us going with him and that made me feel good. We said goodbye and parted our separate ways.

We got back to Carl's house and we took all the pictures we wanted inside and outdoors. The girls even took a picture of the fishing room.

They said every time they needed a good laugh, they would look at it.

We loaded all the bags back in my car. I knew Jan and the girls were glad to be going home, but I think they felt like I did, the time had gone so fast! I wished they lived closer! It was like we were close friends as well as cousins. That made it double nice.

"You got everything loaded?" Carl asked.

"You got your airline tickets ready?" I asked.

"Yes," they answered to both questions. We all hugged Carl and they thanked him for a wonderful weekend and told him they loved Lakeside Church. We got in the car and I had to admit, I don't think that Jag had ever been loaded like it had this trip!

"Are you coming back in the city in the morning?" I asked Carl.

"I got everything caught up when I stayed late Friday night. I'll probably come in late tomorrow afternoon," he said.

"Good! Come straight to my place and I'll take you out to dinner, or do you want to stay in and I'll cook?" I asked. Jan and the girls all looked at each other in amazement.

"You're going to cook dinner for me! I thought you always had one of those business dinners on Monday night, or is that the one you have on Tuesday night? Regardless, you are always busy with work both nights, whatever it is!" he stated.

"Well, I usually work late every Monday night and we have any new clients meet our staff for dinner on Tuesday night. It's about time for Sam to start handling that. He will be taking my place someday and I have taught him all I know," I informed Carl.

He was taken back by my change of attitude toward my job and couldn't say anything for a few minutes. He just looked at me as if he were in shock, but pleasantly in shock. I guess a sudden change of attitude after twenty years would shock anyone! Then he said, "Well, it's about time you start handing it over to him. You are not going to be there forever!" He leaned over and gave me a kiss and said, "You better get going. Call me when you get back from the airport."

We backed down the driveway waving our hands off at Carl, and of course, Pepper. Carl and Pepper turned and both of them were moseying down to the lake as we drove out of sight. On the way to the airport, we just enjoyed the scenery and talked about the weekend. It was fun to have girlfriends again. I felt like I was back in high school.

"Hey, I'll leave you off here. Go ahead and check in and go to your gate while I park. It may take me several minutes and it may not, but just go ahead and I'll catch up with you. We are doing fine on time and

I want to keep it that way." They unloaded and I finally found a parking spot, checked the car to make sure they got everything, and then headed for their gate.

"We start loading in fifteen minutes," announced Amanda as she had walked down to meet me.

"Boy, that is perfect timing if you know you are going to make it with no hang-ups," I laughed.

"Mama, we never did get postcards. Can Amanda and I run over there and buy some real quick?" Linda asked.

"Yes, just hurry up!" insisted Jan, looking at me shaking her head and laughing. Off they went to the little store across from us.

"Jan, I have so much to ask you. I feel like something inside of me is changing. I can't explain it, but it is very evident," I confessed.

"We have been praying for you and I know Carl and those church members have been sincerely praying for you. I see how Carl feels about you and he is very concerned about your salvation. He knows you are totally independent and you act like you would run the other way if he mentioned church or marriage. He stayed by your side anyway because he is so in love with you. He would give his life to have you saved, but he can't do it for you. You have to make the choice. It is all in your hands!" she admitted.

"How awful it would be to be in love with someone, like he is with you, and know they were headed for hell! Also, he knows it could happen any minute. We never know when and how we are going to die. After being around Carl for a while, I can see his undying love for you and really, yours for him. He would have married you a long time ago!" she informed me.

I stood and looked at her and started grinning and said, "Well, I guess you lifted the veil on that subject. No pun intended, of course," I replied.

Jan shook her head, closed her eyes and said, "Sometimes I wonder if you will ever change, but you will. You are changing now, but you are trying to fight it," Jan told me.

"You really think Carl wants to marry me?" I inquired.

She quickly answered, "Carl doesn't want to keep having the intimate relationship you two have like you are married. It goes against his moral belief, but he loves you and desperately wants to be with you. He has been away from church for a long time, probably trying to hide from the truth and justify his situation with you, even though he knew it was wrong. Now that he is back in church, he will have a very difficult time dealing with the lifestyle you two have. Carl will not go on living like this much longer. He knows what is right and what is wrong in God's eyes and he won't hide from it anymore. Why do you think everyone is praying for you! If you don't make a turn around, there will be some changes in your life you won't want to face!" Jan revealed.

"You will totally understand when you make Christ Lord of your life. Your heart changes! You are a new person! Then you will want to do what is right. The Holy Spirit will show you what is wrong, whether you want to see it or not and He will always do it in a loving way. You will never understand until you do what you know you need to do. If you don't, Diane . . . you may just lose everything—and I mean everything!" she warned.

"Mama! We have to go."

"They are boarding. Diane, we love you and thanks for everything. It was wonderful!" they all told me as they hugged and kissed me. Jan gave me a final hug and kiss on the cheek. They had their boarding passes out and Jan scurried behind them and they all yelled back, "Love you! We'll keep in touch," as they got ready to board.

"Jan, what is the rapture?" I yelled, not realizing I was so loud or why I even asked her out of the clear blue!

An old lady behind Jan turned around and pointed her finger in my face and said, "Missy, if you don't know, you better find out and you better be ready!" The whole line of people boarding froze in time and so did I. I couldn't take my eyes off her withered face and steel blue eyes. I knew Jan and the girls were at a standstill, looking at her.

"Yes ma'am," I quietly answered and she put her bony finger down, turned and walked around the corner to board.

All of us that had been motionless began to move again as the white-haired lady disappeared. Jan said, "We love you. Call me!" and looked intently at me and then turned the corner and she was gone. I could hardly move after that, but I finally walked over to the window and sat down in front of it. I watched their plane back up and turn to taxi down the runway. I walked up to the window and waved. I saw a hand frantically waving and off they went and disappeared en route to Nashville.

I stopped at a small neighborhood market and got a quart of milk for my coffee and some deli meat and sourdough bread. Carl sent some cheese back with me for the week so I had enough to make a meal on now. He had sent some different cheeses back with Jan and the girls too. He thought Ray and Michael would enjoy them as much as he did. I noticed the sky becoming overcast, realizing how fortunate we had been to have had such pretty days all week.

I drove into my garage, entered the hall and into my apartment with my groceries. I kicked off my shoes, put on a small pot of coffee, and went over and looked out the windows. It was like I was scanning, to make sure nothing on the streets of Manhattan had changed while I was gone for a whole day and a half. The wind had picked up and I could hear it starting to howl against my windows. The clouds seemed to turn those skyscrapers a cold gray and the city took on a different look.

I decided to call Carl. "Hey, sweetie! I miss you already!" I told Carl.

"Miss you, too," he said.

"What ya' been doing?" I asked.

He replied, "Well, I took the boat out and took Harold and the two little boys for a ride. Then I came back and took Mary and the two big boys for a ride the other direction. It was a beautiful day and I didn't have anything else to do and they enjoyed it. Pepper decided he wanted to sleep on the porch all day."

"Trish didn't go?" I asked.

"No, she had to head back to the city too. She said maybe next weekend," Carl answered.

"I would say Jan and the girls are about halfway home right now," I mentioned.

"Yeah, that would be about right," Carl agreed.

"I'll call them tonight and see how their flight was and make sure they got in OK. By the way, I enjoyed going to church this morning and meeting everyone. I sure do like Brother Darrel and his wife, Judy. I liked everyone I met there. I can see why you love going there," I told him.

"Yeah, they are wonderful people. I'm glad you went today. I have been wanting you to meet them for quite a while. Matter of fact, I better get going, Sunday night services start in about forty minutes. I have to clean up around here and get ready," he said.

"OK. I'll call you later if it is not storming here. It looks pretty bad outside right now. Bye, sweetie!" I said. He said bye and hung up.

I turned on the TV and tried to find a gospel channel, and lo and behold, this preacher was talking about the end of the age. He said he was reading from Matthew 24. He talked about earthquakes, famines, and all kinds of things that are happening right now (Matt. 24:6–7). I mean today! He said time was short and we need to be ready, for the day and hour are unknown as to His return (Matt. 24:36). It was the end of his sermon. I wished I had heard it all! I had to get a Bible!

I laid down on the couch to watch the news. I wanted to see what the forecast was. They were talking about a terrible earthquake that had happened overseas. Then they told about a desolate country and its famines and how many had died so far. Good grief, that is exactly what that preacher was just talking about! How could anyone not see what was happening after listening to that preacher. I had heard all this before, but I had always just passed it off and not paid any attention. My golly, all this was in the Bible and I never knew it!

Immediately, I saw that little old white-haired lady pointing her bony finger in my face. She was staring at me with those intent, steel blue eyes, saying, "Missy, if you don't know, you better find out, and you better be ready, and you better be ready, and you better be ready. . . ."

Salvation in Harlem

CRACK! POP! I JUMPED STRAIGHT UP OFF THE COUCH TO FIERCE lightning darting right by my window and throughout the city. . . . All its deadly electrical limbs lighting up the pitch black sky. I don't remember ever seeing it any worse than this! The TV was still going. What time was it? What day was it? Oh, my gosh, I never called Jan and I never called Carl back.

One o'clock in the morning! Monday morning? Yeah, it was Monday morning. Boy this was crazy not knowing what day it was and what was going on! I must have really been sleeping. I'd just have to call Jan before she left for work.

The sky was quite dramatic, but I didn't care for the horrible popping and cracking. I must have really been tired, but not too tired to know I was hungry! I fixed a sandwich, had some crackers and cheese and iced tea. Here it was one thirty in the morning and I was eating a snack! Well, most people would call this a meal. After all, I never ate dinner. I ate and watched the spectacular show outside. The lightning lit up all the tall buildings. I just didn't want to get any closer to the windows. I could see quite enough sitting over at the kitchen bar.

I finished eating, removed my makeup, and crawled into bed. I was so grateful for such a wonderful visit with Jan and the girls. I was so grateful for many things, even the message from the old, white-haired lady. Her stern eyes and bold words of wisdom still burned in my mind and heart. I shall not forget them!

The morning sun! It was 6:30. I got up and looked out. Clear as a bell! After a storm like that, it always seemed to wash all the pollution out. It was just like the night Jan and the girls arrived. It looked spectacular out there. I needed to get ready and see what was going on at the office. Man, it suddenly seemed like a year since I had been there!

"Today is a new day," I declared. "I'm going to start turning more over to Sam. Even Carl agreed with that. Matter of fact, he thought it was long overdue."

I called Jan and they all made it home safely. She said Ray and Michael wanted to take Carl up on a weekend of fishing. I told her he would keep them posted on how the fish were biting.

"I'm going to start calling you every week or two just so we can chat anyway," I mentioned.

Then she said, "Diane, remember the white-haired lady who told you to be ready?"

"How could I ever forget her!" I answered.

"The girls and I looked all over the plane for her and she was not there. I asked one of the stewardesses about her and they said they never saw a lady with that description get on the plane. They called out front where we lined up to board and they said they definitely remembered her, but she never came back out either. It was like she disappeared into thin air," Jan confessed.

"What!" I shrieked. "Well, it certainly wasn't our imagination!" I proclaimed.

"When she spoke that to you and for you, it left everyone there with quite an impression. There were other people looking for her on the plane besides us. There was one preacher that came up and talked to us about her and he wanted to talk with her, but she was gone!" Jan explained.

"What do you think, that she was . . . an angel?" I asked, and there was only silence on the other end. "Oh, Jan, come on!" I exclaimed.

"Diane, she left an impression on everyone who heard her, an awesome impression when she gave you that word, and she was gone as soon as she turned that corner!" Jan emphasized.

"All I know is that I still see her in my mind, and especially those compelling blue eyes. Something about those blue eyes got the attention of my body and soul, I'll tell you that!" I admitted.

"Well, her words got everyone's attention and everyone heard what you asked me," she giggled. "That is why her words rang through all of us, even the preacher! I believe she was a messenger from God, telling us to be ready!"

"Unbelievable!" I whispered as I brushed my arm and felt goose-bumps.

"The girls and I are still talking about her. It was unbelievable, especially when she disappeared into thin air! It was a word for all the unsaved to get saved and it was a message to all the Christians to witness and lead all we can to Jesus. We all need to be ready!" Jan exclaimed.

That really got my attention. Was I really looking in the face of a messenger from God . . . an angel (Heb. 13:2)? After I talked to Jan I called Carl.

He was eating a sausage biscuit and getting ready to go fishing. I told him not to forget his life jacket. He told me that he was glad that I was around, since he didn't know anything. He told me he would meet me up here this evening and not to cook anything. He figured my first day back would be hectic and we would just eat out. I have to admit, that sounded pretty good to me!

"Good morning, Faune!" I smiled, greeting our head secretary.

"Hey, Missy! How was your long weekend?" she asked with that English accent. There was that word "Missy" again.

"My weekend was great! I feel like I lived a month in four days, we did so much," I said. "What has been going on here?" I asked.

"Oh, it's been busy. We have taken on three new accounts and they are big ones! Franklin has asked me several times if you were in yet," Faune laughed.

"He has? I'm ten minutes early right now! What! Three new accounts!" I exclaimed.

"Yes! I imagine he will have you busy, busy, busy!" Faune laughed.

"Three new accounts! Three—in two working days?" I questioned in disbelief.

Faune just kept shaking her head up and down and laughing, "Yes, can you believe it!"

My heart sank to a new low! A couple of weeks ago, I would have been on cloud nine. Today, blah-h-h. What's the matter with me? I opened the door to my office and walked to the window and looked over Manhattan. I lived on one side and worked straight across on the other side. I knew I had a great job, a great firm, a great boss. I had it made! I just wasn't interested anymore . . . I wondered what Carl was doing about now.

I looked around my office and it was very nice. It had solid cherry furniture, sprawling plants, limited edition prints all around, not to mention an incredible view of the city. I looked out my window that was almost a third of the wall, then back at my office. One end of my office had a plush couch and two side chairs to match, a cherry butler's table, even my own wet bar. I had made it this far and could easily work another fifteen years, yet today I was ready to go bye-bye.

I looked over at the couch, fondly remembering all the times Carl sat there and waited, sometimes for hours, for me to get out of a meeting so we could leave for the evening. If I could count all the hours he had sat there waiting on me over the years, they would add up to weeks! At least he knew to bring his briefcase and work. He would always brag that he probably made bigger decisions and more money waiting on me than I did in those long, drawn out meetings. At least somebody got something out of those meetings!

"Diane, my dear! How are you doing? I hope you rested very, very well!" kidded Franklin as he walked in my office with a big smile. I looked at him and started chuckling at the little dance step he was doing all around my office.

I shook my head at him, took my seat and said, "Well, Mr. Grant, please have a seat and tell me al-l-l about these three new accounts we just received. It is three, isn't it?"

"Yes, my dear," he whispered to me, raising his eyebrows and trying to stop smiling, but he couldn't. His smile was always contagious.

In all his excitement about the new accounts, he still wanted to know all about my cousins' visit. I always enjoyed talking to Franklin, because he was genuinely interested in what you did or what you were doing. He was a detail-oriented man, and he wanted to know where we went, what they thought about New York City, and how they liked Carl's place and Amber Lake. We talked about that for a while and things shifted over to what had happened while I was gone.

He told me we were having a big meeting at ten. We both stopped chatting and kidding and got down to brass tacks on who the new clients were and how we needed to handle them to their advantage. He asked me to bring forth my plans and suggestions at the meeting, then he left to finish his presentation for the meeting. I had to hit it, but I knew what to do. I got up and got a cup of coffee to keep me going. It was already 8:40!

I started to work for Franklin when I came here twenty years ago. His father and two other partners started this consulting business here in a one room office. They gathered their clients from Manhattan businesses and the firm kept growing, gathering more clients from Manhattan. Franklin grew up in it and he had told us he knew when he was a little boy he wanted to take over his father's business. He was very well-educated about this company and knew the ropes.

He came here when he was eighteen years old and started out as the office flunky. He stayed in that job about eight months and he kept moving up and up until he got to where he is now. His father made it a point not to favor him. He had to earn his position. In the meantime his father bought out the other two partners with money he had made through the years on excellent investments. His father told him to be honest and caring, to always give a hundred percent satisfaction to clients, and to be very good to his employees. If he did this, the firm would provide a very good living for his children and their children for generations to come. Franklin took it over when his father retired and has always followed his advice.

His position was well-deserved and he was a big credit to this firm. He had been good to me. He was always a fair man and gave credit where credit was due. If someone wasn't doing their job, he had no trouble letting them know they had to get on course. He was a good manager and I respected him a lot.

There was a knock at my door and it was Sam. "Hey, come on in! How have you been doing?" I asked.

"Oh, just fine. Glad you are back!" Sam said slowly, shaking his head.

I looked at him and said, "Was it that wild of a week? I heard about the three new clients. Three big accounts in two days! Man, that is unbelievable! Maybe I better stay gone more often!" I emphasized and giggled.

"No, don't do that! Whatever you do, don't do that!" Sam said putting both of his hands straight out, palms up like a stop sign. Just what I didn't want to hear!

"Sam, listen to me, you can handle it. It is a lot of intense work, I agree, but you know what to do! That is the main thing, that you know what to do," I informed him.

"Well, it was a little scary without you here. You know, Diane, you are always here for me to fall back on. That gives me great piece of mind. If I go the wrong way, you send me back the right way," Sam confessed.

"I understand! I was there many years ago. It is time for you not to fall back on me anymore. You are ready to go! It is not as if you are by yourself. You fill my shoes when I am gone and Carol and Kent are your co-workers. Neither one of them are going to let you get on the wrong track, much less fall! The firm makes a goof-up, all of us suffer. They are not going to let that happen!" I informed him.

Sam looked at me like he was startled and said, "Don't even tell me! Diane, you are not thinking about leaving are you?"

Good grief, I didn't think I sounded that obvious! My deep thoughts must be speaking out of my mouth, whether I realize it or not. "Well, Sam, someday. I mean, who knows!" I stuttered.

Franklin suddenly opened the door and pointed a finger at me and said, "Ten o'clock, we're ready to hear some knockdown ideas," then he grinned and closed the door.

"What is at ten o'clock?" whispered Sam.

"It is about the three new clients. What is best for them and how to do a super job for corporations of this magnitude. We are on the brink of landing other large accounts if these three remain happy with us. It is a different strategy than what has pleased and met the demands of the average client. In other words, a new day is dawning. The big boys are coming our way now!" I stated. "Sam, you need to be in on this meeting," I suggested.

"Me?" he announced, like I didn't know what I was talking about.

"Yes, you need to be involved in the very first agreement and action on these clients. Believe me, like I have just told you, this is a new day, Sam. There is a change taking place now. It is your turn to take the reins and ride a new horse," I instructed. Sam just looked at me with eagerness, yet a bit reluctant.

"Franklin, I want Sam in on this meeting. Is that OK with you?" I asked Franklin on the intercom. Sam was still looking at me like the world was moving too fast.

"If you think he needs to be there, by all means have him there. See you in twenty minutes," Franklin clicked out.

"Sam, you are on! Let me finish here and I will see you upstairs in the boardroom," I said and looked back down at the papers with my notes thus far. Sam backed out of my office, still staring at me. I laughed to myself after he shut the door.

I got out of the elevator and Carol was standing there waiting on me. She gave me a big hug and asked, "Well, how was your visit with your cousins?"

"Great!" I answered.

"Can you believe these new clients?" Carol asked, still in awe herself.

"No!" I replied.

"I called Faune for you first thing this morning and she laughed and said Franklin was already in your office. I hope you had a very restful four days!" she laughed.

"I had a wonderful four days. I ended the weekend in the country with Carl and my cousins, listening to the birds, going to church and . . ."

"You went to church?" perked Carol, not believing what she heard. "We better go to lunch and catch up!" Carol suggested as she grabbed me by the arm. We chuckled, entered the boardroom and took our usual seats. Kent was already seated and Sam was standing by the coffee urn, waiting for me to arrive. He pulled up a chair on the other side of me and sat down.

Franklin brought the meeting to order, still smiling. He began by announcing we were embarking on a new era now. We would all work together to master a new plan for clients of this magnitude, while still maintaining our one hundred percent customer satisfaction we have been so proud of through the years. The meeting lasted for almost three hours. We all put our heads together and came up with a very refined plan for handling these corporations.

Many new ideas and problems were discussed and ironed out. The bottom line was that we could achieve the demands and have a completely satisfied customer. This was our goal, which would attract similar clients. There was no doubt that our successful firm was about to become very successful!

Franklin suggested that all of us go out to lunch together. Carol and I told Franklin, Kent, and Sam we were going for "girl talk," not "corporate talk." They really kidded us about that, but the three of them took off down the hall, just yapping about, what else, "the three new clients."

Sam was really seeing a new day today! This was good for him. He was a good, honest man and he would stick with the hard work to see it through. He was nervous about stepping up the ladder and taking on decision-making responsibilities, but it was time. His loyalty and honesty for the firm would carry him farther than he realized. Those were very important traits to have! There would be times he would get stepped on along the way for it, unfortunately, but he was tough enough to persevere.

The hostess took Carol and I to our booth and seated us by a window overlooking the busy sidewalks of Broadway. "Oh, sounds like you really had a wonderful time. Diane, Amber Lake sounds so serene. You know, I have a feeling it was hard for you to come back to the city this time. I know you really enjoy it out there," Carol implied. She paused for a minute, then she said, "I think I should say you long for it. There is a difference!" She sat there looking at me, knowing there was a difference. Carol knew me too long and too well.

"I'm trying to fool myself, but I can't fool you, can I?" I asked Carol, softly smiling.

"No," she smiled, almost sympathizing with me. "You need to follow your heart, you know. Are you going to stay here another fifteen years when you want to be out there with Carl? The firm is taking a new turn now and you know everything is going to change. Do you know how much time and work that will take?" she asked, knowing that I knew all too well.

"Yes, I certainly do," I answered, not wanting to think about it.

"I know you, and you will be putting in seven day weeks forever," she implied. I shook my head, affirming what she was saying.

"Carl will not be here anymore. You know he could have left the city a long time ago. He has been waiting on you, but he finally saw the writing on the wall," Carol said, trying to get me to see the light.

"I just figured he loved the challenge of his job and it put electricity in his veins. I never thought of him staying here just for me!" I said.

"Well, think again, my friend! Carl has been competing with your job ever since I have known you. He knew you would have never left for him, or anything else. I know he played a very important role in his company. They needed his advice and expertise every day he was there. Diane, he could have left at least ten years ago! Why do you think he stayed?" Carol asked me, trying to get me to see the real picture.

It was the same truth Jan had just tried to get me to see. I believed in Carol and Jan and had to take every word to heart. I needed to open my eyes and my heart in several areas! I could not walk in the dark anymore, the consequences were too great! What was it I would hear Jan say, "the truth will set you free" (John 8:32). Now, that is a revelation!

"I never saw it. Why didn't I ever see it?" I asked Carol, baffled that I was so blind.

"Maybe you didn't want to. You have had the best of both worlds. You had a top-notch job with a lot of prestige and a wonderful man who truly loved you and was totally dedicated to you. You didn't have to make any decisions or choices," she answered.

I sat back and looked at her and shook my head at myself. "Oh, how we get wrapped up in the hustle and bustle of the world," I sighed.

"Please don't fret. The sun has not set yet, but it is fast approaching! The present and the future are what you need to focus on! As far as the past, you have had twenty fantastic years. If all was over today, there are not many people that have had the exciting life you have had! You still have your job and you still have Carl. You have not lost anything at this point, but by the look on your face, I think you are going to have to make some choices now," she said calmly, justifying what I knew in my heart.

"Yes, you are so right. Now, I regret that I didn't make some different choices years ago. If I had not been so determined about my career, maybe Carl would have asked me to marry him and we would have had children. Who knows how different it could have been!" I said regretfully.

"Diane! We all have regrets and guess what? None of us can change them! Remember what you have always told me? If you keep looking in your rearview mirror you are going to hit something! There is no future in the past. You have today. Make the most of it!" she instructed me.

I looked at her and smiled and said, "You know Carl and I got to talking about prayer of all things. I never talk about religion, but we were talking about it because my cousins wanted to pray for me. I told Carl I had done just fine on my own all these years, so on and so forth. He told me if I had been praying, who knows where I would be," I reflected.

"Carl, all these years what I thought was a big deal may have been nothing compared to what God had in store for me! I never prayed and I never did seek Him or ask Him to guide my life," I told her. She looked at me so serious, smiled and said, "Well, it certainly is not too late, and thank God you realize that. You are getting ready to make some important decisions and I believe they will be good ones. You are so fortunate you are in a position financially, that you don't have to work any longer if you don't want to. You are totally free to make the choice you want. Now don't get so buried in work here that you put your needs and desires on the back burner!" she warned me.

"Carol, another thing you said is a confirmation to me," I stated.

"What was that?" Carol asked.

"When you said, 'if it was all over today.' If it was all over right now, I would be in hell," I said as the waitress stood at our table with our change.

Carol and the waitress both stared at me, not taking a breath. I got up from the booth, thanked the waitress and said, "Carol, you are right! I have some serious decisions to make and I am way overdue!" I announced. We both left and returned to the office.

Carol, Kent, Franklin, and Sam were all working late that night. I had told Franklin I had a dinner date with Carl and would catch them in the morning and work late Tuesday if I needed too. Franklin and Kent were very surprised I wasn't working late, as I always did at the drop of a hat. They were surprised when I said Sam would fill in for me. Sam was more nervous than surprised.

Carol had left the boardroom to compile some statistics and put them on Kent's desk. She had worked all weekend and was anxious to leave and get home to Glenn, her husband, and sons, Glenn Jr., whom she called "G," and Chris. G and Chris were both out of college and G helped in his dad's business and lived at home and Chris lived nearby. Kent would stay long after everyone else left, which was normal. Therefore, he would be the one to go over the final notes of the day and compile them.

I went by Carol's office on the way out and told her I was leaving for my dinner date with Carl. She smiled, gave me a thumbs up and said, "I miss you when you are not here. This is where your heart has been all these years, but I see changes about to take place in your life. They will be wonderful changes for you and they are long overdue." She paused and looked down at her notes she was working on rather intensely. Then she looked up with a smile and whispered, "After all these years, Carl has finally won your heart." She turned her chair around and got up and walked into Kent's office and closed the door quietly.

I felt a lump in my throat. Carol and I had worked side by side for those twenty years and through long hours and many weekends. She knew more about me and what I was about to do than I did! She had always thought I should be with Carl and not take him for granted like I did. She had told me that ever since Carl and I started dating.

I closed her door and walked down the hall and caught the elevator. When the elevator doors opened, I met Nick, carrying dinner to the boardroom. "Are you the one leaving early?" Nick asked, like he was alarmed.

"Yes, Nick! Can you believe it!" I said.

"No, I can't! Franklin called me and gave me the same order I have had for years, except I had one order for a turkey and lettuce on whole wheat, mixed salad, no dressing, and peach non-fat yogurt. I thought you must have gone on a health food kick!" he expressed in that Italian accent and all those gestures.

"No, Nick. That was Sam's order. You better get used to that order most of the time," I said as I stepped in the elevator.

"Why? Where are you going?" inquired a surprised Nick.

"Well, right now I'm late for a hot date," I answered, grinning at Nick. His eyes got real big and then he closed them and put his lips together like he was smooching someone. The elevator doors closed with him acting like he was dancing with someone while holding the sacks of food.

I yelled, "Ain't love grand!" I shook my head and laughed all the way out of the building.

In the taxi, I thought how much you look at everything differently when you are about to leave it. Everything you have taken for granted on a daily basis for years suddenly touches your heart. All the times we talked about how we couldn't wait to retire, or I wished I was here or there and not at work. Now that I was considering a change, at least in my heart right now, everything was sentimental, even Nick!

How we have laughed at him over the years as he would bring us dinner when we worked late. He was always kidding and carrying on. His deli was on the street corner of our building and it had been in his family for years. He was the only one out of seven children that carried on the tradition. His mother had taught him everything about cooking.

I remember when I first started working here, I would go down there and get lunch. His mother would be in the back cooking, and Nick would be taking orders out front and preparing carryouts for his father to deliver. Nick would always put a little candy bar or something in my sack.

Franklin used to say Nick was trying to tell me he was sweet on me. If he was, poor Nick never had time to ask anyone out. When I would leave late at night, there was a light in the back of the deli and Nick and his mother would be preparing for the next day. Then one day Nick's father was killed in a traffic accident in New Jersey, while he was visiting one of Nick's sisters and her family.

After his father's death, Nick's mother finally hired a beautiful little Italian girl, Angelina, to help out. Nick and Angelina were married in less than a year. Now Nick and Angelina run the deli and his mother lives with them in their Brooklyn home and watches their four children while they work here.

Nick was always a pleasant break in our routine when we had already worked ten hours and were in for about three more. Food was his business and he was proud of it. He knew our menus by heart and the food was always delicious! On the holidays we worked, or special days like St. Patrick's Day or Flag Day, he would bring us a dessert of some kind to commemorate that day. We didn't know there were so many days to celebrate, but Nick knew them all and delighted in cooking something special for each one of them. It seemed like he was always at work, just like we were.

Franklin or one of us would call and say, "Nick, the regular," in our best Italian accent to kid him, and he would be right up. No matter if it was a breakfast meeting, lunch, or dinner, he knew what to bring each time without another word.

He knew us and what we always wanted. I don't know why we all kept the same orders through the years. We had our favorites and never wanted to change I guess.

Oh, all the nights we worked late and the long weekends! As I look back, we worked very hard, but we kidded and shared tough times and good times with each other. I think of all the traveling we had to do, visiting different cities, and working to get new accounts. We haven't had to travel much in the last six years. Clients have been coming to us, but only as a result of us flying all over the place to make a name for ourselves.

I have always gotten a kick out of the "new kids" coming in the firm. They all want to go back down roads we have already traveled, but we have already been there and know the outcome. I'm thrilled they are full of inspiration and fresh ideas and new blood is always a plus in many ways. Of course, today things are changing so fast, that what didn't work or was impossible yesterday will work today. What is new one week is already outdated by next week. The younger ones are very sharp and adept at computer technology. "We are living in an amazing time!" I thought.

They would never know what we went through to build the firm into what it was today! I guess Franklin, Carol, Kent, and I were the pioneers that flew all over the nation to put it where it was today—especially Franklin! He knew it when it was just a local firm from his father's day. Franklin knew the firm had to change if it was going to keep up with the times and we were able to pull it off, but we had to travel nationwide and it worked! Franklin traveled with us the first three years and then he turned it over to the three of us.

Franklin stayed here and ran the entire office while we brought in new clients. There were quite a few small businesses on our floor years ago and as they either fell by the wayside or moved on, Franklin would take over their vacated office space. The office space, employees, and clients have grown tremendously in the last twenty years. Both have doubled every five years since I started. Franklin's plan was to grow and serve clients with a "one hundred percent customer satisfaction," as he always called it. My, how it worked! Now it was time for another move, a big move to stay in demand.

"Franklin, Carol, and Kent will handle it through the next big move," I reasoned. "They will keep Sam under their wing until he can solo. He is so fortunate to have them as mentors. They are the backbone of the firm. They know all the history, the mistakes not to make, and the avenues to take and when to take them. To have people with that knowledge, and care and concern for your future is a young executive's dream! Franklin will be here until he either dies or he can't operate his wheelchair. He was born into this firm, and he will probably die in this firm.

"Thank heavens he is training his son, Grant, to take over in his footsteps. His grandchildren are already up here in the summer doing office work. Of course, who knows if they will be interested in taking it over. Far from me to worry about. I don't intend on sticking around that long! I'm just glad I was a link in getting it where it is today. I can be proud of that. Won't be long, these kids can take it and roll with it!

"Carol will stay for several more years at least. She will be a mentor to the new generation coming in here. She is loyal, honest, and definitely has their best interests at heart. She will be the perfect inspiration to a new partner. She will be very difficult to replace in many ways. She can work hours on end and never falter or loose her gusto. She has a great compassion for people, and will be there to help them as well as teach them.

"Franklin and I used to kid her about never running down and we were going to put her in one of those battery commercials. Franklin said he was going to call them and have them film her for the part as long as the firm's name was in there so we could get a free plug. That's Franklin, always thinking ahead!

"There is one thing Carol and I share sentiments on. Her heart is calling her in another direction. She wants to help Glenn with his songwriting business and she has always wanted her own catering business. Boy! If Thornton's Bed and Breakfast ever goes up for sale, that would be perfect. She would only be twenty minutes from me and have a beautiful home and business. Glenn would have a serene and inspirational place to write. Perfect! Listen to me. I have already got myself out at Amber Lake with Carl, and Carol and Glenn at Thornton's! Well, it would be perfect!

"I guess Kent would have to handle it all! Kent is total business. All of us traveled well in the old days and we work great together now. Kent is serious about this business like we are, but he has blinders on and that is all he sees. He has a wife and son who he loves dearly, but nothing takes his time away from this business. His wife, Honey, and son, Eric, kid us by saying nothing like a death, sickness, marriage, or whatever better take place if he is working with an important client, because he will be in the office, no matter what!

"Franklin has to tell Kent to take time with his family and take that long overdue vacation. He frets and finally decides to because Franklin makes him. His wife and son get so excited about getting to spend some time with him, and all he can think about is, 'If something comes up, you better call me!'

"Kent's son is away at college now. Honey stays involved in her job because she doesn't have anyone to come home to until late. Kent works until eight o'clock or later every night. He plays golf every Saturday and Sunday in order to meet new clients. Many times he has dinner with them after playing golf, so there is no time for Honey on the weekend either.

"It was really hard on her when Eric left for college. Thank heavens, Eric is going to college near Honey's parents so she can drive out there on the weekends and stay with Eric and them. They visit and all go to church Sunday morning and even Sunday night. He drives back to college and she comes back home. It is only a one hour drive for Eric and about an hour and a half for her. She says her parents really look forward to the weekend. They just wish Kent would spend more time with his family. Honey and Eric go stay with Kent's parents about once every two months. They are about three hours from the city. Kent sees them maybe twice a year.

"Franklin, Carol, and I all wish he would spend more time with all of them. It is so sad. I feel sorry for Honey and I believe Eric resented it for a long time. The last time I saw him he told me he had forgiven his father for all the time he was away from home. He said his father never asked for forgiveness because he has never seen anything wrong with putting his job first. He would tell them that his job is what put food on the table, paid the bills, and sent Eric to college. Eric said God dealt with his heart and the resentment he had. He said he had to seek God and through Him he was able truly to forgive his father. He seemed so peaceful and so mature!

"Honey and Eric are really involved in church and her parents have asked them to move in with them. They have a large colonial home in a beautiful little town. Their church does a lot of mission work and they would love Honey to help them. She would love that too!

"Honey sees Kent at about nine or ten o'clock at night and a few minutes in the morning. I guess she is trying to hang onto those few precious moments she has with him. I don't know why he can't see what a wonderful little family he has. She has just about begged him at least to come to church out there Sunday mornings and eat lunch with all of them. He says he meets with clients over brunch at the country club and that is one of the best times during the weekend to talk with them.

"When I came to the firm, Eric was just a baby. Honey used to come in with Eric at least once a week and eat lunch with Kent in the office. I remember when she brought him in when he had gotten his first tooth. She was so excited and she said Eric would be sound asleep when Kent got home. She didn't want him to miss the day his first tooth came in. The same happened when he took his first step, said his first word, so on and so forth.

"Kent was so fortunate to have such a wonderful wife that would take a little baby and come into the office in winter snow, hot summer days, not to mention the traffic! Kent got home when Eric was already asleep, so she did what she could to keep some kind of father-and-son relationship. Of course, all of us in the office really enjoyed seeing them and watching Eric as he grew up.

"When you work with people for weeks and years on end they are a big part of your life. I even have sentimental feelings about the building! When I go up there on the weekends, it is so quiet, and I unlock my office and just take time to look out over marvelous Manhattan. All the hustle and bustle of the weekday voices, keyboards clicking, phones ringing, laughing, scampering from one meeting to another—it is but a memory.

"On Saturday or Sunday I can even hear the wind against my window up there. I can hear the elevator going up and down for the few people who come in to different offices to work and catch up. It is nice to be able to work in peace and quiet, with no interruptions, yet it is kind of lonely in a way.

"When I get up from my computer, I stretch and look out the window, searching for people below. I wonder who they are and where they are going. When I see couples walking arm in arm, talking and laughing, I wonder if they will fall in love and get married. I think of Carl and I, then I wonder if they will live here, or if they are just passing through. I see all the cars darting here and there. Where is everyone going and what is everyone doing, and in such a hurry too!

"Sometimes on Saturday afternoon I hear distant church bells ringing and get up and look out. Every once in a while I see a car finally go through the intersection with the newlyweds. Cans are dragging behind the car and white whipped cream or shaving cream is all over it. Off they go, down the road of life . . ."

The restaurant was buzzing with people, but all I could see was Carl and was so glad to be with him this evening. Carl swallowed a bite of T-bone steak and informed me, "If they got three new clients, and major ones at that, I would say your free weekends you were talking about yesterday just got unfreed!"

"I'm not even concerned about it right now. We are enjoying our dinner together and Sam is up there doing what I would normally do.

So, see, it is covered and all is well," I calmly said to Carl, reaching across the table and taking his hand.

"Did Sam take your place tonight?" Carl asked.

"Yes, and he came in and sat in the board meeting this morning. I wanted him too and that was fine with Franklin. Sam is ready for the challenge. He has had his feet wet long enough. It is time for him to jump in!" I told Carl. Carl just gazed at me across the table and smiled. He quickly tried not to be conspicuous, and cut another piece of steak.

I knew he was shocked that I decided to meet with him instead of work. I would usually work if need be, but I would always work if a new client came in, much less three of them! Our evening was relaxing and I looked forward to it like it was the first date with a boy I had a crush on!

"Let's take a taxi back to my apartment and talk about Amber Lake and church and all," I suggested, dabbing my lips with the dinner napkin.

Carl looked at me and chuckled.

"What is so funny?" I asked, grinning at his chuckling.

"Nothing," he grinned. I believe he was tickled to see such a change in me, but he never said a word.

I unlocked my apartment door and we walked in. "What would you like to drink? Oh by the way, I can make a great pitcher of iced tea!" I announced as I walked over and hugged him. He started chuckling again.

"What on earth is the matter?" I asked, giggling at him at this point.

We sat side by side and looked out over the city and talked about the weekend and how nice it was to have Jan and the girls here. We talked about all the people I met at church. Carl told me that Sunday night some of the church members came up and told him what a nice couple we made. I was glad to hear that!

"How long are you going to stay in the city this week, sweetie?" I asked, laying my head on his shoulder. "I'll probably leave out Friday morning and come back Monday afternoon," he answered. "I would like to go to church Wednesday night, but that is kind of tough to do in the middle of the week. It would cut my office time too short right now," he stated.

"Why don't you go to Wednesday night service somewhere here! I could go with you if you wanted me too," I suggested. He looked at me for a while. I guess he finally figured I was serious.

"We'll see," he calmly answered. We both called it a night and he left to catch a taxi back to his apartment. He was only about fifteen minutes away from me.

"Diane, I need your help!" stammered Franklin as he entered my office bright and early Tuesday morning. "We are going to need to work much more than eight hour days for several months on these new clients. I know through all the years you have poured out as many thirteen hour days and long weekends as anyone here. I really need your expertise right now. I'm overloaded on the work. Sam has told me he is willing to put in all the hours necessary. I know you have taught him well, but I have to put these accounts in seasoned hands. We have too much to lose if I don't," Franklin pleaded.

"Franklin, I have to agree with you. I know we are at a big turning point here. The future of this firm lies on how we handle these clients, period. I will help you, and Sam as well. I'm sure Carol and Kent are pouring it on too," I commented.

"Oh yeah, we'll be like we were a few years ago, just having time to go home and change clothes!" Franklin laughed. "Diane, you have always been faithful to the firm and me. There will be a bonus in this for you. I will definitely make it worth your time," he assured me.

"Franklin, I'm speaking prematurely, but I may not be around much after the next six months. I'm starting to think about phasing out gradually. I believe it is time for me to go," I said calmly, looking at Franklin. Franklin looked at me and I could tell he wasn't surprised, but now the words had come to confirm his suspicions.

"I know Carl is leaving the city shortly and I know you have decisions to make. That is up to you. Whatever you decide, you always have an open door back here at any time," he said and looked at me with that reassuring smile. "I just wanted you to know that," he said quietly and turned and closed my door behind him.

I called Carol and Kent and told them it looked like we were heading for old times, starting tonight. Carol was not thrilled about the long hours, like myself, however, we knew it had to be done and we would do it with gusto. Kent loved it! Honey might as well move to her parents now. She will never see him, except for a few minutes in the morning. He was excited about all this work. It was a new horizon to him. It was almost like he was glad he didn't have to give his family excuses anymore for working late.

I didn't get to see Carl at all on the weekends for the following few weeks. He started staying in town Monday and Tuesday, and would leave Wednesday afternoon so he could go to Lakeside Wednesday night services. He was phasing out fast now. I would eat lunch and a late dinner with him when he was here. We both worked very long hours Monday and Tuesday nights, so it worked out well. He would always come up to the office to say bye before he left for Amber Lake. We would all look up from our work and say, "Hi, Carl." I would kiss him bye, they would tell him bye and we would bury ourselves in paperwork again!

I had tried to call Mike, but he was always out in the taxi. He had returned my calls, but we kept missing each other. His boss said he was working a double-shift quite a bit since two of the drivers had been out a lot. I guess he was at least making some extra money, so that was good! I sure did hope he was taking time to go to church with his mother.

It was Labor Day weekend and Franklin told me to take Sunday and Monday and go to Amber Lake and surprise Carl. He told Carol to go home and visit with her family and relax. Kent didn't want to stop working. Franklin told him "orders from headquarters" were that he go to Honey's parents and spend the weekend with his wife, son, and in-laws. It would also be a good idea for all of them to drive over and see his parents too. Carol, Sam, and I took Franklin up on his offer immediately. All of us worked until eight o'clock Saturday night.

Nick had brought us food from breakfast to dinner. He would work Saturdays and usually Sunday mornings in his deli. He said Angelina, the children, and his mother would not miss church for anything. I told him he should go to church with them, but he said so many people were getting used to coming by about eleven and getting his fantastic sandwiches, he felt he owed it to them to be open. On Sunday mornings he would be getting all the food ready for Monday mornings. People kept knocking on the door wanting to know if he was going to open. He finally opened on Sundays against Angelina and his mother's wishes.

Boy, I can hear them now! Pointing their fingers and lashing those dark eyes at him telling him what they thought. He admitted they never got upset with him about anything but not going to church on Sunday mornings. He said both of them kept telling him he would pay dearly for that someday. He told me his oldest son told him he was going to hell if he didn't know God, and that really made him think! I told him he better think! He looked at me, surprised I would take their side, especially since I was working all the time myself.

I got up early Sunday morning, ran across the street to Peggy's, and got some bagels and juice. Peggy and Eugene were in church. She was open on Sunday mornings only with the agreement that the two employees took turns working, so they both could attend either early or late church services. Peggy would cook everything very early and then leave for church. I had always known that, but it didn't register until now. Amazing, all the people I was noticing who were going and not going to church for some reason.

I packed everything and headed for Lakeside Church. It was so beautiful out. An early fall was in the air. It was about my favorite time of the year. I got there in time for Sunday school. Carolyn, our teacher, was out there greeting people. Sharon came up and gave me a hug. Brother Darrel and his wife, Judy, came over too. They all told me they heard I had just about been working around the clock. I told them they didn't know how good it felt to be out of that building and be here!

April was already there with her two cousins, Adon and Ian. They were practicing a special they were going to sing. They remembered me from the last time and told me Carl was back in his class reading over the lesson. I went back there and he was reading and didn't even look up. I asked him if the seat next to him was taken and he looked up and about fell over. He started laughing and stood up and gave me a hug and a kiss.

The entire service was great and April, Adon, and Ian sang "Beulah Land." There were some people in the church that were wiping tears away. Brother Darrel had a wonderful sermon. It was about when Christ gathers His people off the earth to be with Him. He called it the rapture. He said the dead in Christ shall burst out of their graves and rise first. The believers that are living will be caught up with them and meet the Lord in the sky. We who are Christians, shall comfort one another with these words (1 Thess. 4:15–18). That got some "Amens" throughout the church!

It sounded too good to be true to me! Maybe that was my problem, everything sounded too good to be true. You know what they warn you about on a sales pitch. If it sounds too good to be true, then it probably is! Brother Darrel gave the invitation and held up the Bible and said, "If all this sounds too good to be true and you sluff it off, you better read your Bible. I didn't say these things, the Lord said them and they will come to pass. You better be ready!" Boy, was that a confirmation or what! I didn't move, but I felt my heart quicken. When the invitation was over, he asked Carl to close in prayer.

The Goodfellows were in front of us and after the service they turned around and greeted me. They were laughing and talking about the boys and Carl and their fishing trips. Trish was there and the two of us started talking. I asked her about her job as a makeup consultant. I told her at my age I was ready for a complete makeover! I basically hadn't changed makeup for years and had the same look. I told her I needed that face-lift in a bottle.

She laughed and knew exactly the colors I needed and the makeup for my type of skin and all. I couldn't wait! She did makeup seminars all over the country, so she definitely knew what she was doing. Boy, when I came here, I found help in another whole area I didn't expect to find in church!

Almost twenty people from church decided to go to the buffet over at Grinder's Mill. We had a great time! We all ate out on the patio and talked and laughed. The Goodfellows sat at our table and Trish and I were still talking makeup! Sharon looked even better than the last time I had seen her! She sat behind us, and some of the women in the church had lost as much as twenty pounds since she started her seminar about six weeks ago. I told them they had the most beautiful church women in the country with Trish and Sharon seminars. We all laughed and had great fellowship over a delicious lunch.

Carl and I left and drove around the countryside, stopped at the grocery, and got some food for a cookout the church was having that night. It was the last cookout of the season. Carl said they would have a fall festival at the end of October and hayrides around the lake. Sounded like fun to me!

Carl and I took a boat ride and relaxed out on the lake. Pepper sat on the bank and waited on us. We heard the loons, and bluebirds darted around the woods near the pier. We went to church for the evening services. Afterwards, we had a great cookout and it was a good time to get to know everyone better. It was a beautiful evening and we watched the sun go down over the lake and once again, Amber Lake lived up to its name. We all packed up our stuff and everyone hugged me and said they hoped to see me soon. I really felt at home with all of them and I could see why Carl loved it here.

Monday, Labor Day, was a beautiful day. We planned how we could redo the upstairs storage room and free the fishing room from the mess it was in! After all, Ray and Jan and the kids could be visiting soon.

We drove to Thornton's Bed and Breakfast for lunch. I loved that place. There were sailboats on the lake and the hanging ferns were waving in the breeze. I believe the flowers were at their peak that day. They wouldn't be beautiful for very long; we could have freezing temperatures anytime and all that would be gone for the season. After lunch, I wanted to go out to the gazebo with Carl. We walked out there and stood for a while, hugging each other, enjoying the lake and just being together.

We went back to Carl's, and as I packed my bags to leave, I changed my mind. I decided to stay another night and head out at daybreak so I could check on the apartment and still be at work on time. I just didn't want to leave until I absolutely had to, and I was starting to feel like I didn't want to then!

Carl and I sprawled out on the sectional, talked, and had a tray of crackers and several new varieties of cheese he had bought on Friday. We both fell asleep and when I woke up, the night sounds of bullfrogs and crickets were a melody to my ears. The breeze was blowing in the windows, carrying the music through the house. Oh, I thought, the most wonderful things are absolutely free!

At daybreak I tiptoed out and loaded my car, backed down the driveway and took one last look at the house and lake as I entered the road. Carl was still sound asleep on the sectional, but Pepper was on the porch, watching me as I drove out of sight. The dawn was breaking across the countryside and I didn't have to worry about traffic this time of morning, at least not much.

The morning sunrise silhouetted the church steeples, and silos and barns dotted the hillsides and valleys. It was so serene. I stopped at Kinsey's Breakfast Nook and bought a large cup of their delicious coffee. I was really enjoying the early morning and countryside as I drove along. As I took my last swallow of coffee, I drove into Manhattan. . . . Hopefully ready to conquer the piles of paperwork and tasks that had to fall into place.

"Thank you Franklin for letting me loose this weekend!" I was refreshed and ready to pour on the coal. Maybe it wouldn't be long before we would get things ready to move into "another new age" as Carol and I called it. I knew Carol was ready to have a break! I had a feeling that Kent had worked the entire weekend. Man, I hope he didn't! Well, I would find out soon, I thought, as I wheeled into my garage.

I unloaded my car and checked on the apartment. I took a shower and dressed, then rushed back down to catch a taxi. There was Gilbert, holding the door open. I handed him a tip as he opened the taxi door and told him to run over to Peggy's and get himself a blueberry bagel with gushy cream cheese. He laughed and told me he was ready for one.

Carol greeted me at my office. "How was your cherished, and I do mean cherished, weekend?" asked Carol laughing.

"Great, great, great!" I answered.

"Wow, what did you do?" she asked, astonished at my enthusiastic answer.

"I went out to Carl's and went to church and came in early this morning," I replied.

She looked at me and started laughing and said, "Boy, you used to have to go to Europe on a ski trip, attend five international parties, and see the Pope to give three 'greats' as a response." We both started laughing and I agreed with her.

"Not anymore!" I said as we both walked into the boardroom to plan the attack for this week.

"Nick, I don't know what we would do without you!" Franklin announced. We all looked up from our paperwork at the Styrofoam containers of food Nick was carrying in for the second time today. I looked outside realizing another day was coming to an end. Where does the time go?

"Do you want to break for about an hour and go back to your offices, kick your shoes off and relax?" Franklin asked.

"Yes, sir!" Carol, Kent, Sam, and I shouted simultaneously. We always joked like that when he suggested something that there was no doubt we all knew we wanted to do! Yes, Sam was learning fast!

Carol came back to my office, and as we ate we chatted about our weekend and how much fun we had relaxing and being free from the office. She talked about her catering business again and I talked about writing short stories or a novel. We sure were a long way from that!

Carol and I headed back up to the boardroom and all of us worked about another hour. I told them I was going to call it a day and finish cleaning off my desk and check my answering machine. Kent was staying a while and Franklin and Sam were going to leave in about fifteen minutes. Carol and I took the elevator back down and bid each other good evening as we went to our separate offices to finalize things.

"Kimberly! I haven't seen you for a while. Where have you been?" I asked the cleanup lady as she came into my office.

"Oh, honey I've been off for a while. My husband passed away almost a month ago and I had a lot of things to take care of and all. You can imagine," she told me.

"Goodness sake! I am so sorry! I didn't know about it," I apologized. I felt so sorry for her! She would always talk about him and it sounded like they were so happy.

When Flo had retired several years ago, the building maintenance company hired Kimberly in her place. She was always so full of peace and joy! That really impressed me about her. She had a smile that lit up the world! I would hear people talk about her smile and that there was something about it, almost spiritual. That smile made everyone feel happy. Now that her husband had died, I was sure I would see her downside for awhile. That was only natural.

Kimberly pranced around the room, dusting and taking out the trash. "Girl, you all working late again, like you used to?" she asked, laughing and shaking her head.

"Yeah, I'm afraid so," I answered, smiling.

"Well, then, I'll be seeing ya every night then. Ya'll take care!" she smiled and waved at me as she closed the door, flashing that famous smile. I leaned back in my chair, still hearing her humming and singing her way on down the hall.

What is it that woman has? Where in the world does she find that peace after loosing her husband? I knew she was not putting on a front. This was real peace, the real thing. You sure don't see that much, even in people that shouldn't have a concern in the world. "The people that would pay a fortune to have that kind of peace and strength," I said to myself. "What a testimony she is." I was rather baffled by her. No, really baffled! Oh well, I had to get back to work.

"Did you know that Kimberly's husband had passed away?" I asked Carol Wednesday morning.

"No! I saw her down the hall with her cart and she had just left Franklin's office. She waved and smiled and asked me how I was doing. She had that wonderful smile as usual," Carol answered.

"That is what amazes me! How can she be like that?" I asked Carol.

"Well, she had told me a while back that faith in God and prayer gives one great comfort and peace. Now you see that it is true!" Carol revealed. I looked at her. I knew what she was saying was true.

Why, if I knew it was true, did I have trouble believing it? Did I have such little faith? I could truly see God at work in Kimberly. If I didn't see God and didn't feel His presence, did that mean I could not truly believe in Him?

"Carol, I can see it in her and on her face. Why can't I believe it for me?" I asked her.

"You never spend any time with Him to try to find out. You need to go to church and you need to start reading your Bible. You will see a change. I guarantee it!" Carol said as she nodded her head and smiled reassuringly at me. "I'll see you upstairs at ten o'clock," she said and turned and closed my door.

We worked late and Nick brought us lunch and dinner again. I had taken dinner to my office so I could call Carl, then Kimberly walked in. "Hey, girl, how are ya doing?" she asked, just beaming. You could never help but smile when she walked in the room.

"I'm just fine. How are you doing?" I asked.

"Oh, I'm fantastic!" she said as she went about her work, humming a tune.

"Kimberly, I would like to ask you something, if I may?" I asked.

"Sure, girl, what is it!" she answered.

"Well, I may be out of line. Please forgive me if I am. I want to know how you always have such peace and joy about you, even when things are difficult in your life," I seriously asked.

"Oh, honey, that is easy! The Lord is my refuge and my strength (Ps. 46:1). He always has been, or I would have never made it through my husband's sickness and death," she told me. "I was afraid of death until I watched him as he went on to be with the Lord. I'm not afraid of it anymore. I know he doesn't have anymore pain and everything in heaven is absolutely wonderful. No tears, no pain, nothing bad, and I mean nothing bad, only good!" she professed.

"My husband can't come back to me, but I'll go to him someday. Oh, what a great day that will be. I'm ready!" she laughed and jumped around. I watched her in all her excitement. She truly had it, whatever you call it! I couldn't help but laugh. I mean this lady was having a good time!

"Honey, aren't you ready! Aren't you excited that Christ is preparing a mansion for you in heaven. Woowee!" she laughed. She looked at me and she studied my face and became real somber and looked me in the eye and asked, "Miss Diane . . . have you accepted Jesus as your Lord and Saviour?"

We stood there looking at one another. "Well, I have been confirmed and live a good life," stumbled out of my mouth.

"Sweetheart, that is not accepting Jesus as your Lord and Saviour," she whispered, shaking her head back and forth. She looked very concerned. "Miss Diane, if you were to die tonight, do you know where you would spend eternity?" she asked me real slow, studying my face.

"Well, I have been a good person. That I know. I'm certainly not perfect, but I'm as good as anyone else . . . probably better than many," I stuttered.

She looked at me and held her ground and shook her head sadly and said, "Honey, that ain't gonna get it! None of us are good enough to get to heaven without Christ in our hearts! No one comes to God except through Jesus Christ. You don't want to die and have to appear before Him and He tells you to depart, He never knew you (Matt. 7:23). Oh honey, to be cast into hell forever and ever! Girl, you have to wake up before it is too late! You could die tonight! Are you ready to repent of your sins and ask Him into your life? We can do that right here and now!" she informed me as she walked over to me.

"You know, I don't know. I don't feel anything move in my heart. I don't know why," I confided in her.

"Honey, you need some serious praying over!" she said slowly, shaking her head and waving her arms in the air. "We got revival going on in my church right now. I'm going up to the altar and pray for you tonight!"

"Tonight?" I asked. "Yes, honey! As soon as I leave here I'm heading there and who knows when I'll get home," she laughed.

"You need to go with me, Miss Diane!"

"Tonight?" I asked again.

"Yes, tonight!" she stammered back. "I tell you what! If I wasn't saved, I would be scared not to. Then I would be scared I would die before I got there. Girl, you are living dangerously! You got one foot in hell and don't even know it. Woowee! You had better go with me tonight!" she wailed.

"Oh, Kimberly, I can't go tonight. I have at least two more hours of work here. It has to be done for a meeting first thing tomorrow morning," I explained.

She looked at me and put her hands on her hips and said, "Now Miss Diane, you listen to me! How important is that work if you are going to spend eternity burning in hell? Now ya tell me that!" she snapped.

I looked at her and knew she was right, but didn't make a move. "You had better get your priorities straight and real quick!" she added. "OK, so you don't want to go tonight. If you are still living and here tomorrow night, you can go with me then. Unless of course, ya got another hot shot meeting you're working on again. You know, ever since I have known you, your work has always come first," she informed me, pointing at my paperwork and turning her nose up.

"Ya better think about what I said, and ya better think real good!" she said pointing her finger at me, as she turned and closed the door behind her. I sat in my chair a few minutes without moving. She was one of the sweetest ladies I knew, but she sure was bold about "preaching the gospel" as they say!

I resumed with my stack of paperwork and about nine o'clock, I called it quits. I walked over to Kent's office and he was still there, which didn't surprise me. "Man, do you ever go home?" I asked him. He looked up and grinned and said, "Yeah, about ten o'clock each night."

"Whew, that is too much, Kent! I'm glad you went to see your family this weekend," I stated.

"Well, I went out Sunday afternoon and left Monday afternoon and came back to the office," he said.

"You didn't go to church with your family?" I asked.

"They were having about eighteen people baptized and then the service. It was going to last too long. I got a lot of good work done up here first and was at my in-laws when they got home from church," he said.

"You didn't even get to see your parents?" I asked.

"No, maybe Thanksgiving. Honey's parents have invited them to their home for Thanksgiving. My parents are starting to stay over at their home about once a month and they go to church together. They are all having a great visit and Eric loves going to church with both his grandparents," he smiled.

"He would be beside himself if his father went," I added.

"Oh, Eric knows I'm far too busy on Sunday for that! I have formed some good connections with several members of the country club over Sunday morning brunch. Matter of fact, I believe we will soon land an impressive client from those Sunday brunches!" he informed me.

Now I know how ridiculous I looked to Kimberly by the way I felt about Kent always putting his work over all that really mattered. Disgusting! I can see everything about everyone else, why on earth can't I see myself! I need to open my eyes! Thank God I have people praying for me!

"Kent, I'm going on home. What time did Carol leave?" I asked.

"She left around eight, I believe. She said she went by your office and heard someone talking to you and didn't want to bother you," Kent said. That was when Kimberly was talking to me I thought.

"Good night, ole buddy. I'll see you in the morning," I said as I threw my purse over my shoulder and went out and caught an elevator down to the street.

There were not any taxis coming my way and there were three across the street. I didn't see any cars coming and thought I would make tracks across the street and catch one of them. I knew I shouldn't jaywalk, but I didn't like waiting after dark. I liked getting in a taxi right away and making it to my front door where there was a security guard.

I was halfway across the street and I heard a couple scream, "Watch out! Run!" I realized in a split second they were yelling at me and turned and saw a car from out of nowhere with no lights on, heading straight for me! "Oh my God," I screamed and I couldn't move! "Jesus, help me!"

I looked up and the couple and a police officer were leaning over me and the lady was weeping. I was laying on the hood of a taxi and it was like waking up from a bad dream. "Am I all right?" I asked them.

The officer shook his head and said, "Ma'am as far as we know, you are OK." He paused a moment and said, "You weren't hit, but you were hurled through the air a split second before he would have hit you. You landed here on the hood of the taxi. I don't know what force threw you out of his path, but all I have to say is that you must have some kind of guardian angel!"

I looked at the lady, still weeping. Her husband whispered, "My wife is crying because she knew it was a divine power that saved you from death. We saw it with our own eyes. Something pulled you up suddenly right before he would have hit you. It was amazing!"

"You were knocked out for a few minutes when you landed on the taxi. We have called an ambulance and it will be here any minute," the officer said.

"Thanks for warning me," I said to the couple.

The lady shook her head and said, "I can't believe that you are alive! I saw a divine intervention take place right before my eyes," she wept. I could tell she was visibly shaken from what she saw. Her husband hugged her and they turned and walked off into the night.

The officer said, "Just don't try to move. The ambulance will be here any minute."

"Who was the person who almost hit me or do they know?" I asked.

"I don't know yet," he answered. About that time another officer pulled up and walked over to us. Both officers greeted one another and the one with me asked if they found the man who almost hit me.

"By the time we found him he had wrapped his car around a light pole and left one pedestrian dead. He ran right up over the sidewalk at about sixty miles per hour and ran over her. He had stolen the car about twenty minutes before he killed her. He must have been strung out on drugs. He was only a junior in high school. What a waste of two lives!" the officer told him and shook his head. "Lady, I hope you realize how lucky you are. There is another lady two blocks down that is . . . well, it isn't very pretty," he told me. About that time the ambulance drove up. Of course, I knew it wasn't luck. It was a sudden answer to prayer, and sudden like I have never seen sudden (Acts 16:26).

I looked over and saw Kent. "Diane! What in the world happened here officer? Is she OK? Diane, are you OK?" he exclaimed as he leaned over me, shocked by the police officers and ambulance. "Officers, what happened here? She just left the building moments ago!" Kent shrieked.

Kent had come out of the building and seen all the commotion across the street. He was shocked to find me in the middle of it! The officers told him what happened and the fate of the driver and innocent pedestrian. The officers asked Kent to go with me since he knew me.

They told him I had definitely had a brush with death which was terrifying enough, even if I was all right physically.

"We believe she is OK, but she needs X rays to make sure," the officer told the ambulance crew.

"I see she is the lucky one from the stolen car escapade," a paramedic said. "You do not want to know what shape the other two were in," the ambulance driver told them.

Kent climbed in the back of the ambulance with me and sat down, still in disbelief. Off we went to the hospital. "Diane, I just can't believe this. Thank God, you are OK!" Kent emphasized.

Kent looked out the window and shouted, "Oh, my God!" putting his head in his hand.

"What is it?" I asked him.

The paramedic said, "It is the kid that almost hit you. His burned car is still smoking."

"I could see his charred body in there!" Kent whispered, then he took a deep breath.

"Are you OK, sir?" the paramedic asked him.

"Yeah, whew! Diane, I am so glad you are OK!" Kent sighed.

"They will get the driver out in a few minutes. The fire was so intense no one could get near it. The fire department just extinguished it," the paramedic told us.

"Kent, it just goes to show you how quick your life can be over!" I emphasized, looking at him, still shaking. The paramedic put another warm blanket over me. At the hospital, they wheeled me into the X-ray department where the doctors checked me over and after two hours decided I could go home. They told me I would be sore for a couple of days, but that was it. A miracle, indeed!

Kent got a taxi and we got in. "Diane, why don't you come back to our house tonight. Honey and I have plenty of room. I think it would be a good idea. I don't think you need to be alone tonight after all this," Kent pleaded.

"Kent, I really appreciate it. I just want to go back to my apartment and get in bed and maybe stay home in the morning. You understand," I said and patted him on the shoulder. We pulled up to my building and the doorman opened the door and I turned and told Kent, "Thanks a lot old buddy. You know, we both need to reconsider our lives. I have been doing that a lot lately and you know what I came up with?" I asked Kent.

"What is that?" inquired Kent.

"That life is too short and it can be over in a split second. Then we are going to spend eternity in heaven or hell," I said. "I'll call you in the morning. Thanks for everything, Kent," I said as I leaned over and hugged him.

I exited the taxi, went in, and checked my mailbox where I found a package. I entered my apartment and just looked around and said, "Praise you Lord for sparing me!" and then I wept. Yes, I had so much to be thankful for and it could have been all over, all over. The worst part is that I would have been in hell right now instead of my home sweet home. My apartment looked better than it ever did! The package was from Jan and the girls. I opened it up and it was a beautiful Bible! She had written me a note and placed it inside the front cover.

> Dear Diane,
> We have been praying for you. We have
> prayed that God keep His angels around
> you and keep you from harm. We asked the
> Holy Spirit to touch your heart so that
> you may come to know Jesus as your
> personal Lord and Saviour. Now you
> have a Bible. Please study the word
> daily and keep it in your heart.
> > We love you,
> > Jan, Amanda & Linda

I sat down and held the Bible against my heart and wept again. I hadn't wept for a long time. "Dear Lord, thank you for your angels that lifted me from death's door tonight. Lord, I feel so grateful and scared too. I came so close to losing my life. Lord, be with the families of the other two victims. Lord . . . help me and lead my life. In Jesus' name, I pray, Amen."

I put on my nightgown and crawled into bed. I wished I could call Carl so much, but it was 2:00 A.M. I wish he were here to hold me! I took the Bible and held it against my heart and remembered a verse I learned as a child in Sunday school, "I shall never leave you, nor forsake you" (Heb. 13:5).

I opened my eyes to the rain beating on my window. Rain even looked good! I imagined all those people who I would have been in hell with would love to have rain to cool the agonizing fire. Oh, it was great to be alive! I went to get up. Oh-h-h, was I sore! It was an absolute miracle I was alive, much less no broken bones, sprains, or concussion. I slowly got up and hobbled to the kitchen and put on some coffee. I went back in and laid down. It was now eight thirty. I got a cup of coffee and laid back in the recliner, Carl's recliner, and called Carl.

Oh, it was so good to hear his voice! I told him about the whole ordeal. I started to shake again just telling him about what happened to the driver and that poor, innocent pedestrian. "I wish so much you were just here to hold me all day long," I said.

He started laughing and said, "Well that sounds good to me, but you can't get any work done that way."

"Work is the last thing on my mind, after what I have been through!" I replied back, and rather strongly at that.

"I would come in tonight, but the carpenter is coming over this afternoon to work on the storage room with me. This way I will get it finished twice as fast. I will be in town tomorrow and I'll see you then," he said.

"Well, I'm glad you are getting that room done. Then you can get all your thousands of hooks and that truckload of fishing gear moved over there. Sleeping in the fishing room is another way someone could lose his or her life!" I implied.

"That is why I'm working on it," he quietly replied.

I told him that Jan and the girls had sent me a Bible and I was thrilled about that. It was really a nice one. He wanted to know if it had a concordance. I told him I didn't know what that was and he said he wasn't surprised. He said he would look at it tomorrow night. He thought that was a very nice gift. He asked me if I was going to work. I told him I thought I would go in later. I was really sore, but I just needed to move around and get going. I told him I couldn't complain at all. After all, there were two funerals being planned today. It made me wonder if those two people were saved. I told him I would see him tomorrow night and that I loved him and he said, "I love you, too." Man, he must have been more upset about my near-death experience than he let on!

Right when I hung up, the phone rang. It was Carol. "Are you all right?" she asked.

"Well, yeah, thank heavens!" I answered.

"Kent came in a few minutes ago and told us what happened. I couldn't believe it!" she exclaimed.

"It is pretty unbelievable! What happened to the young man who stole the car and the other poor lady was a nightmare," I told her.

"Why didn't you call me? I would have come over and spent the night. You never know how things will be when you have been knocked out," she said. I told her I appreciated that, but all I wanted to do was come back home. I told her I was coming in later. She thought I should rest, but I was ready to get up and get moving. As I hung up, I was so thankful for my caring friends.

I walked over to Peggy's and got a couple of bagels. I mainly went to see her. She wanted to know if I was taking a day off. I told her what happened to me, as well as the other pedestrian and young man. Peggy's husband, Eugene, came out while I was telling my story and he would always kid me if he was there. After he knew I was all right he pointed his finger at me and kidded, "That is what you get for jaywalking!"

I chuckled at him and said, "Yeah, but that other poor woman was just standing on the sidewalk and was killed."

He shook his head and somberly looked at me and said, "We never know when our time is up! That's why you have to be ready. Well, I sure am glad you weren't hurt," and he came over and gave me a hug. Peggy went to the back and he turned and walked back behind the counter, bent down, and grabbed another bagel. Of course he made sure Peggy wasn't looking and then left quickly. I laughed to myself.

Peggy came back out and I kidded, "I never see Eugene much anymore. Do you keep him in the back locked up in the kitchen?"

"Oh no, he just took off today to build some more shelving I need in the storage room."

"Are you sure you can afford him?" I asked.

"Why?" she asked. I pointed to her bagels behind the glass case where she had them all in precision rows, except for the three missing. She looked down and yelled, "Eugene!" and flew to the back.

I ran out the door and went to the corner to cross the street instead of jaywalking. Gilbert was out front and I handed him his blueberry bagel and cream cheese. I told him what happened when he asked if I was taking a day off. He shook his head and said, "Miss Danay, sounds like you came real close to meeting your maker. Whew! I'm glad you are all right! I sure would miss these," he kidded as he held up his bagel, with cream cheese patted on both sides of his face.

"Of course, I would miss you too, you know," he added, with a caring smile and twinkle in his eyes.

Back in the apartment I ate my bagels and drank a cup of coffee and exercised a little bit to get the soreness out. I called Carl again just to tell him I missed him. He just chuckled at that. He was still trying to get the storage room ready to be worked on this afternoon. I took a long, hot shower and got ready to go to work. Then I sat down and looked out. The rain had stopped and the sky was clearing. Dear God, it is good to be alive!

My mind kept going back to the two people who died last night. Oh, I hope they were both saved! I had no grudge against the young man who almost killed me, only sympathy! Golly, he was only a junior in high school. Just a kid! At the emergency room I had found out the woman was young also. How sad for not only them, but all their family and friends!

I opened my new Bible and turned to the New Testament and started reading. It had a commentary and that was a big help to me. I was enjoying reading and studying. I looked up and ninety minutes had passed! I was understanding what it was saying, too! Was it because people had prayed for me and God was revealing it to me, or was it the Holy Spirit working? It didn't make any difference; I was receiving from what I was reading. I don't remember it being this enjoyable before. The Bible hadn't changed, I guess it was me that had changed!

Later, on the way to work, I visited Nick's deli. "Angelina, please fix me my usual," I asked and turned and looked across the street where I almost lost my life last night. People were walking along and cars were bumper to bumper. Life went on as usual. It was the same where the two victims were killed. Nothing remained, just the pictures in the morning paper. Angelina brought back my sandwich and told me she had wondered where I was when my order was not in the regular office order.

I told her what happened and she stood there with those big eyes and covered her mouth with her hand. "Diane, how awful, but how your life was spared! You came so close to being on the other side instead of standing here in front of me. I wonder if the other two people are in heaven or in hell right now," she said as if she was talking to herself and then the phone rang. "I'm so glad you are OK," she said as she turned and ran for the phone.

I got up to my office and people came by all day telling me they heard what happened and they were glad I was OK. Carol came in and gave me a hug and then Franklin and Sam came in and they gave me a hug. Carol already knew the story, but I told all of them what happened in detail. I made sure to mention that the last thing I said was, "Jesus, help me!" and how, according to the couple, I was miraculously hurled out of the path of the oncoming car.

They shook their heads and were thankful I was spared from being killed or hurt. They were so glad Kent was there to be with me through the emergency room ordeal and that he rode home with me. "I tell you, it was an awakening for Kent and I both. He saw the burned car and the young driver still in it. That leaves an impression on anyone!" I told them.

Kent came in and I got up and gave him a hug. He shook his head and told everyone about how you never think of awful things happening to you or your friends, especially right around your own building or workplace. Faune came in carrying the newspaper and gave it to Franklin showing him the story and pictures. All of them put their heads together reading the story and looking at the awful pictures. Faune came over and gave me a hug and talked about how terrible it was.

The paper told the whole story from the time this young man, only sixteen years old, had stolen the car. The paper said he had a high level of drugs in his body. It mentioned what happened to me and that I was released with no injuries. The other lady who was killed was only thirty-two years old and left behind a husband and two children, nine and eleven years old. She had gone to her husband's office to take him dinner and show him the children's school pictures they had gotten back that day.

They all read the paper and told me how glad they were I wasn't hurt. They left one by one, except Carol. I said, "Carol, you can't imagine what an eye opener this has been. Last night Kimberly was talking to me about being ready because you never know when your life will be over, so on and so forth. Then I go out the door and this happens. Carol, it was like suddenly I was laying on the hood of a taxi and I didn't know how I got there!"

"After I got home, I checked my mail and Jan and the girls had mailed me a Bible. Jan had written a letter and put it inside the front cover. It said they were praying that God would keep His angels around me and keep me from harm," I confessed to her.

"I believe in the power of angels. When you read your Bible, you will see all the times they are mentioned. Thank you God for angels!" she announced as she reached over and patted my hand.

"There is a lot being revealed to me, Carol. My heart is being touched in ways I can't explain. Everything I have been hearing and everything that was said after this close call. It is all coming in loud and clear and for the good I must add. Boy, when you have people praying for you, seriously praying, things are going to happen! I just didn't think it would be this quick!" I admitted.

"Carol, everything I thought was earning me a place in heaven was my own lie. Being confirmed, being a good person and all, that doesn't get you to heaven. Only repenting of my sins and accepting Jesus as my Lord and Saviour will save me. You know the Bible says that His people perish from lack of knowledge (Hosea 4:6). Carol, those are the Christians! I have fooled myself. I can tell you this, if I had been killed last night, I would be in hell right now," I confided to her.

"Then you must do what you must do and without delay!" she insisted.

Franklin walked in and said, "Ladies, we have called a meeting at three o'clock, which is in ten minutes. I need you both there. We are having a conference call with the president of Spectrum, to go over some ideas and plans. See you in the boardroom." Then he closed the door and headed for the elevator.

Carol and I both jumped up, pointed our finger at each other and said simultaneously, "Go to the bathroom, and get something to drink." She headed for the door and I went over to my coffee pot and said to her before she left the room, "Why do we do this? It is such a vicious circle," and we both chuckled.

The conference call lasted ninety minutes. We took many notes and we went back to work. It was going to be a late night again. Before we left the boardroom, Franklin said, "I don't care how late or how early you leave, just don't jaywalk across the street to catch a taxi!"

"Don't worry!" we announced. We all ordered dinner from Nick's about six o'clock and all of us ate back in our offices. We were tired of sitting in the boardroom all day, I guess.

My door opened and it was Kimberly. "Hey! How are you doing?" I asked.

"Girl, I'm great. How are you doing is the question. I saw all that mess in the paper. Honey, if that didn't open your eyes, nothing will. Woowee!" She exclaimed, shaking her head and waving her hands.

"It most certainly opened my eyes. I'll have to say that!" I replied.

"You ready to go to that revival with me tonight?" she asked, as she dusted around.

"Yes, ma'am!" I answered. She turned and looked at me and laughed, slapped her leg with her hand and shouted, "Glory be to God! Miss Diane, you meet me on the first floor by the elevators at seven o'clock," she said.

"I'll be there!" I confirmed.

I finished some more paperwork, freshened up, and met Kimberly at seven o'clock. We left the building and Kimberly said, "You let me get a taxi, your taxi luck ain't too hot lately." She had one right away and we jumped in and she told the taxi what church to go to. We chatted for a while about what happened last night.

I looked around and I suddenly realized I wasn't familiar with the area and asked her, "Kimberly, I never even asked you, where is your church?"

"Harlem," she answered.

"Harlem!" I exclaimed as the taxi headed for Harlem. I kept looking at her, sitting there humming a tune, happy as a lark, moving her hands to her own music. "Are you serious?" I asked.

"What's that, honey?" she asked back, not missing a beat.

"Are we really going to Harlem?" I inquired, squirming around a bit, trying not to be so conspicuous that I was reluctant to go to Harlem. I didn't want to be rude or insulting to Kimberly. It had to be obvious to the taxi driver, who was black, that I had great reservations about going to Harlem and especially at night.

"Honey, white people go there all the time and live through it," she stated nonchalantly.

"Yes, ma'am, of course ya might be the first white woman to ever get her throat cut in the back pew," the taxi driver said.

"Child, shut your mouth!" yelled Kimberly and kicked the back of his seat and they both burst out laughing. I sat there speechless and then I started laughing too.

"Well, I didn't know! I've never been to Harlem the whole time I've been in the city and I have been here twenty years," I explained, realizing how silly I must have sounded.

They were both worn out from laughing and Kimberly reached over and patted my knee and said, "Relax, honey, everything is OK. I'm supposed to take you here tonight. God is in control and He don't care who is black and who is white. He is only concerned about all His children knowing Jesus. That's all. That's all!"

"OK," I said.

"Just don't pay no attention to this crazy taxi driver," she said and they both started laughing again.

We got out at her church and a lady by the name of Sylvia came out to greet us. Kimberly and Sylvia hugged and then Sylvia came over and hugged me and welcomed me to their church. The three of us went in and Sylvia found us a seat and returned to greeting people who were still coming in. Everyone in the church was standing and clapping and swaying to the music of the choir. I mean they were really getting with it!

Some people had jumped out in the middle of the aisle and were dancing. Others were waving their hands and praising God. There were some people in front of the altar dancing and reaching for the heavens, but I couldn't hear what they were saying. Some were crying and some were joyous. This Baptist church was sure different than any I had ever been to.

The preacher came up and started giving the sermon. Something started to come over me and when the invitation was given I felt like I was burning up. Like I was on fire, but it was not like a painful fire. I can't explain it. It was "Holy Ghost fire" as I have heard it called. It was on me and inside my heart. The invitation was over. I never moved.

I opened my eyes to a cloudy morning and balmy breezes. It was already seven o'clock! Kimberly and I didn't leave the church until almost eleven. We both caught the same taxi and he left her off and then he went way on down to my place. I got in my door a little before midnight. I was wide awake after that service and decided to read my Bible. I went to bed about 1:00 A.M.

I fixed a cup of coffee and stretched out on the sectional and called Carl.

"Hey sweetie, how are you doing?" I asked Carl.

"Fine," he said.

"How did the room go yesterday? Did you get a lot done?" I asked.

"Yeah, we are going to finish it this morning. We put up a lot of shelves for all my gear and several tabletops to work on my tackle boxes and such. We are doing the final touches on it today. It is going to be real handy to have everything set up in there and it will be arranged nicely too," Carl said.

"When are you going to get here tonight?" I asked.

"What time do you want me to be there?" he asked.

"Be here about five o'clock and we'll go get a bite to eat and I want to take you somewhere," I said.

"Well, I would like to hear this evangelist that is in the city tonight or at least go to a church service somewhere," he stated.

"Just be here at five and don't be late," I said, chuckling to myself.

"You haven't given me a chance to ask how you are doing," he said.

Golly, I forgot all about being sore and . . . I just forgot!

"I'm doing fine! I can't wait to see you. We will get in late. You can bring a change and stay here. That is if you want to," I suggested.

"I may stay at my place tonight and check on it and go straight to the office in the morning to catch up on things. Leave your Bible out on the coffee table so I can see it when I come in. I'll probably get there before you do to relax a little bit before going out," he said.

"OK. Please be careful and I'll see you later. I love you," I said.

"Me too," he replied.

I went to the office and asked Franklin if I could leave around four thirty this afternoon and he said that was fine. Carol and I ate lunch together in my office and I told her about last night. "Harlem! You went to church in Harlem!" she exclaimed.

"Carol, white people go there all the time and live through it," I explained to her. "It was a wonderful service and the choir was moving and grooving, let me tell you! Guess what I'm going to do tonight?" I said.

"I'm scared to ask! Go ahead and tell me, nothing would surprise me at this point. I mean one night you escape death by one tenth of an inch and end up as a hood ornament on a taxi cab and the next night your out with the cleaning lady at a revival in Harlem. Why would I be shocked at anything!" she admitted.

"Carl is coming in tonight," I opened.

She looked at me and said, "And?" waving her hand for me to finish the statement.

"I'm taking him to the revival in Harlem tonight," I said.

"You're taking Carl to Harlem! Oh boy, this ought to be good!" she exclaimed. I started laughing at her. "You mean Carl agreed to go?" Carol asked with a surprised look on her face.

"No, I'm not going to tell him where we are going," I said.

She put her hands over her face and shook her head. "Let me go sit down," and she sat down on the couch and sighed.

"I would offer you something to drink, but all I have is water and it isn't chilled yet, plus I'm out of ice," I said.

"That is fine. I just need fluid," she replied. I don't think she wanted to believe what she was hearing. I watched her take a drink of water and then both of us started laughing.

"Carol, here is my plan," I started out. She looked toward the heavens. I continued, "I'll just get us in a taxi and give the driver the name of the church and we'll start heading that way."

"Boy, what I wouldn't give to see the look on his face when he realizes he's going to a revival in Harlem!" she exclaimed.

"Well, you can see his face. Get Glenn and you two can go with us," I suggested.

"I think you landed on that taxi harder than you think you did!" she giggled.

I told her I couldn't wait to go and how I felt while I was there last night. She kidded me, but she was excited for me, because she knew what I felt was real. I knew that she saw it as a breakthrough for me and that made her happy. I could see it in her face. She was going to tell Kimberly that I was planning on going tonight with my boyfriend, since she would see her.

"Hey, sweetie!" I said as I entered my apartment and saw Carl in his recliner, looking at my Bible. He turned and smiled and got up and hugged and kissed me. I held onto him and told him how much I missed him. He would always chuckle every time I did that. I told him I wanted to take a quick shower and then we would leave. I hurried and got ready while he laid back in the recliner and read the Bible.

"Let's go, honey," I said.

"Where are we going to eat?" he asked.

"Wherever you want to, but I'm kind of hungry for a big steak," I said.

"Let's go!" Carl said. We ate two great steaks and then jumped in a taxi. After a little while, Carl started looking around and said, "Where is this Baptist church at?" I told him the address and he looked at me and frowned.

"Yes, it is in Harlem," I confessed. He looked straight up in the air, shook his head, and mashed his lips together to stop from saying what was on his mind. "Oh, don't be so prejudiced," I whispered so the taxi driver wouldn't hear me.

"I'm not prejudiced! I just don't want to go to Harlem," he informed me.

We pulled up to the church, and as we exited Carl mumbled, "Well, this should be real exciting!" How little did he know! Sylvia was at the door and found Carl and me seats. Kimberly was there with some of the people that worked in our building. She saw me and gave me that famous smile and waved. The place was packed. The choir started singing and everybody got into that. Carl loved music, and he clapped along. I didn't know what he thought, but I wasn't going to let anything interfere with my feelings.

As the preacher began to preach I knew I was going up! All day I was worried something would happen to me and I would die and go to hell. I watched every corner I crossed, I was concerned about getting in a wreck, anything that would stop me from getting to church! I was even worried about the elevator falling and I had never thought about it before. I knew I could repent and ask for forgiveness and accept Jesus in my own living room, but I wanted to make it public (Matt. 10:32).

The invitation came and I went to step by Carl and he wasn't expecting me to move. He thought something was wrong and I needed to leave the auditorium. Then he let me by and I walked down the aisle and I saw Kimberly up in the choir. She looked at me and began to weep. I heard people saying, "Praise God!" and "Hallelujah!" as I passed them. I walked up to the preacher and told him I wanted to repent of my sins and ask Jesus to come into my heart. He prayed the sinner's prayer and I repeated after him. He asked me to sit down on the front pew. I turned and, to my surprise, saw Carl walk up to the preacher. They prayed and then Carl sat down beside me. He grabbed my hand and held it. The invitation ended.

The preacher had Carl and I come up and he told the congregation that I made Jesus my Lord and Saviour and the congregation and choir raised their hands and shouted, "Amen" and "Glory be to God," and then the preacher said that Carl had rededicated his life to Jesus.

They started singing and dancing and Carl and I were crying and laughing at the same time. The choir was singing and some came down and were dancing. Kimberly and Sylvia came up and hugged me and told me they had been praying for me. Then they went up to Carl and gave him a hug. The church was rejoicing because my name had just been written in the Lamb's Book of Life and all the angels in heaven were rejoicing (Luke 15:10).

That night, the church was like a touch of heaven on earth! All these people praising God because I was going to spend eternity in heaven. I felt so wonderful! No words could explain the peace and joy I felt! I finally had true peace!

I knew all these people were my kin! We were all brothers and sisters in Christ and would dwell in heaven together forever! What a night! Carl and I kept our arms around each other while the singing and dancing continued.

The hour that I accepted Christ will always be a precious memory! I will never forget that night! Never! All my sin debts were paid and heaven was to be my eternal home! Hallelujah!

Walking in Faith

MY EYES OPENED TO THE BLUE SKIES OF ANOTHER WONDERFUL day. "Oh, is it good to be alive! I have been reborn! Lord, what awaits me? Thank you, Jesus! Thank you, thank you, thank you for saving me! What a relief to know that if anything happens to me, I'll be in heaven! Relief isn't even the word! Oh, this is so wonderful! No amount of money could even begin to buy what I have in my heart!"

The phone rang. "How are you doing?" Carl said with a heavy voice.

"Great! You must have just woke up," I said.

"Yeah, I've just been lying here thinking," he said.

"What have you been thinking about?" I asked.

"Oh, I'll tell you when I see you," he said.

"Last night was something, wasn't it?" I replied.

"Naturally, you can't compare being saved to anything else, ever!" he answered.

"Oh-h-h . . . I feel . . . I don't know how to tell you how I feel," I exclaimed. I heard Carl chuckle a little bit on the other end.

"When are you going in to work?" he asked.

"As soon as I get ready. I can hardly wait to get there," I answered.

"Why?" asked Carl.

"Well, you know, to tell everyone how I feel, and what happened. What do you mean by asking why? This is something to be excited about if I was ever going to be excited!"

131

"People aren't going to be as excited about you being saved as you might think," Carl confessed.

"Why not?"

"Let me ask you something. If Kent, Carol, or anyone you know would have come up to you six months ago and were so excited because they got saved, what would you have thought?" he asked.

"Well, I would have been excited for them, if nothing else. I would have thought there must be something to it if they were genuinely excited," I answered. Then I thought to myself, would I have been that excited? I mean would I have been excited or just thought they were on a religious high or something.

"OK. You are not supposed to hide your light under a basket, remember?" he mentioned.

"Yes, I remember," I said, both of us knowing that I accused him of that a month or so ago when I was upset with him.

"You are supposed to share the good news with people and what better time than when you are just reborn and have that transition feeling all over you. Then others can see the immediate joy and peace it has given you! You will always have it, and it grows because you are so thankful you are saved and going to heaven," Carl stated.

"Now, today, you are a different person than you were yesterday. You have been reborn, so it is up to you to share the good news. You are not bound for hell anymore, you are heaven bound. That is something to shout about, just like everyone was last night," he acknowledged.

"Well, I guess I'll find out what happens when I get there. I know one thing, I sure can't hold this feeling in! I can tell you over lunch what happened," I suggested, giggling to myself.

"That sounds like a good idea," he chuckled.

"I better get in. We have a lot of work to do. Let's eat about noon. I will have to work until about seven this evening. That should be enough hours for today," I affirmed. "Are you getting ready to go into the office?" I asked.

"Yes. I need to get some things done and since you have to work all day, I'll head to the lake after we have lunch. You know I'm not much of a Saturday worker anymore. It is just that this week was unusually busy," he said.

"Well, I will look forward to our lunch," I said, missing him already. "Honey, you go ahead, we both need to get to work. I want to get enough done, so I can enjoy my time with you at noon and not be pushed on deadlines," I told him. Then I whispered, "I love you!" and he said, "Me too," and hung up.

I had to call Jan and the girls. "Jan, it's Diane and guess what!"

"What?" shouted Jan.

"I accepted Christ last night as my Lord and Saviour," I told her and I thought I would cry just telling her.

"Oh, that is great!" she screamed. "Girls, Diane was saved last night," she yelled. I heard yeahs and clapping in the distance. I started laughing and Jan was laughing and almost crying.

"Oh, thank you for my Bible! I have so much to tell you! I didn't think I would catch you," I replied.

"We were just walking out the door to go shopping. Where were you, out at Lakeside Church?" she asked.

"I was at a Baptist church in Harlem," I answered, waiting for her response on that one.

"Harlem!" she screamed and started laughing again. "How did you end up in Harlem?" she squealed.

"Kimberly, the lady that cleans our offices, wanted me to go to the revival with her Wednesday night. Her husband had died and we got to talking . . ."

"Her husband died?" Jan inquired.

"Yes. The reason we started talking was because I saw a real peace in her spirit, even though she had just lost her husband and I wanted to know about that type of peace, true peace. She started talking about Jesus and salvation and told me I better accept Jesus because we are not promised tomorrow. Well, that was the night I almost got killed, but God spared me miraculously!" I explained.

"Almost killed!" Jan exclaimed.

"Yes! This young man who stole a car was strung out on drugs and almost hit me, and he died in a fiery crash after he ran over and killed a young woman. Oh, it was just awful," I exclaimed.

"Two other people died! . . . Oh my!" Jan yelled.

I told her how God spared my life that night and how it had gotten my attention.

"Believe me, I went with Kimberly the next night! I felt something over me so strong that I went back the next night and I wanted Carl to go with me. I knew I was going to accept Jesus and walk down that aisle!" I affirmed.

"Oh, how wonderful! What did Carl think of all this?" Jan asked.

"He rededicated his life to Christ," I told her.

"Oh, I wish I had been there! Golly, I am so happy and what a story!" Jan whispered, almost overtaken by emotion.

"Jan, all those people in that church were shouting and dancing for us. You can't imagine!" I told her.

"That is the way it is supposed to be when one is won to Jesus. Hallelujah!" she cried (Luke 15:10).

"I will call you later. I had to tell you!" I confessed.

"Thank you for calling us," she cried.

"Jan, thank you for all your prayers. It has made all the difference in everything," I told her.

"Praise God. We love you," she whispered.

"I love all of you too," I replied, with tears in my eyes.

We said bye to each other. I didn't think we would get emotional. I should have known better. I knew Jan and the girls had been praying for me. Boy, I know now that prayer works!

"I don't think I know that song you are humming," Carol whispered from behind.

"I don't think it is one, I'm just humming away. Come on in a moment, I have something to tell you."

She came in the office and I asked her to take a seat.

"Well, first let me get a cup of coffee before I get started," I said.

"Boy, here I am in suspense and you have to run and get a cup of coffee. If the world was coming to an end you would run to the nearest coffee pot and drink a cup down to the last drop!" she giggled.

"Well, now when the world comes to an end, guess what?" I asked her.

"What!" she asked me, wondering what on earth I was going to say.

"You and I will be in heaven together," I affirmed as I saw her jaw drop. "I accepted Jesus as my Lord and Saviour last night!" I smiled, and walked over to hug her.

"How wonderful!" she exclaimed and hugged me back.

We both sat on the couch and talked and I told her all about what happened to me at Kimberly's church. I told her about Carl rededicating his life and how everyone in the whole church was shouting and dancing—just celebrating! I was so excited telling her about it. How wonderful to share this good news!

I told her I couldn't wait to tell Franklin, Kent, and Sam about what happened. She didn't want to dampen my spirits when she said,

"I think you should tell them, because you are supposed to tell the good news. Just remember, they may not share your excitement like you would expect them to." I told her Carl had already told me the same thing.

I went into Franklin's office to tell him about my plans to eat lunch with Carl and then come back to the office. Then I told him about what happened last night. He seemed excited for me even though he didn't really understand the excitement I felt, but I could tell he was very curious because he could see it was real for me.

Then I went to Kent's office and told him about it. At first, I didn't think he would look up from his paperwork long enough, but he did. He listened to me and he had a look on his face like he must have thought I had gone off the deep end. He said he was happy for me, but it was obvious he thought I had lost it, when in reality, I had found it!

"Sam, how are you doing today?" I asked as I entered his small, but nice office. It wouldn't be long before he would step up another notch in the corporate ladder and get a bigger office. Franklin would make sure of it.

"I'm doing fine!" he exclaimed, as he looked up from his paperwork. "Have a seat," he insisted, as he put his hand out to the chair beside his desk.

I sat down and started telling him what happened to me last night. He sat there and listened intensely. He had some questions about how all this came about and what made me start thinking about accepting Jesus. I told him how my cousins had witnessed to me and prayed for me. I also told him about the white-haired lady who mysteriously disappeared after she told me I had better be ready. I said the people at Carl's church had been praying for me and about all the changes that had transpired. I told him about what Kimberly said to me and how she invited me to her church and the rest is history.

I let him know how peaceful and joyous I felt knowing I was going to heaven and not hell. I told him it was a peace and joy words could not explain. He must have seen it in my face because he was so curious! I knew now he wasn't saved, just by the questions he was asking me. I was not as bold as Jan or Kimberly and didn't know how to lead anyone to Christ. I wished one of them were here. I told him I had to leave and that I would pray for him. He told me he wished I would. Even though I was a one-day-old Christian and didn't know much about leading people to Christ, I believe my humble testimony touched Sam. He saw it in my heart and soul. The truth had set me free and that gave God glory!

Faune was hardly ever in on Saturdays, but we had been so busy lately she had to come in and catch up. I invited her into my office for a mid-morning break. This was one Saturday I had brought in a box of assorted bagels from Peggy's. Everyone was enjoying them too! Well, I just felt so good, like celebrating or something! My insides were ready to burst with pure happiness and nothing could take it away. Even if I died, I would be in heaven. Oh, what a joy to be this free!

She came in and I shared my experience with her. She came over and gave me a hug. She said she could see the joy in my face. She told me how she was saved years ago and had become a member of a church which was in essence a cult, but she didn't see it until years later.

They did not want you going to other churches, theirs was the only one that was right. Some of the things the Bible taught, they would not have anything to do with. She told me it was like putting a dark veil over her eyes. She had to get out finally. The other members seemed to have no joy, yet shunned her when she left. She found another church that was like the one she attended when she was growing up, and there she found truth and love again.

She said she couldn't believe she had wasted so many years in the church she had gone to. She should have known when she began to feel like a prisoner, she explained. Being away from church for so long, I had never experienced this and surely did not want to. Now she wanted to go to Kimberly's church one night. I was glad. I wanted to go back.

I ate lunch with Carl and we stuffed ourselves on seafood. It was wonderful! He asked me if I had seen Kimberly today. I told him she didn't work on Saturdays. I told him Faune wanted to go with me one night to the revival, so we would probably go back real soon. Faune didn't have to work late and I could leave in time to go to church if I made up for it the next day.

Carl wanted me to leave early Sunday morning and go to Lakeside Church with him. If I was in agreement, he wanted both of us to go up in front of the church and tell the congregation about Friday night. I was excited about that. After all, they all had been praying for me and I have no doubt that prayer is what brought me under conviction. Thank God for praying people!

He told me he would be calling me, but expected me out there early Sunday morning. He said he would fix me a big breakfast and then we would go to church and lunch with whoever wanted to go to Grinder's Mill. That was a great time of fellowship for the ones who could go on Sunday. Then he wanted me to go to a fall festival in a little town north of Amber Lake before I had to head back. I told him I could hardly wait until the next day and to be careful. I told him I loved him and he said, "Me too." We kissed goodbye and I returned to work and he left for the lake.

Faune came in my office and wanted to know if we could go to the revival tonight. I was on such a high from last night, I couldn't wait to go back. We agreed to leave about five o'clock, eat dinner, and head for Harlem. Franklin, Carol, Kent, and Sam were working up a storm in the boardroom. I told them that Faune and I were going to Kimberly's church tonight and wondered if anyone else wanted to go. There were no offers.

I told all of them we needed to leave work one night and go to church. Carol looked around the room to see their reactions. Kent was frowning and looked back down at his paperwork. Franklin put his hand to his mouth and leaned his chair back, studying me. Sam looked around and smiled and said, "Well, I'd like to go!" We all stared at him. He looked back at us and said "Well, I would. I would like to go!" Carol and I started chuckling. I told him we would definitely go next week and whoever wanted to go was more than welcome to go with us.

Carol said she would go one night with us. She was busy with her own church, plus she worked so much that she didn't get to spend much time with her family as it was. She was anxious to go though and so was Sam. Great!

I told Franklin I needed to leave about five o'clock. He told all of us that everyone needed to take off Sunday. We were getting too burned out. We all needed a day off. They all figured they wouldn't leave there tonight until about eight o'clock.

Kent was disappointed about not working Sunday, but said the country club would be a nice break. I knew what the country club meant. Talking with, hopefully, future clients. I told him he needed to go to church with his family. He frowned and shook his head, and said he was far too busy for that. His excuse was always that there were too many bills and the costs of raising a child. Some day I was going to tell him that all it cost to raise a child was time and love!

He would say his wife doesn't make much money on her job and he has to compensate with "extra work" to make it. Ha! Some day I was going to tell him he made plenty of money on a forty-hour week and the only reason she worked was because she hated to be at home by herself all the time! "Listen to me!" I warned myself not to open my mouth. "I need just to pray for him and quit judging! Kent definitely needed prayer, but all of us do. Look what prayer did for me!"

Faune and I wished everyone a good weekend and left at five. We had a great dinner at an Italian restaurant and then caught a taxi and headed for Harlem. Sylvia greeted us and gave us a hug. She seated us and Kimberly waved at both of us from the choir, and what a choir it was! We all had a great time! We all went out to eat afterwards and Faune and I didn't leave Harlem until about midnight. It moved me so much to see people saved and loved ones rejoicing over them. Also, to hear testimonies as to what the Lord had done in their lives concerning healing, finances, guidance . . . you name it!

I woke up at daybreak. I fixed a cup of coffee and walked in front of my windows, looking at the pinks and purples across the sky. I was thinking about Carl and I. Our lives had changed and it was a new day for us now.

I didn't want to go in front of that church with Carl and tell them I was saved and then stay for the night at Carl's house anymore. The church would love us and support us, but things were different now. I was different and I knew it. I knew Carl felt the same way. That is what he meant the other day when he said he was thinking about things. He feels the same way I do. I know now he always has.

It must have been difficult for him all these years. I just got used to being the way I am. I wanted to do what was right for both of us, but it wasn't up to me to bring up the issue—was it? I knew I needed to let him know I wanted to live my life the way Christ would want me to live it. He already knew I was a new person. I needed to tell him that though. It was probably something he has been wanting to hear for a long, long time!

I got ready and carried my church clothes with me. It was another beautiful September day. Carl fixed me a wonderful breakfast, just as he said he would. He showed me the fishing room as soon as I got there though. More than half of the stuff was out of the bedroom and he had moved it across the hall in the new fishing room.

"What are we, I mean you, going to call the old fishing room now?" I asked, correcting myself. He looked at me and kind of grinned, because I would always say "we" in everything we did to our apartments and his home.

"I don't know what to call the room. You are good at that," he said.

"Well, let's see. It'll be our, I mean your fin and feather room," I said, embarrassed I had goofed again. He looked at me and shook his head in an approving manner. At this point, I believe he would have agreed with any name that was halfway acceptable. He got ready for church and I cleaned up the kitchen and went upstairs to the peaches and cream room and changed. I went down to the back patio and walked around looking out over the lake.

Carl came out dressed in a medium gray suit with a white shirt and charcoal tie. He looked so nice. "What are you thinking about," he asked as he came up and put his arm around me.

"Oh, I was just thinking how nice it would be if you had a gazebo out there at the end of your pier like the one at Thornton's," I answered, proud that I said "you" instead of "we."

He looked out there for a while and said, "Do you think we would use it that much?" with great emphasis on "we." I looked at him and we both started laughing.

"Yes, I think we would," I answered back.

"We'll have to go out there and look it over when we get back," he said. "We better go right now," he said after looking at his watch.

Brother Darrel and Judy greeted us first thing and told me they were so thrilled about my decision. Carl confessed he had called them Saturday afternoon and told them because they had been praying for me. Carl and I stood up in front of the church and Brother Darrel told the congregation about my decision and Carl's rededication. After the service everyone came up and congratulated us and hugged us.

The moment I was saved I saw how important it was by the look in other believers' eyes. How grateful and happy they were, even if many were still strangers to me. After all, who wants to see anyone spend eternity in hell, even if he or she is a total stranger!

Quite a few of us went to lunch together and we had a great time. We talked and laughed. This church family was really a family. I never thought of a church as being like this before. I don't know why. I felt like I was living a whole new life in the last several weeks, and especially since the other night. People praying, loving, full of joy. Why didn't I ever see it before? Everyone at lunch seemed like they were celebrating the coming home of a long lost sister. Well, they were!

Carl and I drove up to the fall festival. What a divine drive in the rolling countryside. We got candy apples and I had it all over my face like a little kid. I thought of Gilbert and his cream cheese after I looked in the car mirror at myself. That is what you get when you talk about people, I thought. I was wearing sticky red where Gilbert always wore his cream cheese.

Carl had introduced me to several residents that lived around Amber Lake at the festival. "Carl, why didn't you tell me I had this stuff all over my face. I wonder what your neighbors thought!" I wailed.

"That you didn't look the part of a business executive!" Carl answered. We both looked at each other and started laughing.

We drove back to Carl's and he fixed a cheese tray and I poured us some iced tea that was in the refrigerator. "Carl, this iced tea is good. Did you fix this?" I asked, out of curiosity.

"Yep, nothing to it!" he replied. We went out on the patio and sat down. We looked out over the lake and talked about the gazebo and how nice it would be. "If I had an occasion for one, I would build it in a minute and then probably enjoy it from then on," he stated.

"What do you mean an occasion for one?" I asked, really wanting to hear this one.

"Well, you know something real special, a reason for building it," he replied, looking out over the lake.

Boy, would I have liked to have said something! Then finally I said, "Looks like you are thinking about something. A penny for your thoughts," I said, as I bent over in front of him and looked him in the eye. He started chuckling to himself. I started giggling and said, "What?"

"Come on, let's walk out there," he said. We walked out the winding walkway and we talked about finishing that too. Carl said as soon as the fishing room was done, that was next. It all should be done within the next two weeks.

"I hope so, October is my favorite month, you know. I love being out," I told him. We stood on the pier and talked about putting in a new pier if he was ever going to build a gazebo at the end of it and how it needed to be an octagon shape.

The pier needed to come out in the lake about twenty feet and that way we could see all the way down the lake both ways and not be out too far. Carl's property set back from the shoreline forming a wide cove with the woods on both sides. We discussed how it would really be nice to build it that way and he wouldn't be too far out in the lake. It would be just enough to clear the bend of the woods and that would be perfect! We talked about how it should be built, everything down to the center knob on top of the roof.

We walked back to the patio and Carl told me to sit down and write down everything we had discussed about the gazebo. He went in the kitchen and came out with two big steaks and put them on the grill. He sat down across from me and we wrote every detail, and I mean every detail, down on paper. I was wondering why he did that. He acted like he was getting ready to build it tomorrow!

It was just like the one at Thornton's except the shingles would match Carl's house. I didn't know what he had up his sleeve, but I was excited. We ate dinner out on the patio and looked out over the lake, imagining the gazebo out there in the sunset. I told him that it would be so peaceful and wonderful to be out there. "It is like you can feel the presence of God in the nature around you. He is the water lapping against the bank and the birds singing, not to mention the loons serenading you." Carl and I both loved nature and being out there was heaven!

It was dusk and I got ready to leave. I got ready to get in my car and kissed him goodbye. "Are you coming in tomorrow?" I asked.

"No, I'm taking a month off," he answered.

"You are taking a month off!" I exclaimed.

"Yes, I'm going to be busy doing a lot of things around here before winter sets in and the next month or so is perfect weather," he said. I just looked at him.

"Boy, this comes as a shock!" I said to him.

"It has to be done. My work is caught up in the city. They know they can call me if they need anything. I will even be tied up next weekend working over at the church. There is some remodeling that needs to be done on the fellowship hall. Several of us will be working on it for the next two weeks. We will have church as usual. The fellowship hall is just off limits. We are even putting new carpet in the sanctuary," he told me.

"Man, you will be running back and forth between the church and home I guess!" I said.

"You use the next two weeks to get caught up at work. Then you need to be able to take some time off and come out here for a while. You have always wanted to go up the eastern coastline. October would be perfect. You be thinking where you would like to go," Carl suggested.

"Well, all right. I will sure look forward to that!" I affirmed, juggling my feelings about the new me. How did I feel about this now? I knew how Carl felt. We'll just have to talk about this later, I thought.

"I love you," I said and kissed him and held him.

"Me too," he said.

I got in the car and looked up at him and said, "We have never been away from each other for two weeks. Boy, I am going to miss you so much!" I said.

He said, "Me too!" I shook my head at him and we both giggled.

I got back to the apartment and decided to call Jan. I told her about the service this morning at Carl's church. I was so happy to see how excited they were for Carl and I. I told her how I felt different about staying over at Carl's now and we both were different. Our feelings for each other certainly hadn't changed. Jan told me I was a new person and both Carl and I had repented the night we went forward. Now we wanted to live like Christ would want us to live.

"You are a new person. It changes you, and it changes you for the better!" Jan said. I told her I didn't understand a lot of things, but I felt different all of a sudden. She told me everything was fine and I had to walk in faith. She said to read my Bible and learn His word. I told her I was confused about Carl's feelings for me. She said confusion was from Satan, not God. She said God was always peace, not confusion (1 Cor. 14:33).

I still wondered what was going on. We had never been away from each other for two weeks. She told me that wondering and reasoning about everything was useless. She said, "Turn it over to God and pray about things. We can't figure everything out and we are not supposed to. Give it to God and let Him handle it. Don't go back and pick it up after you have given it to Him. He is very capable of taking care of your worries and problems. The Bible tells you not to worry but to cast all your cares on Him (Ps. 55:22). It is Scripture. The bottom line is you have to have faith (Luke 17:6). That is the answer!"

"Well, I guess that settles it! Where do I find those Scriptures for what I need?" I asked.

"Look in your Bible and there will be a concordance. You need to look in there and whatever word you are looking for, it will give you Scripture to look up. God is true to His word! When you read it, what-ever it says do it, do it and believe it, and it will come to pass" (Mark 11:22–24).

"I guess I better get off here and get busy reading, learning, and applying," I said, putting emphasis on "learning" and "applying." I told her that I realized that it depended on me to make the truth come to pass. He had already given me everything. She said it was such a relief that I knew Christ and no matter what happened to me ever, I would be going to heaven! She was so excited that we would get to spend eternity together! No matter if we died, were killed, or the rapture occurred, we would all be together in heaven.

"That is what else I wanted to ask you about, Jan! Remember when I asked you about the rapture at the airport, and that old woman turned around and told me I better be ready?" I asked.

"Yes, we must be ready. We don't know when we are going to die and we don't know when the rapture will occur. Either one could be any moment. We know that!" she stated. I told her to keep praying for Carl and me. She said they would. I told her I would keep her posted and that my life was sure making some turnarounds for the best!

Monday morning I was ready to go again. I got to my office and put on my coffee pot and went down to Faune's desk where she was taking phone calls left and right. She finally got a thirty-second break and I said, "You want to go to Harlem tonight?"

She thought a minute and laughed, "Yeah, let's go!"

The phone started ringing again and I said, "I'll call you later, we'll go after work," she affirmed that with a thumbs up and answered another call.

I just got back in my office and Carol came in. We sat down a minute and I caught her up on what happened Sunday. "You have never gone two weeks without seeing Carl! Wonder what on earth he is doing?" she asked.

"My sentiments exactly! I'm not worried about it. He told me to get my work caught up and we would go on a vacation," I told her.

"Well, do you want to do that?" she whispered and we both paused and I pondered her question.

"Wonder what he is doing?" she inquired.

"I don't know. Carol, to tell you the truth, I have been with Carl for twenty years and now I don't want to stay over or go on a vacation unless we are married!" I confessed.

"Well, that is good. I'll tell you, I bet Carl feels the very same way," she affirmed.

"I'm sure he does, Carol. That is what confuses me," I admitted. "I am so different, but boy, does it feel good," I confessed.

"That certainly does not surprise me! Don't try to figure things out with Carl or yourself. Just pray about it and then have faith in what He tells you to do," she instructed.

"Do you hear Him tell you what to do?" I asked.

"You hear it in your spirit or your mind. Sometimes you feel it in your heart, but it is always a feeling you have peace about," she said, trying to help me understand.

Franklin peeped his head around the corner of my door and said, "You two gals ready for the ten o'clock meeting. Petersburg International will be calling in on a conference call. Get your brains and notepads up there at 9:45 A.M."

"Good thing we had a day to get refreshed!" I said as I looked at Carol and Franklin grinning. This was one of our new accounts and the biggest one the company had ever had. Carol and I got up and she looked at me and said, "Go to the bathroom and get something to drink," and off we went.

We finished with the conference call at 11:30 A.M. We had enough to work on to keep us going the rest of the week and through the weekend at twelve hour days. Franklin immediately ordered from Nick's and we all got up and stretched. I told Carol that Faune and I were going to Harlem, but she said she couldn't go with us tonight.

We planned on going Tuesday night though. We both asked Sam and he wanted to go tomorrow night too. We told Franklin and Kent we were going tomorrow night and asked if they wanted to go. Kent frowned and shook his head "no" and Franklin said he appreciated the offer, but he was too busy. We ate lunch and kept going.

Faune and I saw Kimberly and told her we were leaving in a little bit to go back to her church. She was going too. I don't think she ever missed a night. Talk about being full of vim and vigor. I don't think she ever ran down! Faune was excited about going again. On the way we ate at a wonderful Chinese restaurant and got to church right after the choir started singing.

I could see that Faune was enjoying herself. Kimberly came in late and joined us. The Holy Spirit was definitely in this place! The invitation came and Faune went up for prayer. The pastor prayed for her and called several brothers and sisters to come up and keep praying for her. There were many people that came forward for many different reasons.

Kimberly went down there for Faune and she came back with her arm around her. Faune had been crying and yet she looked, well, she looked "free." Yes, that was the word, "free." She looked like a huge weight had been lifted from her. She looked wonderful! What a service! Kimberly, Faune, and I left about 11:00 P.M., all with our arms around each other. I turned and looked back at the altar and Sylvia was still up there praying for people.

I called Carl about 7:00 A.M. "You sound out of breath, what have you been doing?" I asked.

"I was outside working on the walkway to the lake," he answered. I told him about last night. He asked me if I had thought about getting baptized. I hadn't thought a lot about it, but I definitely wanted to. I told him they were having a baptism this Sunday in Harlem and I would like to be baptized there since I was saved there. "You let me know what you decide and if you are going to do it, I'll be there," he said. I was surprised he mentioned it, yet I was glad he did.

"Well, I better go, I got some workers coming to lay rock on the walkway this morning," he replied.

"You do! Man, the fishing room is done and now the walkway! Be careful, and I love you," I said hurriedly.

"Me too," he said and hung up.

I got into work and called Kimberly's church and told them I would like to be added to the list of those being baptized this Sunday. The lady on the other end told me they had plenty of white gowns and to bring a hair dryer, towel, and an extra set of undergarments. She was excited for me and said the list was growing every day, praise God. She was excited! I called Carl back and told him so he could plan on being there.

That night Carol, Faune, Sam, and I left work about five o'clock, ate at a great steak place and headed for Harlem. I told all of them over dinner I was going to be baptized Sunday and wanted them to be there. I had left Kimberly a note on my office couch telling her we were all going to church. She knew where to look for her notes by now. They were always on the couch in an envelope with her name on it.

She didn't know what she started. Well, yes, I guess she did. The Lord told her to bring me and look what has happened! Praise God for people that pray, listen, and do what God tells them to do! God sure had her in my office for a reason!

Sylvia greeted us at the door as usual. She was always at that front door with a smile. We went in and the choir started. Carol loved music and she was enjoying this. Sam was really looking everything over. He was full of anticipation, yet I felt He was going to find Jesus this week. Seek and ye shall find (Matt. 7:7)! He was seeking. We all enjoyed the music and I could see Sam studying the people who were shouting and dancing. I could almost read his mind. He was wondering what they had that he didn't.

That was the way I felt, too. I didn't criticize it, I just didn't understand it. I saw real tears and real joy. How could anyone criticize that? What did it feel like to be touched by the Holy Spirit where you could not stand still? Woowee! "It must be something!" I surmised.

Faune cried during the service. I went up and prayed that God would lead me to say and do what He wanted me to do. I wanted only Him to lead my life now. I wanted to be able to hear from Him and do what He wanted me to do. Carol and Sam enjoyed the service. They said they had never been to a service like that before.

Kimberly and Sylvia came over and hugged each one of us. Kimberly whispered in my ear, "Do not worry about Faune, tears are a cleansing. She needed to do that. This is a release for her. Praise God!" I smiled and thanked her for sharing that as she left with some of her family.

Early the next day, I checked on Carl's progress again. "Carl, how is it going this morning?" I asked.

"Oh, it's busy. We're still working on the walkway," he said. "You remember Sharon at church?" he asked.

"Yeah, she is the one doing the seminars," I answered.

"Well, she is coming into the city to attend a two-day health seminar and she is trying to find a hotel in Manhattan. I figured she could stay at my apartment, but she may not feel safe staying someplace where she doesn't know anyone. I was just wondering if you would mind her staying at your place? She is trying to find a hotel near where she needs to do her work, which is only about ten minutes from you. I haven't said anything to her about your place, but it would be nice if she wasn't in the city all by herself."

"I think that would be a great idea! When is she coming in?" I asked.

"Tomorrow morning," he said.

"I'll be working early, so give her your key to my place and draw her a map. She can stay in the guest room and maybe she would like to go to the revival with me at night! Tell her to come on in and park in the garage space where you usually park. Tell her to be careful. This is not Amber Lake traffic," I laughed.

I went to work and we hit it hard all day. Sam, Carol, and Faune all came to my office and we ate lunch together. Franklin walked in and said, "Don't tell me you're planning another revival meeting!" We all laughed. "What in the world is going on up there?" he asked. We all were telling him about the choir and the spirit moving and people being saved and prayed over for everything they needed.

"By the way, Franklin, you need to come up there Sunday morning. I am being baptized," I told him. He looked at me for a minute. I think he thought I was in a religious movement full swing.

"Well, I'll see if Robbie wants to go. She stays awful busy with our church you know. I don't have to go to church. She makes up for both of us," he laughed.

Robbie was Franklin's dear wife. She was a sweet lady and Franklin was very loyal and good to her. They had one son and two daughters. The son was following in Franklin's footsteps all the way. The two daughters were following in their mother's footsteps and were attending private church colleges and were wonderful girls. Franklin was a very good person and no one could deny that, but I was concerned over his salvation.

The one thing he did not do with his family was go to church with his wife and daughters. Other than that, he was with his family for everything that he could be. It had to be something very urgent for him to be away from things he considered important. He just didn't think church was important. He was not kidding when he said his wife had enough religion for both of them. How sadly mistaken he was!

We were all in the boardroom by 1:00 P.M., ready for another conference call to come in. It was then I invited Kent to come to my baptism. Of course, I knew the answer, but wanted to extend the invitation. He said he would hold the office down for the rest of us that were going to the church service. "Man, we might as well move our boardroom to Harlem!" he suggested to us, not looking up from his paperwork. We started laughing at him.

Franklin got a call back from Robbie in the boardroom. She wanted them both to go to my baptism. I was glad. This would get Franklin in church! We would have to pray that the Holy Spirit touched him during that service! I had learned what the power of prayer could do! His wife and daughters had been praying for him all these years, I was sure!

We all worked until 8:00 P.M. I had seen Kimberly around six o'clock and told her I would probably go home tonight and do laundry, clean my apartment, and get some rest. I told her I was having a guest coming in from Carl's church. I explained to her the type of seminar she had started at Lakeside Church. She said she wanted to talk to her and knew some other people who would love to meet her. She told me that Sharon and I should definitely plan on being there tomorrow night!

I called Carl as soon as I got home and he said Sharon took us up on our offer to stay at my place. She was really relieved she had some company in the big city and she would love to go to the revival. She said she was ready for one! Everything was set for her to come here and I was looking forward to it.

He said he was ready to turn in. It had been a busy day and he finished arranging everything in the new fishing room. Man, I couldn't wait to get out there and see it! I really couldn't wait to see what the fin and feather room looked like without that big mess in it. It was a beautiful room anyway. Tomorrow the men were working on the walkway again. It would probably take them one more day. It was a long and broad walkway and they had not worked on it more than five hour days, but at least it was about to be finished. Boy, he was really pouring on the coal, or in this case, rock.

"We've got a lot of work to do yet, but we have made excellent progress," Franklin said, opening the board meeting. "We are accepted as a top rate firm in the eyes of our new clients. That is the way I want it to stay! Everyone around this table today is responsible for paving the way into the next century. What an exciting time! Each and everyone of you will be written in the history of this firm as the ones who conquered the currents and rapids of the business world and stayed afloat. That is something to be proud of! We have proved to the top corporations we are one of the best firms around today, and we have to keep that image in the years to come. The age of technology is now changing moment to moment. We have to fight to stay on top everyday and you are able to do it! I'm proud of you!" Franklin announced.

With that, we all were dismissed and went to our offices and hit the paperwork again. I called my apartment and Sharon answered. She had just gotten settled in and loved the apartment, especially the view! She was going to catch a taxi to her health seminar. It was about ten minutes by taxi from my apartment and that was perfect!

Carol, Sam, and I ate together. Faune came in for a moment. She was swamped too. I asked them if they wanted to go to church tonight. Sam and Faune were going tomorrow night. They were beat too. Carol was so busy at home and church, she was just coming up Sunday morning with Glenn. I told them I was going tonight with Sharon, a member from Carl's church, who came in the city to attend a health seminar.

I informed them about her great weight loss and battles she fought in her life and conquered them through the power of Jesus. She was starting her own seminars entitled "Your Loss is His Gain" and she was presenting them to different churches all over. The seminar involved not only weight and health issues, but other issues in life and how to get a handle of them through the power of Jesus. As she said, there were many things that could cause us to overeat and not eat healthy. They really thought that would be interesting.

Carol even thought this seminar would be great to hold in the large conference room for all the people in our firm who needed "Your Loss is His Gain." We all thought it might be a challenge and perk some people up and make them feel better in many ways. I told them I needed to leave early, at least early for us, so Sharon and I could eat and attend church. "You are not just going to eat a bowl of whole grain cereal, are you," kidded Sam.

"I hope not!" I answered.

I left at five o'clock and went back to my apartment. Sharon came in about ten minutes later. We both talked a few minutes and decided to freshen up and eat dinner. We ate a great meal and Sharon told me certain things to stay away from and how important it was to eat healthy and not to skip any meals. We got a taxi and headed for Harlem.

Sylvia greeted us and we walked in and Kimberly left her friends and came back and sat with us. Sylvia finally got to join us too. The service was getting better each night! I learned what revival means—revival! Sharon was really enjoying this. She loved music. She loved the freedom to worship and see the spirit moving! We visited with some of Kimberly's friends afterwards for almost an hour. We told them we were coming back tomorrow night. We all were going to sit together and wanted to go out and eat afterwards. Sounded good to me and it even sounded good to Sharon. I thought maybe she wouldn't want to eat again, but she did.

On Friday morning Sharon and I drank coffee and looked out over the city. She only drank one cup of coffee and switched to decaf. She was more disciplined than I was! She had brought some fruit and whole cereals. I needed to learn a lot from her. I knew I needed to eat healthier. I could see she felt good and was full of joy. The way she ate certainly was not a drudgery, it was enjoyable. That is what impressed me. After all, anyone who has lost 182 pounds will definitely get your attention as to how they did it and how they are maintaining it.

I called Carl and he was getting ready to go over to the church. The carpet had come in and was ready to be installed. The men were finishing his walkway today. He was really having a busy week. I told him I would call him in the morning. Sharon was bragging on the church at Amber Lake and how all of them loved Carl. We talked about the service last night and she commented on how strong she felt the presence of God in that meeting. Neither one of us could wait to go back tonight.

She had her seminar at nine, which would last all day. It was only a two-day seminar, and they had a lot of info to absorb. She said this seminar came highly recommended to learn about health issues. She was very anxious to go and I was anxious to hear about it.

I told her I better get ready and head into the office. She was going to get ready and spend time reading her Bible. She really enjoyed her "time with the Lord" as she called it. I had a lot to learn from this lady. I'm sure many other people did too. That is why she was in the city getting ready to set up and start presenting these seminars on a professional basis. Her plan was to visit churches and help people physically and spiritually through her own seminars. What a great idea! It amazes me the wisdom God gives people when all you do is ask and seek Him (James 1:5). I left with her peacefully meditating on the Lord, looking out over Manhattan.

"What's up?" Carol asked, joining stride with me, headed for another conference call in the boardroom.

"Another great day, lady!" I announced, turning and smiling at her. She smiled back, and we both giggled a bit.

"Did you and Sharon go to the revival last night?" she asked. "Yes! We had a great time. We're going back tonight. After the revival, Kimberly, Sylvia, Sharon, and I, and whoever else wants to go, are all going out to eat. It is hard telling when we will get home!" I laughed.

"I can imagine. You will probably come in the office tomorrow straight out of Harlem!" laughed Carol.

We had our usual busy day and accomplished a lot. I saw Nick as he came down the hallway with all of our lunch regulars. He asked me why my order had not been in the dinner regulars. He told me it wasn't like me not to work late. I had worked late all these years when the rest of them did and I was suddenly breaking my pattern. He asked me if I was in love or something. He wanted to know what happened to Carl. Nick was always kidding everybody and noticed everything that went on!

"Yes, I'm in love!" I perked.

Nick's eyes got real big and he exclaimed, "What about Carl?" before he even thought.

"Well, Carl is the one I am in love with and now I love the Lord too. I finally came to know Jesus as my personal Lord and Saviour last week. After all these years I have wasted not knowing Him. . . . Nick, it just changes your life. I am going to be baptized this Sunday," I told him, surprising myself with all that I said.

Nick was all ears and stood there a minute, still holding all the lunches. After staring intensely at me another minute he said, "Well, you have changed. I can't explain it, but there is a change. You have definitely changed your priorities! I have to admit, that was long overdue. You must be looking at everything in a new light!" he replied, inquisitively so.

"Totally!" I quickly replied. Then I said, "Nick you need to start going to church with your family and quit working down there on Sunday mornings. That is the Lord's day anyway. He only asked you for one day out of seven. You need to honor that and spend quality time with your family, not just work time," I admitted.

He looked at me and quietly confessed, "That is exactly what Angelina has been telling me."

"Well, you need to listen to her. She loves you very much and is very concerned about you," I informed him.

"Thanks for sharing that with me," Nick whispered. Whispering was out of character for him. Nick had a lot of flair and expression with his words and personality. He then went on and delivered the lunches to everyone.

We all ate lunch and continued to work. We were all coming in Saturday, but I told them I would probably be in about ten o'clock. I informed them tonight would be a late night and I wanted to spend a little time with Sharon in the morning before she left.

I told them I was anxious to hear what she had learned at the health seminar. I sure needed an update on what I needed to do to stay healthy. You can't take your body for granted. I sure didn't want to wait until something happened from years of neglect. After all, I was on the downhill run. We all laughed and admitted we were all on the downhill run! Then I said, "Except for Sam, he is still a pup!"

Sam was only thirty-eight. He was the youngest of all of us. He wanted to stop smoking, but was having a rough time. I told him he needed to come back to the revival and get some people seriously praying for him. "After the revival they set aside a prayer room with prayer warriors who confidentially talk and pray with you. It is wonderful!" I told him.

As I told him this, Carol, Franklin, and Kent listened. I told him I was going back tonight and pray for guidance in my life. I informed them the reason I was going back was because several people had already come forward and given a testimony as to the results of those prayers. More and more people are going back and they have four prayer rooms available now. The results are astounding.

There is power in prayer, great power I confirmed to them. I couldn't believe I was so bold. Of course, Carol agreed and told them what she had heard as testimonies the night she had gone. Sam said there were about eight testimonies that night. He told them about one couple who had lost their jobs and had been unable to find work for the last two months. After going to the prayer room and being taught by Scripture about praying and walking in faith, both of them started praying every day and believing and not doubting.

Three days later the wife was hired making the same money she had made from her previous job. One week later the husband was hired making two dollars per hour less than his previous job, but with a chance of promotion within six months. Then he found out they had a much better insurance plan and offered him overtime every Saturday that he wanted to work.

Sam said the testimony that really touched him was the couple that came up with their baby girl. She was born with one kidney and had trouble with that one. They had come to this church about three months ago and people started praying for this baby's healing and walked in faith with what the Bible preached about healing. One month ago, the doctors said they were in total awe that the tests showed a new kidney in the place of the missing one!

No explanation from the doctors, because there was not one. It was just a miracle! The brand new kidney and her kidney she was born with are working perfectly. This couple was crying and Sam said so was everyone in the whole church. Carol affirmed that. She said the testimonies were very impressionable, to say the least.

"How on earth can that be?" blurted out Kent. "The doctors must have gotten something mixed up somewhere. A kidney doesn't just grow out of nowhere. As far as those jobs, they just started hustling a little more and then they found something," he said, rather sarcastically.

"In Luke 1:37 it says, 'With God nothing will be impossible.' I would say that settles it, because He said nothing will be impossible!" I announced, amazing myself. I had made a vow to myself to learn at least one Scripture verse every week and keep repeating it ten times a day until it sunk in real good. That was the Scripture I had learned this week. My, how it had paid off, not to mention what it was doing in my life!

All of them looked at me. Franklin was taken back. He looked like he was wondering how I had changed so quick in a matter of days. He looked curious. Kent looked at me like he was thinking, "This has gone too far! Now she is quoting Bible verses!" Sam was silent. He looked at me like he wanted to know more about God. The testimonies moved him and that Bible verse got his attention. Carol just looked at me with a sweet, peaceful smile. She knew God was finally in control of my life. That is a marvelous thing to see happen to someone!

"Maybe they will have some testimonies Sunday morning. That must be quite enlightening to hear. We certainly need to hear some good news once in a while," Franklin replied, softly smiling at me.

I wanted to say Jesus is the good news, but I didn't. I just smiled back and said, "That's for sure!" Something told me to take one step at a time with Franklin.

Sunday morning would be eye-opening for him. Gentle persuasion, I thought. I was moving as fast as I could with Franklin. He was being very tolerable with me already. I just hoped time wouldn't run out for him. It almost did for me. I praised God I was saved!

We all ate lunch as we worked and I got up to leave about 4:30 P.M. I told them I had to clean off my desk and would see them about mid-morning on Saturday. "You know, I think I'll go tonight," said Sam as he entered my office.

"Great!" I said, surprised he had left the boardroom to come and tell me.

"Well, Carol and I went out to get something to drink and she told me I should go tonight if I wanted to. She thought we were going to run ahead of schedule on our deadlines," Sam informed me. That was Carol. She always had her finger on the pulse of wants and needs of the people as well as the company. Her follow-up was never one of procrastination!

"Why don't you meet Sharon and me for dinner and we will all go together. I have to go and meet her right now. Please check with Faune and see if she can go. I'll call you as soon as I get home. We will have a great time! You and Faune really try to go. I'll call you in a little bit," I said, as I darted out the door. Sam was hotfooting it to Faune's office.

"Hey! How did it go today?" I asked Sharon when I walked into my apartment. She was sitting on the couch looking at some of the brochures she had picked up from the seminar.

"Oh, it was great! I had prayed about attending this seminar. I received just what I needed to tie up loose ends. I'm ready now to put together my entire program. Praise God!" she said, as she lifted her hand up and closed her eyes and shook her head.

"This seminar must have been something!" I exclaimed, seeing her prayers had been answered about this seminar.

"It was just what God wanted me to learn to complete everything! We serve an awesome God!" she confessed. "This seemed impossible to me over a year ago. Who would have ever thought I would lose 182 pounds and then put all this together! I had to turn my weight, not to mention a lot of burdens, over to God. I had to learn to walk in faith. While I was on that walk, believe me I learned a lot, but look at the results!" she acclaimed.

I studied her and I could see the real results in her eyes, deep in her soul. I didn't know Sharon that well, but I could see it. "How wonderful that must be!" I thought. "To glow from the inside out! I want to be on that same walk! Oh, to have that and then to be on the road accomplishing what He told you to do. I know what the results will be there!"

I called the office and Sam and Faune were going. Great! We all decided to eat seafood and we all met at a wonderful Friday night seafood buffet. We had a great dinner together and Sam and Faune were all ears listening to Sharon's new venture and what the Lord had done in her life.

Kimberly and Sylvia had saved seats for us at the church. We all got seated and the choir started. We walked around the church and sang. I had never done that before. We just walked down the aisles and clapped and sang. All of us were laughing and singing!

People started coming up and giving their testimonies after we were seated. The preacher preached, and people were crying, praising God, and filling the altar. Mothers were crying over children who went up and accepted Christ and wives were crying over lost husbands, now repenting. Everything and anything was laid at the altar for so many people!

Faune and Sharon were crying and had their arms around each other, standing in the front. Sam and I were standing in the aisle and we felt like we were breathing in the Holy Spirit. I went to one of the prayer rooms and a man and a woman took my hands to pray for me. I told them I wanted to pray to do God's will in all aspects of my life and be a light to other people. I did not want to waiver and be lukewarm. I wanted to walk a straight line in the direction God had for me.

They prayed over me and gave me Scripture to read. These people were praying for my guidance, since I was a new Christian. They told me I needed to study God's word every day for there would be turmoil along the way. They said Satan had no control over me anymore, only if I let him. "For He who is in me is bigger than he who is in the world," they said. They told me not to fret, that God was always with me and would tell me what to do if I listened. I must walk in faith, not by sight (2 Cor. 5:7).

I thanked them for praying for me. I went back out front and Kimberly and Sylvia were praying at the altar for other people. Sharon was praying for Faune. When Sharon and Faune finished praying, I asked them where Sam was. They said he went back to one of the prayer rooms. "Hallelujah!" I exclaimed. They laughed and said they had just prayed for him, Kent, and Franklin.

All of us finally joined together and we all went out and ate. Twenty-three of us bombarded a restaurant just a few blocks from the church. They seated us in the back in an area of our own. We all ordered and then a man by the name of Arnold stood up at his table and started singing "I've Got One More River to Cross." You could hear a pin drop. Even the waitresses stopped, the people at the cash register stopped and turned, the cooks came out of kitchen, silently. There were no dishes being stacked or picked up, no babies crying, and no words spoken.

When he finished singing, there were "Amens" whispered and one man stood up in the front and put his hand up and shouted, "Praise God." One woman over by the windows stood up and put both hands in the air, and then started bending forward from her waist again and again while saying, "Thank you Jesus." The other women at her table started crying. I felt tears rolling down my cheeks.

It was a few more moments before anyone else spoke or moved. Arnold had not moved. With his eyes still closed he started singing "Amazing Grace" and all of us at our tables quietly stood up and joined in. People around the restaurant started standing up and joining in. The music was heavenly. The waitresses, cooks, and cashier joined in. I will never forget that night, as everyone there will not!

I woke up to a wonderful fall day. I went out and fixed a pot of coffee. I walked over to the windows and looked out. That was my morning ritual. I loved looking out at the sky and the movement down on the city streets. Every day was new, with different weather, breezy or not so breezy, clouds or maybe no clouds. I enjoyed it whatever it was. It was good to be alive and blessed, I should add.

"Well, good morning!" I said as Sharon came into the living room. "Isn't this a fantastic day? Are you going to stay in the city today? You are more than welcome to spend the weekend here if you would like," I offered.

"Thank you, but I need to get back today for sure. I have to get all my notes and teaching put into my seminar package while it is fresh and the Lord is moving me to finalize it. When he tells me to do something, I don't procrastinate! That is a big trick from Satan. Satan will always tell you that later is fine, when it isn't at all," she stated.

"Well, then you have a beautiful day to drive back. That's for sure!" I affirmed.

I needed to heed that message myself. When the Lord called me, I wanted to be obedient and not wait until tomorrow. After all, tomorrow might be too late! Boy, I came too close to learning about that the hard way. The epitome of learning the hard way would be to be in hell forever and ever. It makes me shudder to think about it!

Sharon got a cup of coffee and came over and looked out the window. I pointed out some landmarks to her and told her stories about Carl and I over the years we had been in the city. I poured another cup of coffee and we sat down on the couch and talked. I told her I would really miss Carl not being in the city anymore. We had been together twenty years. I also told her we had not been apart in all those twenty years, at least not for more than a couple of days at a time, and that was only due to business trips.

I told her how quickly things had changed in my life in the last month. It all started when people started praying for me! I told her about my cousins visiting me and how that set the stage for making me very aware of decisions and changes I needed to make. Then I found out Lakeside Church was praying for me too. How quickly my life started to change. I wanted it to, but I didn't want it to.

"The 'didn't want it to' was from Satan. I can tell you that! Believe me, I have been there and Satan will always try to get you to go the wrong way, even after you are saved. Once you are saved, you have authority over him in Jesus' name. Praise God!" she acclaimed.

I told her the horrible story about almost losing my life and what had happened to the driver and that poor innocent pedestrian. I admitted that the near-fatal accident had been eye-opening for me. I told her how Kimberly had witnessed to me and prayed for me. I told Sharon that Kimberly was a bold preacher and we both chuckled.

I confessed to her that after all the years I had been with Carl, now I didn't feel I should stay at his place or he should stay at mine overnight. "Sharon, we are just like an old married couple. Why am I so adamant about that all of a sudden?" I asked her.

"Because in God's eyes you are not married and you are acting like you are." She chuckled and shook her head and said, "Believe me, He has a way of letting you know what you should be doing and what you shouldn't be doing. You can count on that! It is the Holy Spirit convicting you about your lifestyle. I would never judge you, I know better than that! I won't lie to you either, because the truth always sets you free, my sister . . . always!"

"I know Carl feels the same way even though he doesn't say it," I told her.

"Sure he does!" confirmed Sharon. "When you get saved, you are a new person. Christ is in you and your views and things you used to do may not seem the right things to do anymore. Listen, it happens to all of us who are allowing God to work in us. Thank God! I had sin in my life to clean up, just like everyone else. Sometimes it seems like it takes a long time, but it doesn't have to," she proclaimed.

"When Christ is in you, you want or have the desire to do right. The Holy Spirit that lives in you will tell you what is right and what is wrong. You are the one that has to make it happen. It can be the smallest thing to an overwhelming decision. He'll even tell you not to litter or to put your grocery cart in the cart rack. All those little white lies that we justify are all right, well they are plain lies in God's eyes!" Sharon exclaimed, affirming she knew all about how God can deal with you.

I told her how I had people pray that I would do what God wants me to do and not what I want to do. I told her I knew it wouldn't be easy. Sharon said, "Well, I know one thing. Carl really loves you. He talks about you all the time. I know he is lonesome without you. I personally got the feeling that he knows you love your job and that you would never tear yourself away from it. He never complains or says that, but he is always telling us how much you work and that you will come out to see him when you are caught up. I think he feels he is a definite second to your job, but he truly loves you, so he has settled for that all these years," Sharon revealed.

"Well, I would love to change that. I would rather be with Carl right now than anything else! In the last month it is like a veil has been lifted off my eyes, Sharon. Maybe it was because he has finally decided to retire and leave the city. He has always been here, and I realized how much I took him for granted. I even took my own life for granted! Boy, when people start praying for you, expect some changes! These changes have been for the good and long overdue. I can't change the past, but today is a new day!" I affirmed.

"We all wish we could change the past. Don't even go there! The Lord tells us to renew ourselves daily (Ps. 51:10). That is why! If you get hung up on yesterday, you'll never get past it. That is the devil's workshop, that 'what if' or 'if only.' Keep those thoughts from your mind, whatever you do!" suggested Sharon. "Does Carl know how you feel?" she asked.

"You know, I don't know. I think he does see a change in me, especially about going to church and now being saved. That was a total turnaround! I know he can tell I miss him and I want to be out there with him. He may still feel that my job comes first, but I have shown him a different side of me in the last few weeks. I know he notices my change in priorities, but after all, I have put my job first for twenty years," I admitted.

"Then you need to tell him he is the most important thing in your life. He certainly deserves that if he has waited on you for twenty years!" Sharon replied. We both started laughing and I definitely agreed with her.

"Pray for me about this," I asked. She grabbed my hand and we prayed right there.

Then she whispered, "Always listen and always walk in faith." That must have been a confirmation, because that is all I had heard lately! We both got ready and I helped her carry out her bags and we went to her car. I told her about my favorite little stops before I got to Amber Lake. "Carl told me you would have me shopping and eating all the way back," she laughed. We hugged goodbye and I said I would see her soon.

I got into the office about ten and Carol, Franklin, Kent, and Sam had their heads buried in paperwork. "Boy, Sam was telling us all about last night. You all must have had a time!" laughed Carol.

"We certainly did! I wished you could have been there!" I exclaimed.

"We worked last night until 9:30," Kent said dryly.

"You need to bring that guy you went to the restaurant with and let him sing and motivate us," Franklin chuckled. We all laughed, except for Kent.

We ordered lunch. I told them I had to go back to my office and make a phone call first. I walked back to my office and knew I needed to call Mike, the taxi driver. I finally found his number and placed the call. He was in and he came to the phone and said, "Hello, this is Mike."

"Mike, this is Diane, you know the one with her cousins who had you drive to the Bowery," I laughed.

"Yeah, of course I remember! I have called you back several times, but missed you," he replied. "I went to church with my mother that next Sunday and she was thrilled to death. She kept telling everyone how she had been praying I would come to church with her. I don't know why on earth I wasted all those years and didn't go to church! If nothing else, I should have gone because my mother wanted me to," he confessed.

"Well, no one could have told me I would be going to a Baptist church in Harlem several weeks ago either. Now I can't imagine not going to this church. The mindsets we get in!" I affirmed.

I went on to tell him in a nutshell what all had happened and that I had accepted Jesus as my Saviour. I told him I was going to be baptized this Sunday and gave him the name of the church in Harlem. I invited him and his family to come up there.

He couldn't believe what all had happened. He said he heard about the accident and about a lady barely escaping being hit and landing on the top of one of their taxis. "I certainly had no idea that was you! The size of this city and here it was someone I knew!" he exclaimed.

He told me he was to start a Bible study class on Wednesday night at his mother's church. He was looking forward to that. I told him to keep in touch with me and that I had to get back to work. He said he had to tell me one more thing. His mother's friends and my cousins had prayed for him and now he was working not only a forty hour week but a lot of double shifts. "Not only that," he said, "I got a raise too!"

"Great! By the way, what number is your car, Mike? If I have to call for a taxi, I'll ask for you."

"I'm number sixty-eight, the year I was born," he answered.

"I'll write that down. When I am around the city I may just spot you. Congratulations on your raise. See, look what prayer has already done for you!" I exclaimed.

"Pray for me to find a beautiful, rich lady, Diane. You tell Jan and her daughters that too!" he laughed. On that we said bye and hung up.

I was shaking my head about him and so thrilled for him and for his mother!

The day wore on. We ordered dinner from Nick and then we all worked until eight o'clock. We all walked out together and Carol, Franklin, and Sam said they would see me in the morning. Kent said he was coming in about six in the morning and was planning on getting a lot done and sticking with it all day. We told him to have a good day anyway! They said they didn't get to see Carl anymore and would be glad to see him on Sunday. We all planned on eating out after church.

We used to eat out a lot after work and Carl would be with us most of the time because he would wait on me to get off work. The rest of the spouses hardly ever joined us because all of them had children to take here and there. We all had a lot of good times over the years! I don't think we realized how close we really were. I had realized it since I had been thinking about leaving. It would be tough to leave them. They were a big part of my life!

Oh, it was good to be home in time to see the sunset. The view from my window at sunset was breathtaking! I called Carl and he said he would met me at the church. He was leaving early to get there ahead of schedule. He said the walkway was finished and the fishing room was totally done now. He said he had had a long day and was getting ready to go to bed.

"Well, you are about caught up with things then?" I asked.

"Oh, there is a lot of work to be done around here before winter sets in! Plus, we got the new carpet at the church down too. The fellowship hall has been painted and we put in all new cabinets and countertops. The ladies picked out new curtains and blinds and some kitchen decorations," he said.

"Wow, I didn't know the church was going to do all that!" I exclaimed.

"We have decided to go ahead and put down a new vinyl floor in the Fellowship Hall," added Carl. "That church is a landmark and that room certainly needed a total renovation. It looks like a different room back there now," Carl said.

"I guess so! I can't wait to see it," I said, thinking about next weekend.

"It looks great! The new carpet was all they needed in the sanctuary. It was repainted last year and so was the outside of the church," Carl said.

"It is a beautiful church! It looks like a picture postcard with that tall steeple," I said.

"Oh, some of the church ladies are in a shopping frenzy now that they have seen the new cabinets and all. They are buying decorations and even buying candle arrangements for the dining tables when we have special occasions. They are having a ball!" he laughed.

"Boy, I wish I was up there! That is right up my alley!" I pouted.

"I told them it was a good thing you weren't up here. You wouldn't sleep at night thinking what needed this and that and what color would look best and on and on," he replied.

"Oh-h-h, that would be so much fun!" I complained, knowing I was too tied up to help. Well, I wasn't a member anyway. I wouldn't want to intrude.

"Those ladies said they wished you were here to help," said Carl.

"They did?" I said with surprise.

"Yeah, Judy called me last week to see if you were available to help with decorating. I told her you were working at least thirteen hours a day for a long time yet," he said. "She said they were going to do the classrooms and restrooms next spring and would like your input," Carl informed me.

"Really?" I said, thrilled they wanted me to help. "Count me in right now!" I insisted.

"You want me to?" Carl asked.

"Yes! I would love doing that!" I replied.

"Well, all right. I thought you might be too tied up at work. You will probably have even 'bigger and better' clients by then as they say," Carl said. I knew he was surprised at my wanting to drop everything to help with a church I had only visited several times. "OK. I'll tell Carolyn. She is heading up that committee. I know she would like your help," he implied.

"Be sure and do that," I said.

I think Carl was surprised and at the same time he wasn't surprised. Even though I was doing things totally out of character for me, he still knew I had undergone a change of heart and mind in many ways. He was beginning to see it now. We talked a little while longer and then I told him I would see him in the morning. I told him, "I love you very much," and he said, "Me too," and we hung up.

I called Jan and told her about all that was happening and that I had called Mike. She was glad and wanted to hear about him. I told her what all he said and to pray for a beautiful rich lady to come into his life. She laughed about that. She said Carl had called and talked to Ray about coming up real soon. "He did!" I said, rather shocked. I wondered why he didn't tell me! "Are you all going to come up?" I asked.

"Yes, we are all planning on it as far as I know," she answered.

Good grief, I wonder why Carl hadn't told me. Oh well, it would be great to get to see them again. Ray and little Michael would love fishing on Amber Lake! We talked for a while and I told her about what had been happening in Harlem. She was excited for me. I told her how important her prayers were to me and to keep praying for Mike too. We laughed about that. I told her tomorrow was a big day and I better turn in. She said they always prayed for me and wished they could come up and go to Harlem.

I told her how important she and the girls had been to me in seeing things in a different light. I knew she couldn't be here, but it wouldn't be long until I would see them all. I told her I would call her later and then we hung up.

What a beautiful morning! I drank my coffee and then ran across the street to Peggy's and grabbed some bagels and low-fat cream cheese. I didn't get one for Gilbert. Sunday was his day off. Gilbert told me many years ago that Sunday was the Lord's day and he wouldn't miss church. Why is it I never thought about him being off every Sunday to go to church until now? I will have to tell Gilbert I am saved the next time I see him. I want to see his reaction.

I got ready and carried my hair dryer, extra set of underwear, and my camera. I wanted some pictures taken of Kimberly, Sylvia, Carol, Franklin, Sam, Faune, and their families. I wanted some taken of the church too. Out the door I went, on my way to Harlem to be baptized.

I met Sylvia and Kimberly at the door. We were talking and I felt a tap on my shoulder and there was Carl with Sharon, Carolyn, April, and Judy! I couldn't believe it! I introduced Kimberly and Sylvia to Carolyn, April, and Judy. Sharon just hugged them both. We all got on the same pew and then Carol and Glenn came in. Sam and Faune followed in right behind.

We were all seated and then Franklin and Robbie came in and sat with us. Lo and behold Nick, Angelina, his mother, and their four children came in! Franklin leaned over and told me he had told Nick he was planning on coming up here today and Nick said he was closing the deli and coming up here too. Franklin said he called Kent real early this morning and told him to bring his lunch to work because Nick was going to the baptism. All of us that knew Kent laughed at that. I could just see his reaction.

Carol introduced Kimberly to Robbie and Glenn. Then she introduced Sylvia to everyone else from the office. We had taken up two pews now. The preacher, Brother Creighton, came back and introduced himself to everyone. Right after that the choir came out.

They started singing and the church was in such a mood of revival, it seemed the winds of it swept out over us, covering us from head to toe. The Holy Spirit was not leashed here! He flowed where He was welcome to flow, and the blessings abounded. Free to flow, free to receive—He touched us and we received much.

There were people here and there that stepped out in the aisles and praised God. I didn't know what they were freed from or healed from, but I knew they were. I knew some of the ones that had come today on my behalf had never witnessed anything like this before. I didn't know what they thought, but they had to see it was real. When God touches someone, you can see it! It is too powerful to be hidden.

Some people were in the aisles dancing, some had gone to the altar. Some were in front and down on their faces, while others raised their hands or got down on their knees. The choir kept singing and I didn't turn to the left and I didn't turn to the right. I just prayed for all my people that were there. "Touch them Lord, fill them with your Holy Spirit."

The choir stopped and Sylvia motioned for me to come with her. I stepped out and the two of us slipped to the back to prepare for baptism. I got ready and those of us who were being baptized were in a line.

Brother Creighton was already in the baptistery behind the choir. All of us were waiting in line, all in white robes. The curtains on the baptismal were opened and Brother Creighton told the audience that we were beginning the baptisms. He said that twenty-three of us were being baptized. There were people shouting and praising God.

We started going, one by one, walking into the water and up to Brother Creighton. As each one went and grabbed his hand he would tell the congregation our name and that we had made a profession of faith. Then he asked each one if they had accepted Christ as their personal Lord and Saviour and that person would answer "yes." He would then say they wished to follow up their profession of faith in the act of baptism.

He said the act of baptism did not save one, but it was symbolic of burying the old person and the rebirth of the new person. Then he put his hand in the air and pronounced his authority in the name of Jesus Christ to baptize this sister or brother and would give his or her name.

With that he would completely immerse them under the water and bring them back up. It was my turn. I waded out across the pool to Brother Creighton and took his hand. As he talked I looked out and saw my friends out there, softly smiling. The old me went under and the new me burst out of the water.

We all went back and changed and dried our hair and went back out front. The choir had been singing songs of jubilee and celebration from the time the last one was baptized. All of us that were baptized ranged from ages five to eighty-four. One lady came back and helped her little girl fix her hair. She said there were people dancing in the aisles out there.

The eighty-four-year-old man who was just baptized was dancing all over the back of the church! We were all so full of joy, but to see him, you would think he was sixteen. One lady started singing "Look What the Lord Has Done," and others joined in. When I got back out there Brother Creighton was standing in the front and there was one more song and then he started preaching. He preached from Luke 16:19–31 on Lazarus and the rich man and I remembered that one well.

He preached from Luke 12:13–21 about the man who was a fool because his soul was required of him that night and he was not ready. He preached from Luke 23:42–43 about the thief hanging on the cross. When the thief asked Jesus to remember him, Christ told him he would be in paradise with him today.

When he finished preaching everyone in there knew from his words that hell and heaven are real. When you die you will be in one of those places when your heart stops beating (Luke 16:22–23). "Remember, you never know when you are going to die. Once you are in heaven or hell, you will be there throughout all of eternity. The fires and torment of hell are real! The magnificence of heaven, we can't even imagine the glory of it! God does not send anyone to hell. We send ourselves. Salvation is a gift, all we have to do is accept it (Eph. 2:8–10). Jesus paid for it when he died for all our sins on the cross. Be ready, my brothers and sisters, be ready!"

The invitation was open and about fifty people went forward. There were many tears of joy and celebration. People were coming to the altar to be prayed over for healing, guidance, and whatever their needs were. There were many prayer partners on hand all through the church. Prayer warriors started quietly coming to the pews, whispering to people, not missing one. "Would you like to know Jesus today? If you don't know Him, you need to know Him. He is waiting, he is waiting."

Somebody behind me moved out in the aisle. It was Sam! He walked down front and went up to Brother Creighton. They talked and prayed and then Sam got down on his knees at the altar. Kimberly and Sylvia saw him and went over and got down on their knees with him, one on each side. I felt my heart pounding. Tears were running down my cheeks. I didn't look at Carl, but I knew he had tears too. I didn't turn to look at Carol or Faune, but I know it was emotional for them too.

Sam stood up and Sylvia and Kimberly stood beside him. All of us that were baptized went up too. I went up to Sam and gave him a tearful hug. After the service, everyone came down and hugged us. Carol, Faune, Angelina, and I were still drying our tears. Franklin gave Sam and I a hug and was speechless. Robbie hugged us and was so happy for both of us. Nick hugged me and talked to Sam just a minute. Sharon, April, Judy, and Carolyn hugged me and Sam and told both of us how happy they were. They had all been crying too.

Then Mike was standing in front of me! I looked at him and shrieked, "Mike, thanks for coming here today!" He had his mother with him and he introduced me and she hugged me and kissed me on the cheek. I knew he must have told her about that day in the taxi and what all was said. I introduced Mike and his mother to everyone. We asked them to join us for lunch and they accepted.

We all left and went out to eat. We had quite a celebration! I was baptized and Sam accepted Christ! Sam was emotional and full of joy at the same time. Franklin was happy for us. I knew he was searching his heart. I could see it in his face. He was being Franklin, professional and charismatic, but I could tell his spirit was stirring.

All of us visited and had a wonderful time. Carl got up and I knew he was going to pick up all the tabs. Franklin quietly got up and went over to Carl and I knew Franklin insisted on paying the bill. Carl came over and sat back down and continued to visit with Glenn. They loved talking about music and didn't get to see each other much.

We all got ready to leave. We asked for our bill and the waitress said, "That gentleman over there wanted to pay for your lunches," and pointed to Franklin. We all told him that was too much and Franklin said, "It was definitely my pleasure. This day was a testimony in many ways to me and very special." We all thanked him.

It was already three o'clock! All of Carl's crew said they would get back to Amber Lake in time for the evening service. I really appreciated them coming down here. They said they would always remember that service. Kimberly and Sylvia said they were both going home for a couple of hours and coming back to the revival. Sharon told them she had to come back down to that revival. Both of them invited her to stay with them anytime she wanted and also extended the invitation to Carolyn, April, and Judy. Kimberly and Sylvia had plenty of room and were sincere in their invitation. They would love having them come and stay.

We all began to part company. Mike was taking his mother home and going to work. I told Sam, Carol, Franklin, and Nick I would see them tomorrow and said bye to Robbie, Angelina, and Glenn and thanked them for being there.

They all said that was quite a moving service and that it was one they would never forget. All of them had left the parking lot except Carl's crew. They were all loaded and Carl came over to me carrying a tray covered with foil. "What in the world. Oh, don't tell me! This week's cheese specials!" I guessed, figuring it out. He laughed. He told me the cheese was already sliced and he had wrapped up some assorted crackers and put them in there too. I shook my head and laughed. I told him I would certainly miss him greatly the rest of the day, but all the cheese and crackers would keep me company. He hugged me and chuckled.

I told him I was moved that Sharon, Carolyn, April, and Judy came down. I told him my day was one to be remembered, in many ways. He said that he better get going and lightly kissed me on the lips. I looked at him and said, "I love you very much," and he softly smiled and said, "Me too." With that he parted and they all drove away waving until they were out of sight. It touched my heart they all came to see me baptized . . . really touched my heart.

I went back to my apartment and it was almost four thirty. I felt fulfilled and wonderful, yet a little lonesome for Carl at the same time. If he was here right now, he would be bored. He would be over in his recliner reading the Sunday paper for several hours. After that he would fall asleep and when he woke up we would go get something to eat, go to a movie or he would watch TV. As for me, I always had something to do! I had laundry, cleaning, or projects I seemed to never get around to. It was different for him.

He was tired of being in a city apartment. He was definitely an outdoors person. Now that I think back, I don't know how on earth he stayed in the city as long as he did! He must have really loved me to stay here. Some of his friends told me years ago that Carl only came to the city with a plan to work for about seven years, make big bucks, and buy him a place in the country and fish and hunt. He told them he didn't know if he could even stand seven years. Then he met me about five years into that seven and stayed twenty more years! Oh, he wasn't bored because we were busy all the time. We did up the town, saw all the sights, and went to every social event.

I knew all along his heart was not in the city. He just made the most of it to be with me. I never told him to stay. He just did. I never told him what to do. Carl did what he wanted to do. Of course, he made a big pile of money, but money is not really what he was after. His desire was only to be comfortable and do what he wanted.

"Am I seeing this now because God is revealing it to me? Dear God, I hope it is not too late. We have always loved each other greatly. I still love him, but I wonder if he has given up on me? Carl is a man of few words. Has he finally wandered away quietly, breaking off the relationship little by little?

"No, I must not think this way! He has wanted me out there at Amber Lake, but I kept working all the time. Maybe he thought if he bought such a beautiful place, I would give up the city and this crazy rat race. He knew I was able to leave financially at this time, so he probably thought if I was going to come with him, I would.

"He even let me call the shots on decorating the house in and out. Well, he still does, come to think of it. He wrote down everything about the gazebo. Wonder what that was all about? Is he really going to build one? He said he would if he had an occasion. I have to stop all this reasoning. This is crazy!

"I know one thing for sure. I let what wasn't important take over what was important! I see it in Kent. Why didn't I see it in myself? It was my fault. All I can do now is try to correct it starting today. Jan, Carol, Kimberly, and Sharon have tried to get me to see the light. I need to pray, that is what I need to do!"

I picked up my Bible, and started on the first page of the New Testament and started reading. After about two hours of reading and searching, I realized that I had no idea what all was available to me. I got up from the couch and fixed a glass of iced tea and a small cheese tray. I sat at the window and ate, looking out at the evening sky. I got up and stretched and fixed a cup of coffee and resumed my spot on the couch and started reading the Bible again.

I looked up and saw the evening sun setting. I laid back a minute and just watched the colors melt together. I walked over to the window and watched the sun disappear behind the buildings for another day. I went back to reading and started writing down Scriptures I wanted to remember. You never know when you need to quote one to somebody, I reasoned. You never know when you need to quote one to yourself. A verse of Scripture can save your life!

I called Carl after church and we talked for a while. He told me to plan on coming up next Sunday morning real early. I asked him why so early. He said we didn't get to spend much time together on Sunday and he just wanted me to.

"OK. I'll be there by 7:30," I said. He said he would fix me a big breakfast. He told me he would be very busy this week working on things. He said he had to get up early and make the most of daylight.

"I can't wait to see the house, yard, and the church! I am really looking forward to that. Not to mention getting to see my sweetie!" I exclaimed. I told him I loved him and he said, "Me too," and we said bye and hung up.

I resumed reading my Bible and realized what peace and companionship it gave me. I wasn't really lonesome! I can't explain it! All I know is that it gave me blessed assurance. . . . Yes, I believe that is what I would call it. I kept reading until I looked at my watch and realized it was eleven o'clock! I couldn't believe it. Man, it really had been *some* day—all of it was wonderful. I got ready for bed and then I got down on my knees and prayed for His guidance in every step I took. I praised Him for all that He had done in my life. I thanked Him for touching Sam's heart and everyone's heart that was there. I praised Him for such wonderful friends and all the blessings.

The next week was busy! We were trying to get a handle on a new way of doing business for the twenty-first century. We worked twelve hours every day. Nick was keeping our lunches and dinners coming. We got a lot done. We were winding up a lot of loose ends. On Friday, Franklin told us if any of us wanted to take some time off, we could start thinking about it. We had hit it long and hard and he knew we were ready for a break.

I was so glad he said that since Carl mentioned taking me on a vacation. How could I go somewhere with Carl for a whole week if I wanted to live a Christian life? I knew he wanted to live a Christian life too. There I went reasoning again! I had already asked God to guide my steps. I needed to walk in faith . . . walk in faith!

We worked all day Saturday, but Franklin said it was time to call it quits at five o'clock. I was glad and everyone else was too. Kent said he would get to bed early and be back here at six in the morning. Boy, he never learned!

Sam had left around noon in order to get back home. He was going to be baptized at the church he grew up in tomorrow morning. It was a five-hour drive. When he had told his family about his profession of faith, they were moved to tears. He said his parents, both sisters, and eighteen other members of his family were going to be there to see him be baptized. I was so happy for all of them! Franklin told him to take off Monday and enjoy his family a little bit.

I got up at four Sunday morning and hit the road at five thirty. It was a beautiful morning! I pulled into Carl's driveway at 7:15 since there wasn't much traffic. Carl came out the front door before I got down the driveway and motioned for me to stop in front of the garage instead of pulling around back. He came up to the car and opened my door and gave me a kiss.

"Wow! You look nice. I love that suit!" I said, admiring how handsome he looked. "OK. You want to surprise me and show me the walkway and see the look on my face. Right?" I asked.

He laughed and said, "Well, yeah."

I jumped out of the car and said, "Let's go! I can hardly wait!"

We walked around the other side of the garage where the patio was and I looked out over the backyard and lake. In shock I exclaimed, "Oh-h-h, I can't believe this! It is absolutely beautiful!" I stood there entranced by a gorgeous gazebo at the end of a new pier and a new walkway. It was built just like the one at Thornton's Mill, and it was something! I mean it was really something! It looked like a picture postcard, sitting out there at the end of the pier. Ferns were hanging around the edge of the roof, blowing gently in the breeze.

I couldn't take my eyes off of it!

"I take it you like it," Carl chuckled.

"Oh, Carl, everything is just beautiful!" Carl had set some large concrete planters on each side of the walkway just like we had planned. There were three sets of planters and each pair sat across from each other in the places where the walkway straightened out for just a little bit. He had them filled with the same trailing flowers that were on the patio. I couldn't believe he put them out this late in the season. They were a sight to behold!

Carl put his arm out and said, "Well, my lady, are you ready to stroll out to the gazebo and take a look." I put my arm in his and we slowly walked down the rock walkway, plenty wide enough for two people to sashay down. It was like heaven! Walking down this beautiful flowered walkway, over the pier, and into this huge gazebo fit for a queen. The water was gently lapping against the pilings and the breeze was so refreshing against my face.

We were silently standing in the gazebo, listening and feeling the wonder of nature all around us. Carl turned and looked at me so serious and took both my hands in his. We stood there for a minute, looking at one another, so intensely.

"Will you marry me?" he asked, as his emotions stirred.

I felt my heart suddenly leap and tears rush to my eyes and I answered, "Yes!"

He looked at me, trying to steady his voice and whispered, "I have always loved you since the very beginning and I love you more every day."

"Me too," I whispered, as we both held each other tight. We stood there, harbored in that gazebo, and nothing else in the world mattered to us, but each other. It was a moment that would last for a lifetime in our hearts. We didn't want to let each other go. Peace and love just kept flowing through us as we embraced.

He kissed me and took my hand and we silently walked hand in hand back to the house. We walked in the back door and he took both my hands again and told me we had plans to make and it was time for us to get married. He didn't want to wait another week.

"Are you serious?" I whispered.

"Yes, I want to get married next Saturday if that is OK with you," he said. Then both of us started laughing.

"Good grief, Carl, we have been seeing each other for twenty years and now we don't want to wait one week to get married!" I laughed. We both felt the same way.

"Would you like to be married at Lakeside Church?" he asked.

"Yes, I love that church!" I answered.

"I thought we could have the reception in the fellowship hall if it rains. If the weather is nice, we could have it here and have it catered either way. How does that sound?" he asked.

I looked at him and grinned and said, "Sounds to me like you have been thinking about this for a while!"

"Well, it doesn't hurt to plan ahead if you think it might go your way," he said as he chuckled and leaned over and kissed me.

"You sit down here and start writing things we need to get done before Saturday. Now, what do you want for breakfast?" he asked.

"You are going to make such a wonderful husband," I kidded. We ate a great breakfast and were planning every detail we could think of before church.

"The first thing we have to check is if the church is available next Saturday," I announced, rather concerned to think it may not be available.

"It is available. I already checked with Brother Darrel," he answered.

"You already talked to Brother Darrel about proposing to me?" I asked, very surprised.

"No, I had to make sure nothing was planned for a three week timeframe before we could tear into the remodeling of the sanctuary and the Fellowship Hall. We weren't sure how long it would take, but everything moved like clockwork, which is unusual!" he replied, like he was surprised it all fell into place so quickly.

"We can announce our wedding plans in front of the church this morning if you want to, and make it an open invitation," suggested Carl.

"Oh, we better see first if Darrel can marry us," I replied. "You can't get married without a minister. I sure hope he is available next Saturday!" I told Carl.

"We need to get ready and get to the church early. Brother Darrel is always there at least thirty minutes before Sunday school starts," Carl suggested.

"OK. Let's hurry up. I just need to brush my teeth," I replied.

Carl took off to his bedroom and I ran upstairs. Oh, my gosh, I had never even looked at the fishing room or fin and feather! I would save that for Carl to show me when we get back. He was so proud of all the work they did to it, I didn't want to peak and spoil his surprise.

"I can't believe this! We are getting married!" I kept saying that over and over in my mind. I looked out the octagon window to see the gazebo again. Oh, I never asked Carl what the occasion was for building the gazebo. He had told me before he would build one if he had an occasion. I need to ask him about that. I want to hear what he says. I got ready and went back downstairs and fixed a cup of coffee. I was so happy I couldn't believe it. I just couldn't believe it!

"You ready to go?" Carl said as he came around the corner smiling.

"Sure am, sweetie!" I announced. "I have one thing I want to ask you," I said, grinning.

He looked curious and said, "What is that?"

"You had told me if you had an occasion to build a gazebo, you would build one. What occasion was on your mind when you built it?" I asked, as I couldn't wait to hear what he would say.

"The proposal," he answered.

I looked at him and then replied, "You built the gazebo just to propose to me in!"

He smiled and said, "Yes. I knew that moment would be so special. I had a vision of us in that gazebo when you said how beautiful one would be over the lake. I wanted it just to be us with peace and serenity all around us," he said, and he paused to get a hold on his emotions once again. "It was just as I envisioned," he whispered.

We hugged each other again and held each other so tight. "It's nice to have the memories right in your backyard," I smiled. "Every time I look at that gazebo, or walk in it, I will be fondly reminded of the moment you asked me to be your wife," I whispered and reached up and kissed him.

We stood there for a moment in silence and then Carl announced, "Let's get going," and kissed me on the forehead.

We jumped in his Jeep and took off. We got to church and Brother Darrel and Judy's car was there. We walked in and went back to Brother Darrel's office. He and Judy were sitting in there looking at their Bibles. We knocked at the door and they were surprised to see us. "Hey, how are you two doing this morning?" they both said. They both came over and hugged us.

Carl said, "Brother Darrel, we have something to tell you and Judy," he said as his emotions surfaced again. Carl came over and put his arm around me and said to them, "This morning I asked Diane to be my wife," and his voice started to quiver, then he continued, "and she said yes!"

Brother Darrel said, "Well, congratulations!" and Judy said "Oh, that is wonderful!" They both hugged us again.

"Now we have something to ask you," Carl said as he looked at Brother Darrel.

"What's that, Carl?" inquired Brother Darrel.

"Would you marry us?" asked Carl.

"Well, sure! It would be my honor to marry the two of you," he answered.

"Now I have something else to ask you," said Carl.

"Go ahead, Brother Carl," he replied.

"Are you available next Saturday?" asked Carl, and we all started laughing.

"Yes, I'm available," he assured, shaking his head and laughing.

"I knew the church was available, but we wanted to make sure that it was OK for us to be married here," Carl stated, wanting Brother Darrel's approval.

"Of course! The church is waiting and ready for a wedding. The remodeling and cleaning up are all finished. It was finished way ahead of schedule, which surprised all of us. I would say the power of prayer is at work here! Next Saturday is ready for you two to become one!" he grinned.

"Oh, what time will the ceremony be?" he asked.

Carl and I looked at each other and I said, "How does two o'clock sound, Carl? That way we would have plenty of daylight for pictures and the reception outside if it is nice weather."

"Sounds good to me!" Carl agreed.

Brother Darrel said, "Two o'clock it is then!"

Judy said, "That is a perfect time for an October wedding."

We looked at each other and Carl laughed and I said, "God prepared our hearts, our minds, our spirits—everything from the gazebo to the sanctuary!" All of us agreed and chuckled about that. It was true. We did serve an amazing God! Carl and I proceeded to tell them about Carl building the gazebo for "the proposal" and what happened this morning. Carl told them the gazebo was finished ahead of schedule too.

The crew he hired showed up with three extra men who were laid off of a previous job. Carl said that worked out wonderfully and the roof was finished Saturday afternoon. I told them he even had the walkway all the way to the pier rocked, and concrete planters put in and filled with flowers to boot!

"That was close since the proposal was scheduled for Sunday morning!" Carl laughed. Brother Darrel and Judy were in amazement over the church being finished, now they were really amazed after hearing about the gazebo, walkway, and planters full of flowers!

They just kept shaking their heads and saying, "Whew! God is amazing!"

During the service, Brother Darrel was going to announce our wedding on Saturday with an open invitation to the church. He asked us if he could give a little sermon about us and our testimony over the last month or so. He wanted to tell them how God had worked in our lives so quickly and miraculously. We both were in total agreement with that idea and were honored that he saw the hand of God working in our lives. I knew our testimony would touch someone that would be there today. Praise God!

It was time for Sunday school class and Carl made the announcement about our marriage on Saturday with an open invitation. Of course, Carolyn wanted to know what our reception plans were and the ladies would be glad to help with anything we needed. Carl thanked them and told them it would be catered and our family was serving.

Carolyn asked about the decorations for the sanctuary. Carl said he hadn't thought about that. Carolyn said the ladies of the church would take care of decorating the church as soon as they found out what we wanted. Boy, I couldn't believe these church members! They would do anything for you. Not to mention the extra time they would take to make it just perfect!

After Sunday school we went out front and Brother Darrel had Carl and I come up after the announcements. We stood together with our arms around each other and he told the church that Carl proposed to me this morning and I accepted. He then informed them we were getting married here next Saturday at two o'clock and all were welcome. They started applauding to show their sentiments. Carl and I almost started crying! After that, Carl and I took our seats as everybody was smiling at us.

Brother Darrel told everyone that he was moved to preach about Carl and I. I couldn't wait to hear what he had to say. He told the congregation how Carl had asked people in the church to pray for me since I wasn't saved. He told Brother Darrel he had always been in love with me and he wanted God to lead our separate lives as well as our lives together.

"Carl said that since he started coming to Lakeside and had been reading his Bible more, God showed the verses to him about being unequally yoked (2 Cor. 6:14). Carl felt like God was showing him how important it was not to be yoked with an unbeliever. If God said it, that settles it. Carl started praying and seeking God in this matter," Brother Darrel told them.

"Diane's cousins came to visit her and many of you met them the Sunday they were here. They had not seen each other for twelve years. They witnessed to her and prayed with her while they were here. They have continued to earnestly pray for her ever since. She attended church service here because they always attended church on Sunday, so she came with Carl and them. Then she received an excellent sermon here," Brother Darrel chuckled and the congregation chuckled too.

"When Diane took them back to the airport, she asked Jan as she was boarding what the rapture was. She had heard Christians talking about it and didn't know what it was. Before Jan could answer, this old white-haired lady pointed her bony finger in Diane's face and told her she better find out what it was and she better be ready! She better be ready! Diane said she will never forget her steel blue eyes or the words she spoke," he told them.

"When Diane called Jan, Jan said the old white-haired lady who gave Diane that message and boarded with everyone else was nowhere on that plane to be found. No one ever saw her again. There was even a preacher on board who had overheard her, as many did that day, and he was looking for her. Her message moved him so much. . . . there was just something about her, and he wanted to talk with her. She just vanished. They checked everywhere, even back at the boarding gate to see if she turned and went back out. No sign of an old white-haired lady with steel blue eyes. Jan believed she was an angel God sent to deliver a message. Praise God!" he shouted.

"Carl finally got her here for several services and she got another dose of the plan of salvation," he chuckled.

"Then Kimberly, the cleaning lady who works in Diane's building, lost her husband, but the Lord gave her peace that surpassed all understanding (Phil. 4:7). That aroused Diane's attention greatly. When Diane asked her about it, she told her only Jesus gives you that kind of peace. She invited her to a revival going on at her church. She was too busy that night to go. Kimberly informed her you never know when your life is up and you better be sure you are ready," he informed them, pointing his finger quickly over the congregation.

"Minutes later she had a brush with death involving a drugged teenager in a frantic high-speed chase in a stolen car. He killed another pedestrian and died in a fiery crash. She told Carl the last words she said before the racing car was about to hit her were, 'Jesus, help me!' Witnesses said it was like something supernatural hurled her out of the path of that oncoming vehicle. That was an eye-opener to her, to say the least," he said and shook his head.

"She went with Kimberly to the revival the next night. She was under conviction then, but didn't go up, and the next night Carl went back to the revival with her. She walked down the aisle and accepted Jesus and Carl rededicated his life that night. Thank God He let her live until the next night. She said all that day she was scared to death something would happen to her. She knew by then that she could pray the sinner's prayer and be saved, but she wanted to make it public. She knew all too well how quickly life could be snuffed out. The following Sunday morning they stood up here and professed to that," he said, walking back and forth.

"Diane invited her coworkers to this church where she was saved, since they were having revival there. May I add that it was quite a revival and is still going on. People are being saved, healed, and set free from a multitude of problems. Now that is revival, folks! Last Sunday when she was baptized, one of those coworkers walked the aisle and accepted Christ," he announced to them, with "Amens" being spoken.

"Judy, April, Carolyn, Sharon, and Carl went down to that church to see Diane baptized and witnessed that man's profession of faith. By the way, this church is a Baptist church in Harlem. Our members who went said it was a blessing to see twenty-three people baptized in one service. They said it was a loving church, full of the Holy Spirit, and matter of fact, our people that went, well, they can't wait to go back! I better go down there myself and see what is going on," he confessed, throwing his hands up and everyone started laughing.

"Everything I have just told you, happened in less than six weeks. Now they are getting married next Saturday. That is the power of prayer, my brothers and sisters! Never deny the power of prayer! All things are possible through God! All things! There are many lessons to be learned from this story . . . many! Just think about it," he paused and wanted us to search our hearts.

"Just think if that car had killed her, she would be in hell, a burning hell for now and forever. I hope that teenager and young pedestrian were saved. If they weren't, they are in hell today and forever. Prayers were answered when Diane accepted Jesus and now look at all the blessings she and Carl have received," he preached.

"God is still in control!" he shouted raising his hands in the air, a Bible clutched in his right hand. There were "Amens" spoken throughout the audience. With that he opened the invitation telling people, "Be ready! Be ready! Now is the time, before it is too late!" and the music played. A couple walked the aisle. Many of the church members wiped tears away as Brother Darrel talked with them.

After the music stopped, Brother Darrel had them both stand up there with him. They were both wiping the tears away. Brother Darrel said James had asked Jesus to come into his heart and be his Lord and Saviour. Dena had come with him to rededicate her life. How wonderful, I thought! We all went up after the service and greeted them and said a few words to them. I found out later that they had been dating for years and church members had been praying for them.

Brother Darrel and Judy wanted to take Carl and I out to lunch. As it ended up, several carloads of us went to Grinder's Mill: Carolyn and Ralph, April, Adon, Ian, all the Goodfellows, Sharon, James, and Dena to mention a few! We ate out on the patio again overlooking the mill dam. We all were rejoicing talking about various things that the Lord had done in our lives.

Carl and I got back to his place about 2:30 P.M. I leaned over and kissed him before we got out of the Jeep. "OK. I can't wait to see the fishing room!" I yelled as I jumped out of the Jeep.

"Oh, how could I have forgotten about that!" Carl exclaimed, not believing he hadn't shown me that room. Pepper was lying on the front porch waiting on us to get back. He looked up and wagged his tail and laid back down. I guess a Sunday afternoon nap was more important.

We went upstairs and he showed me the new fishing room and I couldn't believe it! He had tables installed completely around the walls and had his different gear laid out neatly on top of all of them. There was a drop light in the center of the room over a huge work table with drawers in it. He had racks built on one wall just to hold fishing rods, his fishing hats and his bags and stuff. He had also put down a sandy pebble stone vinyl for the floor. It looked great! He was so proud of it.

He said he had never dreamed he would have a workroom that nice. He could work there all year around. No cold garages in the winter if he had a desire to get fishing equipment ready for spring! All his waders, nets, and baskets were already hung neatly in the garage. He had some old antique bamboo fishing poles he had from forty years ago. He said he wouldn't use them, but wasn't sure where they should go.

"I know! I will polish them and hang them up in fin and feather as antiques," I announced.

"Whatever you think," Carl replied. "Are you ready to see fin and feather?" asked Carl.

"I can hardly wait!" I exclaimed, as we walked across the hall. He flung open the door and I sighed "Oh-h-h, I never thought I would love a room of fish and ducks, but this is beautiful!"

"You definitely had a fabulous decorator!" I kidded, looking at him inquisitively.

"Well, yeah, pretty good," he said nonchalantly, not wanting me to get the big head.

"I have to admit, I don't know how you could find a better fin and feather than this!" I exclaimed, so proud of this room. Ray and Michael would love this room when they came to stay.

"Oh, by the way, they can come in any time. How about next weekend so they can be here for the wedding and then they can watch the house while we are on our honeymoon?" he suggested.

"Perfect!" I exclaimed, shocked at how good that would work out for all of us.

"I told Ray he could use my fishing gear and not to bring any. Brother Darrel would go with Ray and the Goodfellows have been wanting to go fishing. That would be good since they know Amber Lake and all the good fishing holes. Ray knows how to operate my boat, so they are ready.

"I need to call my brothers and sister and see if they can drive or fly in for the wedding. Hopefully, they all can," he said. Carl's mother, Mama Nan as everyone called her, was ninety-two and unable to make such a long trip. Carl and I had called her and told her about the wedding and she was thrilled for us, and sounded as good as she always did. Carl's dad, Daddy Ross we called him, passed away several years ago at the age of ninety-three. He was always active and drove until just months before he left and went on home. That is what Carl would always say, that he "left here and went on home." Now I could see clearly that was exactly what he did!

"Well, when everybody gets here there is enough room for everyone. The den sectional is big enough for Ray and Jan's kids to sleep on and then some. They would love being in that room anyway," I assured Carl.

"We can figure it out when they get here," Carl closed the subject.

"Carl, I just thought of something!" I exclaimed.

"What?" he asked.

"I don't even have a dress yet! I know exactly what I want if I could find it!" I implied.

"What do you want?" he asked.

"I want an ivory Victorian dress to the floor, a fitted waist and lace all at the top with a high neck. Oh-h-h, I see it now. If only I could find it!" I dreamed. "My fiancé could pick out an antique brooch I could wear in the center of the high neck. Perfect, huh?" I kidded Carl.

He came over and put his arms around me and kissed me and said, "I guess so."

"Thank heavens, things are caught up at work. I need to find that dress and a Victorian hat to match," I envisioned. "Oh, good grief!" I wailed.

"What now?" asked Carl.

"We have to get our blood tests and marriage license right away!" I insisted.

"I know. We will get on that right away," Carl agreed.

"You sure we have time?" I asked, wanting to be reassured that everything would all fall together. "Oh, we need a cake too!" I remembered.

"Can Peggy do that at the bakery?" Carl asked.

"Yes, and she is the one I want to handle the cake, mints, and the punch, if she is available this Saturday. Oh, I hope she is!" I said.

"Go see her first thing in the morning and find out," Carl insisted.

"OK. We have the church and minister. We have Jan and Ray coming in. She could be at the guest book, if she would. Oh, we have to get a guest book and pen too! The girls could serve at the reception. We'll place Michael with the other boys helping at the reception. You could have Alvin be the best man and Don and John sing a few specials. My sister could be the maid of honor. Jean Marie would be a perfect wedding coordinator. I better get a notebook and pen and start writing this all down!" I exclaimed.

Carl and I sat at the kitchen bar and started writing everything down. He called Carolyn and they talked for a while. She was taking care of the church set-up from the front steps throughout the church. If it rained, she would be prepared to fix the fellowship hall. Carl told her we would be back over for the evening service and look it over again and finalize what we could.

I called Carol and gave her the news. It was a little emotional for both of us. I told her since her desire was to organize weddings and cater, now would be a good time to learn. Of course, she had to do it perfect the first time out. We both laughed. I told her Carl was going to try to get Thornton's to cater it. I suggested to her that would be a perfect place for her and Glenn to stay. I said, "You need to see if it will be for sale in the near future anyway. You are going to love it out there, Carol. Absolutely love it! It would be perfect for you and Glenn. Plus you would only be twenty minutes away from us!"

We talked about what a difference that would be from the city. "What are you going to do about work after you two lovebirds are married?" she asked.

"Golly, Carol, I haven't even thought about work! I can't imagine that!" I said amazed.

"I guess you know now where your heart is," she giggled. "Glenn and I just have to buy Thornton's, that is all there is to it," she sighed.

"Yeah, then we would have matching gazebos," I mentioned.

"Matching gazebos?" she questioned. I told her what happened this morning and she thought that was really special, not to mention romantic. "Oh, I can't wait to see it!" she replied.

"I better go right now. We have to go over to the church in thirty minutes," I said.

"I know. . . . plus you have to go to the bathroom then get something to drink," she said and we both giggled.

"When you are ordering our wedding announcements to pass out to everyone at the wedding, you should order your new business cards too," I kidded.

"What do you want on your wedding announcements?" she asked.

"Carl and I need to have a picture taken of us in the gazebo and then I want to write about how long we have known and loved each other, and how the Lord made a difference in both our lives. How walking in faith changed our lives and our priorities became what God wanted them to be. We will say that the gazebo our picture was taken in was built for the proposal and then put the date and Lakeside Church. We will thank them for sharing our special day with us and put Carl and Diane Frost at the bottom. How does that sound?"

"Great! Give me some more ideas for announcements. Couples will love that one," Carol laughed.

"I'll see you tomorrow. I have got to leave," I said.

"Are you coming home tonight?" Carol asked.

"Yeah, I'll be home about ten or so," I answered.

"Be careful!" she insisted. I told her I would and that I couldn't wait to tell everyone tomorrow. I wanted to see the look on their faces. We chuckled and then said bye.

I grabbed my notepad and Carl and I jumped in the Jeep and took off. We left Pepper lying on the porch, still wagging his tail. He probably wondered what on earth was going on.

Carolyn, Judy, Carl, and I talked about decorating the church. I knew I wanted huge ferns on podiums and brass candelabras all around. Large vanilla candles in hurricane glass would sit in each window, adorned with silk fall arrangements with nuts and cranberries scattered throughout. My bouquet would be all fall decorations, such as orange and red maple leaves and chrysanthemums, fall berries, and such. All other flower decorations would be of the same combination. All the corsages, maid of honor's bouquet, and boutonnieres would match. Carl and I loved fall and we loved nature. This was perfect!

The front doors of the church would have huge grapevine wreaths decorated with all the same fall arrangements. The black wrought-iron railings would be intertwined with silk maple leaf runners. It would look like Thanksgiving. We were very thankful and that was very appropriate for this wedding!

They knew exactly where to get everything and that was a miracle. We all said bye and Carl said he would be back and forth assisting. They said they could not wait to see what it looked like. Carl told them to leave all the fall decorations up until after Thanksgiving for the church to enjoy. David, Glenn, Adon, and Ian came up to us before we left church and volunteered to help at the wedding. We told them they would make the perfect ushers and they were thrilled about being chosen for that.

We got back to Carl's and while I packed up, Carl fixed me a cheese tray. That would have to be a must at the reception. He called Thornton's, and lo and behold, they could cater the reception! They would plan on having it outdoors at Carl's if weather permitted, otherwise in the church fellowship hall. I told Carl I wanted the wedding cake to be on a table in the gazebo. Carl said he would probably buy a black wrought-iron glass table to sit out there with matching chairs anyway. I told him that would be perfect with candles and fall decorations. Oh, I was so excited! We got a lot done just today.

We walked to my car and we kissed goodbye. It was a long goodbye! "Just think, next week this time we will be married! I still can't believe it!" I whispered to him. "Carl, I never did ask you!" I exclaimed.

"What?" he asked.

"What do you want me to do about my job?" I asked.

"I want you out here. You don't have to work anymore. Start phasing out of the firm so you won't leave them in a sudden bind. They have been very good to you. I don't think it will come as a total shock to them that you will be leaving," he replied.

"You won't have any trouble selling your apartment. If you want, you could sell it furnished and I think that would be very appealing. There are a lot of people going to the city to work that would like the convenience of having a ready-to-move-into apartment. All your furnishings are basic, but very tasteful, so it would appeal to a man or a woman. The view would sell anyone, plus the location is great," he added.

"We can fix up the storage room across from peaches and cream into your writing room if you want to. You have a nice big window in there overlooking the woods. I'll even buy you a coffee pot to put in there," he chuckled and kissed me again.

I couldn't believe my ears. I looked at him and asked, "You haven't been thinking all this out have you? You probably know what brand of coffee pot you are buying, don't you?" We both started laughing. I was so happy, happier than I had ever been, and Carl was too!

I backed down the driveway and Pepper and Carl stood on the porch. We waved bye until I was out of sight. Oh, I can't believe this! I thought about the wedding all the way home. "I don't even think I can sleep tonight! Oh, I can't wait to tell Jan and the girls! Tomorrow I tell my friends at work!

"I can't wait to tell Kimberly and Sylvia. Sharon wasn't at church today. She had a seminar in another church. I believe she is coming in the city to stay with Kimberly this week. Kimberly wanted her to do a seminar during the day and go to the revival at night. I'll have to call at the church in the morning. They will all be over there about nine or ten.

"My gosh, I wonder where we are going on our honeymoon. I didn't even think to ask! It doesn't make me any difference, as long as we are together. Oh, my gosh, it's time for me to buy lingerie for sure now. Oh, I need to buy my ensemble for my wedding night. I want something in cranberry satin and lace. I can go on and on! I haven't had time to buy clothes for ages. Now is the perfect time. The perfect time! Thank heavens Franklin told us we could start thinking about taking time off. I sure need it now, if I ever needed it!

"I will go in tomorrow and announce my wedding. I'll have to have a meeting with Franklin and tell him my plans about leaving first thing.

I know I will have to just start phasing out slowly. It might take me at least two months. Thank heavens Sam started filling in when he did! God was putting everything in motion!

"I'll have to put my apartment on the market. I need to sell all my furniture with it if I can, just like Carl suggested. If I had just arrived in the city, I would love an apartment already furnished! The furniture that is in it would suit most people. What all I went through getting it selected and set up. What a wonderful convenience for someone else. I hope it won't be hard to sell.

"I know, I'll just pray about it! I bet someone that is praying for a nice place to live in the city will get it, too. Matter of fact, I know that it all will work out. All they will have to do is move in and start living. I just need my personal things. Boy, I sure will miss Gilbert and Peggy's!

"Oh, I need to see Peggy in the morning. I want her to do my wedding cake, the candies, punch and all. I need to tell her about all the decorations we are going to use and build the theme around that. The candies need to be little maple leaves and the punch made with a peach sherbet. I want the top of the cake to be made like a gazebo with the couple inside. Miniature silk fall leaves, button mums, and berry sprays around the tiers. At least that is a start! She told me she has always wanted to see Amber Lake ever since I told her about it. They will just have to load the cake and goodies in their van and take off for Amber Lake Saturday.

"I have to get my wedding dress and accessories. Carl and I have to get our blood tests and marriage license. I better just go into work and talk to Franklin and tell everyone and then leave. Oh, Carl and I have to get a picture in the gazebo immediately so the announcements can be done. I hadn't even thought about that! The rings! How could I have forgotten about that! All I wanted was a huge solid gold band. That shouldn't be too hard. I need to see what Carl wants."

I wheeled into my garage and unloaded and got in my apartment, cheese tray and all. I put on the coffee pot and grabbed a notebook and wrote Wedding Plans on the front and started jotting down everything I needed to do. Thank heavens the church was working on all the decorations and preparing the sanctuary.

I was thrilled Thornton's was available. Carl was going over there to look at the menu and pick out the food. I had to give Carol the picture and verse to go in the announcement and she would follow-up with Thornton's. She and Glenn probably would want to go out there and stay Thursday night.

I needed to go out there and stay at Thornton's Thursday too. I needed to pick out the dinnerware, tablecloths, and all. Praise God I wanted a fall theme. Everything is geared to decorate for that anyway and it is all available. I looked up and said, "Thank you God for making everything so perfect. I ask you to be with us this week and make everything perfect for Saturday. Let our wedding be a testimony to you. In Jesus' name I pray. Amen."

Monday morning. Kind of an overcast morning. I sure hoped Saturday will be nice. Whatever kind of weather it was, we would manage. I had too much to do to worry about it. Besides, God tells us not to worry about anything. Saturday I would be married to Carl! A new life and a new name! How I loved Amber Lake and Lakeside Church . . . not to mention having a nice home and new gazebo!

Oh, the proposal. What a moment to remember. Carl said after the wedding was over he was going to put a lounge chair out in the gazebo. He said until I quit work, he would lay out there and think about me until I got back to Amber Lake. He said he would take a glass of my iced tea and Pepper out there to keep him company. He mentioned the bluebirds were starting to nest out there and he enjoyed seeing them darting all around.

I was greeted at work by Carol the minute I hit my office door. She gave me a big hug and told me how happy she was for me. "We better hurry up and get Thornton's in the selling mood. I don't even want to think about you leaving here!" she said hurriedly and immediately looked down at her notes she had to discuss at our ten o'clock meeting.

"Don't even go there, Carol," I pleaded. "We'll get something worked out. You are as ready to leave as I am. It is time both of us did what our hearts are calling us to do," I stated. "You know, now that I look back at us being here—where did twenty years go?" I asked softly, amazed at how fast those years had gone.

"I don't know! I just can't believe it! It is like a whirlwind of memories!" she confessed, shaking her head.

"I wonder if we will say that after we have all been together for ten thousand years and have thousands more to go!" I sighed, and we agreed how wonderful that would be. "Carol, at least we can both say we have been blessed to have had and still have a wonderful job, a great boss, and great friends to work with. Most people can't say all that. Plus, the pay was pretty good too!" I added. She agreed how fortunate we were in many ways.

"When are you going to tell Franklin?" Carol asked quietly.

"I'm going over to his office as soon as I have a cup of coffee," I answered. We both laughed.

"That figures!" Carol laughed.

"By the way, I am mixing almost half decaf in my regular coffee now. The Lord has been dealing with me about it. I can't pull off caffeine all at once because of the headaches. I missed my coffee late one morning last week and I got an awful sick headache. That is when I realized it was withdrawal symptoms. Caffeine is a drug, and boy did I realize it when I got that horrible headache!" I confessed.

"It amazes me how the Lord deals with you on everything. I knew I needed to cut back and sure enough that headache confirmed that what I felt in my spirit was right. I want to even eat and drink what He wants me to. I'm sure Sharon is teaching some people in Harlem that right now!" I implied. Carol thought that was wonderful that Sharon was down here doing a seminar and Kimberly, Sylvia, and she had become such good friends.

"I need to talk to Franklin before I go into the meeting. I might as well face the music. This is not a meeting I am looking forward to at all. It will be emotional for me. Franklin has been really good to me through the years," I replied, feeling my heart quicken at the thought of it.

"I can understand that. You have been good to Franklin too, you know. You have been there to back him up through some tough times and he always knew he could count on you. That means a lot!" Carol confessed.

"Both of us have done that through the years, Carol. It was tougher on you because you had a family at home," I replied. We both giggled and agreed we had been dedicated to our work through the years, but also had the best of times any coworkers could have.

"I can't wait to be married to Carl and live the rest of my days out at Amber Lake, but it is very difficult to leave dear friends!" I replied.

"I know," whispered Carol.

"We won't start on that again!" I shook my finger at her, laughing. She laughed back. "I better go see Franklin right now, before he goes in another direction. Pray for me. I don't want to get emotional," I said as I headed for the door.

She turned and said "I will. See you upstairs at ten o'clock."

"Thanks for your prayers!" I told her.

"Oh, Carol, don't forget to fix a pot of coffee before the meeting. I do hope it tastes better than the last one you made," I said so serious, shaking my head at her.

"There will be some things I won't miss!" she sighed and we both stuck our tongues out at each other and she turned and left.

"At least we both have kept our professional air about us through the years!" I yelled down the hall at her, knowing she heard me.

"Yes, we certainly have managed to do that!" I heard her reply as she hurried down the hall. I laughed to myself, as I walked to Franklin's office.

"Well, Miss Danay, how are you today?" announced Franklin as I walked into his office.

I grinned at his enthusiasm and said, "Just great, Franklin."

"Did you have a wonderful weekend?" he asked.

"Yes, sir, I believe I had the best one I have ever had!" I answered. That got his attention.

He pushed his chair away from his desk and leaned back and looked at me seriously. He changed his expression, smiled and said, "Well! I think you better tell me about the weekend. I want to hear about this one for sure!"

I felt my heart pick up and start pounding. We were looking straight into each other's eyes and I was telling myself to get a grip on this. Don't let your emotions show! "Well, Carl proposed to me and I accepted," I blurted out. Complete silence for ten seconds that seemed like an eternity.

"Well, heaven sakes! Congratulations, my dear!" Franklin exclaimed. He got up from his chair and came over and gave me a bear hug. He took a hold of my shoulders and quietly asked, "When is the wedding day going to be?"

I whispered back, "This Saturday," I answered.

He jolted his head and his eyes blinked wide open and he shrieked, "This Saturday!" I started laughing at his expression. "Well, we have been dating for twenty years and now we are getting married six days after the proposal," I laughed. "God works in mysterious ways!" I replied to Franklin, who still was looking at me with amazement.

"He most certainly does," he whispered, and shook his head. He turned and sat down in his chair and asked me to take a seat. I sat down and looked across at Franklin. He sat there and looked at me a minute and I could tell he was a man with a lot of thoughts running through his mind.

"Well, first of all, I am truly happy for you and Carl. I have always thought a lot of Carl. He is a good man, a true professional, and has always been the one for you," he smiled. "I know you will have a good life with him, as you already have and always will. I think the world of both of you. You know that," he quietly said.

"Thank you, Franklin," I stated.

He paused and pulled up to his desk and then looked at me and solemnly asked me, "What are your plans as far as here?"

"Franklin, I want to move on out as quickly as I can without leaving you in a bind. I believe Sam can take over within the next few months. I know he still has a lot to learn, but he is a dedicated and loyal employee. He is a fair and honest man and that goes a long way," I commented.

"I agree with you about Sam," he said. "You want to be out within a few months?" Franklin asked.

"I want to aim for that, but I don't mind another month or so if need be. I am ready to get the finalization process moving into gear here. I am going to go ahead and put my apartment on the market," I answered.

"Oh, boy, this is moving fast! I will work with you as best I can to help you retire to Amber Lake. We have accomplished more in the last month than I thought we would ever accomplish in three months! As soon as I feel comfortable with our new strategy for these large accounts, feel free to head for the country."

"You made a smart move when you had Sam come in with us a while back. He has been able to learn more in a few weeks than he has the nineteen months he has been here. Those nineteen months he was just learning about the firm and the ropes. In other words, he just got his feet good and wet. It is astounding how he has progressed. Everything that has happened in the past several weeks has absolutely amazed me!" he proclaimed.

"Franklin, that is the power of prayer. The Lord paved the way for all this to fall quickly into place," I confirmed. Franklin looked at me and I knew he was rethinking everything that had happened in the past weeks. "Think about it, Franklin. Have you ever seen a whole new way of approaching business come into being so quickly and completely?" I asked.

"No, I haven't. I'm still in awe of it. Especially since everything we have come up with is one hundred percent effective. That is what is amazing!" he admitted, knowing it was nothing short of a miracle. "Were you praying for this to happen the way it did?" Franklin inquired.

"Well, yes and no. I had people praying for me to come to know Jesus and accept him as my Saviour. Carl and his church members were praying for me. After I was saved, people were praying for Carl and me. God has his own perfect way for everything to be fulfilled. I just asked him to guide my life. I didn't specifically ask for everything to happen at work like it did. Now I see that was part of his plan in guiding my life," I answered.

"Franklin, you have always heard 'The Lord works in mysterious ways'. Now you know that He does. He let all this happen here so I could be free to get married like we were supposed to. I could go on and on in all that I have seen Him do. It is absolutely beyond belief. We serve an awesome God!" I responded.

"I'll go along with that!" Franklin confirmed. I was so surprised to hear Franklin say that.

"Franklin, you said last week that we could take time off if we would like to. I would like to take two to three weeks off starting as soon as possible, like after lunch!" I said, hoping nothing major was planned for the next few weeks.

Franklin looked at me, then he started laughing. "I guess so! You have many things to do before Saturday. Oh, then there is a honeymoon and all! Well, heavens yes! You better get going right after lunch!" he laughed. "I would just like your input on the ten o'clock meeting, please. That will gear us in the direction we have to go this week and next. I will have to tell you it will last several hours," he said.

"That is OK. Thank you so much, Franklin. I better go and get my thoughts together for that meeting," I replied.

"By the way, who knows you and Carl are tying the knot?" he asked.

"Only Carol," I replied. He nodded his head.

"I will let you make your announcement at ten o'clock if that is all right," Franklin inquired.

"That will be fine," I replied.

I turned to leave and Franklin said, "Diane," and I turned around and he said, "Tell Carl he is a lucky man," and lightly smiled and then returned to his paperwork.

"Thank you. I will tell him," I said softly, as I closed his door behind me. I walked on to my office, thanking God my meeting with

Franklin went so well. I didn't want to become emotional, but if I had, the Lord would have taken care of that anyway.

I entered the boardroom and Carol was already seated. She looked up at me and smiled, knowing the rest of them would be told shortly about my wedding plans. I poured my coffee and took my seat beside Carol. Sam came in and looked at Carol and me and smiled and went over to pour himself a cup of coffee.

Carol leaned over and whispered, "Yep, he is ready to take your place, he is following right in your caffeine steps. Look how comfortable and assured he is now that he has poured a cup of coffee."

"He won't be assured and comfortable long if it tastes like that last batch you made," I whispered. She hit me on the arm. Sam took his seat beside me and greeted me.

He took a sip of coffee and whispered to Carol and I, "Whew! I don't remember the coffee being this strong before," shook his head, and went on about his notes. I leaned over to Carol and whispered, "Stronger isn't necessarily better. Don't try to buy Thornton's unless Glenn can make coffee." We both looked at each other with a put-on smile and returned to our notes, laughing inside.

"Good morning everybody!" Franklin announced as he walked through the big double doors. Faune came in behind him and closed the doors. Both of them sat down. Kent was sitting left of Franklin and had looked up from his notes long enough to say, "Good morning," and went right back to writing. Franklin talked about the meeting we were about to have.

"I believe Diane has a very important announcement to make to all of us," Franklin announced.

"Well, yes I certainly do. I wanted to tell all of you that Carl asked me to marry him and I accepted," I announced.

"Oh congratulations!" came from voices around the room.

"Oh, how wonderful!" Faune exclaimed. "When are you getting married?" she asked.

"Next Saturday," I said. Then there were shrieks of "Next Saturday!" Carol, Franklin, and I laughed out loud. "Yes, this coming Saturday at Amber Lake. I hope that all of you can be there," I announced. "Carol is in charge of directions and overnight reservations if you need them. It's only about a two-hour drive. We are getting married at two in the afternoon at Lakeside Church," I told them. I stopped to laugh again as did Carol and Franklin, after looking at the faces around the room. They were in shock I was getting married. Maybe it was the twenty years of courtship, then finally the big question, the right answer, and six days later the wedding.

I told them I would be off from work for maybe three weeks. I also told them that Carl wanted me to retire to Amber Lake. I would phase out of work as soon as I could, but it would take several months. Faune looked happy and sad at the same time. Sam sat very quietly. He knew this was his chance to be promoted, but he knew it was a big step in many ways. Carol looked at her notes and I didn't want to look at her face. Franklin just looked at me like he was happy for me and no matter what his feelings were, he would keep his chin up.

Kent looked at me like he couldn't believe I was leaving. He looked like he was reliving twenty years of memories by the look in his eyes. Kent, Carol, and I had been the three with Franklin through thick and thin for all these years. Why did we all think things would never change? Well, we just never gave it a thought. We were lucky we worked together that long and that well. Things finally do change in one way or another.

Franklin broke the silence with, "Diane, we all love you and you will be greatly missed. Not only as a partner, but as a dear friend. We are very happy for you and have seen some wonderful things happen for you lately." There were heads shaking in agreement to what he said.

"We will all plan on being at your wedding Saturday. That will be quite a day for all of us. We have just about known Carl as long as we have known you," Franklin said. I was barely hanging on inside. The waterworks were right on the verge with the pounding heart. Franklin looked at me and pointed his finger at me and said, "Just remember, when you get back from your honeymoon we will have stacks and stacks of work for you to do. Tell Carl you can only rest on your honeymoon."

Everyone broke into laughter, including me. I replied with, "I'm certainly not going to tell him that!" I thanked God for that bit of humor right when I needed it. Everyone got up at that time and came over and gave me a hug and congratulated me.

We dove into our meeting and broke for lunch two hours later. Nick came in with lunch. Franklin told Nick I had something to tell him. Nick ran over and looked at me and I told him Carl and I were getting married next Saturday. He jumped back and squealed. Everyone started laughing at him and his expressions. Then he hugged me and told me whoever replaced me would have to order the same thing I had been ordering for years. He said he was getting too old to remember new orders. I invited him, Angelina, and his family to the wedding.

We ate lunch in the boardroom and all of us talked about the wedding and where Amber Lake was, so on and so forth. We had to get back into the meeting and it finished about two o'clock. I was running a little later than I thought, but this meeting was far too important.

There was a knock on the door and it was Nick. He brought in a box and sat it in the middle of the table. Nick told me to open it up. It was a white cake that had Diane and Carl written on it with hearts in red icing. Everyone got a kick out of that. I got up and gave Nick a hug. He said Angelina made it as soon as he got back and told her we were getting married. We asked Nick to join us and we all ate a piece of cake and talked about the years and memories we had shared again.

After that I told them I had better leave and get things planned for the wedding. Thank heavens I had Carol there and she was going to take care of directions and all. Carol came out in the hall with me and I told her I would be in touch with her and get the announcement and picture to her to be printed. She said she already called Thornton's and she and Glenn were staying there Thursday and Friday night for sure.

I left the office and stopped to look at wedding gowns. I wanted a Victorian gown in ivory. They had several with hats to match. The fifth one I tried on was the one I fell in love with! I loved the hat, but we had to change the ribbon. Then I had them wrap a strand of pearls around the ivory ribbon on the hat. I bought a pair of round pearl earrings and a bracelet to match. They had pearl clip-ons for shoes and I bought them. All I needed now was a pair of ivory shoes.

I wonder if Carl will be able to find me a brooch. They had some, but they were not quite what I wanted. He would probably have better luck at the antique shops where he was. They packaged up everything and I was so thrilled I found my dress. I loved it and the sales lady just went on and on about how beautiful that dress was with the hat.

I was in the mood to shop now. I dropped off my dress, hat, and accessories at my apartment and got something to drink and took off for Macy's. They had given me a swatch from the hat ribbon to compare the color. I went to the shoe department and found an ivory medium heel in a plain pump, which is exactly what I wanted.

I went to Ladies Lingerie and bought ivory lace pantyhose and undergarments. Now my wedding ensemble was complete, except for the brooch and wedding ring. I looked at their selection in night wear and found a beautiful cranberry satin and lace robe and gown. I found slip-on low heels to match the outfit. Across the aisle was a rack of velvet and satin lounging pajamas. I picked out a black outfit and slippers to match. In the back was a display of satin sleep shirts. They looked so comfortable and were really pretty. I picked out one in gold and found a gold satin jacquard robe with black velvet cuffs to match. I could wear the black slippers with that too. I figured that was enough for the honeymoon.

I was already picturing Carl and I relaxing in the den in front of the fireplace this fall and winter. Oh, what fun it will be at Christmas this year! Carl never bought any decorations and I just put up a three-foot tree in my apartment. We were always out and about during the holidays. We just enjoyed everyone else's decorations. After all, I could look out my windows and see decorations on buildings, on the streets, and all over. I have to admit, Manhattan at Christmas was quite fantastic! I want one of those nine-foot trees in the den, decorated to the hilt. "Boy, don't get into Christmas now!" I told myself. I will do good to get ready for the wedding. My life is so exciting now . . . thinking about all the things we could enjoy in our home and just being together.

I went into the women's department and bought a pair of soft brushed denim jeans and a jacket to match. These were very comfortable and looked real nice. I figured if Carl and I went up the coastline this time of year I would get a lot of use out of them. I bought a harvest gold turtleneck to go with it. I was getting pretty loaded with bags and it was already eight o'clock. I stopped back by the shoe department and bought a pair of brown leather lace-up boots.

I would have to find out from Carl where we were going and tell him I found my high neck Victorian gown. I decided to get him a pajama and robe ensemble and a pair of slippers. He never bought that kind of thing for himself. I decided to go on home. I would start putting everything in the spare bedroom. Thank heavens I had a good set of luggage and plenty of sweaters and jackets.

I finally wrestled all the boxes through the door of my apartment and into the bedroom. Gee, this reminded me of the shopping trip with Jan and the girls. I believe this was worse! At least I had one of them to tell me if I dropped something.

I changed clothes and put on a comfortable cotton nightshirt. It was a good thing Gilbert wasn't out front, he would have laughed his head off at me trying to get out of the taxi tonight! I think that is why he loved his job so much, because he got a kick out of all of us that lived here, coming and going.

I fixed a cup of coffee and looked at the things I had bought. I hadn't tried on everything, or I would have never gotten home. I tried on everything and it all fit great. I cut the tags off and folded them up and kept them laid out on the bed until I packed. I looked in my closet and found plenty of fall and winter items.

I went in to call Carl. "How you doing, sweetie?" I asked.

"Real good," he answered. "How about yourself?" he asked. I went on to tell him about my shopping spree and that I found my dress and everything. I told him all I needed was the brooch to fit on the high neck. I told him about the pearl accessories so that he would have an idea of what would look best to match everything.

"Carl, I need to know what to take on the honeymoon trip, so I can plan," I said.

"Just yourself," he laughed.

I laughed and said, "That is all, huh?"

"Don't forget all your coffee supplies. I want you in a good mood for sure," he laughed.

"Golly, I better make sure all that stuff is packed," I said.

"Let's just plan on going up the coastline and enjoying the fall colors. Just relaxing and enjoying the ocean and eating seafood and doing what we want," he suggested.

"Sounds great to me," I agreed.

"You need to drive out here tomorrow so we can get our blood tests and marriage license and take our picture in the gazebo. It is really supposed to be nice tomorrow, so let's get the picture done." We both decided to wear what we had worn that Sunday morning during the proposal. I wore a black turtleneck dress and Carl wore a gray and black tweed jacket with a white shirt, black tie, and slacks. The photographer Carl had hired for our wedding was coming out to take some pictures and develop them right away. That way I could take them back and pick one for the announcements.

"Judy and Carolyn picked out all the fall decorations. Judy called the store and they had gotten in their second fall shipment last Friday, so there was plenty to pick from. She has them in the church," Carl said.

"I didn't think they would have all that done this fast! I'm glad she does. I can't wait to see them," I replied. "I will go over there and pick out what I want for my bouquet and have the florist there in Amber Lake make it up for me," I said. "I will drive out early in the morning and bring my black dress. Maybe we can go to Thornton's and eat lunch and look at the selections they have in plates, tablecloths, and such," I hinted. "I can give my ideas to Carol. I want to look, just to have an idea of what is available," I suggested.

"That sounds good to me," Carl said. "The wrought-iron set for the gazebo is being delivered tomorrow and I want you to pick out the chair and chaise lounge pads. We will just put the table and chairs in there for the wedding. I'll keep the lounges on the patio until after the wedding. I was fortunate enough to be able to get the same type we already had on the patio, so it all matches. I thought we were lucky there," Carl admitted.

"Luck isn't the word," I replied.

"Amen to that," Carl laughed.

"Oh, I can't wait to see you!" I sighed. "I am so excited about all this coming together that no words can explain it!" I admitted.

"Well, just keep praising God and we will use it as a testimony at the reception. We'll tell how He brought everything to full circle, and I mean everything!" Carl testified.

"Oh, we must do that. Give God the glory, because He certainly did it all!" I exclaimed, with emphasis on "all."

"Oh, that is another thing, we need to pick out our crystal flutes for the toast before we cut the cake. Maybe we will find a pair in one of the antique stores. I would like an amber, berry, or emerald base flute. Any of those would work with our fall colors," I said.

"We shouldn't have any trouble finding those," Carl said.

"No, everything is and will come together perfectly. We just always need to pray and believe in His promises. We are a testimony to what God has done in our lives. This wedding will all fall into place quickly and perfectly, because we know He wants us married and to live like Christians. You had prayed about next Saturday before you asked me, and you felt that was the day, so all will be fine."

"I hired two ladies from church, Cassie and Joy, to clean the house. They have their own cleaning business and they are going to do an overall cleaning. They said they were going to do spring cleaning in the fall. I trust them and they do a super job," Carl said.

"Well, that gives me more time to enjoy my hubby when we return from our honeymoon. No house chores for a while!" I laughed.

"I hired a yard crew to do the outside. They also do landscaping and they are going to put down mulch and clean up the bank. They need to trim out some trees and pick up from that storm we had a couple of weeks ago. It is called Casey's Landscaping and everyone is very happy with their work. He is a member of the church too. He and his wife Susan have come into our class and talked about healing and what the Bible says about it. They have been attending Bible seminars and classes around the country. They are ministering to us on passages God has showed them about this in depth. Our eyes are being opened to promises in the Bible we never saw before," Carl reported.

"Their ministry is called It Is Done Ministries. They both said when Christ died on the cross He paid the price for our sins as well as our sickness, poverty, and so forth. He did not miss anything that binds us and destroys us. He paid for it all two thousand years ago. It is done. All we have to do is learn we already have it," Carl explained.

"Is there anything that little church doesn't have? I can't wait to become a member and go every time the doors are open," I affirmed.

"Well, that is your next step, that you become a member," Carl stated.

"Well, I already know I want to. I'll take care of that after we return from our honeymoon. We can be at church and do all they need us to do since the house and yard is done. Not to mention the fishing room!" I laughed.

"Of course I haven't cleared out of the city yet. That will take several months. I am figuring if I can work real hard Monday, Tuesday, and Wednesday, I can head back Wednesday afternoon and be here in time for the seven o'clock service. Then possibly I can head back out at daybreak Monday morning and go straight to work. We'll just have to see," I said.

"Don't worry about any of that now. The next few weeks are all ours and we have enough to think about right now. It will all work out," Carl acknowledged.

"Praise God!" I said softly.

"Well, we better say goodnight. I will get up early and be out there," I said.

"The photographer will be here at eleven o'clock. The morning sun will be up and that will be a good time. Afterwards we can head to Thornton's," he suggested.

"Sounds great! I will see you in the morning. I love you!" I said.

"Me too," he said and hung up.

I went back and looked at my wedding dress again and held it up and looked in the mirror. I had to put on my hat too. I just thanked God I found my wedding dress and everything. I decided to make a list of what I needed to pack. I would check it off as I packed it. I found that always worked. Once again, I went to bed not believing all this was taking place. Only God could have put all this together. Thank you Jesus!

Another beautiful morning! I fixed some coffee and drank one cup while I looked out over the city . . . my morning ritual for twenty years. Where the blue sky meets industrious mankind and the two come together. . . . You could certainly see it in Manhattan if you saw it anyplace.

I slipped on a jogging outfit and ran down to Peggy's. She was there and everything was on go for Saturday. She showed me a picture of what my wedding cake would look like. She and Eugene would be at the wedding and have the cake ready to set up in the fellowship hall or at Carl's. I grabbed a couple of bagels and one sack for Gilbert. I didn't even ask Peggy for Gilbert's anymore, she just automatically fixed it for him. I told her I would talk with her later.

I zoomed across the intersection and handed Gilbert the sack. He had been laughing watching me jogging down the street to the front of my building. "You trying out for the Olympics?" he laughed.

"Yes! I have to fit into my wedding dress and go on a honeymoon," I panted as I laughed.

"What? Miss Danay, you and Carl finally tying the knot?" he exclaimed.

"Yep! This Saturday. We decided that last Sunday," I told him and I couldn't wait to see his reaction. He took his hat off, shook his head, and put his hat back on.

"Good heavens above, Miss Danay, you never cease to amaze me!" he shouted.

"You know how it is. When you proposed to Tiffany, you couldn't wait until you were married, right?" I asked.

"That's true. Believe it or not, I remember," he chuckled, shaking his head back and forth.

"I would love for you and Tiffany to come to the wedding. We are getting married out at Amber Lake at Lakeside Church. Carl has retired and has a home there now. He is back and forth once in a while and will probably sell his apartment soon," I informed him.

"Well, surely you're not leaving that man out there by himself once you're married!" he kidded.

"No, but I have to work here for several months, at least part of the time until I can phase out," I told him.

"You tell whoever buys your apartment about me and these blueberry bagels and cream cheese. You have me far too spoiled!" he kidded, shaking his finger at me. "Miss Peggy doesn't want me coming over there. I always stay too long and keep eating bagels. Then I visit with everyone that comes in and tell them they ought to try this flavor and buy a few more of this kind, and so on. She says I'll end up getting fired here, and it's all because she makes the most tempting bagels in the city," he laughed.

I shook my head and said, "Peggy and Eugene are coming to the wedding and know how to get there. She is baking my wedding cake and all the trimmings."

"Well, she wouldn't let me ride with them. She would be afraid I'd eat the cake by the time they got there," he chuckled.

I laughed too and said, "I'll give you an announcement. You and Tiffany need to come up. You'll be off work and you need to be there. You would love the countryside. It is so beautiful up there!" I explained. "You were here and opened the door for Carl when he came to pick me up for our first date," I laughed.

"Oh yeah, he got out of that taxi and smoothed his suit jacket and was carrying a plant for you. It was a gloxinia, with beautiful dark red blooms," he remembered.

"You still remember that!" I said in amazement.

"Oh yeah, he was the distinguished businessman all right, and looked as nervous as a boy going to the prom. You came back out with him looking like the prom queen. You two couldn't stop looking at one another. I knew you two were in love before you did!" he laughed.

"Really?" I asked.

"Oh, yeah! When you see true love, you just tend to remember it. It is one of the sweetest things you can have happen to you in this old life," he affirmed.

I smiled and said, "Thanks for sharing that with me, Gilbert." He just waved his hand and shook his head and turned to open a taxi door for someone.

Back upstairs, I ate my two bagels and drank some juice and got one more cup of coffee. I showered and slipped on a cream silk jogging suit and leather slip-ons to match. I wanted to look nice but I wanted to be comfortable and casual. I got the color swatch that matched the ribbon on my hat, my black dress, gold jewelry, and black pumps. I wanted to dress for our picture in exactly what I wore when Carl proposed to me.

I put my things in the car and pulled out into the streets of Manhattan en route to Amber Lake. The drive was beautiful and I was hoping it would be that nice on Saturday. Just pray about it I thought! We were set, rain or shine. We were not going to let anything dampen our spirits!

I pulled into Carl's drive a little after nine o'clock. I pulled around back and he came out of the kitchen and across the patio and opened my door. We kissed and held each other as the autumn air whispered about us. Pepper stood there wagging his tail. We both looked down at him and started laughing. He needed some attention too and we both patted him on the head.

We both went in the kitchen and sat for a minute and drank a cup of coffee, then decided to go to the church and look at the decorations and pick out what I wanted for my bouquet. I wanted to get that done and make final arrangements with the florist.

We got in Carl's Jeep and headed for the church. We arrived there to find Casey and his crew cleaning up the bank by the lake. There were several cars there. We went in the sanctuary and Cassie and Joy were shampooing all the red cushions. I remembered them once I saw them again. It was still taking me a while to know everyone in the church. We started talking with them and Carl kidded them about having to work a whole week to get ready for this wedding.

The church had hired them to do the weekly cleaning and they had to do a complete cleaning after all the remodeling had been done. They said they usually stopped here during the day and ate lunch when they were out cleaning houses. Both of them enjoyed that because they said that Brother Darrel, Judy, and Susan were usually there. Casey would try to make it if his work wasn't too far from the church. He liked having lunch with his wife, Susan, as well as the others.

"We have a regular prayer meeting every day at lunch and we love it!" Cassie said.

Joy said, "You two will have to come over and join us when you get back from your honeymoon."

"I would sure like that," Carl announced. I agreed, and I told them I would be there when I could.

Brother Darrel and Judy came in the door and greeted us. They had been walking around the church and down by the lake. They hired Casey to do the weekly yardwork and any landscaping or seasonal work that needed to be done. Brother Darrel told us that two of the men Casey had working for him, Jesse and Gary, were not saved. Casey always brought them by for lunch when they were in the area.

When he did bring them, Susan and Casey would go out and join them in the church shelter. They would talk with them and pray with them. Brother Darrel said Gary was starting to come around, but Jesse had certainly built up a wall. He said they were chipping away at it as fast as they could without upsetting him. Casey informed us he was known to have a bad temper and was full of resentment from an abusive childhood. He was hard-hearted and closed his eyes and ears to anything he considered "religious."

"Prayer is the key and walking in faith is what opens the door!" Brother Darrel affirmed. We all agreed.

"We all know that we are responsible for our own actions no matter what has happened to us. When we stand before God, He will see only what we did in our lives. We won't be able to blame and use excuses. That is a trick Satan uses on this earth to get us in hell. He is always reminding Christians of their past or problems. Everybody has had things happen in the past and will continue to have things happen, but praise God, He is greater than he who is in the world," Brother Darrel proclaimed (1 John 4:4). We all agreed and shouted amen!

I could see the concern for these men on all their faces and it touched my heart. I knew now how the Holy Spirit touched my heart. When you have serious, loving Christians praying for you, something is going to happen! Of course, you have to open your heart as well as your eyes. Like it says in the Bible, the man who remains stiff necked after many rebukes will suddenly be destroyed—without remedy (Prov. 29:1).

Judy told us she had gotten so involved with Casey and Susan's ministry that she tried to come over here every day during her lunch break and work with them. She said that Sharon was already being invited to different churches and she was going with her and they were ministering to quite a few people.

"Sharon called me this morning and said her prayers had been answered. She has found the assistant she had been needing to complete 'Your Loss is His Gain.' She said this lady will be an inspiration to people who are suffering and need the joy of the Lord in their lives. Sharon said she has already seen her help several ladies who were grieving from the loss of loved ones," Judy said.

"Those ladies saw how the Lord had taken her grief and totally restored her and given her great joy. He took her loss and turned it around into His gain. She and Sharon will make a great testimony together. Whatever we lose, our jobs, our loved ones, our dreams—God can turn it around, into His gain! Praise God! This lady is bold in the Lord and not ashamed to witness to people she told me," Judy informed me.

"Boy, that sounds exactly like someone I know!" I admitted.

"She told me I knew who she was. She was going to bring her to your wedding. They are working on finalizing this ministry. They are going to rent or buy an office or home here in Amber Lake for their headquarters. They plan on being ready to go wherever God leads them to give these seminars within the next couple of months," Judy implied.

"I'm anxious to meet her," I responded.

"Are you ready for this big day?" Susan said, smiling. She had come up through the front of the church from the Sunday school rooms.

"Yeah, I'm ready!" I told her and she hugged me.

"I can't wait to hear all about the ministry you and Casey have," I told her.

"Well, we are excited and this is something the Lord has had on our hearts for a long time. Casey's business is doing well. We are able to work on this together since all his work now is within twenty miles of the church. People here really have pride in Amber Lake, the town, and their own yards," Susan said.

"That is for sure!" I agreed.

"I come here almost every day now. I am able to work part-time and devote more time to this, now that his business is going well. I come here about mid-morning and go to the Sunday school room and work at the table there. I usually open the window and listen to the birds and the breeze from the lake is so refreshing. That is my time with God and He enables me to plan the services and gives me guidance," she told me.

"Susan and I are both part-time workers now!" Judy announced as she put her arm around Susan. "I work in town at the bank. I'm at the front desk. They hired another lady part-time and I have trained her and she will replace me when I quit. Her name is Leanne and she is another one who is not saved."

"I am trying to get her over here to church. I tried to talk to her while I was training her, but she was not interested. She said her parents had so much religion she could float into heaven on their coattails. She said she had to go to church all the time when she was at home. Then she told me she had already had enough for a lifetime!" Judy explained. We all shook our heads.

"She is dating the mayor's son, Reggie. Reggie says his mother has enough religion for him and his dad both. He feels the same way Leanne does. Oh, Diane, you will probably meet Reggie's mother today. She owns the florist shop. Her name is Millie. She used to go to church here. She only has an aunt left on her side of the family and she takes her to her church every Sunday now," Judy informed me.

"Susan, Casey, and Sharon qualified me for part-time," Judy bragged on them. "Now Darrel and I are working together to prepare cottage prayer meetings several nights a week. We work on that here at church during the day. There are about eight of us that eat lunch together now. We take turns fixing meals. We are really enjoying our newly decorated Fellowship Hall!" Judy smiled.

"I can see why! It is beautiful and homey. Not to mention looking out over the lake and all," I replied.

"Darrel is thinking about being open for lunch and serving lunch for three dollars and having a fifteen minute sermon during that time. Our town is so little that it would be by word of mouth. There are a lot of people that work right here in town who are not saved. We feel this would be a great witnessing time," Judy informed me.

"Maybe the fellowship they enjoy at lunch would get them interested in coming on Sunday. If the Lord leads him to do lunch here, I will quit my job and be here with Darrel all day. He is behind his desk in his study at least five hours a day now," Judy said.

I was interested and excited about what all was going on in this church. I knew I wanted to be a part of it. I couldn't wait to be here all the time! Carl and I could have a cottage prayer meeting one night a week. Oh, we could have them in the gazebo when the weather was nice. Talk about being peaceful and feeling like God is all around you!

"Oh, I better go look at the fall decorations. I forgot what time it was," I told them. Judy, Susan, and I went back to one of the Sunday school rooms where they had set up three large tables and had laid everything out on it. The decorations were beautiful! They looked so real and rich. I picked out what I wanted for a beautiful bouquet. Carl and I would come back later and look everything over the final time. We walked back out through the sanctuary and said bye to everyone.

I would leave off all the decorations to make up our bouquet at Millie's Florist. Carl and I went back to the house and proceeded to dress for the photographer. We had gotten ready and looked out and the sun was perfect. Pepper was standing on the patio looking through the French doors at us. I think he wanted to be in the pictures too.

The photographer drove up and off we went to the gazebo. He took two rolls of film and said all of them looked good. He told us we shouldn't have any trouble finding a good one. He laughed and said we may have trouble making up our minds. Carl and I had stood against the railing of the gazebo with part of the woods and the lake behind us. He told us to come by his studio in town about two o'clock and he would have them ready. He said the gazebo was perfect for taking pictures in.

He left and Carl and I slipped back into our casual clothes and headed for Thornton's. We were starved. We walked in Thornton's and asked for Charmaine. She greeted us and we told her we wanted to eat lunch first and then we would look at the table selections. She seated us by the window in my favorite booth. If Carol and Glenn ever buy this place, they can keep this booth reserved for Carl and me. Anywhere in the dining room had a beautiful view though.

"When are Ray and Jan coming in?" I asked Carl. Thornton's reminded me of Jan and the girls and how much they enjoyed it.

"They are coming in early Saturday morning. Brother Darrel is going to pick them up at the airport," Carl answered.

"Well, that is nice of him!" I answered.

"Yeah, they will probably be talking fishing all the way back. Brother Darrel, Ray, Michael, Harold, and his four grandsons are all going fishing."

We ate way too much, as usual. Charmaine gave us our check and had the selections ready to look at in the back dining room. They only used that room when they were overcrowded. We went back there with her and she opened all the antique cupboards where all the tablecloths were. I knew already I wanted the harvest gold tablecloths.

Carl and I chose the ivory porcelain dinnerware with gold scrolling and gold-plated flatware. The gold scrolling was one inch deep around the edge of all the dinnerware, including the cups. It was very shiny and rich. How it would set off all the harvest decorations! We picked the crystal punch bowl with the gold rim and cups to match. There was a gold-plated ladle that matched the set.

We would have coffee in their beautiful antique urn with the ivory porcelain creamer and covered sugar set. Carol was ordering our napkins in ivory with a church and tall steeple in the center with our names and wedding date all in gold. Carol would pick out all the casserole dishes, servers, and bowls Friday.

Carl and I went over the menu and proceeded to pick out our items for the reception. We turned in our order to Charmaine. Carol and I would finalize everything Friday. She would make sure everything was finalized and set up wherever we were having it. If it was at Carl's, we would bring the banquet tables and set them up on the drive beside the patio. The patio would be set to receive guests as well. Carl had his drive covered with pea gravel and it looked nice and would work out perfectly.

Besides, Carl had six other park benches in black wrought-iron scattered about. One was overlooking the lake, down by the gazebo. Two were on the north side of the patio and two were placed along the rock walk to the pier and one was in the gazebo. One sat back beside the woods where several of the bluebird houses were. Also there were the rockers on the front porch.

The yard was being manicured all day Friday by Casey and his crew. They were putting a flower garden in across the front porch. Mums of yellow, white, crimson, lavender and pink were being planted Wednesday and fertilized, then midnight mulch would be put down. Oh, I could not wait to see all those colorful mums! Talk about setting off that brick home with the black shutters and roof.

The blooming flowers were at their peak. We were blessed again! The ferns were still flowing and beautiful. Cassie and Joy were making sure the patio and all the furniture was washed. They were going to do the windows too. Now that would take them more than a day, as many windows as Carl had. At least everything would be done for all the guests and for us when we came back home.

Carl and I had our blood tests done. We drove back to Amber Lake and went to Millie's Florist. Carl and I met Millie and she told Carl how much she loved his home on the lake. She had lived here all of her life and took a lot of pride in this place and the surrounding area. She was pleased how well the lake and its shores had been kept up by people such as Carl, the Goodfellows, and others who had built on the lake.

I gave her my decorations to make a bouquet. She said they would make a unique bouquet and that she felt fall weddings would become popular after they saw how mine was done. "That is a wonderful time to be married. The fall of the year is a perfect temperature and is so beautiful. Then you can come back from your honeymoon and buy everything to decorate your home for your first holidays together," she smiled.

"Now for Roger and I, our home was a very small apartment above Clancy's hardware store. The honeymoon was staying overnight fifty miles down the road," she laughed. "We were so in love we didn't even care," she confirmed. "The years have been good to us and we have three beautiful children. Roger is the mayor and his life is dedicated to this little town," she affirmed.

"Our sons, Reggie and Jack, are following in Roger's footsteps. Reggie is already assistant to the president of Amber Lake Bank. Of course the president is Roger's brother, Wayne," she laughed. "Jack works at city hall and will probably take over Roger's job someday. That is, if he is elected. The people around here really like him. I have to admit, he is a hard worker and has a lot of charisma even if he is my son!" she chuckled.

"My daughter, Nancy, owns Nancy's Cafe, the little narrow building that sits between the beauty shop and the real estate office," she said.

"Oh, that is the one that has the window box on the front window, brimming over with flowers. It is so cute!" I said.

"Yes, that is it. You think it is cute outside, wait until you go in. There was an alley there years ago and Lou McClaney decided to fill that spot in. He built a cafe there for his wife, Mary Alice. She ran it until she passed away. Her son, Mitchell, took it over and he ran it until he fell in love with a beauty from Louisiana," she giggled.

"Annie Mae, was her name. She came into town to visit with her aunt, Lucille Pryor. Lucille brought her in the cafe one morning for breakfast. It was love for her and Mitchell at first sight. The old timers around here still kid about it. They said once he saw her, his food wasn't worth eating anymore. That morning she walked in, he burned the pancakes, eggs, and all. He came out to talk with her and a fire started back in the kitchen. Doc Martin and Pete Snively were sitting near the kitchen and they ran back and beat the fire out with their jackets!" she laughed. Carl and I laughed too.

"One July afternoon, my Aunt Dora and my sister, Tammy, were sitting in the gazebo over there," she said as she pointed out the window to the huge, white gazebo. The gazebo had grass and flower bushes all around it, like a miniature park and was very inviting. "Tammy said several of the school teachers were in there having a picnic and talking about the next school year," she continued.

"They looked over and saw Mitchell and Annie Mae come out the front door of the cafe and locked it up. He was finished with his lunch crowd, but he still had on his apron and white hat. They walked across the street to the gazebo and they both were whispering and holding hands. Aunt Dora said they came right in the center of the gazebo and Mitchell got down on his knees and proposed to Annie Mae right there in front of God and everybody!" she told us.

"Gee, that sounds familiar," I whispered to Carl. "Except you didn't get down on your knees," I giggled.

"I figured if you had to help me back up, you would have changed your mind about marrying me," Carl answered back. We both laughed and I reached up and kissed him on the cheek.

I looked at Millie and told her Carl built a new gazebo at his place just so he could propose to me there. She sighed and said, "There must be something about those gazebos. Word got around like wildfire about Mitchell's proposal. It was Amber Lake's love story that summer. All the girls in town were daydreaming about their beaus proposing to them in that gazebo. Some did and some didn't," she laughed.

"Young lovers would drive up here just to see it. They would go in there and sit or take a picnic lunch. They acted like it was something magical concerning matters of the heart. It wasn't just young folks either. I could tell you stories of folks around here who had one foot in the grave and would go sit in there during the day and many times meet someone there. They had quit their complaining and grumbling and gone there looking for love. It made all the difference!" she chuckled.

"I don't know how many weddings we had over the years after that. Grumpy old maids, stubborn bachelors, lonely widows and widowers were all getting hitched! They didn't have one foot in the grave anymore! I mean that foot was kicking, and I don't mean the bucket!" she exclaimed. Carl and I were about to roll on the floor laughing.

"How do you think my business got going? Everyone was going down to Meadow Creek to order all their flowers. Roger said Amber Lake needed to have its own florist. He said I was the perfect one to do it. When Roger and I first married we were too poor to buy decorations. I would walk along the lakefront and roadsides and pick wildflowers and gnarled limbs, rocks and such. I would come home and put arrangements together," she explained.

"Roger and the children loved it. I couldn't believe Jack and Reggie noticed, being such rough and tough little boys. I started bringing arrangements into Roger's office at city hall. Word got around and people started asking me to decorate for special occasions and all.

I was staying busy just doing that. I loved flowers and always had a green thumb and loved to decorate," she said.

"We went on and bought this building. Wayne got us a small business loan and it was a great move. It used to be Ivy Reed's Produce Store, and when he passed on, it just sat here empty. We went to see his daughter, Candice, and she sold it to us. To this day she is so happy to see life in these old walls again," she grinned.

"Candice grew up here behind this counter. She says she would sneak candy out of this glass case when her dad, Ivy, was waiting on a customer. I guess they named her right! Her dad nicknamed her Candy. She still comes in several times a week to talk and reminisce," Millie informed us.

"All five of her children were married over there at Lakeside Church and I did all the flowers for their weddings. I have been doing flower arrangements for births, weddings, graduations, anniversaries, and funerals for generations of Amber Lake families," she told us.

"Matter of fact, Candice's mother just passed away a few years ago. She was one hundred years old! We had a birthday party for her . . . where else but the gazebo! They had her sit in the center in a rocking chair. Nancy baked her a huge cake and Roger, Wayne, and Nancy started lighting all the candles. Candice's mother, Miss Abbey, told us she had to blow them all out at once to keep the gazebo from going up in flames," she laughed.

"Then she said, 'Now I want to tell all you old men something. Just because I'm sitting here in this gazebo, known for its romance and all, I'm not gonna jump up and grab up any of you men. If any of you out there are single, in good shape financially and physically, and under eighty, I might consider looking at you.' The townspeople, close to two hundred people, liked to have died laughing at her," she told us.

"Roger put a microphone in front of her and said, 'Miss Abbey, you mean in good shape physically first and then financially.' 'No,' she stated, it was just like I said. That way I know up front I will be rolling in the dough. If they keel over, I have big bills to dry my tears on!' she stammered. Everybody laughed and laughed. Some of the old timers were slapping their legs laughing," Millie chuckled.

"Then Roger asked her, 'Miss Abbey, you are our oldest living resident. Do you have any words of wisdom to share with us? Other than we know now you are interested in young, healthy rich men.' Everyone chuckled. She took the microphone and it was so quiet you could hear a pin drop," Millie continued.

"She slowly stood up and said, 'I'm thankful to be here today. God has been good to me. I studied and knew His word and tried to live by it. Everything is in the Bible you need to know, so you better seek Him. I was saved when I was nine years old. I was ready to leave here if my life had been taken, but He gave me ninety-one more years. I had a lot of bad things happen in my life. The good things I praised him for and the bad things he lead me through and blessed me. The main thing I want to tell all of you is to know Him and trust Him (Ps. 37:3–5). Then remember, prayer is the key and walking in faith is what opens the door. In every matter, you must always walk by faith, not by sight (2 Cor. 5:7). So, walk in faith my dear people, walk in faith,' she instructed. With that she sat back down," Millie concluded.

"There were many tears falling at that moment. Roger whispered, 'Miss Abbey, thank you for that wonderful insight. We all love you!' and he hugged her. You see, I have it all memorized to this day. I just wish Roger, Jack, and Reggie had done more than listened. They won't open a Bible or go to church," she stated with regret.

"God said our life is like a mist that appears for a little while and then vanishes (James 4:14). Believe me that is just the way it is! My grandparents on both sides, aunts and uncles, mom and dad, and my brother are buried over there in Amber Lake Cemetery. They all lived to a ripe old age, except my brother, Ronnie. He was killed in Vietnam. He was only twenty years old," she confessed.

"His death tore our hearts out. I couldn't understand why someone like Ronnie had to die. The Lord helped me to quit asking why and to stop trying to figure it out. My family and I had to turn it over to God and believe in His peace. It was then the Lord gave it to us," she revealed (1 Pet. 5: 7–11).

"Praise God Ronnie knew Jesus so we know where he is! Ronnie was the one who lead me to Jesus. I was eleven years old. Everyone needs to be ready. You never know when it is your time!" she attested. Carl and I stood there somberly listening to her story. It was a sad, yet beautiful story of how God touched their lives in a time of despair and grief.

"Have either one of you been through Amber Lake Cemetery?" she asked. "No," we both said. I told her I had seen it from the main street and it looked like a beautiful cemetery.

"It is absolutely beautiful and so peaceful back there. It backs the lake. There is a huge cross built by the bank of the lake. I keep the flower garden that is at the base of it," she said.

"We have an Easter ceremony there before church every Easter. Nancy and I cook and bring out breakfast to the cemetery. There are concrete tables and benches scattered throughout the garden by the lake bank where the cross is. There have been azaleas, dogwoods, and cherry trees planted out there too," she explained.

"People plant something that will bloom in honor of a loved one who has passed on. It reminds us of how they grew and bloomed here on earth, and yet they live and bloom on the other side. We rejoice for that and see the beauty and grace of God's plan. Some people thought it was strange we have fellowship in the cemetery. Then they found it gave them a new outlook on death. They didn't look at it as morbid, but just as a crossing over. You need to know where you are crossing over to. Many people have been saved after those Easter services. Many people that were lost and grieving experienced a mighty change in their lives!" she proclaimed.

"On Easter morning we worship our risen Lord and praise Him for dying on the cross for our sins so that we may have life. We eat and have fellowship together out there in joy, not in remorse for the ones who have gone on. They won't come back to us, but we will go to them someday," she confirmed with a reassuring smile.

"Oh, honey! I didn't mean to make you cry," she whispered, so apologetic.

"That's OK," I whimpered back, wiping the tears from my face. "They are tears of joy, not remorse," I explained, as the three of us chuckled.

Then she perked up and announced, "I tell you what! I would love to be in that cemetery when the rapture occurs. When the dead in Christ burst out of their graves and the living in Christ are caught up with them in the air with Christ, our Lord (1 Thess. 4:13–18). Wouldn't that be something?" she yelled slapping the top of the counter. The three of us were ready to have revival when she said that. We all just kept laughing and Carl had tears in his eyes and said, "Praise God!"

We finally settled down, and I said, "Well, you never did tell me what happened to Mitchell and Annie Mae." Then we all started laughing again.

She continued with, "Mitchell left for Louisiana at the end of that summer and just closed the restaurant. He was an only child and Lou and Sara had passed on. Annie Mae's father hired Mitchell to work for his company. He had a boat and yacht business down on the gulf. They were married that fall, just like you two are going to be."

"Well, how did Nancy get the cafe? You got my curiosity up," I commented.

"Well, two years went by. One day we saw Alex Banner and Jonathan Snow in there cleaning the place up. Mitchell didn't have any family living. Alex and Jonathan were his best buddies in high school and they chummed around until Annie Mae came to town," she said.

"Mitchell had sent them the key to the cafe and told them to clean it up real nice because he wanted to sell it. He had sold all the food and dry goods to the Hillside Inn and Restaurant over in Millerstown. Allen told me he and Jonathan cleaned up all the equipment and got the place in good shape as far as being clean. He said Mitchell sent them a check for one thousand dollars! He told them to give Max, my son-in-law, who owns Amber Lake Real Estate, the key," she continued.

"He contacted Max by phone and said he wanted to sell it and told him what he wanted for it. It was so cheap Max and Nancy jumped right on it! Nancy had been praying for her own business, and bingo! Mitchell calls out of the clear blue and made an offer she couldn't refuse. Ain't God great!" Millie shouted, shaking her head.

"Oh, yes, I have met Nancy!" Carl announced. "Max is who I bought my land from on Amber Lake. He sure is a nice guy!" Carl told her. "He would take me next door to Nancy's when I was up here. We had several great meals and the coffee was the best," Carl told her. "Every time I was in there she was running her legs off!" Carl laughed.

Millie laughed and said, "It only holds about twenty-five people at the most. She serves all three meals and still has the blue plate special as they call it. She has a young lady, April, helping her now. She goes to college over in Springfield, but helps Nancy from about eleven to one, during the lunch rush. Nancy said she is great and she makes enough in tips to make her car payment. She received a music scholarship, so that takes care of most of her college expenses," Millie said.

"She goes to Lakeside Church. I can believe she received a scholarship, she's such a fine young lady," Carl affirmed.

"Nancy also hired April's two cousins, Adon and Ian, to clean tables and do dishes on the weekend and after school. They love making their own money!" Millie said. "Nancy is a great cook and is known for her fabulous desserts and people say she has the best coffee for miles around," Millie advertised.

"I will have to try Nancy's," I affirmed.

"Yeah, Diane can truly rate coffee on a scale of one to ten," Carl implied.

"Nancy has to turn people away at lunchtime. I sure wish there was another place that could handle the overflow. She says it hurts her feelings when she has to tell people there is a thirty minute wait when they are on their lunch breaks," Millie told us. Gee, I thought, this is a confirmation for Judy! Lakeside Church needed to get ready to open the fellowship hall at lunch for spiritual and physical feeding.

"Matter of fact, I'll be ready for dinner before too long," I said to Carl as I looked at my watch. We had been talking to Millie an hour! I apologized to her for taking so much of her time.

"Are you kidding me? I enjoyed getting to catch you up on some history here, neighbors!" she laughed. The last thirty minutes she had been working on my bouquet behind the counter while talking with us.

She came out and said, "Diane, you are the originator of this fall bouquet idea, but I guarantee there will be many to follow once people see this!" She held it out in front of her and she had maple leaves, berry sprays, and ivy draping down the front and sides. Mums in many colors and baby's breath would be sprinkled throughout the bouquet. The baby's breath sprinkled throughout would set my dress off. Cranberry lace wired ribbon, edged in gold, would tie it all together in a huge bow with twirled streamers.

The bouquet was like one I had never seen before, but exactly how I had imagined it. I couldn't stop looking at it! Carl couldn't get over how elegant and unique it was. "We'll have to take pictures of you in the front yard with the mums. They are the same colors as those in your bouquet," Carl suggested.

"I love it!" I squealed.

She was going to make up the bouquet for my sister, a corsage for all the ladies, and a boutonniere for all the men involved in the wedding. We thanked Millie, paid her, and told her we were coming back to eat at Nancy's later.

We left and jumped in the car to head for Springfield. Carl said he found out from Cassie and Joy that they had several nice jewelry stores. We needed to pick out our rings. We stopped by the church first, to leave my bouquet on the table with all the other decorations.

The same ones were still there. Casey, Gary, and Jesse were still cleaning up the lakeside. Susan and Judy were ready to leave there for the day. They had a prayer meeting with the women of Maplewood

Church, which was forty minutes from here. Cassie and Joy had just finished shampooing all the cushions and it smelled so fresh and clean! I went back to Carl's Jeep and gingerly picked up my bouquet to take it in to show the ladies. I couldn't wait to see their reactions!

I walked in the back door and Susan, Judy, Cassie, and Joy's mouths flew open and they couldn't believe how beautiful the bouquet was. Brother Darrel came out from the back and had to see what was going on. We all started laughing when we saw him. "What is going on out here?" he laughed. About that time he saw the bouquet and he said, "Well, there is nothing more beautiful than nature. God created it!" he said as he shook his head and commented on how beautiful it was. I laid it on the back table and Carl and I left.

We stopped by the photographer's. He had our pictures ready. They were fantastic! "I can't wait to see our wedding pictures already!" I commented. He was right. We had a difficult choice to make. They were all different and all excellent. I was anxious to see how the announcements looked.

Carl wanted an eleven by fourteen full shot of us in the gazebo. It showed the ferns hanging and the beautiful lake and woods in the background. I knew we would not pick a full length shot for the announcement. The one Carl picked would make a beautiful portrait though. Carl wanted it matted and framed to have up at the reception. Great idea I thought!

Carl and I found the rings we wanted at the second store we stopped at. I wanted the biggest gold band there was. I got Carl a gold band with inset diamonds in a diamond shape. That is what he liked the best. We locked them up in the glove compartment.

We passed a huge department store and for some reason I just thought about the tables being set up at the reception. I thought brass planters with button mums in each one would be beautiful! Afterwards we could have Casey plant them in the long flower bed along the rock walk. The flowers that were in there would be gone in a few weeks anyway. The silk fall decorations could grace the main table with the brass planter and candles in the center.

"Carl! I never thought! Who will be the flower girl and ring bearer?" I panicked.

"Don't panic! I don't know, just pray about it!" Carl said. "Jan is going to be at the guest book. David, Glenn, Adon, and Ian are going to usher. John Jr. will set up the music. Amanda and Linda will serve punch and cake. Brian and Thomas can serve refills throughout the house and grounds. Michael can pass out all the bubble bottles to everyone to blow bubbles upon our departure."

"If the weather is nice, Carol, Glenn, and the boys will set up the reception right before we get out there. Thornton's will be right there ready to serve food wherever we have it. They will have it ready in nothing flat. They know what to do," Carl implied.

"My nephew, Isaac, can be the ring bearer. The whole family is driving out anyway for a fall vacation after the wedding," Carl said.

"Hey! You remember Kimberly's little niece, DeAndra. She was there the day I was baptized," I stated. Carl shook his head yes.

"I wonder if she could be the flower girl? Wouldn't that be cute! I know Kimberly is coming. Her other niece, Jessica, along with Calvin and Nathan could serve dessert to people in the yard and house. That would be great if they were available!" I told Carl. "Not everyone will want to wait in line for cake," I suggested.

"Sounds good to me. You better call Kimberly right away and ask her," Carl said.

We got back to Nancy's. April was there and we talked to her. She worked there at lunch but only worked two nights a week. We saw Adon and Ian running around and cleaning up. April waited on us and we told her all that we had done in two days. She laughed and said, "You can tell the Lord is behind this wedding!" We all laughed.

Nancy came up and said, "I heard you got the history of Amber Lake today," and started laughing. We ate a wonderful dinner and Carl got homemade banana pudding. I took a couple of bites. I would make up for it when I didn't have to fit into a tailored Victorian wedding dress!

Carl and I went back to his house. We talked and planned at the kitchen counter to make sure we were tying up all loose ends. We picked out the picture we wanted for the announcement. Then we went out and watched the sunset over Amber Lake. Pepper sat with us during the sunset ceremony. He just wagged his tail and looked at us.

Carl and I walked back to my car. We stood there and held each other. "Whew! What a day. I will be so glad when this is my home. I love Amber Lake, Lakeside Church, and everybody here," I whispered. We kissed good night.

"You be very careful. We have had a full day. I know how you get sleepy when you are driving. You have two hours in front of you, you know!" Carl said.

213

"I'll just drive faster," I whispered through a yawn.

"Oh, that is a big help!" Carl announced. I started laughing.

I got in my car and rolled the window down and told him I loved him and he said, "Me too." I backed down the driveway and headed for Manhattan. Back to a different world! I had to stop several times and walk around and get coffee. I finally made it back to my apartment. I got a glass of water. That tasted so refreshing. The skyline was clear and beautiful. I felt wonderful, yet my life seemed like it was a whirl-wind, an awesome whirlwind, yet still a whirlwind.

I took off my makeup. That reminded me! I needed Trish to do my makeup and see how I liked it. If I liked my new look, I might have her do my makeup for the wedding. Carl had said she must be at her parents since he saw her out in the boat with the boys after school. I would call her tomorrow and see if we could meet later in the week. I had to make all the necessary phone calls tomorrow. I would go by and give Carol the picture and check in at the office. After all, I wouldn't be back for several weeks. Oh, my old bed felt so good! I wouldn't have any trouble sleeping tonight.

"Good morning world!" I said rising early to a cloudy day. If it was going to rain, I wished it would go ahead and rain now and be nice for Saturday. I went out and turned the TV on. Saturday was looking perfectly clear with a high of sixty-eight degrees. That would really be nice! Crisp and clear! I sat down at the dining table and went over my notes of what needed to be done. Then I took a shower and dressed casual. I picked out about six fall casual outfits, two dresses, and two dressy pantsuits. Everything from treaded boots to pumps! I spent two hours matching up turtlenecks, sweaters, socks, etc. I was checking things off my list. I packed my camera and plenty of film. It was only nine o'clock!

I called Carol. She had just gotten to work. We set up a lunch date and I told her I would be in about one hour before lunch to talk to Franklin, Kent, and Sam. Especially Sam, since he was filling my shoes. Carol said he was doing a good job. She said on some aspects he was still a little rough around the edges, but was shaping up very fast. She said they were very impressed at how quickly he had taken on all that responsibility and was sailing smoothly. I was glad to hear that!

I called Kimberly and she was glad to hear from me. She told me she would be at the wedding and she was bringing both her nieces. She said she was coming up Friday and stay the night with a friend she had up there. "Great! I have a favor to ask you," I said.

"Sure, girl, what is it?" Kimberly asked.

"I would like DeAndra to be the flower girl and Jessica to help serve at the reception. I know this is last minute notice. I didn't even think about it until yesterday afternoon," I apologized.

"My nieces would love to be in your wedding! What color dresses do they need?" she asked.

"Anything that goes with fall colors," I answered.

"They just got beautiful dresses for the holidays. They wanted to shop early. They are burgundy satin and lace and they are tea length. Would that be OK, or do we need another color?" she asked.

"That is perfect!"

"They have satin flats to match. Now I know why they were supposed to get them!" Kimberly laughed.

"All three of you be at the church for rehearsal Friday night at six and then we will have the rehearsal dinner at Thornton's in Silver Lake at eight o'clock. I will make sure Carol gives you a map, but there will be plenty of room for you to ride with someone to Thornton's. You will get to meet our family and many Amber Lake folks. You will love it up there!" I told her.

"Oh, I can't wait to see that wedding, honey!" she laughed. She told me she would see me at the church Friday evening and we said bye.

Carl was calling his brothers, Alvin, Don, and John, and his sister, Jean Marie, this morning to make sure they were all coming in. Mom, Dad, Sis and her two sons, Brian and Thomas, were driving. They would get to Thornton's about noon Friday. My Uncle Robert, his wife Dorothy, and my Aunt Annabelle were driving in too. I wasn't sure if any of my cousins were going to make it or not. They all had a long way to travel if they did. It was a good thing Thornton's had nine rooms! No one would be disappointed staying there. Whatever you were going there for in the fall, the sightseeing was worth the drive alone!

I got ready and went into the office. I talked an hour with Sam alone. We worked out some of the problems he was in question about. I gave Carol the picture and she had color samples for the announcement. I picked out the buff with black print. Carol was running it out to the printer and would be back in one hour.

I visited with Faune. She and Sylvia and several other women from Sylvia's church were coming up Saturday. Faune had really gotten involved with church there. She was having a great time and had met so many new friends. I was happy for her. She even had a new hair style and a new outfit on too. She looked so nice and seemed full of joy. She was hoping her daughters would come up with her. Her husband and son were busy working Saturday.

I went by to see Kent. "I hardly see you look up anymore!" I announced.

Kent looked up from his paperwork and smiled and said, "Hey! How is the bride-to-be these days?" He came over and hugged me.

"Just great! I wanted to come by today for a little while. I'll leave tomorrow and stay at Thornton's out there at Silver Lake," I told him.

"Carol and Glenn are coming out Thursday night. Glenn is going to play golf over at Mountain View Friday with his old songwriting buddy, Russ. Russ wrote a couple of successful songs and bought a beautiful chalet on Pine Mountain. He and Glenn still write songs and keep in touch so this will be a nice visit for him," I said. "Why don't you and Honey come out and take a second honeymoon and enjoy the fall colors and beautiful weather?"

"Well, Franklin and I have decided to stay here through Friday night. We will have everything in fine shape for a meeting with Ancon at nine Monday morning," Kent explained.

"Whoa! Ancon is a big account! That is great!" I replied.

"That is why we are making double sure we have all bases covered and we will if we work on it through Friday," Kent answered. "Then Franklin, Robbie, Honey, and I are leaving Saturday and plan to meander through those little towns and antique shops you always talk about," he said. "Carol set us all up for staying at Thornton's Saturday night, so we're making a weekend out of it," Kent smiled.

"Really! Well, that is neat. I'm so glad you are doing that. I bet both the girls are excited to be out with their hubbies!" I said.

"Oh, yeah, they have been giggling and planning what they are wearing, where we are going, where we are eating—you name it. They are like a couple of school girls!" he laughed.

"I can't wait for them to see Amber Lake, Lakeside Church, and Carl's place. Looks like the weather is going to let us have the reception at Carl's," I said.

"Honey said she and Robbie were making a beeline to the Victorian room and peaches and cream. They even went out and bought film and they are both taking their cameras," he chuckled.

"They need to. . . . Amber Lake and Silver Lake are absolutely beautiful," I told him.

"Of course, I think they did want a couple shots of you and Carl too," he kidded.

I could truly see Kent was looking forward to some time with his wife and being away from the office, although he would never admit it. Maybe he would lighten up a little bit after this weekend and make some time for his family. I certainly hoped so. Kent had plenty of money and had invested well. No one needed to neglect their family like he did whether they had money or not! I hoped this weekend would open his eyes. Kent was a great guy. He just didn't see that he never put God first (Matt. 6:33).

"Honey and Robbie said it had been so long since they had been out with their husbands, they were definitely taking pictures of the event," he laughed and shook his head.

"Kent, you and Franklin both have such wonderful wives. You need to do this more often. Kent, life is just too short! You don't know how glad I am that you are planning such a wonderful weekend and coming to the wedding," I told him.

"Now, don't stay here until midnight Friday, then fall asleep and sink down in your pew during the wedding," I instructed him. "You remember back in the seventies when Carol, you, and I went to Milwaukee to meet with Milco, Inc.? You fell asleep in that leather boardroom chair and slid down until your chin was almost on the table. I was across from you and Carol was next to you. She kept nudging you and you would just jerk and nod your head around again!" I laughed.

Carol knocked on the door and walked into Kent's office. She had just gotten back from the printer's and heard us laughing. "What is so funny?" she giggled. When we saw her, we started laughing even harder. We told her what we were talking about and she laughed and said, "How could I forget that! I was so embarrassed!" I told her I remembered that her face turned as red as a tomato.

I reminisced about how I tried to reach under the table far enough to kick him, but couldn't reach that far. Carol said, "Oh I remember what happened next. You kicked at him anyway and your shoe flew off and landed way past Kent's chair. Then the company president asked you to come up and give the presentation to the vice president, who came in late."

"Diane just sat there and looked at him!" Carol told Kent. We were all exhausted from laughing.

Then Carol continued with, "I backed up my chair and crawled behind Kent and threw her shoe back under the table at her. He asked her what was wrong and she said she was sorry, but she had a horrible cramp in her foot. Her foot was dancing under the table trying to locate the shoe. Finally, she found it and went up and gave the presentation again," Carol sighed.

Kent caught his breath and said, "Why didn't I ever know what all you two went through?"

"You nodded and slept through the whole meeting! When you woke up, we had the account sewed up!"

We were all worn out from laughing and then Franklin peeped his head around the corner. We all started chuckling again. He wanted to know what had been so funny. He had heard us laughing clear down the hall.

We told him the story, although we didn't think we would ever live through it being told again. When we finished Franklin said, "Good heavens! It is a wonder we ever got that account!" and he burst out laughing too.

Faune came around the corner and knocked on the door. "What is so funny?" she giggled. It started all over again and Franklin told her the story. If laugher was like medicine to the body, we had over-dosed.

Carol and I went to lunch and she had a sample run of what my announcements would look like. They looked great! The verse said exactly how we felt and was not too long. The picture was perfect with our names and the date of our wedding at the bottom. What a nice keepsake to have made up.

I told Carol I wanted three hundred made up. I didn't expect more than two hundred, but those who were unable to make it to the wedding would receive one in their Christmas card. Carol thought that was a great idea. Carl and I both had family and friends who were not able to travel that far for one reason or another.

Carol said she and Glenn were excited about the weekend and were staying Saturday night also. She had made an appointment to talk to the owner after lunch Sunday. She wanted to talk to her about running a bed and breakfast and gain some knowledge. "Well, it doesn't have to be Thornton's. They are always busy, yet never frantic. That would ruin the whole meaning behind it. You go there to rest, relax, eat good food, and have peaceful surroundings. That is exactly what you need to look for in a place," I implied.

"You talk with her Sunday and she may even know of one for sale. They all know each other in that area. When you go over to the church Friday, go by Amber Lake Realty and see Max. Matter of fact, Carl and I will plan around so we can eat lunch with you at Nancy's Cafe. It is right next door to Max's office, and Nancy is his wife," I informed her. She liked that idea.

"You have to start somewhere. This would be a perfect time. Keep praying, listening, and walking in faith my friend!" I said.

"I know. I will!" she whispered back.

We went back to the office. I told everyone bye and I would see them Saturday. Sam spoke with me privately and asked me if it was all right to bring a date. "Sure!" I said. "Who is the lucky lady?" I asked.

"You remember when I went back to my home church to be baptized?" he asked.

"Yes," I answered.

"Well, she was my nephew's Sunday school teacher. Jamie is her name. I felt my heart race the first moment I saw her and I'm no teenager anymore!" Sam said.

"That can happen at any age Sam. Thank heavens for that!" I laughed.

"Yeah, but it is a lot more than that. A lot more!" he emphasized.

"And?" I tempted him to tell me the story here.

"She is the one I want to marry. No doubt in my mind!" he said.

"Does she know that?" I asked.

"Well, not yet," he stuttered.

"What are you waiting on?" I smiled.

"Well, my future here looks good. I have changed my life and now I have put the Kingdom of God first. I can't believe what a difference it already has made. Of course, I have a lot to learn and a long way to go, but at least I'm on the right track this time," he informed me.

"Just pray about it, Sam!" I said.

"I'm saving my money right now for a diamond engagement ring for her," he told me.

"Don't wait too long, Sam," I told him.

"I won't. I will have the money saved within six weeks," he said. He said her cousin worked here in Manhattan and Jamie was coming to stay with her on the weekends so she could see Sam. He said it made for a very lonely week though. I told him I certainly understood how he felt.

He told me I was the only one that knew about this and he wanted me to pray for him and Jamie. Of course, I told him I would and I was honored he confided in me. I hugged him and told him I would see them Saturday. I told him to have her in the front line to catch the bouquet. We both laughed.

"Franklin! I'm heading out. I'll see you Saturday," I announced.

"We'll be there with bells on!" he laughed.

"You better have bells on to keep Kent awake!" I giggled. Franklin shook his head and chuckled.

"We are going to sightsee all morning and change into our fancy threads at Thornton's. You knew Carol got us reservations for Saturday night, didn't you?" he asked.

"Yes, Kent just told me. I'm glad you are making a weekend out of this. You'll love it out there!" I acclaimed.

"Yes, Robbie is thrilled. I tell you, I am looking forward to it myself!" he grinned.

"By the way, you picked an excellent time to be gone," he smirked.

"OK. What is going on?" I asked, curious to hear his reply.

"Our present computers and programs are not going to be able to keep up with all the changes we are going through. We all had a meeting Monday morning and decided to change everything over to a completely new system. We will go through that transition for the next two weeks," he informed me.

"Thank heavens I am missing that!" I exclaimed. Franklin laughed. He knew I hated changing when I was comfortable with the current way of doing business.

He got up and hugged me and said, "We'll see you in a couple of days. I just can't wait to see Amber Lake. It sounds like heaven!" he smiled (Rev. 21:10–27).

"It's absolutely beautiful, but I'm sure it wouldn't even begin to compare with heaven," I said, softly smiling.

"Probably not," Franklin whispered. I waved bye as I closed the door.

"Faune, I'll see you Saturday. I understand you are coming up with Sylvia and some others," I said.

"Oh yeah, and both my daughters are going. I am so happy about that! We have a carload!" she laughed.

"I wanted to see Kimberly, but I need to get going. I'll just call her. You knew she was coming and her nieces are going to be involved in the wedding and reception?" I questioned.

"Oh, yeah she told me. She was excited! She told me all about their dresses and all," Faune said.

"You would not have caught Kimberly today anyway. She is only working two nights a week now. That just became effective Monday. I look for her to quit entirely within the month," Faune informed me.

"What!" I shrieked. "I leave the office for two days and the whole world changes!" I proclaimed. "Why is she doing that?" I asked.

"She is working with a new friend and feels the Lord has lead her to help her with her business. She seems real excited and confident about it. You know Kimberly. She seems to know where she is going and why!" Faune laughed.

"Well, this is true. I wonder why she hasn't told me about it. I just talked to her Monday," I told Faune.

"She probably wants to tell you in person," Faune replied.

"I guess so. I can't wait to see what she is up to. I know it will be doing what the Lord wants her to do!" I implied. I hugged Faune and told her I would see her Saturday.

I left and got in a taxi and went straight to Macy's. I bought Carl a navy velour robe, light blue pajamas, and navy leather slippers. I found him a brushed denim jacket and jeans in a medium blue and a denim shirt to complete the outfit. I couldn't resist the braided black belt or the tan woven one. He had plenty of boots. I knew he had at least two pairs of black ones and a brand new pair of tan ones.

I went to men's loungewear and bought him a silk lounge shirt and boxers to match in light gray. I didn't know what he would think of them, but they looked comfortable! I laughed knowing the look he would have on his face after he opened that package.

It was already five o'clock. I stopped and ate a huge salad and drank a glass of iced tea before I went back to the apartment. When I did get home, I didn't want to have to go out again, especially after dragging all these packages around! I caught a taxi back to the apartment and was so glad to get home!

I kept Carl's presents in the gift boxes and planned to wrap them after I got to Thornton's. It would be so much easier to go out and buy little things once I was living up there. I had gotten used to the city after all these years. In the small towns, you just drove your car, parked without any trouble, ran in and got what you wanted, and went out and drove off.

Not quite that simple in Manhattan! One thing was sure, you had quite a selection to pick from in the city! I was ready for the simple life though. Of course, Carl already told me I never needed to buy another thing for myself or the house unless it just plain wore out! That was true, but that just didn't sound like any fun! I couldn't wait to buy Christmas decorations already! I never cared to buy any just for me. This year was different!

I drank a cup of decaf and started packing and checking items off my list. Then I was hungry again. Why was I always so hungry all the time? I was going to pig out on seafood on my honeymoon! When I got back, I would have to attend Sharon's seminar! No one needed this much food. I knew that!

I called Carl. "How you doing, sweetie?" I asked.

"Whew! Casey and his crew set the mums out and put midnight mulch all around. The front yard looks totally different," he said.

"Well, you like it don't you?" I asked.

"Oh yeah, it looks like it ought to be on the cover of a magazine now," Carl said. "Cassie and Joy cleaned windows all day. They will be here doing windows in the morning and then cleaning the house. They will get done Thursday afternoon. They are even cleaning out the oven and refrigerator. I'm glad, because with everyone that is staying here, they will be using every inch of it!" Carl chuckled.

"Can Isaac be the ring bearer?" I asked.

"Yes, I called John this morning and he can do it. I am getting his tux rented," Carl said.

"DeAndra can be the flower girl," I told Carl. "We will talk all about everything tomorrow and we will see everyone Friday evening at six," I told him. "You have enough detergent, towels, toilet paper, sheets, pillows, and so forth for all the house guests?" I asked.

"I don't know. I better take a survey in the morning and go to the that huge discount store in Springfield. I will just buy some more white towels, washcloths, sheets, pillows, and blankets and put them in the foyer closet. We will know we have them whenever we have extra guests. I'll stock up on everything else too," he told me.

"Make sure you have enough life jackets too. That boat of yours can handle four people if need be. The kids will all want to be on the paddleboat. You better take a total survey of everything you need. That includes people food and dog food too," I reminded him. "Pepper will be ready to jump into the lake after being used to peace and quiet!" I laughed.

"I'll just take him over to the Goodfellows. I'll get his food. The boys love having him there. Ray and Jan are only going to be here a week anyway," Carl said.

"That is a good idea," I agreed.

I told him I would be out at least by noon and we would get our marriage license then. Also we would get the flutes for our reception. Carl said he already found an antique pair that were crystal with amber stems. I couldn't wait to see them! I told him I was doing my final packing in the morning. I was taking it slow so I wouldn't forget something. I would get my car serviced tomorrow and cleaned. We agreed we might as well leave the Jeep for Ray and Jan to get around in. I told him I loved him and couldn't wait to see him. He said, "Me too," and hung up.

The next morning, I woke up and stretched to the sun shining over Manhattan. Only two more days, I thought to myself! That was my last morning in the city for a while. I slipped on some clothes to run down to Peggy's and get a bagel. She was there and she said everything was on go for Saturday. Gilbert and Tiffany were riding with them.

I told her I would give her a key to my apartment and wanted her to check on it once in a while during the next several weeks. I gave her Carl's phone number too. She handed me Gilbert's sack and she said, "See ya there. Carol already faxed me the map and all."

"Great. See ya then!" and I raced out and down the street.

I raced up to Gilbert, handed him his sack, and said, "I'll see you Saturday. I've got to get out to Amber Lake!" and ran to the door.

"All right, bride-to-be. Anxious bride-to-be I should say!" he laughed and sunk his teeth into that bagel. Of course I had to look back. Yep, cream cheese on the cheeks!

I packed everything and made three runs to the car. I checked the apartment and carried out my coffeemaker last. I locked up the apartment and headed to Amber Lake.

I got up to Carl's about eleven.

"Wow!" I said out loud as I pulled up and saw all those huge mum bushes. They were beautiful! Casey's crew was doing the final touch-ups to the yard. I pulled up in the back at the garage. Everything looked tremendous! Carl even had the American flag hanging from the front of the gazebo, over the water. Now it really reminded me of Thornton's!

Carl came out just grinning. I hugged him and kissed him. I told him the yard looked like he was expecting a national TV show to do a garden tour any minute.

Cassie and Joy were done with all the windows and were seriously cleaning everything. I couldn't believe the windows looked so good! Carl had only built the house several years ago, but everything gets dirty so quickly. We talked to Cassie and Joy several minutes, then went to the church to see what we needed to do there.

All the brass candelabras were already up with the candles. Huge ferns were arranged on podiums and the pews were already decorated with silk arrangements and burgundy wire laced bows. It was absolutely beautiful! Brother Darrel and Judy came in. We hugged them and talked a minute. Judy said they were decorating all the window sills this afternoon with the pillar candles and hurricane globes. They wanted to make sure they had enough decorations for the church and reception too. They were ahead of schedule, so I wasn't concerned. They had already done everything perfectly!

Brother Darrel and Casey were bringing over about seven banquet tables to Carl's and store them in his garage until Saturday morning. They said they would be back to set them up on the drive and patio. The pea gravel drive behind Carl's garage was perfect. It was a very large area, it was spotless and joined the patio. Also the view was perfect, overlooking the gazebo and Amber Lake! They were bringing folding chairs too. Carl had a long wide drive and the road out front had wide shoulders. No one would have any trouble parking and there wasn't much traffic anyway. The only cars that came by were the residents on this side of the lake and whoever came to see them.

Everything was in perfect shape at the church. Judy was preparing lunch for the lunch bunch from church. Susan was coming in any minute as were Cassie and Joy. Casey and his crew were delivering the button mum bushes and sitting them on the patio at Carl's. They would put them in the brass containers Saturday morning. Judy said Casey, Gary, and Jesse were coming to the church for lunch too. Judy asked us to stay for lunch. We thanked her for the invitation and everything they had done, but we had to run.

Carl and I stopped by Millie's and she had all the boutonnieres and corsages done. She was working on the bouquet for my sister. Also, she was decorating a basket for DeAndra. She would have deep red rose petals to sprinkle on the white runner. The men's boutonnieres were a yellow and crimson mum staggered. They were backed with a fern frond and a small cluster of berries with baby's breath throughout. She said Carol was picking up everything tomorrow and taking it all to church.

She had a beautiful white guest book and gold pen in a gold filigreed stand. We got that, returned to the church and put it on the podium at the back. We could hear our friends talking and laughing. They were having good food and having a good time too! I knew that Carl would be over there every day that he could be after we got back. I didn't blame him!

We got back in the Jeep and drove back to Carl's. Casey had delivered all the button mum bushes and they were so perfect they didn't look real. The colors were so vibrant! I couldn't wait to see all this come together. Carl's sister-in-law Suzanne was videotaping the wedding and reception from the back of the church. James, one of Carl's former business partners, was taping it from the front. I was so glad. When we came back from the honeymoon, we could sit back and watch it.

We got in my car and headed for Thornton's. I had to unload everything into my room. My gown was in a long white bag and my hat was in a hatbox so Carl didn't know what they looked like. He had probably imagined it from what I had told him, but that was all. I wanted to surprise him when I walked down the aisle. It did look terrific, especially with the hat, and I couldn't wait to see the look on his face.

He helped me carry my luggage in. We each made two trips and finally got everything. "Next time I carry all your stuff in, I won't have to leave!" he laughed.

"Well it won't be long now!" I smiled.

We had a wonderful lunch. He had finalized everything with his brothers. Alvin would be his best man. His other brothers, Don and John, would be singing songs Carl had picked out.

Alvin and his wife, Jean, were driving in and would be here sometime Friday. Don and his wife, Barbara, were driving too. They had already been on the road sightseeing for several days. John, his wife Suzanne, and their three children were driving in and said they would be here sometime Friday. I was curious to see what times they would arrive. I prayed their angels would guard them the entire trip (Ps. 34:7 and Ps. 91:10–12).

Carl had all the equipment there for his brothers to rehearse and had the music picked out and set up. Of course, they would have to check it all during the rehearsal. We were going to have quite a rehearsal dinner tomorrow night. At least thirty people! We had a huge banquet room reserved at Thornton's. It was decorated with old-fashioned wallpaper and antiques everywhere. It looked out over the lake, too.

"Carl, you know what would be neat?" I exclaimed.

"What is that?" he asked.

"We need to go through the albums and pick out pictures of us through the years and put them in frames and set them out!"

"Yeah, that is a good idea," he agreed. "We need to do that now. Tomorrow will be too hectic. Everyone will be coming in and it will be wild!" I implied.

We got in my car and went back to Carl's. Joy and Cassie were back there. They were putting finishing touches on the downstairs. They had done a super job. They had worked all morning on the entire kitchen. The refrigerator and stove were spotless in and out. They said they would be attending the wedding and reception. They were going to eat in the house so they could hear everyone comment on how spotless the house was. We all laughed. Carl and I said they deserved every compliment that would be spoken.

We started looking through the albums. Every picture I had at my home I had always duplicated for Carl. We came up with fifteen pictures we wanted framed. We had several we wanted enlarged. Carl knew a printer in Springfield that could do that from the picture. We carefully put all the pictures in a folder.

I took one last look to see if there were enough napkins, toilet paper, towels, washcloths, soap, shampoo, etc. Yep! Just as I thought. We needed more supplies. Carl made the grocery list out. He had forgotten to buy tea bags, butter, pancake mix, oil, and salt. Heaven knows he had enough "aged" cheese available.

I asked him what all that cheese was doing in his lunch carrier. He said it was for us to take on our honeymoon and this was the "really" aged cheese. The real good stuff! I looked at him and put on a fake smile and whispered, "Oh, how romantic."

He looked at me and then said, "Well, I like it. You don't have to eat any!"

"Don't start acting cheesy or I'll eat limburger!" I warned, laughing inside.

Carl said he would check in his bedroom and bath to make sure there was shampoo, soap and such. I thought I would take one last look in the refrigerator. Cassie came around the corner. "Cassie, the refrigerator just shines inside. I had to get past all Carl's cheese before I could see," I explained.

"Boy, he really likes that cheese, doesn't he!" she whispered.

"That is a story in itself!" I exclaimed in a low voice. We both giggled.

"Well, I need to supply the bathrooms. We better get going and buy what we need. Getting our pictures framed will take a while. Cassie, you and Joy just lock up when you are finished. I left your checks on the dining room table. Where is Joy, by the way?" Carl asked.

"Probably upstairs cleaning the bathroom corners with a toothbrush. I hope it is not yours, Carl," I answered. Carl was still waiting for Cassie's answer. I don't think he liked mine too well!

"I believe she is cleaning the bathroom off the den," Cassie answered.

"You two did a fantastic job! If you need any references, have them call me," Carl told her.

Carl and I left in my car for Springfield. We got all the pictures done and bought unique frames for each one. Then Carl had to stop at the grocery where he bought several vegetable and deli trays, huge ones! We bought another truckload of supplies and groceries. We didn't want our guests to go without anything.

We got back to Carl's and put all the supplies and groceries up. We took the frames apart and washed both sides of them. How did so much dirt get inside a new picture frame? I fixed a cup of coffee and fixed Carl a pitcher of iced tea. We really enjoyed putting our pictures together.

Two hours later we were all done and had them all set out. They looked terrific! We also had the laundry done, folded and put up, along with all the supplies. We just kept admiring the pictures. They really added a special touch. Twenty years of memories! Most newlyweds can't show that many years of courting.

Carl had several on his den desk and a couple in the foyer, where people would see them when they came in the front door. He had the rest of them spread out on those bare shelves in the den which were such a popular subject when Jan and the girls visited. After we got our wedding and honeymoon pictures back we would regroup and have room for all. It would really look good! It already did.

I called Trish and she came over and did my makeup and it looked great! I was so happy with my new look! I picked out the colors I wanted for my wedding and she planned to do my makeup at the church.

If my sister wanted to have her makeup done also, and liked it, I already knew I wanted to buy a kit for her. Trish would fix her up with a kit for her skin type and one that would compliment her perfectly. That would be my gift for her being my maid of honor. I thought she would love it!

Trish and I agreed that after everyone saw my new face Saturday, she would have a lot more business! I thought I should let Carl see my new look. I didn't want to shock him Saturday, plus I was wearing different colors to complement my dress anyway. He really liked my new look. It was a very natural look. Just what I liked!

I wanted a complete kit! Trish went back home and put together one for me with facial care items and makeup. She brought it back over and showed me how to use everything. Now I would look so nice for my family and friends coming in tomorrow, for my wedding, and honeymoon. I was so glad she had everything over at the house! I was thrilled that it all worked out and just in the nick of time!

After Trish left, Carl and I spent about an hour going throughout the house and making sure everything was in order and supplies were plentiful and in place. After all, tomorrow everyone would start coming in. Carl and I decided to eat a sandwich and salad for dinner. It would be our last evening to relax together.

We checked the lists both of us had made. We had everything ready for the wedding and the honeymoon. Of course, Carl said all I ever made sure we packed were the coffee supplies, the camera, and film. Of course, after looking at all the albums and pictures sitting out, he was very glad I had always had a camera with me!

It was already eight o'clock. He walked me out to my car. We kidded and hugged and said "goodnight" to each other. We agreed to get a good night's sleep and that I would return early for breakfast. It would be our last chance to be by ourselves until our honeymoon.

I drove back to Thornton's. I went to my room and sat up my coffee pot. I had my sugar and the milk was chilled in a small cooler. I wanted to lay everything out for the wedding to make sure I didn't forget anything. I had brought one of the framed pictures of Carl and I back to set on my nightstand. It was taken eleven years earlier on Long Island.

We had been guests at a wedding for one of Carl's business partners. He married a young British lady and they were going to live in England. They had met in New York City. The reception was at his parents' home. I remember their home was a mansion!

The bride was a runway model and had come to the city to gain fame and fortune. She said when she met him, fame went out the window. All she wanted to do was be his wife. Well, she got the fortune when she married into that family. She didn't know that up front though.

Carl said his partner told him the day he met her he was walking through Central Park in a pair of jeans and an old shirt. She was sitting on a park bench reading a book. He sat beside her and started talking to her. He asked her out and then they went out the next night and so on.

They would go to movies, or museums, eat at inexpensive places, walk in the park and do things that didn't cost much. He didn't want her to know he was wealthy. He told her she was so beautiful that she could date any rich man she wanted. She said she had dated rich men, but she never fell in love with one. About six months went by, and he asked her to marry him. She accepted and he took her home to meet his parents at their mansion on Long Island. The rest was history! I hoped they lived happily ever after.

It is funny how you don't forget fairytale romances I thought as I laid my wedding dress out. I laid out my hat, lace hose, pearl earrings, and blue garter. Mom said she would bring something old. I thought that when I saw them I would say "Gee thanks for bringing something old" and point at Dad and say, "I meant something old to wear." Of course, they wouldn't be surprised at me saying that.

"Well," I said to myself, "I better get some sleep. I can't be thinking about everything or I'll never get to sleep! I still can't believe this is really happening. Let's see, I have enough film and an extra battery for the camera. I have to stop this!" I walked over to the window and raised it up. I could hear the lake lapping in the distance. I could hear nature's sounds of the night. Oh, the moon was shining over the water and the gazebo was silhouetted in the moonlight. How beautiful! I sat by the window and wrapped Carl's gifts I had bought him . . . each one with a loving touch!

One more day I thought as I woke up! I showered, then got ready while I drank a cup of coffee. I slipped on a bronze silk casual suit and a pair of bronze slip-ons. I wanted something that was comfortable, but looked nice.

I thought about seeing my family. I hadn't seen all of them in such a long time! I had not seen some of Carl's family for years! I was anxious to see all of them. I couldn't wait until they saw Carl's home, Amber Lake, and of course, the church. My family was so excited when I told them Carl and I were getting married. Not only would they get to see us get married, they would get to see our new home too.

This was more than a wedding. It was a reunion of two families that were uniting in marriage. It was the fellowship of friends and family that shared love for a husband and wife. When would we ever have a get-together like that again? So far, just about everyone would be able to attend. That was unusual in itself!

I pulled up behind Carl's garage. He came out immediately and opened my door. Pepper was beside him, wagging his tail. Carl gave me a kiss and was ready to fix breakfast. That sounded good to me. He fixed me sausage, over-easy eggs, and biscuits with butter and black-berry jam. Both of us ate hearty, but I only ate one biscuit.

He wanted me to come into the den and sit down with him on the sectional. He put his arm around me and kissed me. He took a jewelry box off of the coffee table and gave it to me. "Honey, what is this?" I whispered. "Open it and you'll see!" he encouraged. I opened it and there was the most beautiful brooch! It was heart-shaped, made from fine pearls. It definitely looked like an antique to me. It was about one and a half inches across and just as long. Absolutely stunning! It was perfect for my dress!

"Carl, this is absolutely beautiful! Perfect! Where on earth did you find it?" I asked, stunned that he found this.

"Something just told me to stop in this little antique store in Clear Creek one day. I went in and told them that I was looking for a brooch. She brought out a display case and there it was, sitting right in the center. I told her I wanted the heart-shaped brooch. She laughed and said several people had wanted it and just never came back to get it. 'It must have been waiting just for you,' she told me. I told her it definitely was!" Carl said, thrilled he had found it.

"I wonder how old this is and who had it?" I asked as I examined it.

"She told me it was probably one hundred years old. A British lady that lived in Clear Creek years ago had it. That lady is the one who built that beautiful Victorian home there that you admire so much. It is the one that sits at the very end of Morrey Street. The street dead-ends right in front of her house," Carl answered.

"Oh, that beautiful three-story pink house with the cylindrical room on the third floor?" I asked.

"Yes, it is trimmed in white with the gray porch and roof. You know, you love the wrought-iron fence and that unique gate. It has every kind of tree and flower imaginable on the grounds," Carl answered.

"Is she the one that owned the brooch?" I asked.

"Yes. Her great-granddaughter lives there now. She sold it and some other fine jewelry belonging to her great-grandmother. She said she had so much they only kept the ones with precious stones. She told the owner of the store they had sold enough to restore the home and grounds. She was so pleased and said that is what her great-grandmother wanted," Carl said.

"Wow! I would love to know more about this brooch. I wonder what the British lady's name was?" I asked.

"Her name was Lady Chandler and she was given the brooch by her husband on her fiftieth birthday. He had a garden party for her at their home and she wore it on a flowing ivory Victorian dress," Carl said smiling, knowing I had picked out the same for my wedding dress.

"I understand there is a portrait painted of them in the garden as a remembrance of that day. The store owner told me that portrait hangs above the mantle of the sitting room in the home. She is wearing that dress and this brooch," Carl said.

"Then why would they want to sell the brooch?" I asked, thinking I surely wouldn't if I was the remaining family.

"The lady in the antique store said they kept all her precious stones and there were many! Her husband had a shipping business and traveled quite a bit. He had the brooch designed and made in the Orient. He told Lady Chandler that it was a token of their many years of wedded bliss," Carl replied.

"Oh, I want to see that portrait of them some day!" I exclaimed. "I bet they look just like us!" I giggled.

"I wonder whatever happened to them?" I asked.

"The lady told me he died later that year. It was late fall and she found him lying in the gazebo on a lounge. His Bible was open and laying in his lap," Carl said.

"What! I don't like this story too well, Carl," I informed him.

"Well, just wait. She had him buried in the backyard."

"Buried in the backyard!" I interrupted harshly.

"Just let me finish," Carl said, putting his hand up. "She had a beautiful memorial garden built way in the back," he explained.

"She is buried there with him now. He was about twenty years older than her. She joined him only a day after she turned eighty-five. They say the garden is beautiful and peaceful. Her home and the gardens are open in the spring along with the other historic homes in Clear Creek. The good news is her home is always open during the week for prayer meetings on certain nights," Carl said.

"I would love to go!" I answered.

"Here is what I wanted to tell you. They said her husband was a man of God. In his will he asked that the first floor of the home and the west garden be devoted to at least two prayer meetings a week. They would not interfere with any church service. Lady Chandler had the first prayer meeting scheduled a week after his death. She held it in the front room of the home. That is where the portrait is hanging above the mantle. The lady told me people came and many of them were curiosity seekers and then the Holy Spirit touched them," Carl smiled.

"The prayer meetings became very popular and many people were saved. She had a small pool built in the backyard for baptizing. It is only four and a half feet deep and had steps leading in and out of the water on both sides. She had concrete sculptures of angels and one life-size sculpture of Jesus with His hands reached out. There are flowers and ferns everywhere. Concrete benches are placed all around the pool for family and friends to attend baptizing services. Lady Chandler was very happy attending to her husband's wishes. The lady in the store told me she was joyous and peaceful until the day she died," Carl said.

"Now to the brooch. In her will she instructed her family to continue the prayer meetings. She instructed them to sell all her jewelry, with exception of all the precious stones her loving husband had given her. With this money they were to renovate the home and gardens. While the remodeling was going on, they were supposed to have the prayer meetings at Clear Creek Baptist Church those two nights. She had already talked to the church and they were happy to do that," Carl said.

"She wanted others to be blessed by buying the jewelry, which paid for the beautiful home to be open for God's work there. She felt they would be blessed with the love she and her husband shared all those years on earth. She also felt God would touch them for the cause they gave to. Every time the new owners of her jewelry wore these pieces they would be reminded of their love for each other and God's love for them," Carl replied.

"Carl, you told me all that just like you were reading it from a book. I'm amazed you remembered every detail. What a beautiful story! It must have been difficult losing the man she loved so dearly," I said in amazement of this story.

"Well, I am not done yet. She had this etched on her tombstone," he said and he paused. "'I walked in faith on earth, now I walk with Jesus and my beloved husband in heaven,'" Carl said, his voice cracking. I couldn't say anything. I looked down and lightly rubbed my fingers over the brooch. I was thankful beyond words Carl found and bought this brooch! I couldn't look up. I just reached over and hugged his neck and held him tight.

"I love this brooch for all the reasons," I whispered.

I backed up and looked at him and told him we definitely had to go the Lady Chandler's home for a prayer meeting as soon as we returned. Carl was in full agreement. I told him I was so excited about Amber Lake, Lakeside, and now Lady Chandler's. It would be very difficult to be back in the city even two months. "What about me?" Carl grinned.

"Oh, yeah, I knew there was something I left out. Thanks for reminding me!" I grinned. Then I reached up and kissed him.

About that time we heard a car pull up in the driveway. It was Carl's brother, Alvin and his wife, Jean. We both ran out and hugged them. Alvin and Jean said the rest of them were en route somewhere and laughed. They said it was a beautiful drive, but they were glad to get out of the car! We went in and put them in the Victorian room. They loved the house. We visited and then we heard another car. It was Carl's brother, Don and his wife, Barbara. We all ran out and greeted them. We all took their luggage and put it in the peaches and cream room.

Carl fixed a cheese tray and all kinds of crackers and started pouring iced tea. Then he brought out a huge vegetable tray and deli tray of every different kind of sliced meat. He sat them on the kitchen bar. He had about five different kinds of bread and about seven boxes of different party crackers. Then he sat out a cream cheese pie, chess pie, pecan pie, and a huge sheet cake—carrot cake with cream cheese icing. He even had to have dessert with cheese in it! Oh, I wanted to sample it all, and thankfully I couldn't gain that much weight before tomorrow anyway.

I called Thornton's. Mom, Dad, Sis, and the boys had just gotten in. I told them to come on to Carl's and we would visit and eat a bite. They had just unloaded. They had directions to Carl's and said they would be on their way. I fixed a pot of coffee. Carl sat out fruit tea and had the refrigerator full of juices and soft drinks.

Carl called Brother Darrel and Judy and told them to come on over and meet everyone. They got there about the same time Mom, Dad, Sis, Brian, and Thomas did.

I was so glad to see my family! The boys looked like they had grown five inches since I had seen them. They took off for the paddleboat. They were real good swimmers and knew water safety. I looked out the window and made sure they had on their life jackets. They did and both of them had about three little sandwiches and a soft drink. Mom, Dad, and Sis loved the house, especially the gazebo! That was Mom's favorite. Dad liked the lake and woods. Sis liked the Victorian room.

I called Thornton's back and Carol was there getting everything in order for tomorrow. She was almost finished. I told her to be on the lookout for my Uncle Robert, his wife Dorothy, and my Aunt Annabelle. I asked her to bring them out to Carl's. She said she would. She said Glenn had been up at Russ's cabin at Pine Mountain. She said they played golf all morning and had a few songs they were trying to put together this afternoon. She was expecting Glenn back any minute. Russ was going to bring him back to Thornton's.

I told her everything sounded like it was right on schedule. I told her I had called Max about available bed and breakfasts or homes that would easily convert into one. He didn't have anything right now and knew this entire area very well and what was for sale. He said he would definitely keep Carl and I posted when something like that came on the market. I told her I would see her whenever the rest of my family arrived there and she came out with them.

Another car pulled up. It was Carl's youngest brother, John and his wife, Suzanne, and their children: John Jr., Alexis, and Isaac. We all went back out and greeted them. We had their car surrounded. "I bet you never had a welcoming committee like this," I laughed. We all carried in their things and put them in the fin and feather room. Isaac would sleep on one of the cots Carl used for overnight fishing trips. Also Alexis and John Jr. were going to stay in the huge den with Amanda, Linda, Brian, and Thomas.

Jean Marie was brave enough to volunteer to stay out there with the young crowd. She and several others would sleep on the very comfy sectional, since it was huge. Carl always had extra pillows and extra thick sleeping bags, so all the kids would fare well. Plus there was a half bath in the back of the den.

Not only that, there was pizza, popcorn, and hot chocolate Carl had bought just for them. It was a good thing Jean Marie was in charge of the "Slumber Party." It wasn't the slumber I was concerned about, it was the party! They were all good kids and loved it here. They were all getting along great and talked nonstop, comparing their schools and how one differed from the other.

There was so much visiting and talking. It was a good thing Carl's home was in the country! Pepper greeted each car that pulled up and then would go lie back down. Carol and Glenn drove up and they had Annabelle with them. Robert and Dorothy were just behind in their car. We all went out again and greeted them.

All of us visited and ate all afternoon. I couldn't help but watch the teenagers with the paddleboat. They seemed to all be having a ball! The adults reminisced, looked at pictures, went out to the gazebo, or sat in the yard. All the women loved the house. The men loved the lake, woods, and the den. Everyone loved the gazebo!

Later that afternoon, we all left and traveled to Lakeside Church in what looked like a caravan. Brother Darrel and Judy picked up David and Glenn at the Goodfellows. They would be our ushers along with Adon and Ian. John Jr. would enjoy having some boys around his own age.

We arrived there and Kimberly and her two nieces were sitting at one of the picnic tables with Sharon. Carl and I got out and went up to them. Brother Darrel and Judy took everyone around the church-yard and the lake. "Sharon, how are you doing?" I chimed. She got up and we hugged. She said she was doing fine. I hugged Kimberly and the two nieces. I asked them how long they had been at Amber Lake, and she said they came in that morning.

I asked her where they were staying and she told me she was staying at Sharon's. "You are!" I exclaimed with great surprise. "Well, how nice! Faune told me at work you were only there part-time now. She said in a month or so it may not even be that. I was so shocked!" I told her. Kimberly and Sharon laughed.

"Honey, that is true," Kimberly said. "I'm keeping really busy with Your Loss Is His Gain. Sharon and I talked that Sunday you were baptized. When you brought her up for the revival and I met her I told several of the church ladies about her seminar. They were really interested. Sharon said she was so busy trying to tie all the loose ends together. I told her I would help her and she accepted. God lead me with the input and both of us started finalizing this seminar," she informed us.

"Grief and depression leads us to destroy our bodies as well as our minds. I knew how to get people over that hump! God lead both of us to understand all types of problems and how to overcome them mentally, spiritually, and physically. In other words, your loss is His gain!" Kimberly laughed.

Sharon yelled, "Amen to that!" She continued with, "God showed me that both of us are needed to put this together and totally accomplish this vision and mission. This way we can help and lift each other up and encourage each other. We will have a ball going everywhere and preaching to these ladies and gentlemen. We are ready!"

"Praise God!" Kimberly laughed and waved her hands. Sharon looked at her and started laughing.

"Are you serious? You two are both putting this together to hit the road?" I asked.

"Yes ma'am!" they both chirped. "We will stay here or go wherever God leads us to go. No problem!" Kimberly giggled.

Carl was laughing and said, "Amen to that!"

I was so happy for them! I thought how wonderful the Lord worked all this out! I felt like I had been instrumental in arranging their meeting and that made me feel good. Of course, the only reason I was instrumental is that both of them had been praying for me. I was so excited for them.

They said they had paperwork all over Sharon's den and were in the process of putting all their notes together to form a study and planning guide. The Lord would take them to the next step after they put the guide together for publishing.

Sharon had a good size home she had bought at an auction about two years ago. It was two miles north of Amber Lake and sat on one acre of land. She had been living about thirty-eight miles from here and heard about the auction and came down here. She got it at a good price and said she loved Amber Lake the minute she saw it. She had been working in Springfield as an administrative assistant for a corporation, but was about to quit and let her seminars provide for her living. After all, put the Kingdom of God first and everything else will fall into place

(Matt. 6:33). She said the Lord had not told her to quit her job yet, so she wouldn't until she knew that was right and she had peace about it. Good idea!

Kimberly was thinking about buying the Hitch'n Post in Amber Lake. It was a two-story home that was on the main street, but away from the center of town. It had been a boutique for antiques and local crafts. The family that owned it lived upstairs and used the whole downstairs for their business. They were moving to Boston to refinish and sell antiques with some of their family. They would be doing the same type of work on a much larger scale and to a larger market of people.

This home would be perfect for her. Sharon and Kimberly would use the downstairs as their office, study, and headquarters for mail, calls, and seminars if necessary. Kimberly would have the entire upstairs to live in, and it was beautiful! It was all ready to live in. It had a huge state-of-the-art kitchen in it and a huge bath. Kimberly loved the enormous tub! There was one room set up on the main floor that was perfect for local seminars or meetings.

It was a beautiful old home that was painted in sunshine yellow with white shutters and a gray roof and porch. It had a white fence around it and perennials planted everywhere that bloomed from early spring to late fall. You felt joy and sunshine when you looked at it! I was so happy and excited for them I was beside myself. I hoped Kimberly would buy it. Wouldn't that be something, I thought, Kimberly living here and she and Sharon working together. Like Sharon would always say, "Ain't God good!"

"You all ready to rehearse this wedding folks? Let's go, I'm ready to eat again already!" Brother Darrel shouted from the church steps. Everybody heard him from the lake, the yard, and the picnic area and started laughing. We had only stopped eating about two hours ago!

We all gathered together and went into the church. It was so beautiful and serene! Everybody loved the church and all the decorations were perfect! It turned out as beautiful as we had pictured in our imaginations.

Judy took everyone on a tour of the church. They all loved the fellowship hall. She informed all of us they were going to start serving lunch to the public next Wednesday. All lunches would be three dollars and Brother Darrel or Casey would give a fifteen minute sermon. Carl said he would fill in if both of them were unavailable. He taught Sunday school years ago and really loved teaching and knew his Bible very well. Judy had a beautiful voice and she would sing a song. If April was around, she would sing a song, too.

Everybody whispered back and forth what a good idea that was. Many thought they would take that idea back home to their church. It was amazing to see how the Lord works! How he gives us wisdom when we ask him and then all of a sudden there is a solution or an idea (James 1:5). Who knows how many would be saved from those church lunches!

It was a beautiful evening and the sun mellowed and lit the windows in amber hues. We all rehearsed and the songs were practiced and all the music was set-up and ready to go. We had finalized everything. Everybody knew what to do and when.

All of us then drove to Thornton's. Charmaine greeted us. She had tables set for thirty people. It worked out perfectly. We talked and laughed and the food was delicious! There was a fire going in the fireplace and the windows were barely open.

The lake and woods serenaded us with the sound of lapping water and rustling leaves in the night breeze. The moon was shining on the lake and it looked like a huge silver glistening blanket laid in the middle of the rolling countryside.

We talked and laughed and then we all walked through the gardens and out to the gazebo. We started parting our ways after three hours of visiting. A caravan headed back to Carl's home and Amber Lake. I headed to my room at Thornton's. Carol, Glenn, and my family were all there. We finally said goodnight and turned in.

I looked out my window over the lake. The gazebo was silhouetted in the moonlight. "Tomorrow night," I thought, "I'll be married!" I turned and looked at my wedding dress and remembered what all God had done in my life. I remembered how quickly He spared me from death and hell! He turned my whole life around, and suddenly (Acts 16:26). Praise God!

My eyes opened fixed on the clock—six o'clock. "Today is my wedding day!" I realized excitedly. I lay there for a while and relaxed. I fixed a cup of coffee and drank it while I looked out the window and over the lake. I finally took a shower and washed my hair.

I called mom and dad about eight o'clock. We all decided to meet for breakfast at nine o'clock. Carol, Glenn, Robert, Dorothy, Annabelle, Mom, Dad, Sis, Brian, Thomas, and I all ate breakfast together. Praise God it was a beautiful day. We talked and laughed over old times, and brought each other up to date on our recent activities and future plans.

In the midst of the laughter, my heart realized how precious life was and that we cannot take anyone or anything for granted. I didn't know when we would be together again or if we ever would. Time goes so quickly and none of us are promised tomorrow. As long as all of us are saved, we will spend eternity in heaven. That is the only thing that is everlasting! "Lord," I prayed, "let us realize the life that we have through your precious Son, Jesus Christ." I treasured these moments and that we were all able to be together.

We finished about eleven and I hugged my family and they said they were going to drive around Silver Lake and look at some of those antique shops for about an hour. Then they would come back and get ready for the wedding.

Carol and I finalized everything with Thornton's. Glenn and Carol were going to get ready and go to Carl's and make sure everything was ready to be set up as soon as the wedding was over. She said Carl had called her this morning and had gone to the airport to pick up Ray, Jan, Amanda, Linda, and Michael. She said they would get back to Carl's about noon. They were all going to stay in Carl's bedroom tonight.

She gave me a hug and said she would see me over at the church and help me with whatever I needed. She said Judy had picked up all the boutonnieres, bouquets, and corsages. They were all in the fellowship hall in the refrigerator.

I went upstairs and freshened up and redid my hair a little bit. Trish was going to meet me at the church and do my makeup. I packed and carried all my things to my car. I left and headed to Lakeside Church.

Judy was already in the fellowship hall. She fixed a pot of coffee for those of us in the wedding party. Carol came in and said that Glenn was going to Carl's to help transport people that had to be at the church early. He was picking up David and Glenn too. We had two Glenns with us today! Jan would be at the guest book. Carl and Alvin were already on their way over.

Trish did my makeup. It looked great! I started getting dressed. I put on my lace hose and blue garter, and Mom brought me an old bracelet my great-aunt had given her. I slipped on my dress with Sis and Mom's help. I pinned on the pearl brooch and checked the clasp.

Sis got in her dress with Mom's help. It was a gold Victorian dress with a fitted waist and high neck. It was beautiful! She looked wonderful in her new makeup. She was definitely getting a kit from me.

Trish was going to put it together and bring it to her at church tomorrow. She was so happy about how pretty she looked and she should have been! Mom and Dad would be proud of their two daughters. The photographer came in and took pictures of Mom and Sis making sure my dress and hat were just right. Carl and Alvin would be in black tuxes, white shirts, and gold cummerbunds.

I heard the music start! Dad came back and grinned and said, "Well, if you are going to change your mind, you have about ten minutes." We all giggled. I took Dad's arm and walked to the back of the church. I had heard John and Don singing. Then I heard Carl, Alvin, Don, and John sing, "Shine On Us." After that, April sang, "If You Could See What I See." It was time for the flower girl and ring bearer to walk down the aisle. They looked so cute—just like little models! The guests were all smiling and there were many ohs and ahs. The church was full!

I saw Franklin, Robbie, Kent, and Honey sitting up there. Nick and Angelina were there with his mother and all the children. I saw Peggy and Eugene with Gilbert and Tiffany. There was Mike, his mother, and on the other side of him, a pretty young woman. I guessed she was his girlfriend! Sam was in front of Kent and Franklin. The young lady with him, Jamie, was so pretty. Carol and Glenn were sitting on the other side of him.

The wedding march started! Everyone stood up and turned. Dad and I started down the aisle. My heart was in my throat! There was Carl, Alvin, Sis, and Brother Darrel. They looked a mile away! Don sang "The Lord's Prayer" as we lit the unity candle.

I repeated the vows after Brother Darrel, never taking my eyes off Carl. "I now pronounce you husband and wife. You may kiss the bride," Brother Darrel said. Carl and I kissed and smiled at each other. "Ladies and gentlemen, I give you Mr. and Mrs. Carl Frost," Brother Darrel said as we turned to a church full of smiling faces. Everything was so beautiful, all the happy faces, the sun streaming in the windows, all the decorations . . . everything glowed inside me and throughout my new world. I couldn't stop looking at Carl and his smile.

The photographer took the family pictures and our pictures. All the children were passing out maps to Carl's house for the reception. It was only fifteen minutes away and most of the people knew where it was. Everyone taking care of the reception had already left for Carl's house.

Carl and I kept looking at each other. Once we knew we were getting married, I felt like the day would never arrive. Now, I felt like I was eighteen again! Carl must have felt the same way. We kept giggling at each other.

We finally got in my car which all the boys had decorated. There were tin cans tied to the back bumper and shaving cream foam spelled out "Just Married!" We could barely see out the window!

At Carl's we pulled up to a mass of people on the patio. The tables were decorated beautifully and the food looked and tasted fantastic. We all ate and talked and everyone was thoroughly enjoying the outdoors. It was gorgeous weather! Jan and the girls all three hugged me and said, "Now do you believe prayers are answered?" and laughed. "Can you believe this!" I shook my head. A reception line was formed and cameras and videos were clicking and running.

Carl and I walked to the gazebo, and everyone gathered around. We told them that we were saved by the blood of Jesus, we dedicated our marriage to God, and we would always ask for His help and guidance in our marriage and our lives. We would pray for each other and we would pray together and we would walk in faith. With that we toasted to our lives together. We fed each other a piece of wedding cake. I didn't want to cut it because it was so pretty. Peggy had outdone herself and had decorated it exactly like I asked her to. It was also delicious. We all ate cake and had punch. I joked that I knew Gilbert hadn't got into the cake on the way here since he didn't have icing on both cheeks!

We took more pictures in the gazebo and throughout the yard. There were people sitting on the park benches enjoying the lake as well as the woods, which were full of crimson, orange, and yellow trees. It was perfect.

April caught my bouquet. Sam caught the garter. I don't think he needed to catch the garter to know he would be the next one married. When he and Jamie looked at one another, sparks flew. It was the same with Mike and his girlfriend, Renee.

After another hour, Carl and I went in the house and changed into our denim outfits. He put his bags in my car. He went over and talked to Ray and Jan and put him in charge of the household. Ray and Jan had Carl's Jeep and they knew about the boat and certainly knew where all the fishing gear was!

Carl had bought groceries to last through Monday. He had bought everything from steaks for the grill to pancake batter. Carl's family were leaving out Monday morning and heading back. His brothers had promised Brother Darrel they would sing Sunday morning at Lakeside. Both of our families were all going to Lakeside Sunday morning. Ray and Jan would stay most of the week. Brother Darrel and Judy would be back and forth and would take them back to the airport. Ray would tell the Goodfellows when he was leaving and they would check on the house. Pepper was already over there and felt right at home.

All the families seemed to be enjoying each other's company. Carl's family, my family, and our church family were having a great reunion. . . . Yes, a wonderful reunion!

Carl and I made sure we had everything in the car. As we walked out the back patio door everyone blew bubbles. They looked great against that royal blue sky with drifting white clouds. Everyone gathered in front of us and waved. We backed down the driveway, tooted, and waved back at them.

I will never forget that sight. All the family and friends of our lifetime, waving to us as we started off on our life together. I waved until we rounded the bend, heading down the road of life as husband and wife.

A Thief in the Night

ABOUT TWENTY MINUTES LATER WE STOPPED AND TOOK THE TIN cans off the car. We had gotten enough laughs from people looking at us, not to mention the commotion we were making. We drove until we hit the coast. We traveled up the coastline and the first seafood restaurant we came to we stopped. It was a buffet and Carl knew that was my favorite and we ate to our heart's delight. We asked our waiter about hotels and places to see up the coastline and he gave us some great places to see and stay. We told him we had just gotten married and he brought us each a luscious chocolate dessert on the house.

We left and drove up the coast to a place he had mentioned, which was a very unique, luxury hotel. We told them we wanted a wedding suite and there was one available. We went and looked at it. It was beautiful, so we took it. It was on the third floor and looked out over the ocean and was totally private. It had a balcony all to itself. The ceiling was vaulted, the bed was king-size, and the bathroom was huge with a red heart-shaped Jacuzzi.

I gave Carl one of his gifts. He opened it up and he went into the bathroom and slipped on the gray silk lounging pajamas. He came out, and they looked nice on him. I slipped on the cranberry ensemble and he said it was beautiful. We turned all the lights out, except for one low light in the bath. We stepped out on the balcony and listened to the ocean.

The moon was shining across the waters—a sight to behold. The balmy breeze was coming in across the beach and upon our faces. We stood there and held each other in the night. I had not known a togetherness like this in the twenty years I had known Carl. This was beyond words. It was peaceful, loving, and reassuring. God had His hand on this marriage, because we turned ourselves and our marriage over to Him . . . and the two shall become one (Matt. 19:5–6).

We had a leisurely morning. We opened the door to the ocean and lay in the bed and talked about what we wanted to do. We figured we would ride the coastline and stop when we wanted to. I laid my head on Carl's chest and I could hear his heartbeat as I looked out over the ocean. It reminded me how awesome God was. The rhythm of the world He set up to keep life going. The tide coming in, the heartbeat, our breath. All moving, flowing, giving, and sustaining life. How we take it for granted, and how beautiful and glorious it is!

I fixed my cup of coffee. Carl made sure I had my whole milk and sugar. I drank a cup of coffee and stood out on the balcony in awe of the majestic and powerful ocean. I just could not imagine how powerful God must be. He was the one that created the oceans! My mind could not fathom His greatness, and I couldn't believe we actually worried and wondered if He could do things in our life! How sad! How ignorant we are and how insulting to the Father.

I leaned over and kissed Carl. He was lying there enjoying the ocean breeze coming in. It was refreshing and relaxing! I took a shower and washed my hair and got another cup of coffee and looked at Carl again. He was totally resting and so full of peace. I thought about the rat race we had been in and how we were always trying to do everything ourselves. How stupid we were! Yes, we were successful in the business world, but what a price to pay. We should have been married years earlier!

It wouldn't have worked if we had not given it to God, however. Now I felt we had it all! Most people never got to have what we had right then. How blessed are those who trust God earlier in their lives and how dreadful for those who never know God.

How it must grieve God, I thought, to have given us everything and we keep doing it our way and never let Him lead our lives. That isn't even to mention what it does to us. We just complain, blame people, and think we had bad luck! A trick from Satan. God can turn it all around to His glory! "Thank you, Jesus!" I said as I looked out over the ocean.

"What?" called Carl.

I turned and laughed. "I'm just thanking God for what He has done in our lives," I whispered to Carl.

He laid there motionless and whispered, "Well, you should be thankful." I giggled at him. He finally decided to get up.

"I want to call the front desk and ask about the church around the bend. I can see the church steeple from the balcony. It is on the same side as we are about a mile down the road," I told him.

I called and they gave me the name. It was a Baptist church, and they had a service at eleven o'clock and said to come as you are. Carl was up by now. "Let's go eat some breakfast and go on down there. Checkout isn't until one o'clock here," I suggested.

"OK," he said.

We ate breakfast and then went to church. It was a beautiful church inside. The service and people were great! Several of them talked to us afterwards and gave us all kinds of places to see, visit, and dine. We came back and checked out and walked up and down the beach for about an hour. I realized how much I had missed it. I hadn't been to the beach for at least five years and I wasn't that far from it. It just renewed me. Amber Lake renewed me too. The Lord said to renew yourself daily. I sure saw why. Why on earth didn't we do what He told us? Oh well, I thought, He is wondering the same thing, I am sure! Boy, we think we are so smart and we are nothing without Him!

We got in the car and drove up the coast. We ran across some of the quaintest, unique little towns and villages. We ate lunch along the ocean and it was another great buffet. Food even tasted better when you were at peace. Carl and I sat there and talked about the things we needed to buy for the kitchen. Carl loved to cook. I knew I would if I had the time.

Oh well, it wouldn't be too much longer before I would be out of the rat race. He wanted to plant a garden in the spring. Then he wanted to have a small orchard on the north side of his land. He said we would really enjoy it. We would have more fruit than we needed and he would let the neighbors and church members have most of it. He said I would love all of those spring blossoms. That I would!

"Can you imagine what heaven must look like if we are awe struck over what things on earth look like? Can you imagine what the fruit and vegetables look like? Remember in the Bible where it said it took two men to carry a cluster of grapes (Num. 13:23). Can you imagine how delicious the food must be!" I exclaimed.

"The Bible also says we cannot even imagine how wonderful it is! Think about that a minute!" Carl suggested.

"Now that I know what I know it scares me to think anyone would go to hell rather than accept Jesus as their Saviour! We spend eternity in hell for not taking a couple of minutes to repent and ask Him into our hearts! It only takes a few minutes to spare us from eternity in Hell . . . eternity! Then there are all the blessings and promises He pours on you while you are here!" I replied, shaking my head. "I was the same way for years and only through prayers was I saved. I would have never seen it on my own! I shudder to think of being back where I was. . . . To think I thought I was doing so-o-o good in life. Ha!"

We found another beautiful place to stay on the ocean. We walked along the beach at sunset and gathered up some shells. We had seafood again at a restaurant overlooking the beach. What a wonderful night. Carl and I both lay in the bed with the balcony doors open and listened to the music of the ocean.

We spent the next couple of days riding the coastline gathering shells, eating seafood, and touring places that sounded interesting. Wednesday evening we ended up in a unique little fishing village and attended church services there. It was a very small, old church. It was like stepping back in time.

They had candles lit in every window and at the altar. I could hear the seagulls outside. It was like a place you only read about and never have the opportunity to visit. I could smell the salty breeze every time the back door opened and someone quietly took a seat in the back.

We sang old hymns and the preacher preached a fire and brimstone message. If anyone didn't want to be saved after that message, they were asleep. He said most preachers didn't preach like that anymore. He said hell is real! Many preach what people want to hear, not what God wants to tell them (2 Cor. 4:1–5). You know, he was right! We found out afterwards he was eighty-five years old. He was full of fire. God sure wasn't done using him!

The church members told us there was a bed and breakfast about ten miles down the road. They said the food was great and there were usually rooms available. This time of year there were not many travelers anyway. That made me like it even more. The preacher said if we hadn't eaten supper yet we needed to stop at the Lobster Pit. Wednesday night was a big night there, even if it was a hole in the wall. He told us it was only three miles down the road. He and his wife thought it was the best around.

We invited them to supper as our guests. He said he and his wife had eaten a sandwich before church, but they sure would like to have some lobster, so we followed them down there. Everyone in the restaurant knew him and his wife. His name was Brother Medlock and his wife's name was Ruth. We ate and talked and Carl told him about us and how God had changed our lives.

He said God had not told him to quit preaching the Gospel. There were too many people that needed to hear the message. The real message, not the watered down version. He said God told him time was short and there was no time to water down or mix words. I knew then why God had blessed them with good health and boldness. He takes care of His people!

We had a great fellowship with them. He gave Carl his card and Carl gave him his business card and scratched out the office number and wrote the Amber Lake information on it. He and his wife hugged us and they went to their car. He looked back and said, "If we don't see you here again, we will see you on the other side." They just laughed and drove away waving.

Carl and I stayed at the bed and breakfast we were told about. We had a huge room upstairs overlooking the ocean. The room had a twelve foot ceiling and it was painted in white with a large cherry wood parlor fan. The walls were painted bubble gum pink and all the trim and the huge fireplace were painted in white enamel. I never thought I would like that color of pink, but I loved it in this room. I couldn't stop looking at everything!

The bathroom had a claw foot tub and old wood floors. In the bedroom, there was a queen-size iron bed. There were big throw rugs and runners with flowers on them in pink and burgundy. The bed was very high and had a white crochet dust ruffle. The curtains were white crochet and hung at two tall windows with a huge fern on a cherry plant stand between the windows. The furniture was all dark antiques and highly polished. They had candles in the room and told me I could light them. All the intricate white enamel glistened in the candlelight . . . so beautiful . . . so romantic. We opened both the windows about two inches and the salty breeze moved in.

I woke up about two in the morning and just looked at the beautiful old room. The large white candles were still burning and the breeze rustled the curtains. I blew the candles out and went back to bed and snuggled up to Carl. I could tell he was at peace in his heart and mind. He was sleeping so soundly every night. So was I for that matter!

We had a wonderful breakfast downstairs and then drove on up the coast. We had decided to stay at bed and breakfasts along the way if possible. They were so unique. We ran upon a harbor town and the fishing boats were coming in. We got a kick out of watching them unload their catch for the day. We visited old shops and stores and we strolled along the beach for about one hour. We had collected quite a few shells by now. It was a breezy and cloudy day, but it was still beautiful. The ocean seemed to have a different color every day, depending on whether it was cloudy or sunny.

The next day we turned inland to head home and we decided to take the back roads. We wanted to experience the flavor of the country and enjoy the little towns and villages. I had taken about five rolls of film already. We stayed at bed and breakfasts all the way home. We picked up specialty food items for Carl's friends and family along the way. I picked up local craft items for the ladies. I found things that were unique but would go in any style home.

On Saturday we came upon a fall festival in a beautiful valley town. It was so much fun! We ate pumpkin pie and homemade ice cream, and there were beautiful crafts everywhere. I picked up some handmade Christmas decorations for our home as well as gifts. My car was crammed full of stuff. Carl said it was a good thing we didn't bring the Jeep! I laughed at that. We were having a ball shopping though.

We went through beautiful little towns nestled in valleys. There was always a church steeple or two rising high above each town. We were finding something intriguing about each town. No crowds, just friendly local people. I had taken so many pictures! The kind of simple nostalgic pictures I loved to see on the cover of sentimental greeting cards.

I was enjoying a type of life I always knew existed. I had touched the edge of it before, but never got to step in and let it fulfill my spirit. At least the pictures I had taken would let someone touch these treasures with their eyes and relax their thoughts.

We stayed at a beautiful bed and breakfast Saturday night. It was a huge two-story white house with black shutters. It had a very wide staircase and our room was upstairs. It was painted a sunny yellow and the woodwork was shiny white enamel again. All the furniture was antique oak and the curtains were all white lace. The throw rugs matched the comforter, which was black and white checkered with yellow sunflowers throughout. The bed was king-size in massive oak.

There were black tin trays hanging on the wall with flowers painted on each one. They must have been antiques and each one was different. There were white enamel shelves hanging between the trays and they were full of rare bird houses.

A black wrought-iron parlor settee sat at the side of the room. The seats were black and white checkered and there was a chess game on the table with black and white pieces. Two huge ferns adorned the room on oak plant stands. The sun was just setting and the golden rays came through the windows, making the room quite dramatic. Carl said next he would have to buy a bed and breakfast just so I could decorate it. Boy, would that be fun!

We had already found a church to go to in the morning. We drove around the old town a little bit before it got totally dark. There were many old homes and all of them had artistic fall decorations, yet they were all different. "Oh boy, I have a home I can decorate now. I can do up the front yard, the porch, and the gazebo too!" I announced to Carl.

"I can imagine!" he sighed as I chuckled. He knew I loved to decorate!

We found a nice restaurant in town, known for its great steaks. Oh, that sounded good to us. We had a hearty meal. We got back in the car and drove up and down a few more streets. People had their drapes wide open and the homes were so pretty inside. The residents in this town were very proud of their homes and it showed. They didn't mind letting people see in either, which was fine with me.

We stopped at a little bookstore. I bought some magazines about decorating your home for Christmas. I bought another one that was loaded with Thanksgiving recipes and decorating tips. Carl bought a hunting and fishing magazine. How our lives had changed in the short time we had been at Amber Lake! Well, I wasn't there quite yet.

We went back to our room. The owner had candles sitting around the room and she gave me permission to light them. I lit about three of them in the big hurricane glasses and I lit one in the bathroom. All the colors looked so romantic. We relaxed and read and talked about what we wanted to do for the holidays.

I knew one thing we needed to do when we got back. We needed to get Carl's furnished apartment sold! Carl agreed. He said there were a few new men who had come into the company and he thought they may be interested. I had to keep mine until I cleared out of the city. That didn't mean I couldn't start looking at prospects.

I got up to a beautiful sunrise. That yellow room really lit up when the sun hit the east window. I fixed my coffee on the large counter in the bathroom and drank a cup while I looked out the east and then the west window. The backyard was pretty too. There was a picket fence in the back painted stark white and an old double wash tub sat in the corner with flowers pouring out and about. There was a flagpole and the flag was flying in the morning breeze. There was a little circular flower garden around it not wider than eighteen inches brimming over with red begonias.

By the time I got out of the shower, Carl was up and looking out the windows too. We went down and ate a great breakfast and then we checked out. We enjoyed the church service and were having a ball meeting new people in these different churches. Each place we stopped was a wonderful experience and each church had its very own personality and style. I really enjoyed that!

We traveled through the tranquil countryside all day. I used up another whole roll of film just today! We saw red barns, rambling creeks, old farm houses, and country stores with fallen leaves lying around them like a flowing full skirt. There were little children in bright colored turtlenecks and blue jeans swinging on old rope swings and jumping in crunchy leaves. I was sure that mothers were fixing pumpkin pies and hot cider with a cinnamon stick in their kitchens too.

I could see children laughing and darting about with the family dog at their heels. Soon their back doors would swing shut for the evening with bicycles and wagons at the bottom of the steps. Dads were lighting fireplaces and stretching out in their favorite recliner to read the evening paper. Yes, that was America to me.

We saw a bed and breakfast right before sunset and thought we would check to see if they had a vacancy. They did and back upstairs we went again. The room we had I would have called the lilac and lavender room. It had tall ceilings, an ivory painted ceiling with antique white wallpaper with bouquets of lilacs throughout. It was very rich and very dramatic with whitewashed oak furniture. There was a huge crystal vase full of lilacs, silk of course, on top of the dresser. It was taking up most of the mirror and gave reflections of a hundred lilacs.

The comforter was lavender satin with a dust ruffle to match and ivory satin pillows in every shape laid at the top. Creamy satin curtains hung from the windows and draped dramatically onto the floor, like thick vanilla icing flowing off a warm cake. Lilac satin balloon valances hung above. There were shelves painted in cream, hanging throughout the room with either china plates or cups and saucers. All the china had the colors of lilac, lavender, or purple in them. They were very delicate and beautiful—real attention-getters.

The bathroom had an ivory claw foot tub and a cream marble counter with all gold fixtures. The towels and clothes were the palest lilac. The room was painted a light lavender with a beautiful lilac border about a foot deep. The border was of flowers in country gardens and of wisteria hanging above the heads of seated lovers in romantic gardens. The floors in the bedroom and bath were old wide planked oak, with the bath gracing a deep plush lilac runner.

In the center of the bedroom was a huge circular rug in cream with a small whitewashed circular table and two side chairs to match. It was set with antique plates, cups and saucers in pale lilac trimmed with a deep lilac border with splashes of gold. Gold plated flatware lay on ivory linen to serve dinner for two. Five gold plated candle sticks were staggered in height and held French vanilla candles.

Carl said, "Well, this is really different!"

I laughed inside and ironically stated, "It is rather outdoorsy though," and waited for his reaction.

"Ha!" he exclaimed. That night there was a terrible storm. Lightning flickered at the windows and the wind howled through the trees outside. Even a storm was beautiful if you were not afraid of it. It passed as quickly as it came.

I woke to an incredibly clear morning. I guess the storm was God's way of clearing the air, literally! As usual, I fixed a cup of coffee and looked out the windows. I went on and got ready with my second cup of coffee on the bathroom counter. When I came out Carl was sitting up in the bed reading his Bible. "Good morning, sweetie," I said. He looked at me and smiled. He got ready and we went down and ate breakfast. I took pictures, as I had done with every bed and breakfast we had stayed in.

We drove through the countryside all day and ate lunch and dinner at two quaint little restaurants. The place we ate dinner was only two hours north of Amber Lake. They had the best salad, ribeye steak, and apple dumplings I had ever had in my life. That was their specialty and we had to go back soon! We arrived home at dusk.

22222222

Oh, it was so good to be home! Yes, home! We unloaded what we could before it got dark. It felt so wonderful to walk into this beautiful house and know it belonged to both of us. I felt different about everything in my life. I don't think Carl really knew how I felt inside. All I could say was, "Carl you will never know how happy I am. No words can express it!" He looked at me and chuckled and kissed me on the end of my nose. "Kissing me on the end of the nose. Gee, I guess the honeymoon is over and the minute we hit the doorstep!" I exclaimed.

He laughed harder then and held me and whispered, "You couldn't be farther from the truth."

Ray and Jan had left us a note on the kitchen table. It read:

Dear Honeymooners,

We know you had a wonderful time. Can't wait to hear where all you went! All the bedding has been washed and put back on. All the food has been marked and put in the freezer. We all had a ball! Ray, Michael, Harold, and Brother Darrel went fishing every day. David, Glenn, Calvin, and Nathan went with them after school was out. They all pitched in and cleaned fish and had a big cookout every night! Harold and his grandsons, Ray and Michael, all got tents and camped out by the lake one night. The girls slept out in the den almost every night, watched TV, and had the fire going. We all went over to the church a couple of times and ate lunch.

Alvin, Don, and John sang Sunday morning at Lakeside and brought the house down. All of them left early Monday morning. Both families visited the whole weekend. Carl, your family left early Monday morning. Diane, all your family checked out of Thornton's and stayed here Monday night. They sure did love this area! They went to church for the luncheon Monday.

All the fishermen cooked dinner Monday night and we all visited. Judy, Mary, and Trish joined us too. Diane, your family all left early Tuesday morning.

We all really had a great visit! Our time here at Amber Lake has been a real vacation! It is Saturday morning and Darrel is getting ready to take us to the airport. Thanks for everything and we are so happy for both of you. We continue to pray for you, and remember, look at what the Lord has done! Praise God!

> Much love,
> Ray, Jan, Amanda, Linda & Michael

P.S. Carl, I believe you finally "hooked" Diane when you cleaned up the old fishing room. Ha, ha! The wedding was beautiful!

I was glad to be home! It was like Carl said, we're getting to the point where we can go to Amber Lake whenever we want to pretty soon. A few more months I kept telling myself, just a few more months and I would be out here forever. However long forever is. At least forever on earth.

Carl and I turned on the news and laid down on the sectional. I drank some French vanilla cappuccino and Carl had some iced tea. We were really relaxing, sitting next to each other. Then the news showed a horrible car wreck that happened about forty miles from here. Five people were killed. There were three vehicles involved.

I told Carl it made me think how blessed we were that none of our family or friends were involved in any accidents. There were many people on the road to attend our wedding and many drove for several days. I thought of all the miles we had just traveled. I thought about those people who had just died and wondered if they were lost? They didn't know when they got in their cars that it would be the last drive they would ever take. So quickly our lives are gone! I immediately thought about Franklin and Kent. What if they had been in an accident last Saturday and killed. Their wives would go to heaven and they would go to hell!

"You have a chill?" Carl whispered.

"No," I whispered, as he looked at me. "You know, I was just thinking about Franklin and Kent. Their lives are like time bombs, ticking, ticking. Bang! Their lives are gone! It is like their hearts could stop beating any second and they never know when it is going to happen. Their bodies are gone and into hell they go and they can never, never get out. They need to come to Jesus while they are still ticking!" I thought out loud.

"Looks like you or somebody has their work cut out for them. You better get on it!" Carl replied.

"Do you think I should approach them? Good grief, Carl, I have never come right out and led someone to Christ. I don't know what to do. Someone needs to talk to them who knows what they are doing!" I implied.

"Why do you think there are so many lost people? Everybody is waiting on someone else. You better learn how to lead someone. You talked to me about hiding my light under a basket, remember? I was horribly wrong by never witnessing to you. Don't tell me you are doing the same thing!" Carl stated. Boy, did that hit home!

"First of all, you better start praying for their salvation. Pray the Holy Spirit brings them under conviction so they come to know Jesus in their hearts. You better be about God's business. You don't know when the ticking is over. It could be tonight!" he informed me.

"Oh, Carl, don't even say that!" I scolded.

"Well, do you know when it will be?" he asked.

"Well, heavens no!" I replied.

"Exactly. That is what is scary, isn't it?" Carl said softly.

I got the point and yes, it was scary, real scary! "You didn't just come up with all this. The Holy Spirit is dealing with you on their salvation. You don't just think things like that and then dismiss it. Oh, most people do, but they don't do anything. Just like I did! Learn to listen. He is telling you something. Maybe their time is short. Maybe their souls are required of them tonight. What fools, to leave here and never accept Jesus!" Carl emphasized. We both sat there a minute in silence.

"Let's pray right now for them." I told Carl. We did that. We also prayed for whoever we knew who needed to know Jesus as their Saviour. It made me realize I had more unfinished work in the city than I realized! The kind that was of utmost importance!

"I need to recruit people who know how to lead someone to Christ. People who are bold in the Lord!" I told him.

"You need to do that yourself! God said to go out into the world and preach the gospel," Carl replied.

"Yeah, but when they fire all these questions back at me that I cannot back up with Scripture, then I look like a fool!" I stated.

"That is why the Bible says to study and show yourself approved," Carl said (2 Tim. 2:15).

"Well, I can't do that overnight!" I replied.

"No, you can't do it overnight, but tonight is a good night to start. Start praying for the unsaved. Go get Kimberly to talk to them. She came boldly to you! Start hanging around strong Christians and learn something. You need to read the Bible and learn and pray and

God will empower you! He will give you the strength and the words (2 Tim. 2:15, John 14:26). You just don't think He will, and that is another trick from Satan," Carl said as he picked up his Bible.

"What is another trick?" I asked.

"Wait until tomorrow. Let someone else talk to them. You better pay attention here. You have two friends that you know are not saved. You better take action!" Carl said.

"Do they have a class at Lakeside where I can learn to witness to people? I need help!" I admitted.

"No, they don't, but they should have. Matter of fact, they should have a team of individuals available to go and witness to people. That is what it is all about. If you are not witnessing you are missing the whole point anyway!" Carl affirmed.

"I'm going to call Kimberly in the morning. She is either in the city or out here working with Sharon. I need both of them to pray for Kent and Franklin. Then we will go from there," I said.

"I'll call Brother Darrel in the morning and see what we can do to get a witnessing class or a witnessing group started," Carl replied.

I woke up looking out over the lake. Pepper slept right outside the French doors on the patio. Carl was still asleep. I got out of bed and went into the kitchen, fixed a cup of coffee, walked into the den, and looked out over the woods. I saw several pairs of bluebirds flying around. They were so beautiful and blue as blue could be. I looked out the front and the mums in front of the porch were so brilliant in the morning sun.

I sat down in the den and started reading my Bible. Then I went over to one of the windows looking out over the woods and got down on my knees and prayed. I came to the Lord with thanksgiving and praise in my heart. He had been so good to me. I could still have been unsaved and working overtime in the city. I still would not have realized how good my life could be when I let the Lord have it. Oh, it was horrible to think where I would still be! I had thought I was really cooking too. Yes, I was cooking all right and would have been cooking in hell for all eternity! I just can't imagine burning all the time and never dying. I can't possibly think of anything worse. Absolutely nothing!

"Good morning, sweetie!" I announced as Carl came around the corner.

"Good morning. What are you doing," he said softly.

"Oh, I read my Bible a little and prayed. I enjoyed looking outside too," I replied. He said he was going to fix some breakfast. We decided to get ready and put into action what we talked about last night. I would call Kimberly. If Sharon, Kimberly, Susan, Casey, Brother Darrel, Judy, Joy, and Cassie were around, we could all eat lunch together. At that time we could talk about witnessing classes or groups and pray about it together.

Carl called several people at work about his apartment. One of them had a client who was interested and wanted to see it first thing tomorrow morning. The lunch bunch was at Lakeside and we all ate lunch and talked and planned about witnessing to the lost and how to put it into action. Carl and I got back home about two o'clock.

We had a good meeting and a witnessing class would be started next week. Brother Darrel was getting material together and two people he knew would lead the class, called "Prepare and Lead Study (PALS)." It was a start and a great idea. A great idea if we did witness and we would.

Carl and I went into the city early in the morning. We met with a Mr. Herring at Carl's apartment. He had been in the city about fourteen months and had been renting a place. He was a client of one of Carl's co-workers. His business had done well and he was going to stay here. He was on his way up the ladder of success.

Mr. Herring was divorced and lived by himself. He had two children and they came to stay with him whenever he wanted them to. I figured he and his ex-wife had a good relationship and that it was good for the children to share equal time with their parents. He told us he was going to be a success and when he got to the top he was going to rub that in his ex-wife's face. He said that would serve her right since she left him to marry a millionaire twice her age. He went on and on about her. I could see the bitterness and resentment he had. He said they had been married fifteen years, had a boy and girl, and divorced three years ago.

After hearing him talk, I wondered how she stayed with him fifteen years! No wonder she found someone else! Of course, I didn't know her. He had just met us and his hatred over this divorce was so obvious. I felt the only reason he was on the road to success was to show her up. He said when they divorced she told him she wished him the best and wished their marriage could have worked out. She told him she had forgiven him because Christ had forgiven her. She had peace about their turbulent years and only love and concern for him. He bitterly laughed and asked us if anyone could believe someone talking like that. I could. After all, they did have two beautiful, healthy children and both of them needed their parents' love, not hatred and remorse.

I was glad she felt that way because he was carrying enough hate for two miserable people! Carl calmly told him the Lord does have a way of filling you with joy once you forgive whoever it is you have fought against. Herring turned his lip up at that and told Carl that may be true but she was a religious fanatic! Not only that, he claimed his two children had been brainwashed by her too.

He said his children keep telling him that love is the way, not getting even. He said they were just jealous. This year he would surpass their stepfather in his business. He laughed and said his ex-wife would go haywire when that happened. It sounded to me like he had his wife figured out wrong! It was bitterness and resentment talking!

I asked him what his business was and he said he had a computer sales business. He sold computers and all kinds of business equipment. He had a store only about ten minutes from Carl's apartment called Herring's Business Equipment. Carl told him how he had enjoyed living in this neighborhood all these years. He informed him that he would like to sell it furnished if possible. Mr. Herring said he liked the way it was furnished. He said it looked rich and distinguished and he definitely liked that look!

He asked Carl what the bottom line was for the apartment and the furniture. Carl quoted him a price for the apartment and the furniture and he shouted, "Sold!" Carl and I stood there. "Let's get the paperwork done. I'm ready to move in as soon as possible!" he laughed. Carl gave him a fair price, but I was still surprised that he didn't even counteroffer.

Carl had all his personal things already moved out. Of course, it was a blessing to have sold the apartment and furniture right away and all together. I felt sorry for this man! I wasn't excited about selling the apartment because he was buying it for the wrong reasons.

Carl had wonderful neighbors, a glamorous view, and people in the area he knew and cared about. Mr. Herring would never see any of this. When he looked at the view he would think how jealous his wife would be. He was obsessed with making her jealous and for what? I bet she felt sorry for him too.

Carl and I stayed at my apartment that night so everything could be finalized tomorrow. I started calling some of my friends to see if they knew of anyone interested in my apartment. I knew now I could sell mine furnished too. I sure didn't need the furniture nor the headache!

If someone had offered me a nicely furnished apartment when I came to the city, I would have loved it!

The next morning Carl left to meet Mr. Herring to finalize the sale. I talked to Carol and she said they were working over a lot. She said the pressure wouldn't hit until late next week because there were two new accounts coming in. They were both clients Kent had rounded up. I asked her if it was from the Sunday morning brunches at the country club and she said it was. I was disappointed in that now Honey would never get him to church. He had just proved to her that his Sunday mornings away from church had paid off and paid off well! I guess it did in this life. The love of money was a trick from Satan (1 Tim. 6:10). God could have blessed him in every way and with riches far exceeding these accounts!

Carl came in the apartment about noon. "Well, how did everything go?" I asked as I put my arms around him.

"Oh, he has the apartment now. Everything went smoothly and that is settled," Carl answered.

"Well, great!" I said.

"Do you know what he said when we signed all the paperwork and I handed him the keys?" Carl asked.

"It is hard telling!" I replied.

"He said when his ex found out how much he paid for the apartment, she would croak knowing he had that kind of money to spend," Carl said.

"What! You are kidding!" I exclaimed.

"No, that is exactly what he said. That is why he didn't counter-offer. He wanted to impress her with the price he paid. That man really has a problem!" Carl recognized, shaking his head with sorrow.

"Oh, my! Can you imagine being that miserable. I'm serious. That is sad!" I said, shaking my head too. "Just put him on the prayer list at church and give his name to our PALS group," I said.

"I told him about the revival up in Harlem and what all had happened. It went right over his head. The only thing he said was 'Revival! I wouldn't go. I would probably run into my ex and holier than thou kids!' and then he laughed," Carl said.

"Carl, I wonder how many people are out there like him. People who are bound by remorse, hatred, and such. That would be hell on earth! Jesus can free them from all that!" I affirmed (Luke 4:18).

"He can't see what he is doing to himself. We never can. We need to pray for him for sure. The Lord can show him if he won't listen to us," Carl said.

"I agree!" I replied.

We went out to eat a bite. We went up to the office to get some of my personal belongings. I wanted to take them back to Amber Lake and go through them. We saw everyone and they hugged us and said married life must be agreeing with us, since we looked so happy and content. They all talked about the wedding and how beautiful Amber Lake was. Carl and I gave them all an open invitation to visit. I told them I would be back next week and they were glad because it would be a busy time. We visited and talked and then we left.

We saw Angelina out on the street. She talked about the wedding and how they enjoyed being there that day. Then she asked Carl and I to pray for Nick. She wept and told us he was lost and my heart went out to her. Now I know how Carl must have felt about me all these years and I didn't even realize it. She said she would see Kimberly tomorrow night and ask her to pray for him. She knew she needed believers to be in prayer because she knew what the power of prayer would do. I hugged her and we told her we would pray for him and put him on the prayer list at church. She wiped her tears away and thanked us.

Carl and I left the city and headed back to Amber Lake. We had filled the car up with things from my office and apartment. We had a relaxing dinner and got home at dark. We unloaded the car and Pepper walked every step with us. I told Carl it was too bad Pepper couldn't carry stuff because we would have used him a lot lately! We relaxed by the fire as usual. Yep, we already looked like an old married couple.

The next morning was sunny and cool. I had my two cups of coffee, still half decaf, about the time Carl got up. We were right on schedule. He fixed a great breakfast. I started going through the stuff I brought back, throwing most of it away. I laughed at much of it. All the notes about the firm and all the self-help books I had! The real self-help book was the Bible. Now that was real self-help! I had found books about different subjects that were Bible-based and they were excellent. You better know your Bible well enough to know whether things are Bible-based or not!

The photographer called that did our wedding pictures. The proofs were ready so we went over and looked at them. They were all great and

Carl wanted to order every one of them. So that is what we did. Those bare shelves Jan, the girls, and I kidded about not so long ago would be full now. Oh, I couldn't wait to pick them up! I was so thrilled they turned out so good!

We went over to the church the next day for lunch. Brother Darrel said he had gotten in the material for PALS, as we called it now. I told him I needed help fast. I now knew three people that were not saved and who knows how many more I would run into. He gave me one of the books to study.

Carl grilled steaks that night out on the patio. We ate early since it was getting dark earlier. Pepper seemed happy we were home together now. I told Carl we needed to find Pepper a wife too. "Maybe in the spring," Carl kidded. We both laughed and Pepper wagged his tail.

We went to Springfield in the morning and bought all the frames and albums for the wedding pictures we had coming in. I bought a notebook and went home and started making notes on my witnessing book. We had also bought quite a few groceries since the next day it was our turn to fix lunch at the church.

Carl wanted to fix chicken strips with a special seasoning he had developed. It was a dry seasoning and did not contain any preservatives, which was real important to him. He had been working on it since last year when he started phasing out of the city and it was really good! Who knows what he, now we, would end up doing with that seasoning. We decided to call it "Carl's"! Carl said the Lord just gave him the idea and he blended and mixed until he got it just right. Believe me, it was just right too! It was more proof that we serve an awesome God!

We ate lunch at church and everyone was excited about PALS. We knew we would be on our own mission trip right here at home! There were hundreds of thousands of people right under our nose who not only weren't saved, but were depressed, grieving, sick, and suffering. We had a full-time job without a doubt!

At least the lunch program was helping. Carl and I found out that Gary, who worked with Casey, accepted Jesus last week right after the lunch meeting. He was baptized last Sunday. What a miracle! I hoped that Jesse saw the light too. Brother Darrel said Jesse had stiffened his neck and hardened his heart. We just needed to keep praying for him. He was the one that had to make the choice. We couldn't do it for him, or we certainly would.

Carl got our wedding pictures and it took us almost a whole day to clean the glass and get them framed and set up. They looked so good on the shelf. I couldn't stop looking at them. I reflected back again about Amanda and Linda saying Carl was saving the bare shelves for our wedding pictures. I remembered that day so well, and now, only weeks later, our wedding pictures were covering the shelves. I thanked God for powerful, dedicated Christians! Bless them Lord, I prayed, for they are the salt of the earth (Matt. 5:13–14).

We fixed the lunch at church. Carl had chicken strips with his special seasoning and everyone loved it! They were amazed he had created this, yet they were not amazed God gave him the idea! I fixed french fries, a salad with buttermilk dressing, and for dessert a cherry cheesecake, pumpkin pie, and coconut cake. There were twenty people there. They loved the food, especially Carl's seasoning, but mainly they loved the sermon. I could see the real hunger was for God's word. Praise God! We had a great time and about seven of those people didn't go to church at all.

The weekend went very quickly. The people at church were all commenting on our wedding. I showed them the mini-album. They said it must have been a wonderful honeymoon. We looked happy and relaxed. We told them it was a wonderful honeymoon and we had enjoyed our week at home too. I was as happy as I had ever been, but I had to go back to the city in the morning.

Carl was going to Prepare and Lead Study and then give me the notes and feedback. We started calling the people attending PALS. Yes, they were certainly pals of the best kind and were preparing to use what they were learning!

I kissed Carl on the cheek and said, "Honey, I'm leaving for the city. I'll see you Saturday morning unless I can get away earlier. This is a very busy week."

"I hope it is before Saturday, but if it isn't, I understand," he whispered. Out the door I went, carrying my second cup of coffee for the ride in. I would drive straight to the office. It was really tough leaving him, but soon we would be together all the time. We waved bye to each other and Pepper stood beside him in the early dawn, wagging his tail.

Now that I was back in Manhattan during the week, I had plenty of time to read my Bible at night. I needed to be in prayer and ask God what he wanted me to say and do. Instead of dreading being away from Carl, I was going to use this time in the city to witness to Franklin and Kent. Carol and I got in the office at the same time. She gave me a big hug and said she missed me and asked me about the last couple of weeks. Then she told me about Glenn. He was going back up to Pine Mountain to write songs with Russ this week. They were writing gospel songs and felt they already had one that would be a hit. She was so excited. She had gone along and stayed there two weekends ago. She and Russ's wife, Janet, went antique shopping. Carol smiled and said, "Guess where we ate lunch?"

"I wouldn't have the slightest idea!" I kidded. Of course, I knew they went to Thornton's.

I told her about the bed and breakfast inns we stayed in during our honeymoon. "If you can't get Thornton's, go ahead and get an old house and fix it up. I can help you. I have plenty of ideas. Carl said that is what I will want to do next. You know how I love to decorate! Max is on the lookout for you and Glenn," I said.

She said Glenn loved going up there and he felt they would have a hit on the radio before long. He said the writing they were doing now was better than ever. Carol said they could sell their place here and move up there. She knew if she could operate a bed and breakfast that she could swing it financially. If Glenn got a hit record that would be icing on the cake.

I told her Carl and I would also look around for the perfect place for them to have a bed and breakfast. That would give me a good excuse to visit all the surrounding towns and have some fun too. We laughed at that one since both of us knew I loved going to the little towns. We planned on eating lunch together this week, so we could catch each other up on our news. We would be working until about eight o'clock every night she informed me. We would all order from Nick's and eat dinner here, but we agreed we needed to get out at lunch.

Kimberly came in later in the week. I asked her to close the door when she came in my office. I told her about Franklin, Kent, and Nick. She said Angelina had spoken to her about Nick. She said she would drop "seeds" as she called it and move as the Lord told her to. She said she was not ashamed to witness and she felt today might be the day to see them. I knew she was not ashamed. Thank God for people like her!

I never failed to tell Franklin and Kent how good the Lord had been to me when they asked how I was doing. They had never heard me talk that way before. I knew Kent never wanted to look at anything but his job. He was scared if he got distracted he would not be as aggressive as he liked to be. He knew I was a workaholic before I was saved, but now other things were much more important to me. He didn't want that to happen to him, but he didn't know what joy the Lord had for him either.

Sam's life had changed since he was saved. He was really involved in the firm, but he enjoyed church now that he and his fiancée were both saved and truly happy. He would talk about how different his life was and how thankful he was that it had changed.

I could tell that Franklin would ponder thoughts of finding out for himself what we were talking about, but he would never cross over. At least he hadn't yet. He was interested, but reluctant. Kent would be irritated when we would talk about how good the Lord was. I mean just a general comment and he would bristle up. He was scared of the light and he didn't know he was living in darkness. It made me shudder to think, oh, I decided not to think about where he would be if . . . no, I wouldn't think about it!

I went home early Saturday morning. Carl was waiting for me and yes, Pepper too. It seemed like I had been gone at least a month! I had brought home another carload of stuff to go through and took it upstairs to the room that would be my office. I found out I was throwing out at least eighty percent of what I was bringing home. I had business handbooks, notes, and updates about the firm from years ago.

Carl told me that we were going to go today and pick out what I needed to finish my office. I wanted a flat textured paneling in a very light color. Then I had to pick out what flooring to use. We headed back to Springfield. I found a paneling in an off white with a rough surface, kind of a barn lumber effect that I liked. Then I saw a sandy berber carpet for my floor that would be perfect. Carl said he would have it done next week. I was so excited. He said he wanted me to be able to come home and put everything up where it belonged.

He said the next weekend or so we would pick out the shelving, desk, and chair. He knew it wouldn't be long before I would bring my computer and office supplies from home. That would be last, but it wouldn't be more than a couple of months. I wanted the area by the window to be used for my Bible study and my PALS information.

I saw Kimberly and Sharon at church Sunday morning. They were speaking at a church in Silver Lake Sunday night. I told them to go early and eat at Thornton's. Kimberly said she had talked a little with Franklin, but Kent left his office as soon as she entered his door. "Woowee, honey, Satan has got a hold of that man! He can't stand me being in the same room with him. He doesn't know it is

Satan, but honey, I know exactly who it is. Satan has him right where he wants him—bound for hell!"

"What are we going to do?" I asked, knowing he was so faraway from God.

"I'm going to go down and confront him before he leaves his office next week. I'll stand in front of the door if I have too!" she laughed. "I'll keep talking to Franklin too," she affirmed.

"Oh, I wish this was easier. Why are they fighting so hard?" I muttered.

"Honey, Satan doesn't give up easy and he is full of trickery! He'll tell you anything to keep you from getting saved! Satan is telling him we are a bunch of religious fanatics and to stay away from us. After all, Kent is a professional man and he is taking good care of himself. Why does he need God? I mean how would he look to his clients having religion and all and going to church instead of being with the Sunday country club bunch!" she stammered.

"Honey, you know there are some people that put on a religious face and go to church, because there are clients there too! Some play that game thinking it improves their status and all, you know, being a good church member. They are playing the game and think they are so cool. I mean cool! Ain't none of them fooling God. You are either saved or you are not saved!" she preached.

"I tell you, what He has done in my life! I just fall to my knees and humble myself! That is why I go and do what He tells me to do. I don't care if they think I am a religious fanatic or even if they fire me. I'm going to please God, not man (Gal. 1:10, John 8:29). In other words, I am about my Father's work! Praise God!" she confessed.

"Kimberly, what brought you there to work? I know now you can do anything you set your mind to," I asked.

"I can do anything because I go where he sends me and when He sends you to do something, He has already prepared you to do it! He told me to come to that building because He said He needed light where there was darkness. That is why I came there. There was a janitorial job open and I took it. I got to come right into everyone's office and talk with them, which is exactly what I was supposed to do," she admitted.

"Honey, I was to let my light shine. That light that only Jesus can give you! I'll do what my God tells me to do. He blesses me for obeying Him! There is no room for pride. Pride is a sin when you want to lift yourself up to suit man and what he thinks. I'm on a mission in this life and He will bless me and care for me, especially when I am obedient. Remember, man didn't die for your sins, Jesus paid it all. Honey, He paid it all! He didn't miss nothing on that cross. He paid for your soul, your healing, your needs, you name it!" she exclaimed.

"Just keep praying for Kent and Franklin. I'll keep talking to them. You can't make anyone get saved. It has to be from their heart! It has to be their choice. We can't lead them if they refuse to be led. You may have to kick the dust off your shoes and go on to someone who will listen (Matt. 10:14). We don't have time to waste!" she proclaimed.

"You need to prepare yourself. Carry the sinner's prayer and Scripture with you on the plan of salvation. At all times, be ready! We need to be ready to witness and we definitely need to be ready to met our Lord!" she affirmed.

She and Sharon hugged me and said they were praying for all the unsaved they knew. After church, Carl and I went home and ate out on the patio. It was an unusually nice day, but storm clouds rolled in by afternoon. I went through the stuff I had brought home and Carl and I went back to church Sunday night. There were about sixteen members attending PALS. Everyone was really enjoying it. Carl said this was something every church in America should have available!

I took Monday off and Carl and I looked in Springfield at office furniture. We wanted to start getting an idea of what to put in my new office. Late Monday afternoon we took the paddleboat out on the lake and it was so relaxing. Carl and I spent about two hours studying our Bible by the fireplace that evening. We had started going to bed about nine or ten o'clock. That sure was different than all the years we had spent together before we were married. Both of us agreed we wouldn't want to live that way again!

Early Tuesday morning I drove back to Manhatten. At work Sam and I dropped our usual little "seeds," but Kent was not listening. Sam didn't know he was dropping seeds. He was so joyous in the Lord, he just bubbled over without a thought about it. I knew what I was doing. I wanted to witness to Kent when I would go in his office, but I just wasn't sure how to get started. I was mad at myself for that, and of course, he would hardly look up anyway.

Franklin was always wondering what I was going to say. He was intimidating for some reason, but why should that make a difference? Why didn't I have any backbone, I wondered! I could talk about anything else. Why was this different? Was that Satan filling me with a spirit of fear?

We worked hard all week and we would leave about eight o'clock at night. Kent said he had another possible client. Oh boy, just what I needed! I was in Kent's office waiting on him and the phone rang, so I answered it. It was Honey and we talked about the wedding, then she wanted to know if we were working Sunday. She said Kent's niece was being baptized and she wanted her Uncle Kent to be there. I told her I was happy for his niece and that I would tell Kent. We talked a little and then we hung up. She was such a fine lady!

Maybe this is my opportunity I thought to myself. Kent came in and I told him she called and what it was about. He said he was busy Sunday and that Honey should know that. I told him his niece wanted him to be there, but he immediately said he couldn't make it. He said he had a meeting over brunch with another possible client this Sunday.

"And that comes first?" I asked, not believing the words I just spoke. Kent was surprised at my boldness and just looked at me. Kent and I had been friends for years and we kidded a lot, but I had never spoken like this to him before.

"Yes it does. I have to take hold of my future now. I am going to let nothing interfere with that, and I mean nothing!" he affirmed, as he looked me straight in the eye.

"I'm sorry you feel that way," I whispered. I knew not to say anything else.

I saw Kimberly later in the week in the building. I asked her about Kent. She said this week he must have made it a point not to be found when she came in. I asked her what to do next. She said, "He had stiffened his neck and hardened his heart and you know what that means."

"What?" I asked.

"He is left without remedy," she answered (Prov. 29:1). We both stood there and looked at each other.

"We'll try again next week," she sighed.

I left for Amber Lake Saturday morning. Carl and Pepper were awaiting my arrival. While we were working on my office, I told Carl what happened with Kent. He said just to pray for him and not to worry about it. I have to admit I was so upset with him I didn't even pray for him. We went to church Sunday morning and many of us ate lunch together. I was still upset with Kent, thinking about his niece being baptized this morning and wanting her Uncle Kent to be there. I finally admitted to Carl Sunday night that I hadn't prayed for Kent all weekend I was so outdone with him. He told me praying for him was the most important thing to do. He told me I had said all I could say to him, but that didn't mean to stop praying for him. I listened, but inside I was still too upset with him. Maybe I would feel different if I just got my mind off of him for a while.

The phone was ringing. Carl reached over to get it. I looked at the clock. It was six in the morning. Who would be calling at this hour? Carl said, "It is for you. It's Franklin," he said.

"Franklin?" I whispered, wondering what on earth was going on. Carl shrugged his shoulders and handed me the phone across the bed. "Franklin. Is everything all right?" I asked.

"No. I'm afraid I have some bad news," he said.

"What is it?" I asked, my heart quickening.

"Kent had a massive heart attack and died about two hours ago," he said.

"Oh, my God!" I wailed. "Franklin! I can't believe it!" I sobbed. Carl was looking at me. I couldn't talk.

"I need you and Carl to come in. I have to help Honey with the arrangements. It has all happened so quickly. Kent's whole family is in a state of shock. I am too for that matter," Franklin said, his voice giving a little.

"OK," I managed to blurt out somehow. "We'll be at my apartment no later than noon," I managed to utter.

"I'll call you over there when I know more about the arrangements," he spoke softly.

"Thank you," I mumbled through tears.

I handed Carl the phone. "Kent had a massive heart attack and died two hours ago," I cried. Carl looked at me with deep remorse. He was thinking what I was thinking. We both knew where he was. "Oh God, help me," was the cry in my mind and heart. Carl held me and I finally got some control over my emotions. Carl fixed me a cup of coffee and brought it to me in the den.

I took it and halfway smiled and turned and looked back out the window. Carl just went on back to the kitchen. He knew I needed to be by myself. I had buried my head in the sand with Kent! I didn't want to think about him going to hell!

How stupid I was. How stupid! Knowing the state he was in, which was hellbound, I should have taken the devil by the horns in the name of Jesus! I had authority over him. Why did I sit by and be so passive? Oh, yeah, I did things, but I didn't tackle the problem. I just sat on the sidelines and made some comments. Big deal! Oh Lord, forgive me! Forgive me!

Carl fixed breakfast. He quietly called me when it was ready. I sat there looking at my plate of food. "You have to eat something," Carl said softly. I took a deep sigh and started eating. I didn't want to, but I knew I needed to. Nothing tasted right, but I had to keep my body going.

I called the office. Faune answered. I could tell she had been crying. Carol was there and she picked up the phone and we both cried. I was finally able to tell her we would be at my apartment by noon. I told her Franklin said he would call me. Sam and her were trying to keep the office going, and although their hearts weren't in it, they were doing what they had to do. She said Franklin had already gone to the funeral home to be with Honey and Eric and help them anyway he could. I told her I would call her when I got to my apartment.

Carl and I packed clothes and no words were said. Then I told Carl we better take clothes for several days since we didn't know when the funeral would be. We got packed and loaded and Carl carried Pepper over to the Goodfellows. When he came back we left for the city.

We unloaded everything in my apartment. About fifteen minutes later Franklin called and said viewing would be tonight. "It will?" I questioned.

"Yes. All his family is close. This is so hard on all of them. There is no reason to carry it out any longer than need be. The funeral home had everything in order quickly and Honey bought plots years ago."

I talked to Faune and Carol again. Sam was holding down the office so they could leave and be there as soon as visitation started. I asked her if Kimberly knew. She said she had called her and she would be there tonight. I told them I would see them there. We were all still in shock.

Carl and I stopped on the way to the funeral home and ate dinner. I still didn't have an appetite. I told Carl, "You don't know how awful I feel. I know there was something I could have done. Why didn't I leave him tracts to read, if I couldn't talk to him? If I had prayed for him everyday," I cried. I couldn't finish my sentence.

Carl said, "Remember what it says in the Bible. If a man stiffens his neck and hardens his heart . . ." (2 Chron. 36:13).

"'He is left without remedy,'" I finished.

"That is what happened here. His family and his friends have all been trying to witness to him and especially in the last month!" Carl assured. "Yes, I'm sure there was more you could have done. You have to remember, even though he didn't listen to anything, you did try to tell him. You have to stop blaming yourself," Carl affirmed.

"It hurts so bad, so bad!" I wailed.

"Yes, it does. You must think of Franklin now. There is still hope for him," Carl whispered softly.

We got to the funeral home. I dreaded going in. I wanted to be strong. "Lord, give me strength," I whispered. We walked in and Carol and Faune and their families were already there. We all hugged and cried. Franklin and Robbie came up and they hugged us too.

"This is so awful!" Robbie cried. I knew what she was thinking about Kent when I looked into her eyes. How tormented she must be knowing Franklin wasn't saved!

Carl put his hand on my shoulder and said, "Let's go in and see Honey and Eric."

Carol whispered, "I'll go in with you."

"OK," I muttered. We walked up there and hugged Honey and Eric and she walked with us to the casket. I didn't want to look at Kent. Honey was trying to bear her grief and talk about how much our friendship had meant to Kent.

I looked at him. All of a sudden I felt intense heat hit me in the face and it quickly got hotter and hotter. I saw his face with fire all around it. Then I heard, "Help me! Help me! I'm burning up in this fire. I can't stop burning! I can't stop burning!" was Kent's screaming, tortured voice. He was screaming and screaming. I could hear the flames raging as they engulfed him. I felt I was burning alive! Burning alive!

"Diane, are you all right?" Carol asked as she had grabbed my arm. Honey stood there looking at me with such a worried look and she grabbed my other arm. Carl put his arm around me. Carl told Honey it was just the shock of it all. Somehow Carl and Carol both got me over to a chair and sat me down. Honey came over and I told her I was so sorry. It was just a shock to me. Carl told Honey I would be all right. She finally dismissed herself and went back to her visitors.

"Are you all right?" Carol whispered, shocked that I had reacted the way I did.

"Yes, let's get out of this room for a while," I said quietly. Carl and Carol walked with me and we went several rooms away and sat down.

Carol looked at me and inquired, "Diane, what happened in there? Your face turned pure red and then you looked like you were going to faint." Carl and Carol were both looking at me waiting for me to speak. About then Kimberly and Faune walked up to us.

We were the only ones in this back room and Kimberly looked at me and softly asked, "Honey, what is it? What did you see up there?"

Now all of them were looking at me and I said, "Kent is in hell. I saw him in the flames and heard his tormented screams," I whispered and began to shake all over. "It was the most awful thing I have ever seen. I felt the heat and it was the flames of hell all over his face, but he wasn't burning up, but he felt the pain like he was (Mark 9:43–48). I could tell by his screams and the horrible look in his eyes. It was worse than a nightmare. No words can describe it! Look, the hair on my arms is still standing up," I showed them. They all looked at me and they were so silent.

"I saw it too," confessed Kimberly. We all looked at her. "I have seen it before and you never forget it. I was hoping between yesterday when I talked with Kent and this morning that maybe there was a change in his heart. Oh, Lord! When I saw him in his casket a few minutes ago, I felt hell's flames and heard him screaming for someone to get him out of his torment," she tossed her head back and forth and began to weep. She patted my hand and cried, "I know, I know, you will never forget that sight! Never!"

Carl, Carol, and Faune sat there in sorrow. There was nothing any of us could do. Nothing now! There will never be another chance for Kent and we will never see him again. Never, for all of eternity! He would burn forever and ever and never die. No matter what agony we have on earth, it is only temporary. I could not imagine burning forever and it would never stop and he could never get out of it! Carl, Carol, and Faune knew what we saw was real, even though no one else could see it. No one wanted to believe it, including Kimberly and I, but hell is real! Yes it is! Hell is real . . .

The Rapture

THE NEXT FEW WEEKS WERE VERY TOUGH. I KEPT REFLECTING BACK on that night in the funeral home. Kent hadn't even been dead twenty-four hours when I saw his body. Of course, he wasn't there. He was in hell! The voice and the torment were real. Kimberly saw it too. Why didn't anyone else see it? Were we the only ones who were supposed to see it? Were we the ones chosen to witness how gruesome it was? Hell is real! Hell is real! His voice and those flames made the hair on the back of my neck stand up! I had only seen an image. What would it be like to really be there?

At the funeral the preacher had spoken on heaven and how wonderful it was on the other side. "Someday his family will join him and they will all be happy again," he said. He didn't know Kent! Kent didn't want to know anything about Jesus! He was on the other side all right! The side none of his family wanted to go to! There certainly would never be happiness there! People always kidded about how all their friends would be in hell, shoveling coal, and partying. Tell me how much someone could enjoy their friends if they were burning alive for eternity?

I had lost ten pounds in two weeks. I just didn't have an appetite. That was not like me at all! I felt bad for Carl. He had not done anything wrong, but he was suffering because I was suffering. Brother Darrel and Carl were putting PALS into first gear. They knew what I saw that night was real, but they didn't talk about it around me. They knew it was true and that I experienced for a second what hell would be like.

I could see and feel Kent's unbelievable torment at only a fraction of what he was feeling. All I knew was that Brother Darrel had definitely sped up PALS to witness to the lost. PALS had several groups prepared to visit and witness to people now and they took this very seriously. If they had seen what I did, they would be asking everyone they met if they were saved! Matter of fact, that is what needs to be done. If only everyone could see what hell is like.

I had worked in the city and many late nights as usual for the past several weeks. I was only coming back to Amber Lake three days a week. Now that Kent was gone, we were covered up even more! It was tough being there everyday where we worked with him for twenty years. It was a constant reminder. I pitied him greatly in the anguish he was in . . . and would be forever.

Even though he was gone, I was upset with him. We tried to witness to him, but he was stubborn and in control, at least he thought he was. Satan was the one in control all along, manipulating him and tricking him and he went right along with him. He avoided the salvation Jesus wanted to give him and jumped right into the devil's frying pan—literally. What a sad mistake. One he would pay for for all eternity! A lot of good all of his clients were now! Money can't buy you out of hell, but the love of it can end up putting you there (1 Tim. 6:10).

I went straight to Amber Lake Thursday night after work. We got up Friday morning and started work on my new office. It was late Friday afternoon and Brother Darrel called and wanted to know if Carl could come over to the church and help put together some study guides for PALS. Carolyn had some friends in visiting from out of state. She had told them about the class our church started. They were so interested they wanted to have a mini-course on PALS so they could witness to the unsaved. Carl went right over to the church.

He knew how important this was. After all, what is more important than where you are spending eternity! Our life on earth is so short compared to eternity. The Bible says our life is like a vapor, and then vanishes away (James 4:14). That is pretty short!

I decided to fix him dinner for once. He had thawed out catfish strips for deep frying. I called the church and talked to Carl and he said they were having a meeting with Carolyn's friends. He said he and

Brother Darrel might even drive to their church in Pennsylvania and get them started on it. He said he would go during the week, while I was in the city. I told him to go, by all means. Always do what the Lord tells you to do. I asked him when he would be home and he said in about another hour.

I hung up the phone and thought about PALS. This had been a horrible ordeal with Kent, but at least it prompted PALS to save others from hell and not to wait! It forced us to move forward with PALS more intensely. Since they started making visits to the unsaved, fifteen people around Amber Lake had been saved.

When I saw Kent in hell and felt the heat of the flames, it made an impression on Brother Darrel and Carl. They had seen the weeks of anguish I had gone through for a sixty-second view of someone in hell.

Well, I was going to surprise Carl and fix him dinner for once. I had always been so busy when I got here, he just automatically fixed dinner. I plugged in the deep fryer and got the oil hot. I cooked the fish strips. I looked in the freezer and found a quart of frozen sliced okra. I had potatoes cooking on the stove too. I broke the frozen okra apart and dumped them in the oil.

The oil immediately boiled up and out of the deep fryer. I thought it would run off the counter and into the nearby stove eye. All I could picture was the house catching on fire. I grabbed the handles of the deep fryer and threw it into the sink before it hit the stove. The boiling oil sloshed out onto both of my hands. The pain was so great I couldn't stand it.

I ran to pour cold water on my hands. That didn't help. The pain was so bad I could hardly breathe. I called the emergency room and was gasping with pain. I know I sounded frantic. I told the lady I needed to talk to a doctor. I burned my hands with boiling oil and I needed to know what to put on them. A doctor came to the phone and told me to put them immediately down in ice, keep them in ice, and get to the emergency room. He said it was very important I keep them in ice starting now. It stopped the burning that was going on under the skin. The damage would be far less critical if I kept the burn ice cold.

I called the church, switching the phone and dipping one hand in ice and then the other. Carl had already left. I kept both my hands in the ice until he drove into the driveway. He came in the back door and caught a glimpse of the kitchen. "What on earth happened?" he asked frantically. Then he saw me with both my hands pushed down into an ice bucket. I told him what happened and to be careful walking in the kitchen. I had sloshed oil all over the floor and hadn't cleaned it up. Right now, I needed to go to the emergency room!

He loaded me and the ice bucket into the Jeep. We headed for Springfield. The ice had almost all melted. The pain was so intense. "Carl, you are going to have to stop now and get a bag of ice to pour on my hands!" I shrieked. He had to wait in line for one person and I thought I was going to go through the ceiling of the Jeep. I was tapping my feet, humming, anything to distract myself from the pain I was feeling.

We got in the emergency room and the doctor looked at my hands and said I may have to have physical therapy to get my fingers working good again. I could not believe I had been burned that badly. He lathered my hands with a white miracle cream for burns, and then he put gloves on my hands. I could not wait to stick them back in ice! I told him what happened and that I was scared the house would have burned up if I had let the boiling oil run into a hot burner. He told me I would have been better off to have let the house burn up. I looked at him and I could not believe, once again, that my hands were burned that badly!

Carl and I finally got home. He had to stop and buy another bag of ice. I thought if I was burned like that and could not get the relief the ice gave me, I would just as soon be dead. I was serious. What about people that are burned all over? What if there wasn't any ice, or medical attention? I immediately thought about Lazarus and the rich man. The rich man asked Abraham to let Lazarus put one drop of water on his tongue, for he was in torment in hell. One drop of water! When he looked up into heaven he must have known what just one drop of God's water would do (Luke 16:23–24).

That night I slept in our bed with a bucket of ice on each side of me and my hands dipped in them. I slept that way through the night. Carl went upstairs and slept in the fin and feather room. It was absolutely amazing how the ice numbed the pain. I prayed my hands would be all right. It made me realize how absolutely wonderful it is to feel good!

When I woke up the next morning the ice was melted, but the water was still cold. All night packed in ice made a big difference! I still had those gloves on, but I could move my fingers. It was eight o'clock. I had a slight headache. I never slept that long. I guess it was the exhaustion from the pain.

I got up and fixed a cup of coffee. I would find out if I could stand being out of the ice water. Carl came down the stairs and wondered how I was doing. I said, "It is a good thing we got married before I burned my hands. I can look back at the pictures of our hands and wedding rings and remember how nice my hands used to look," I said, just to see what he would say.

Carl looked at me and frowned and scolded, "Don't jump to that conclusion."

Carl fixed breakfast and we ate. My hands felt better and the burning pain was gone and I was glad! Thank God for doctors and miracle drugs and creams! My doctor was going to look at my hands this morning. I didn't know what to expect. When he took the gloves off and I looked at them I was pleasantly surprised. They were red and there were blisters, but they were not nearly as bad as I thought they would be. My doctor said it was a result of keeping my hands in the ice water, which cut the damage back, and the miracle cream. Praise God! I told him I had prayed about my hands after the emergency room doctor told me I may need physical therapy. He told me my hands were going to be fine, even though I had a lot of blisters. He said he couldn't imagine a worse pain than being burned.

"Why are you so quiet?" Carl said as we drove back home.

"I was thinking about this incident and the horrible pain. I thought if I was burned all over I would rather be dead. Then I thought about the people in hell. They have that burning pain every minute and will never die and never get out of it! The Bible says you are in a constant fire (Mark 9:43–44). I just absolutely cannot imagine! We jump all over the place in torment over a burn like this. People don't take five minutes of their life to repent and ask Jesus into their lives so they don't have to spend eternity burning! Eternity! I wasn't any different, but now I could sure see how terribly wrong I was!"

Carl just sat there, then he sighed. He realized how much we needed to be out there winning souls. Hell was no joke! The lake of fire, the torment, all that is real (Rev. 20:10–14). All I would have to do was remember how horrible this burn was and I would be bold enough to witness. Who would want anyone to suffer like that for eternity?

I found out that Sharon and Kimberly were very busy with Your Loss Is His Gain. Every time they gave a seminar they got at least three more invitations to go somewhere else. They had a study guide and a book for sale and they were always paid for their visits, or given a love offering. What really made them happy was doing the Lord's work and they knew the Lord would always provide. The Lord was taking care of all their travel money, their mortgage, and all their living expenses. Praise God! He will provide!

Kimberly had bought the Hitch'n Post and was remodeling a couple of the rooms downstairs. The upstairs had already been beautifully remodeled and had about eighteen hundred square feet. She had plenty of room to have family and friends stay and visit. I was so glad she was moving to Amber Lake. Who would have ever thought both of us would leave the city and live out here in this tranquil little town?

She and Sharon were traveling quite a bit and loved every minute of it. It was a great joy to see people find happiness and freedom in their ministry. After all, working for the Lord is the best job around! Great benefits, great pleasure, unbelievable satisfaction, and a chance to put all your treasures in heaven (Matt. 6:19–20). That pays way better than any 401K plan! You receive proceeds on all the above for all of eternity! Put the Kingdom of God first, and everything will be added unto you (Matt. 6:33).

Casey and Susan were growing in their ministry too. They were preaching to people with words of encouragement and hope, teaching them that they were somebody important. They instilled in them that they were winners and God could use them. Susan and Judy would go to these seminars together when Casey was working. Susan would preach on healing and show them the passages pertaining to that. Judy would minister in song and testimony of what she had seen God do. Miracles were still happening!

Casey would go every time he could and let Gary and Jesse handle the landscaping business. Casey was getting more new customers every week, so business was good and all three of them were prospering.

Casey, Susan, and Judy were busy working for the Lord and loving it, and Brother Darrel was leading a growing church. It was wonderful to see a church prospering and its members reaching out and accomplishing so much for the glory of the Lord. Individually they were blessed and on fire for God.

It wouldn't be much longer before Casey would let Gary operate his landscaping business. Casey and Susan were about ready to be full-time ministers. After Gary was saved and baptized, he completed PALS and was witnessing everywhere he went with the landscaping. Everyone was thrilled about how he turned his life around, especially Susan and Casey!

Jesse was not too happy about Gary witnessing to people when they were on the job, but several were now coming to church as a result of it. Jesse and Gary had been friends for a long time and were thriving financially, so Jesse wasn't about to jeopardize anything over Gary witnessing to people. All of us were praying Jesse would finally see the light, but he was determined to hang onto his bitterness and stubbornness.

It was time for Casey and Susan to fulfill their dream of full-time ministry. They had studied and shown themselves approved (2 Tim. 2:15). Anyone that was lead by God and bold enough to do all He wanted them to do was in demand! People were hungry for God's word and wanted to feed on it.

Judy would be very busy helping her husband and that was her dream. Lakeside was becoming a very important worship center to Amber Lake in many ways. They were helping their members in their works for God and reaching out to those who needed Jesus. It is no wonder the church was growing! You just wanted to be there, and not just Sunday or Wednesday, but during lunch or whenever someone was there.

Carl and I pulled into our drive and I wanted us to walk down to the gazebo. The trees had lost most of their leaves now. One more hard rain and wind and they would be gone. We stood out there, looking across the lake, listening to the wind blowing through the woods. The wind was captivating, almost spiritual. You could feel it and know the awesome power and results of it, but you couldn't see it. It was good to be alive, feel good and just enjoy life. I was home out here.

We strolled back to the house and went in through the kitchen. I had forgotten what a mess I had made the night before with all that oil! I looked and Carl had cleaned all of it up. I told him I was sorry and that he must have had to use half a bottle of soap to clean it up! He said he would fix dinner tonight and I looked at him and we both laughed. I told him he would never trust me in the kitchen again. I went in the den and sat at Carl's desk and did some of my paperwork. I could at least read while these blisters were healing. My office would be ready within the month, so I might as well get rid of any clutter I didn't need.

I decided to call Carol and see how they were doing. It was about three in the afternoon. I thought they would still be working. I called and she answered and was surprised to hear from me. I told her about my cooking experience. She said, "Oh, I can't imagine the pain! It must have been awful!" I told her I was thinking how awful hell must be to have to burn for eternity. That was hell for sure! I told her I was so thankful my hands were going to be all right. She said to tell Carl to stay in the kitchen where he belonged and we laughed.

She said Glenn had gone back up to Russ and Janet's at Pine Mountain to write songs. She was going to drive up tonight right after work. "I'm taking a bunch of groceries for tonight and Sunday. They are so good to let us come up. I at least wanted to fix some meals," Carol said.

"Don't deep fry anything, especially your hands!" I kidded. She said she was staying away from that.

"I have to admit we are having a good time. Glenn and Russ sit out on that huge front porch in those big old rockers and play their guitars and write. They sit their coffee mugs on top of their stacks of paper so the wind won't blow them away," Carol said.

"They must take a sip of coffee or iced tea between wind gusts," I said. We both laughed.

"I am so glad all of you are having a great time! I believe Glenn and Russ will come up with a hit or two," I said.

"I hope so!" Carol replied. I told her I would see her Monday and we hung up.

Carl was outside grilling two huge steaks. We had not even eaten lunch. We had a big salad and baked potatoes to go with our steaks. Of course, Carl had fixed iced tea, the best in Amber Lake. He used his Carl's seasoning on our steaks, baked potatoes, and salad and it was delicious. Carl was quite the chef! His seasoning was very popular at the church lunches, and people were beginning to ask if he would start selling it.

We sat outside and ate, but we needed our sweaters. It was a beautiful fall evening! Pepper laid there and looked at us. Carl and I decided since we were so happy, Pepper needed someone too. Carl started calling people that night who raised registered blueticks. He located a Mr. Harry, who lived about one hundred fifty miles away. His hounds were known for their bloodlines and he had a female about two years old that he hunted with. She was an excellent dog and he would sell her. He said he was overstocked with dogs and most people wanted the puppies.

After church, we drove over to visit Mr. Harry. Carl looked at the dog and looked over her papers. Sue was her name and she had beautiful markings and was so gentle. Carl knew this breed well and knew what to look for in a bluetick. She met with his approval.

Within the hour, Carl, Sue, and I were on the way home. We got in the driveway and here came Pepper. Boy, was he going to be surprised! Their eyes perked up when they saw each other. Yes, love at first sight! Carl said he was going to Springfield and get her a collar, bowl, and a bed. Knowing Carl, she would get a few toys and goodies too.

November was a beautiful month that year. Thanksgiving was to be quite a celebration since it was our first holiday as newlyweds. We had a lot to be thankful for in many ways. Thank God my hands had healed perfectly! Mom, Dad, Sis, Brian, and Thomas flew in and we planned turkey and all the trimmings. It was so nice to have my family there. We didn't get to visit as much as I would have liked through the years. Now that I was phasing out of work, I wanted that to change.

On Thanksgiving Day, we also invited the Goodfellows, Brother Darrel, Judy, Carol, Glenn, Russ, Janet, Casey, Susan, Sharon, and Kimberly. The ones who could not eat the noon meal with us tried to stop by some time during the day. It was a great fellowship and food a plenty. I had baked a twenty-three pound turkey and it was delicious and so was the gravy! I had oyster dressing, green bean casserole, sweet potatoes with brown sugar and butter, rolls, and pumpkin pies with whipped cream. Even Carl was impressed with my cooking! Thank God for great cookbooks!

He and I had both cooked desserts for two days before Thanksgiving. It was fun being in the kitchen together. Pepper and Sue looked in the French doors at us, hoping we would throw them some scraps. My family all flew back Sunday after church. They were glad to see everyone at Lakeside again and sure did enjoy being at Amber Lake.

That was the last time I would see all of them until spring. We didn't travel much when the weather was bad. We had all learned the hard way. There was nothing worse than driving home in blizzards or having flights delayed when you needed to get back home. We always celebrated Thanksgiving together if we could.

It was a lot more fun staying out at Amber Lake than in my Manhattan apartment, especially for Dad. Mom and Sis liked to shop, so Carl and I would take them out and about a lot. My first five years in Manhattan they had enjoyed the city because we took them to see all the sights. Through the years I would fly to their home in the spring or summer. Carl and I would stay there. After all, they had five bedrooms. I planned on seeing them more once I quit working.

I had the house all decorated for Thanksgiving with fall arrangements from the reception. Lakeside Church had left up our wedding decorations and everyone had enjoyed them. We were the best decorated church in town! Our church had hosted the community Thanksgiving church service on Wednesday night before Thanksgiving. All the candles in the hurricane lamps were lit in the sanctuary and it put a heavenly glow throughout.

After the service, we had two banquet tables full of food in the fellowship hall. The other visiting church members certainly made over our new fellowship hall. Some of them said they wanted to start coming to the lunch program too. I enjoyed the service. It was so touching to see the community all come together. There were at least two hundred people there, maybe more.

We packed up all the Thanksgiving decorations and put them in the big closet Carl had built in my new office. I turned to him with a smirk and said, "Now, it is finally time to buy all those Christmas decorations for our first Christmas!" He said it looked like I was foaming at the mouth and joked that he wanted all the credit cards so he could cut them in half right now! We only had a couple of credit cards and we hardly ever used them. Carl had shown me the Scripture where God didn't want his people in debt. If the Bible said it, we certainly needed to pay attention and do what He said.

I was still in the city four days a week. Although I never complained, I could tell Franklin had not planned this for me. All of us knew we had to pitch in when Kent died. He always put in at least seventy hours a week and never looked up. He was a hard worker and it left a great void, not to mention we lost a dear friend.

My heart sank just thinking that if he could come back he wouldn't have to have anyone try to convince him how important it was to accept Jesus! If only he could come back and have another chance, but that was impossible. If only things had been different!

As I imagined hell's torment, I remembered that I had gone crazy not having buckets of ice just for my burnt hands for a matter of several hours. Kent would be able to look up and see Honey, Eric, Carol, Sam, Faune, and I in heaven. That would be another hell all to itself! When he saw Kimberly and I he would be tormented knowing we tried to tell him and he wouldn't listen. What Kent wouldn't give just to live an earthly life for eternity. He would love it even if he worked twenty hours a day and slept on the floor of his office. That would be absolute heaven compared to burning alive every minute for eternity!

I hoped Franklin would be with us. I knew we would not be able to see Kent. There are no tears in heaven. If we could see all our friends and loved ones who were not saved, we would weep seeing them constantly burning and tormented in hell. It made me realize that for all of us who are saved, our lives here on earth are as close as we will ever be to hell. For all the people who are not saved, their lives here are as close as they will ever get to heaven.

Franklin, Carol, Sam, Faune, and I always checked on Honey and wanted to see how she and Eric were doing. Honey had been promoted in her job and she was now manager of Tilly's. It was a unique women's clothing store. She had been there a number of years and had built quite a following of customers. She knew what looked good on people and how to help them pick styles and colors that flattered them.

She was doing a lot of special orders for many ladies now. They were very pleased with her because they were extremely satisfied with the way their clothes made them look great. Eric was helping her with her orders, deliveries, restocking the racks with new shipments, or whatever needed to be done. He was a wonderful, handsome young man and thank God, they were able to be together during the day.

Carol, Faune, and I would get him on the speakerphone sometimes and then we would kid him about meeting some young, beautiful rich girl in there someday. Kent had left them in good financial shape, but they also had jobs they enjoyed and made them feel they were fulfilling people's needs.

December rolled around and we all decorated the office for Christmas as usual. Franklin moved Sam into Kent's office about a month after his death and that was so much better than seeing it empty. We had packed up all of Kent's personal items and had taken them over to Honey's home about three weeks after Kent's death. She had never been back to the office. She said she wasn't ready and just driving by our building was rough enough.

I knew I needed to have her attend one of Sharon's seminars. Kimberly would be a good one for her to talk to. I thought some of those ladies that shopped at Tilly's would enjoy their seminars. Honey said some of them were obsessed with their weight and worried to death they were going to gain a pound. Better yet, Sharon and Kimberly needed to hold the seminar in the back of Tilly's. They had a first-class meeting room there and Sharon and Kimberly could stay at my apartment. That was a great idea!

At the office, Franklin had been real intense lately on fixing up an old boardroom that was next to his office for his son, Grant. Grant was traveling all the time visiting clients like Carol, Kent, and I used to do. He was very seldom here, but was home every weekend. He was married and had two children in high school and both of them came up here and helped with office work during the summers. It was a business to pass on to his family as far as Franklin was concerned. There was plenty of money in it, along with a lot of headaches and hard work.

Grant was very good to us, after all, he knew it was the partners that kept the wheels turning in many ways! Unfortunately, Grant followed Franklin in the respect that business was first in his life. Grant was very good and loyal to his wife and children, just like Franklin, but there was no room for God in his life either. I guess it was hard for both of them to understand, because they were such good people in every way. A lot better than some Christians.

Oh, what a devastating day it would be when they appeared before Jesus, and he told them to depart, for He never knew them (Matt. 7:23). "Lord, I pray that you touch their hearts and reveal to them that they need to know your Son as their Lord and Saviour. I ask for you to guide my words and actions to witness to them. In Jesus' name I pray. Amen."

It was a week before Christmas and Franklin called all of us in front of this room he was fixing up for Grant. None of us had been allowed to see what was going on in there. Franklin had been like an excited little kid getting this ready for his son. We had all gotten a kick out of it. It was good to see some excitement again! It had been such a down time for all of us after losing Kent.

There was a big red ribbon and bow across the door with a huge tag that said "Merry Christmas, Grant!" We told Grant to get up to the door and look. Santa had been here a week early. He shyly came up and looked at the tag. Franklin was all excited and looking at all of us and winking. "Open the door, son!" encouraged Franklin. Grant looked back at us and grinned. His face was so red and we told him to hurry up. We wanted to see what was on the other side.

He swung the door open and we all gasped. Grant just stood there and looked. "Go on in, son!" Franklin said, moving his hands forward, like he was shooing him in. All of us were standing there laughing at both of them.

Grant looked all around and came up to Franklin and said, "Wow, Dad, thanks a lot! I love you," and they hugged each other for a minute. No one said a word. I immediately felt tears come to my eyes and I wasn't the only one. We had been so lucky to have people like Franklin and Grant head up this company. They were wonderful, compassionate, loyal people.

Franklin had the room fully furnished with cherry furniture, a wet bar, plants, limited edition prints, you name it. He had put some of Grant's awards in there. Franklin and Grant gave a lot of money to different charities in town. They gave so much they would be publicly acknowledged for their contributions. I personally knew they had helped many people through the years and remained anonymous to many other receivers.

Franklin had a buffet lunch brought in and it looked scrumptious! Before we started to eat, Franklin asked me to say a prayer. I felt my heart jump to my throat. I asked that we all join hands.

"Dear Lord, we come to you with thanksgiving. We praise you for our well-being, our family and friends. I ask that you give peace to those who have lost loved ones and let them know you love them and you are their strength and refuge. I praise you for this firm and a very successful year. I pray that you keep us happy and safe during these holidays. Above all, I thank you for your Son, Jesus. He gave the greatest gift of all, His life, for our sins. May we all come to know Him as our personal Lord and Saviour and live in heaven for all eternity. In Jesus' name I pray, Amen."

We all ate that wonderful buffet. Then Franklin had someone dressed as Santa come in and give us our Christmas bonuses. We ate, laughed, and exchanged gifts with one another. Sam yelled, "Hey everyone, look it is snowing!" We all ran to the windows, looking over Manhattan in the snow. The snowflakes were huge and silently falling. All of us got quiet for a moment and just watched the snow. All of a sudden carolers came down the hall singing "Silent Night." Our building managers had groups of carolers do that every year. They walked throughout the building singing. It was perfect timing and very touching.

Franklin hugged each one of us and told us to head for our homes for the holidays. "A Merry Christmas and Happy New Year to one and all!" he shouted as he waved his hand and left, wearing a Santa hat. We cleared off our desks, turned the office machines off and left the building. We all walked out to the garage and were hoping we would not have any trouble getting home. I hugged Carol, Sam, and Faune one more time.

I asked Carol if they were going to Pine Mountain. She said they were flying home to Missouri for Christmas and then they would be back. She said she would call when she got back. Sam looked at me and whispered, "Say your prayers for me during the holidays," and grinned. I smiled back and I told him I would. I knew he was talking about his proposal to Jamie. Faune was going to be busy with her husband and three children. She said she was looking forward to just being at home with her family.

We were all lined up going out of the garage and then onto the snowy streets of Manhattan. I knew I should have called Carl to see what the weather was out there. I guess I knew I was going to make it home or else. I didn't want to stay in my apartment with him out there! I wanted to be home and be home tonight!

The snow got blinding at times, but I prayed out loud for God to lead me home safely (John 14:13–14). I called Carl on my cellular and he was glad to hear from me. He said it was snowing heavy out there, but if I kept coming straight on in I should be OK. He said he had our dinner on hold, the fireplace going, and only Christmas lights on and some candles. Oh, how I wish I was home!

Three hours later I pulled into the driveway. I saw Carl dart by the window to the garage. He had been sitting in the den watching for me. I pulled around back and went into the garage. I usually never used the garage when I got home, but I sure did tonight! Carl was in the garage waiting on me. He opened my car door and it was good to be home and in his arms. No one could have paid me enough to be anywhere else in the world!

The house looked like a picture on the front of a Christmas magazine. I had gotten a nine-foot mountain fir tree for the den. It had a huge gold bow and angel at the top and gold ribbons trailing all the way down to the floor. Clear lights covered it, with huge red bulbs and handmade antique country ornaments.

We had pine greenery and candles on the mantle. I put a six-foot tree upstairs at the end of the hallway in front of the Victorian room. It was in front of the hallway window. It had clear lights, mauve and burgundy shiny bulbs, and gold ribbons and angels with a Victorian style angel gracing the very top.

We had a three-foot Christmas tree in the kitchen on an antique butcher block table Carl had just bought from his favorite cheese store. It had clear lights, miniature kitchen ornaments, as well as miniature pears and apples hanging on it. There were red gingham ribbons all over and a miniature chef's hat on top with the words "Merry Christmas" in red blinking lights.

We had taken a picture of us together in front of our tree the first week of December. We took it with our camera, sitting the timer. It turned out great and I had a hundred Christmas pictures made and addressed them while I was staying in the city at night. Our family and friends who were not at the wedding received a wedding announcement too. We had an eight-by-ten of the Christmas picture made and framed on Carl's desk.

Carl had stocked the refrigerator and freezer that day. He said if we were snowed in we could still eat well. "As long as I have coffee, milk, and sugar," I teased. We watched some Christmas shows as we ate dinner. We retired to the den and turned on the big TV and laid back and relaxed as the snow came down. Carl checked on Sue and Pepper and they were bundled up in their house too. It was so funny to watch them. They acted like an old married couple already.

We did a lot of visiting around Amber Lake during the holidays and had a lot of people visit. We called all of our family members too. I called Jan and they had a big Christmas. I kept telling her how happy I was and thanking her and the girls for all their prayers.

"We serve an awesome God!" she laughed.

"We certainly do!" I exclaimed. I told her I just never knew what the Lord had in store for me, but I had never given him a chance before. We talked and laughed and we both were looking forward to seeing each other next year.

She said there had been revivals going on in Tennessee ever since they came back from New York City. She said there was a great move of the Holy Spirit taking place. She was telling me all about signs and wonders she had seen and how awesome it was. I wanted to see some of those myself, not that I hadn't already in many ways!

Carl had gotten all my office furniture and shelves for my new office as my Christmas present. The store delivered them two days before Christmas and carried all of it upstairs to set up. First thing, I took a damp cloth to all the drawers even though they were new. I started unloading all my boxes and putting everything away. This truly was Christmas! I was having a ball!

On Christmas morning he had a box under the tree, and it was a coffeepot and coffee cup for my new office. That was the first morning I took my cup of coffee and looked at my new office instead of looking outside. The second cup I took over to the window and looked outside.

I had bought Carl some outdoor clothes for Christmas and some keepsake items celebrating our first Christmas together. I had bought him a fancy cheese tray with a dome cover and all. He got a kick out of that. We bought Pepper and Sue some new toys too.

We got so we didn't even want to leave the house. We had never relaxed and enjoyed each other like this before. We spent time together reading our Bibles and talking about what we read. I felt closer to him in a different way than I ever had before.

There was about a foot of snow on the ground throughout the holidays. Carl had bought Harold's grandsons sleds and we took them over there. They were so excited and they all headed over to Windy Knoll to go sledding. We took Harold, Mary, and Trish a ham and a container of Carl's Seasoning for Christmas. We thanked them for watching Pepper and always keeping an eye on our place.

The boys were thrilled when we got Sue and they kept asking when they were going to have puppies. We had a nice visit and Trish was working on the spring line of new cosmetics. There were some beautiful colors. She always used her upstairs bedroom to lay out all the new samples and colors. I placed an order for several items.

Mary was always cooking cakes and pies, or something. She enjoyed that and was always busy in the kitchen. Trish was having more people work for her and she said by spring she should be able to be home four days a week. She was going to go with Sharon and Kimberly sometimes and do makeovers for church ladies. The three of them were giving women a new look from the inside out! It seemed like everyone was making changes and really, rather quickly. Look at me!

The snow was perfect for sledding on Windy Knoll and Carl and I drove up there when we left the Goodfellows. The boys were with several other Amber Lake kids and they were having a ball. Some moms and dads were watching as well as sledding too.

The boys saw us and waved, cherry faces and all. I knew all of them were saved and it did my heart good. Matter of fact, all those boys were already witnessing to their friends at school. I remembered that verse "and the children shall lead them" (Isa. 11:6). Some children did better than we adults!

Carol and Glenn called us from Pine Mountain. We went there one afternoon and visited with them, and Russ and Janet. The chalet was rustic and had a terrific view from that mountain. It was about one hour from our place. Carl always enjoyed listening to their music and hearing about what they were doing.

Janet worked in Springfield and she and Carol said they wanted their husbands to write a million dollar song so they could be at home or have their own business. Carol wanted to have a bed and breakfast where people could enjoy themselves quietly and relax and Janet wanted to help new churches that were just getting started. She had just been very instrumental in the starting of one church, from the building to getting together all the classroom literature. They were both hard workers and extremely organized.

I could see all of us heading for different avenues in our lives. I wanted to write my book on how God had changed my life. I thought couples would take a different look at marriage after reading my book. I believed God wanted me to tell them about that. Everything all of us wanted to do had Jesus in the center of it.

Carl and I brought in the new year at our church. Many of the members brought games and food and all ages came and joined in the celebration of New Year's Eve and we all had a big time. I never thought of the church doing something like that on New Year's Eve, but it was a great idea. Some people were doing puzzles, others playing checkers. The teenagers were playing guitars or games and brought dates or friends. A great way to bring in the new year!

After the holidays I went back to the city. Sam announced to all of us at the board meeting that he proposed to Jamie over the holidays and she accepted. He was hoping she would, since he already bought her an engagement ring for Christmas. "Now I know why the prayer request!" I whispered to him as we both got a cup of coffee at our break. Everyone was kidding about the boardroom being used to announce matters of the heart instead of business dealings lately.

Franklin called me in one day and told me he needed to talk to me. He said he had brought his nephew, Justin, on board. It would take him a couple of months to catch on and then he would be able to play an important role. He had experience, being trained by Franklin's brother, Harris, who was Justin's father. Harris operated a company similar to ours and it was in located in southern California.

He just needed to learn our company's policies and way of doing business. After he was trained, Franklin said I should be able to come in only three days a week instead of four. He said it would get better little by little. I knew Franklin was looking for one more good partner before I would be free. Grant would take Franklin's place someday and had the knowledge to run the firm now if he needed to. Now if Carol decided to leave in a couple of months, that would leave Franklin with another major position to fill. Franklin might as well stay in the recruiting business! Of course, the firm was growing too. He would need new people if none of us were leaving.

Franklin was right. After Carol and I worked closely with Justin for two months he was ready to solo. He was very smart and a real go-getter. Sam was doing great. He was a hard worker and loyal, although not quite as aggressive as Justin. Sometimes Justin was a little too aggressive, but he was not out to step on anybody.

Once again, this was basically a family business, and Justin followed suit with Franklin and Grant in many ways. There was no room in his life for God either. He was all business and even more so than Franklin and Grant. It made me glad I was phasing out. This business-comes-first lifestyle was certainly not for me anymore!

Carl was really involved now in Lakeside Church. They had a revival in February and thirty-four people were saved. Sharon and Kimberly were busy too. They had seen many lives changed and were in constant demand. They came home two days a week to catch up on paperwork and calls.

Sharon had put a podium in their "Your Loss Is His Gain" office and she would stand up there with all her papers and practice her speech. She was getting used to speaking now. She would just stand up there with papers and pantomime to tease Kimberly when she was on the phone. Kimberly said it was all she could do to keep from laughing.

Casey and Susan were busy with "It Is Done Ministries." Casey would usually get Gary and Jesse started on a new job and they would take over and finish. If it was a two or three day job, he would let them handle it. If they were at the church, he stayed right with them. Casey usually did all the weedeating and Gary did all the mowing. Jesse kept the lake bank clean and trimmed the trees and picked up.

Susan was at the church everyday putting together her meetings in the adult Sunday school room. They all ate lunch together here. The church was having more and more activities and different types of services. Sharon and Kimberly would talk one night if they were here and Casey and Susan would minister one night. People were coming to these meetings from all around. There were always new faces Carl said. I had only attended a few because I was in the city too much.

PALS was going full steam. Two groups had been formed and were going about and witnessing—already! Brother Darrel and Judy would each go with one of the groups, no matter what time of the day or night. I needed to attend this class and wanted to so much! Carl and I were going to revivals in the city and around the Amber Lake area. We were meeting people and passing out cards from our church. Our church had a business card made up with the church info, address, and number. "PALS—Soul Winners on call" was listed on the card too.

People were calling and sending PALS to hospitals, colleges, homes, even other church services to introduce the PALS program. More and more people were attending the classes and God was moving! There were so many unsaved people and not enough workers! It reminded me of what it said in the Bible about the harvest being full and there were not enough workers (Luke 10:2).

At least I could pass out cards to everyone I ran across. Also, I had the opportunity to let them use my apartment at least twice a month. I had given PALS the names of Franklin, Grant, Justin, Nick, and Mr. Herring and their work hours. Judy, Brother Darrel, Casey or Susan would come in with a group about every other week and witness in the city.

They were getting more and more names and they would soon be there every week. I felt fulfilled just knowing my apartment was helping somehow in this mission. When I went to Amber Lake they used my apartment. Of course, I told them to look up Gilbert, Peggy, and Eugene. Brother Darrel, Judy, Susan, and Casey made the very first trip together. Brother Darrel headed over to Peggy's the first morning and they remembered each other from the wedding. Eugene was there working again. They were both surprised and glad to see Brother Darrel.

He told them what they were doing in town and Peggy wanted several of the business cards to pass out. Eugene was helping Peggy all the time now. They were getting ready to put in another store across Manhattan. Eugene said he needed to carry several cards to where he used to work. They said they loved Amber Lake and Lakeside Church and wanted to come back up there. Now, they wanted to come up and attend PALS.

I had told Brother Darrel to pick up a blueberry and cream cheese bagel for Gilbert. He did that and needless to say, picked up several for all of them. He handed Gilbert the little sack at the front door of the building and Gilbert remembered Brother Darrel from the wedding and shook his hand. Gilbert peeked into the sack and started laughing.

They talked a while and Brother Darrel said he went in the building and then turned around to look at Gilbert just like I told him to. He said he started laughing at Gilbert with cream cheese smeared on both sides of his face, but he was smiling and enjoying himself!

Brother Darrel, Judy, Casey, and Susan knew New York City well after several trips. They stayed in my apartment when I was not there. They were getting more calls with each visit and had a long list of people to visit and witness to. They were even going to another revival up in Harlem that had been going on for weeks. Kimberly told them about it and when they were in the city they were inviting people to it and went every night.

When I was in the city I went and so did Faune and Sam. Carol and Glenn went several times and all of us would eat out and have a ball. Franklin never went back, but one night we got Grant to go with us. Grant went back several times and we were all praying for him! Justin would stay in the office with Franklin and work late. I was scared to confess these words, but Justin was following in Kent's footsteps. Justin had even started going to his country club for brunch every Sunday morning!

My apartment must have felt like it had life in it again. One Wednesday night I was halfway home and passed Casey, Susan, David, and Glenn tooting and waving, heading for my apartment. I was sure glad I hadn't sold it! Casey and Susan had a much needed ministry. They were witnessing to many sick people, leading them to the Lord, and praying for their healing too. David and Glenn went with them when it involved young people or teenagers.

The number of lost and hurting people astounded me. They were calling out and many Christians didn't know what to do, but there was someone to call on who knew what to do. Christians needed to learn what to do and what was already available to them through God's word. They were perishing from lack of knowledge (Hos. 4:6). "Learn and study the Bible and do ALL it says to do" was our motto!

It was spring already and Carl and I decided to go up to Clear Creek. Lady Chandler's had prayer meetings every Monday and Thursday night. It was four o'clock Thursday afternoon and I had just gotten into Amber Lake from work. I had worn a high neck blouse to wear my pearl brooch from Lady Chandler's collection. Susan, Judy, April, and Trish had gone to the city to stay at my apartment. Trish knew a lot of women there since she worked in Manhattan and still had many connections. Now she was doing all of her work from Amber Lake. She only traveled to buy new lines of makeup and attend workshops and seminars now. I was so happy for her and the boys liked having her home.

We left early for Clear Creek and ate at the Clear Creek Buffet there. It was scrumptious and they had the best fried chicken I believe I had ever eaten, except for Carl's. I couldn't wait to see Lady Chandler's and especially that portrait. We got there forty-five minutes before the meeting and a lady greeted us at the door. She was the great-granddaughter and her name was Carlene. We introduced ourselves and I showed her the brooch and her mouth flew open and she smiled and shook her head.

"Come with me," she said as she breezed around the corner of the foyer and into a huge sitting room. We followed and she put her hand up as if to present that magnificent portrait and turned to us and said, "Look! My great-grandmother, Lady Chandler, and my great-grandfather, Elliston Chandler. She is wearing your brooch!"

Carl and I got as close as we could to the portrait. It was at least five feet tall and four feet wide. There was my brooch, around the Victorian collar of her flowing dress. I felt like I had stepped back in time. Lady Chandler had a very pretty, gentle look about her. She was tall and slim and had her hair up and a beautiful hat on to match her dress. Elliston Chandler was a distinguished man. He reminded me of Carl, except he had a mustache. They were a very striking couple! We talked to Carlene and then she asked another lady to greet people and seat them.

She took us through the house and out back to the gardens. It was dusk and she wanted to show us the memorial gardens. It was breathtaking to see the headstones since I knew the story behind this couple. The memorial garden had weeping cherry trees, blooming hyacinth, and tulips in every color. The scent was heavenly.

Elliston Chandler's stone was a life-size statue. He had his hat on, along with his gloves and cane and he looked like a fine English gentleman. Her statue was life-size and she had on a Victorian gown and hat, just like the portrait. The garden was immaculate and I felt at peace here. As I looked at their statues, I looked forward to seeing them when I went to heaven. I loved what they had done with their beautiful estate and gardens, leaving them to glorify their Lord and Saviour.

Carlene took us back through the baptismal gardens. The pool was so still and clear and it looked like a mirror in the twilight. There were flowers blooming all around and the smell was heavenly once again. I saw all the concrete benches around the pool area. Oh, there was the statue of Christ with His arms stretched out, looking over the pool! He stood in the pool about two feet at the center edge. It was like He was looking over everyone who was baptized and was pleased. I could almost see the Spirit of God descending like a dove over His head (Matt. 3:16). How magnificent it was. I felt tears come to my eyes. Carl and I couldn't even speak when we saw His statue.

There were statues of angels throughout the gardens. They were life-size and there were men, women, and children. Flowers adorned their feet and there were stone walkways throughout these gardens so you could walk under and past the angels. Some were standing on stone pedestals with their arms reached out over the walkways like they were blessing you as you passed under. It was a feeling I can't explain. I felt reassurance, peace and holiness just walking through the garden. God planned this garden and the Chandlers were obedient and completed it. The money they acquired on earth was still working for the glory of God! What a blessing!

As we walked back Carlene said all the jewelry that was sold would keep the estate in total care and upkeep forever. "As long as forever is here," she smiled. "Thanks for contributing to our cause," she said graciously as we walked back in the home. We thanked her for taking us through the memorial gardens and took our seats. There were about twenty people in attendance.

A gentleman came to the podium and started preaching about the Holy Spirit. He talked about being baptized after you accept Jesus and then he talked about being baptized in the Holy Spirit. He talked about the Day of Pentecost and when they were baptized in the Holy Spirit they came up speaking in different tongues as the Spirit enabled them (Acts 2:4).

I wasn't sure what he was talking about and had never experienced that. I wanted to know more about this. I wrote down all the Scripture he quoted so I could look it up and study it. After the service he asked people to come up who needed healing in their bodies. About seven people went up. He laid hands on them and prayed and praised God for their healing (Mark 16:17–18). This reminded me of Casey and Susan. Another gentleman stood behind the person being prayed for and as several fell backwards he caught them and laid them on the floor. Four of them immediately started shouting, "Thank you, Jesus for your healing!" and some laughed and some wept.

"Boy, what a wonderful service that was!" I told Carl as we walked through the French doors and into our kitchen. "I see we have a lot to learn!"

"Why haven't we been taught in our church to be baptized in the Holy Spirit?" I asked.

"Well, we just haven't," Carl said.

"Well, it is scriptural! If it is scriptural, why aren't we practicing it?" I asked, amazed we weren't.

I had heard Kimberly and Sharon talk about it before. I had no idea what they were talking about and didn't ask. I had heard Casey and Susan talk about the laying on of hands and anointing with oil in their healing services, but why didn't we practice it in our church services (James 5:14–16)?

I asked Carl questions that night and looked up Scriptures as to what the pastor preached on. Sure enough it was all in the Bible! Carl said many people did not want anything to do with a Pentecostal movement. They thought people would be running around the church, jumping up and down, screaming, jerking and such. Carl said it didn't bother him if they did, but it did for a lot of people. After all, there is not anyone preaching the plan of salvation any more than our church.

"I know the most important thing is to be saved from hell, but why not be saved from sickness, debt, depression, and all that is evil? 'Whatever you bind on earth will be bound in heaven, and whatever you lose on earth and will be loosed in heaven' (Matt. 18:18–20). If good health is 'loosed' in heaven, I would love to know it is 'loosed' here too. I don't know much about the Bible, but I do know I don't read the part I want and leave out the part I don't want to know about!" I explained, rather exasperated.

We had heard about a revival in Springfield. It had gone on for two months and was still going strong. I immediately thought about

Harlem and that precious church and the fire they had going there all the time! I had to go to Springfield tonight and Carl was in agreement.

We had my office upstairs just about done. It was a rainy day so we got a lot done up there. We kept checking on Sue who was about ready to have puppies any minute. David, Glenn, Calvin, or Nathan called almost every day to see if they had been born yet. I guess they were embarrassed to keep calling, but they wanted to know so bad they made each other take turns. We laughed every time they called. We were going to give them one, but it was going to be a surprise. I couldn't wait to see their faces. That would really be fun!

Carl and I got ready and decided to eat at a Mexican restaurant in Springfield we liked. I wore a nice slack outfit and told Carl if I was going to roll and jump all over the place I better wear slacks. He really frowned at me then. Boy, did I love to tease him, acting so serious when I did. If I had the Holy Spirit touch me and I wanted to dance and jump all over I figured that must be something! What does it feel like, I wondered, to be so touched by the Holy Spirit that you want to jump and dance!

We got to the church and it filled up quickly. They had to bring chairs out. I saw people healed, people come out of bondage from all sorts of things, and people prayed for everything people needed. There was singing and dancing. I kept taking in everything. The look on their faces was real and their laughter and tears were real.

Then the evangelist said whoever wanted to be baptized in the Holy Spirit to come forward. I went right up to the altar. He prayed over me and laid his hand on my forehead. I felt different than I had ever felt, but there was no evidence of speaking in tongues.

We went every night through Sunday night and I went up for prayer, but didn't feel like I received the baptism of the Holy Spirit. Several prayer warriors told me I had it, but Satan was just telling me I didn't. I felt a different feeling inside, but didn't see any evidence. I just gave it to God and I went back up to the altar while people were praying and told God I wanted the baptism of the Holy Spirit and I wanted evidence of it. I wanted to feel the power and the fire of the Holy Spirit working in me.

I finally had peace about it and left it with Him at the altar, vowing not to pick it back up. He had it now and I had asked Him for it and He would take care of it. I didn't think about it anymore, or let's say I refused to think about it. Satan wanted to jab me with not having the evidence I wanted to see, but I was resisting his words in Jesus' name, so he had to flee (James 4:7)!

That was something else I had learned from these revivals. When you heard something negative or a put-down, you needed to know who that really was. If you told Satan to flee in Jesus' name, he had to flee! I needed to know how to discern spirits (1 Cor. 12:10). That would be vital in my walk with God!

We had gone to Lakeside Church Sunday morning and we had a packed house. About twenty of us went to Grinder's Mill and ate lunch. Kimberly and Sharon were back in town. Kimberly said Sharon was a pro at speaking now, but she still pantomimed at the podium when Kimberly was trying to conduct business calls. We all laughed. I talked to them about the baptism of the Holy Spirit and they explained how different they felt when it happened to them. Everybody was leaving and I wanted to talk to them more but they had to be at a meeting at Willow Creek. They both hugged Carl and me and said they would be praying for us.

I headed back to the city early Monday morning and went straight in to work. We all were in our usual frenzy and Grant and Justin were just part of the group now. I went back to my desk at lunch, and Mike, my favorite taxi driver, was on my mind. I called and asked for Mike, taxi number sixty-eight, and he came to the phone. When he heard my voice he started talking about the wedding and how beautiful it was.

I told him I was glad to have met his mother and that he had a very pretty lady with him. He thanked me and said she was his girlfriend with real enthusiasm in his voice. I told him again she was pretty and then I teased him and asked him if she was rich too. He said he was so crazy about her she could have been a street person and his feelings would have been the same for her. When he said this it took me back to where Mike had driven us that day in the Bowery.

He said he thought about her day and night, but there was still a void in his life he couldn't explain. I was bold enough to tell him maybe it was God that was missing from his life. He said that couldn't be it because he went to church every Sunday and was also going to classes they offered at church. He said his girlfriend went with him, but she seemed to enjoy it and feel a real depth with the church that he didn't feel.

I listened to him and knew what he needed. Sometimes it is a lot easier to talk with an acquaintance than a family member or a close friend, especially over the phone. I could hear someone call his name and he said he had to go and would call me later and thanked me for listening.

Franklin called me over the intercom and told me he needed to see Sam and I in his office. Sam and I got there at the same time and Franklin told us to take a seat. He had just gotten a call from a company in Atlanta; they wanted to have us visit them and take over their account. Franklin went on about what all they needed. He wanted Sam and I to go and handle it.

I could tell this would take a whole week of hard work. Sam had never gone to another company and worked on-site before, so he definitely needed this experience. I had been there many times and knew what to do. Franklin knew this would finish Sam's training. He still wanted Carol here for Grant and Justin. He wouldn't tell them that, because they were doing such a great job. Carol had years of experience in every situation that could come down the road and knew what to do if there was a roadblock.

Franklin told me to go ahead and tie up loose ends here this week and take off for Amber Lake. We had to leave on a flight Sunday night and would return Friday night. Franklin told me not to come in until the following Tuesday. That would be a perfect time to have PALS come in here and talk with Franklin, Grant, and Justin on a personal basis, I thought. You couldn't get them in church, except for Grant. He was at least starting to listen.

Sam said he had something to tell Franklin and me. He and Jamie had set their wedding date for the last Saturday in June. That was not far away, and Franklin told him to take off as he needed and we could cover him after this Atlanta trip. We both told him how happy we were for him. All of us had a meeting at three o'clock and the wedding announcement would be made to everyone. He and Jamie were getting married back in his hometown. It was five hours away from here and we would all make a weekend trip to his hometown and see the area too.

I worked hard to get everything caught up and called Judy and told her I was leaving the city Wednesday afternoon for Amber Lake and then I would be in Atlanta all next week. My apartment would be available for whoever was coming in to witness. I told her about Mike and gave her his number too. They already had Franklin, Grant, and Justin's names, but this week or next would be perfect.

Before I left the office Wednesday I sent a message to Franklin, Grant, and Justin about my church's PALS and that they may come up to visit since they were in the area. I said a prayer over the message before I sent it. I told Carol, Sam, and Faune by e-mail and told them to say a prayer for this visit. I told Carol I would see her after next week and told Sam I would see him at the airport Sunday night. I left the office and headed for Amber Lake.

Carl, Pepper, and Sue all came to the car when I pulled up. I was so glad to be home! I wanted to be home all the time, but it just hadn't worked out that way. God was in control, so it would work out. I do know one thing, my apartment was vital to our soul winners witnessing in the city. It was in their use whenever I wasn't there, at least three days every week now. Sylvia was kind enough to let one of our groups stay at her home at least twice a month.

Soul winners were in high demand; people were crying out and reaching for the Christians who were going out doing God's work. There weren't enough of them who were willing to visit, hit the streets, and witness wherever they were and that was a horrible tragedy (Matt. 28:19–20).

Did Christians just think they were supposed to sit in their favorite pews religiously and never do anything else? The multitudes were crying out silently, but I could hear them. Yes, there were some of us Christians who could hear them . . . and it pierced our hearts.

It was the rich man who everyone thought had everything, but he didn't and no one came to share the gift of Jesus. It was the teenager down the street who was a troublemaker and no one wanted to hear his cursing and anger, yet the battle in his mind was plotting suicide. It was the young and old alike in nursing homes and hospitals who thought God had forsaken them, and no one came to tell them about Jesus and how He loved them. It was the children who wanted to go to church and know more about Jesus, but parents didn't take them and no one else did either. It was the ones who were dirty, living in a shack, or not respectable, who needed to hear about Jesus, but many didn't want to associate with them (Mark 16:15).

How sad that we are the way we are, I thought, we Christians that know better. All of us know better. Some of the people PALS were contacting couldn't be contacted at work, but were coming up to the apartment after work. My apartment was in a great location and easy to find. There was always food and drinks available, those visiting were on their own time, and sometimes they stayed for hours. It was a very relaxing and inviting atmosphere and the church was giving money for food and drinks and there was plenty for all who came in.

Many who came there were bringing back others and Casey and Susan were setting up weekly meetings at my apartment for Saturday night which was becoming a church night for many. It was a very inviting and relaxing atmosphere. Peggy, Eugene, Gilbert, and Tiffany were telling everyone about it and sometimes they would be there with guests.

The latest report was that twenty-seven people had been saved in my apartment alone! When I went back there I praised God for that apartment and that he was using it for His glory. I wasn't supposed to sell it. Matter of fact, God had blessed us with selling Carl's apartment and we were doing great financially. I made up my mind I would never sell it as long as it was being used for the glory of God. Some of the neighbors I had had for years said it had been a blessing and they were bringing guests. One of them said it was an answer from God to have a church service right next door to her. She said, "Diane, who would have ever thought of this! All these years we have lived in this exclusive apartment building, and then God shows up and has a Saturday night meeting right here, I mean right here under our noses!"

She and two of her dear friends were among the ones saved. She told me her friends were over for dinner one night and they were visiting and heard quite a few people walking down the hall. She said it sounded like they were all going in my apartment, so she stuck her head out the door and Susan saw her and told her to come on over, they were having church. She said curiosity got the best of her and over they went. She thought she had better find out what was going on, especially since it was next door to her. All the neighbors were good people and of course we weren't a rowdy group anyway, but there was music and "Amens" and hallelujahs!

Brother Darrel, Judy, Kimberly, Sharon, Casey, and Susan were so busy going and doing God's work it was astounding. All of them were baptized in the Holy Spirit. They all had that boldness and fire! Joy and Cassie were handling the noon lunches and church business during the day when they were gone. Carolyn and Ralph worked during the day, but helped as much as they could bringing food and such.

I wanted to be out with all of them, but I guess God needed me in the city for something. PALS had four groups now and they were all busy. The lunch group was growing and Judy estimated at least twenty-three people had been saved as a result of those luncheons!

Months ago God had told them to have the fellowship hall remodeled and the money was there. Then the idea of the business luncheons came up immediately. Brother Darrel and Judy were very well thought of in the community and everybody loved them. People that were saved kept telling their unsaved loved ones to stop there for lunch. Nancy's Cafe and Lakeside Church had the best meals around! Millie kept telling Roger, Wayne, Jack, and Reggie to go to the church for lunch. Roger and Jack went because they enjoyed seeing everyone there and enjoyed the delicious homemade food, but they didn't go for the worship time.

I realized, after studying my Bible more, about tithing. Tithing was very important and it was a blessing to give and a blessing in return to the tither (2 Cor. 9:8–11). I didn't think too much about it at first, but I had to keep reminding myself of what the Scriptures said. I finally became a cheerful giver and couldn't wait to give (2 Cor. 9:7). After all, it was a privilege and a blessing in many ways!

Thursday morning Sue had her puppies. There were seven of them. They were all fine and so cute! We called the Goodfellows after the boys got home from school and Nathan answered. Carl told him Sue had seven puppies and for them to come over. Nathan put the phone down and yelled, "The puppies are here!" Carl heard the rest of them scrambling around and running out the door and Nathan never did hang the phone up.

They all walked down the road with Harold. Mary and Trish had gone to Springfield to buy office supplies for Trish. They all got a big kick out of the puppies. They sat out in the garage and kept watching them. Harold, Carl, and I kept chuckling at them. It was so cute. They didn't want to miss one move the puppies made. Of course, they weren't as cute as they would be in a few weeks. They stayed almost an hour and walked back home.

Carl and I came in and he told me when the puppies were six weeks old he would let them pick one. He sat down at his desk and proceeded to get all their papers ready and take care of that. I went upstairs and continued filling up shelves in my office.

We ate lunch and Carl and I agreed to go back to Springfield tonight to the revival. It was in the tenth week and going stronger than ever. We asked Brother Darrel and Judy to join us for dinner and go to the revival with us. Casey and Susan had left with about three members of PALS early this morning. Brother Darrel laughed and said they had checked in at my apartment and hit the streets about ten o'clock this morning.

I always called Carl when I knew what day I was leaving the city and told him when the apartment would be free. There was so much demand in the city now, that Casey and Susan or PALS members were using my apartment during the day while I was at work and then they were gone on visitations all evening. I would never see them. When I was at my apartment, usually Casey and Susan would stay in the extra bedroom. I would get up and find a letter on the kitchen counter about what all happened last night and the excitement was so obvious in the letter—who was saved, who was healed, and so on.

I had my own bedroom and bath and so did they. Usually they wouldn't get in until the wee hours of the morning anyway. They were ministering healing mostly and there were many testimonies about their ministry. In turn, the people that were healed saw God's power and were able to be led to Christ. They saw His signs and wonders and knew He was real (Mark 16:17–20). Kimberly and Sharon came in once in a while and either stayed at my place or at Sylvia's.

We picked up Brother Darrel and Judy at the church. Sharon and Kimberly were holding a meeting there tonight with Your Loss Is His Gain. They were all back in the kitchen fixing recipes they had in their new book. They were expecting at least thirty women. Some were traveling from as far as eighty miles away.

Joy and Cassie were coming to church in a few minutes to help them. Trish was coming in for dinner and to do makeovers for all of them who wanted one. They all laughed and said women were calling in and said, "A free dinner and makeover, we'll be there!" They didn't know they were going to leave there with a lot more than a full stomach and a new face.

They would also be fed on the Word and their faces would have a new glow provided by the Holy Spirit. Their ministry was in high demand. Women were having a ball and being saved, set free from bondages and mindsets and weight control problems. What woman at any age doesn't want to look great and feel great and know that she is going to be in heaven for eternity! Whew! Those meetings were truly life changing!

Brother Darrel, Judy, Carl, and I got in Carl's Jeep and we headed to Springfield. They were talking about Your Loss Is His Gain and said when all the women come to those meetings you have never seen so much laughing and crying in your life! Brother Darrel said they all leave smiling and want to know when the next meeting will be. They said Sharon tries to schedule one night a week if possible, but she said she and Kimberly were traveling a lot now.

Cassie and Joy were helping part-time with all their paperwork. Between Cassie and Joy cleaning, cooking, helping at lunch, and working with Sharon and Kimberly they were very busy! Judy said they were having a ball and were able to get paid from all three of their jobs. They had cheerfully volunteered to help with the business lunches and help Sharon and Kimberly, never expecting to be paid, but things took off and there was good money coming in. The Lord was taking care of everybody doing His work in every way! He was blessing the givers as well as the receivers. Receivers were becoming givers and givers were becoming receivers! Hallelujah!

We all ate a wonderful dinner at a steak house and went on to the revival. It was a packed house and we got there thirty minutes early. Carl introduced Brother Darrel and Judy to Brother Creasy and his wife, Joyce. The church was beautifully decorated and another building program was about to take place there. Brother Charles Thompson of Jesus Is Lord Ministries was the evangelist. His ministry team included Bernice, Rena, and Angie. They had come all the way here from Heber Springs, Arkansas.

We took a seat. Carl was beginning to know a lot of people here at Northside Christian Center because he had started going almost every night. They sang and everyone was really enjoying praise and worship. I noticed how many teenagers and young people there were. I told Carl we needed to bring David, Glenn, Calvin, and Nathan next time. Every seat was packed. People were giving testimonies and it made me weep!

Brother Charles started preaching and he was wonderful. They had an altar call and I went up. I just felt it was time and I was ready to receive the baptism of the Holy Spirit. He came up to me and prayed over me and laid his hand on my head and the next thing I remember I was on the floor. There was a lady leaning over me telling me to start speaking and something about living waters will flow from within me (John 7:38–39).

I didn't know who she was and it didn't make any difference. I felt like I was in a half-sleep and it was so peaceful. I started uttering something and she encouraged me and suddenly I was speaking an unknown language. Speaking in tongues, evidence of the Holy Spirit! Oh, it was unbelievable! She was laughing and saying, "That is it, you have it, keep speaking!"

I got up and went back to my seat, uttering this unknown language. I don't know how I felt. I knew the Holy Spirit had given me this gift because I sure knew I couldn't speak that on my own!

From that moment on, something inside of me changed. I felt like a little child excited over a wonderful gift I was given, and I couldn't believe it! Nothing could take it away from me. It was mine forever and it empowered me for the glory of the Lord. I felt bold in the Lord. I realized I wasn't nervous to witness to anyone anymore. Whew! It was amazing! Of course, what should I have expected, a gift coming from the Lord!

After church the four of us stopped and had coffee and dessert. I was so excited and bubbling over I had to tell them what happened and how I felt. Of course they were there and saw me go up and go down. They listened and could definitely see my excitement and knew it was real!

We agreed we would all go tomorrow night and see if we could gather up some folks to go. Brother Darrel knew a family in Springfield that wasn't saved. Judy knew some ladies in Springfield who had been to Susan's seminars and she knew they both had lost children. She was going to call them and tell them there were a lot of teenagers that attended, plus it was right there in their hometown. We talked all the way home about everything we were going to do. I felt like I had the power of a mission group all by myself.

The next day we made phone calls and got people lined up to go. Carl was taking Harold's grandsons and one of their friends. I was carrying April, Millie, and Nancy with me. They got the biggest kick out of my gold Jag. It was kind of unusual to see a car like that around here. Most of the people they knew had recreational vehicles, vans, and such.

Judy was meeting several ladies and they were bringing their teenagers with them. She offered to take them all out and eat pizza before the service. That got their attention! Carl and his teenage group met them there so they could all have fellowship together. Brother Darrel called the family he knew there and brought Cassie, Joy, and Carolyn with him. They all met at a restaurant, had dinner, and went to the revival. My crew all ate at my favorite Mexican restaurant. We were definitely helping all the restaurants out in Springfield!

It was a wonderful service and of everyone we brought, two of them accepted Jesus as their Lord and Saviour. Every one of those teenagers went up and wanted Brother Charles to pray over them. The Holy Spirit touched every one of them. One of the women Judy brought could not stop crying. Brother Charles told her to go ahead and cry, that it was a release and cleansing for her.

Brother Charles asked for all the ministers to come up. Brother Darrel went up along with about ten others. Judy was right up there with him. The church had even taken out the two front pews the previous week so there would be more room.

He prayed, laid hands on, and prophesied over Brother Darrel. I knew Brother Darrel would know God had touched him when he came up. When the Holy spirit touches you like that, you are never the same! It is something you don't forget. I saw people healed and set free, and then I saw a spirit of laughter come over several people. I had no idea what that was. Church members there said they were full of new wine (Acts 2:13–18). I was learning something new with each visit. This was amazing!

We went the next night too. Carl and I left mid-afternoon. We had heard about a religious bookstore in Springfield and we wanted to visit there. We spent about ninety minutes in there. They were very helpful and they had a lot of little books that dealt with spirit-filled material as they called it.

I wanted to take several of these books on my trip with me. I wanted Sam to read them too. We bought a bunch of the one dollar books. They were only about thirty pages long and quoted Scripture and told about healing, the Holy Spirit, finances, speaking in tongues, and so forth. Then I found one on the rapture and I wanted to read that.

Carl and I got a lot of the little ones for Brother Darrel and Judy to have too. Carl and I bought books totaling over one hundred dollars. I couldn't wait to read them! We decided to eat dinner and went to a nice buffet in town. In came Casey and Gary with some other men they were bringing to the revival and we all sat together. I was hoping I would see Jesse, but they said he wouldn't go. Casey said Susan had people she knew in Springfield and she was having dinner with them before the revival meeting. They were people she had come to know through her ministry and meetings.

The meeting that night was wonderful. One of the men Casey brought accepted Jesus and so did two of the ladies Susan brought. Some of the teenagers that were here last night came back with some of their friends. Fifty-five people accepted Jesus that night. Trish came and brought all her boys and one of their friends. The friend went up and accepted Jesus. It was some night! We didn't start leaving until eleven o'clock.

We went to church the next morning and it was full. There were several new people as a result of the business luncheons. They gave testimonies and then Brother Darrel read testimonies that were sent to him from Manhattan and Harlem. One of them was a young lady that was saved in my apartment. It made me weep, it was so touching. I wasn't the only one weeping.

They were giving praise to our soul winners, which was a result of PALS. What a wonderful class that was and look what all had happened. We as a church were getting so excited about all these testimonies. We had morning and evening PALS now.

Judy, Cassie, and Joy were in the kitchen from ten until two each day. The public and the class members would all eat there now. We always had at least twenty people on a daily basis. Several days they had as many as forty! Brother Darrel and Judy were as busy as they could be, and people were being saved because there was a great movement of the Holy Spirit. You could feel it and you either were in it or you weren't. The lukewarm people didn't seem to be feeling God's presence at all (Rev. 3:15–17). A lot of them were saved, but had just fallen by the wayside. They didn't want to do anything or change anything. There were people who criticized the laying on of hands, speaking in tongues, and all the "carrying on" as they called it, and that was a dangerous thing to do (Mark 3:29). Of course, there were people who abused it and were full of imitation, but I knew I was supposed to look at the Bible and do all it said.

Laying on of hands and speaking in tongues was biblical, so how could I argue that? I sure couldn't take the Bible and leave in what I wanted and take out what I thought people might consider controversial. If I took a cake recipe and left out certain ingredients it called for and used only the ones I wanted, I would have a flat cake! Why even bother unless you put in *all* the ingredients and followed *all* the directions? I found out I had to do what God said to do and learn to discern spirits.

There were rumors that some of these things that had happened were fake and people weren't really healed. Some people said preachers weren't supposed to have all that money, they were supposed to be humble. The Bible taught me that God owned the cattle on a thousand hills (Ps. 50:10). "Well, He owns it all! It is all His! If we, His children, weren't supposed to have it, who was?" I professed.

We're supposed to have it and more abundantly. The Christians, of all people, are supposed to be prosperous above all things (John 10:10). It is the devil that tells us the opposite. The atheists sure don't want what we have if we are driving around in dirty, dilapidated cars with Jesus stickers all over the bumper! They did much better than that without God!

I hear Christians all the time grumbling and complaining, saying "I hope God gets me out of this mess. I'm begging Him to help me. He hasn't done nothing yet. I guess I'll have to take care of it all by myself!" Woe is me! We are supposed to be full of praise and thanksgiving, not murmuring and complaining (Prov. 18:20–21). I haven't found anywhere in the Bible where He tells us to beg for anything!

He tells us to ask and we shall receive (Matt. 7:7–11). He tells those who are heavy laden to come to Him and give Him their burdens (Matt. 11:28–30). We keep carrying our burdens because we don't think He can do it. That is right, He *can't* do it if we never give them to him. Cast your burdens on Him and leave them there. He is perfectly capable! Then walk by faith and not by sight (2 Cor. 5:7).

God is not a liar. He has to honor what He told us He would do. We need to know what He told us! You can't water it down, leave part of it out, or mix words. In other words, do what God told you to do, not what man wants you to do (Acts 5:29).

Carl took me to the airport Sunday afternoon for my business trip. I met Sam at the gate. I had brought about fifteen books to read. Sam and I boarded and started reading when we got on the plane. He had been going back up to Harlem to the revival. It had been going on for months now. I told him Brother Darrel and several men were staying in my apartment next week and witnessing around the city.

Sam told me he knew Franklin, Grant, and Justin got my message because he heard them talking about it. Sam said Franklin and Grant would see Brother Darrel but Justin didn't want to hear what he had to say. He was just too busy. Sam said Franklin informed Justin that he would greet him and listen. I was surprised and elated at the same time.

Sam and I worked hard the whole next week. We got the new account in good order and ready to take over. We put in twelve hour days so we could get done and get back. We really missed Nick, but several of the client's partners worked with us and they would go out and bring back whatever we wanted. They were very gracious.

Sam and I got to drop a few seeds here and there. I gave our church card to about ten people. I told them it was like the card said, they were on call anytime and anywhere. Several of the people I talked to seemed interested and said they had many unsaved family members and friends. PALS needed to be taught everywhere. We just have no idea how short time is. The more I read the book on the rapture, the more I realized the unsaved were playing with fire—literally!

At night I would read about thirty pages before turning in. It was difficult to get in touch with Carl. He was going to the revival every night and taking people with him. I called him early Tuesday morning and he said Peggy, Eugene, Gilbert, and Tiffany were staying a couple of days. They were going to PALS and to the revival at night. Carl had invited them to stay at the house and he said he wouldn't have had it any other way.

He said he had bought a ton of groceries and Peggy and Tiffany were great cooks! He said Peggy was going to start selling Carl's Seasoning in her bakery. Eugene was about to have the other deli ready in a month or so. He was doing the shelves, counter, and all the inside work in the afternoon.

At breakfast Sam and I would talk about what we read and how God was showing us so much we had never seen before. I told him about being baptized in the Holy Spirit and now I was on fire to do the Lord's work. I had a book about being baptized in the Holy Spirit and gave it to Sam to read. We were still reading when we flew out Friday night.

Sam was driving back home to Mount Sandy and he and Jamie were going to pick out the invitations, talk to the minister, the photographer, and you name it. He was coming back into work Wednesday. He said Jamie was a wonderful Christian woman and God sure had blessed him in many ways. I agreed with him and told him we both were blessed and in many ways. We laughed wondering how blessed Carol felt after a week of dealing with Justin!

Carl was waiting at the airport for me. Sam and Carl talked a while. Carl had not missed a night of the revival and had to share his excitement with Sam. He said his guests had a big time. Gilbert and Carl went fishing in the afternoons with Harold. Peggy and Tiffany had to run to the antique stores on shopping sprees. They drove over to Lady Chandler's one afternoon. He said they told him they wept when they saw that statue of Jesus and all the angels in the baptismal gardens.

We told Sam he and Jamie would have to come up in the fall and spend some time with us. He said they were already looking at an apartment not far from mine, and Amber Lake would make a great getaway in the fall. We finally said bye to Sam and left for Amber Lake. It was still cool out, but this was an exceptionally nice day.

Oh, it was good to get home! I had to go look at the puppies. They were so cute! We unpacked and put everything up. Carl cooked two huge steaks on the grill and I fixed a salad and baked potatoes. We ate a delicious dinner out in the gazebo.

Carl had put his lounge chair out there just like he said he would. He said he would lie out there with a tall glass of iced tea, relax, and think about me. Boy, had I missed being here with him! I imagined how Sam felt being five hours away from Jamie. He wasn't even home yet! We watched the sun set over Amber Lake and then came in.

I couldn't wait until tomorrow. I called Brother Darrel and asked him what happened with Franklin, Grant, and Justin. He said when he went to my office he saw Faune first and talked with her. She took him in to see Franklin. He talked with Franklin and he said Franklin agreed with him about making a decision and he had been dealing with these feelings in his heart for a long time now. Brother Darrel wanted to lead him right then, but Franklin wanted to wait until he saw the preacher at his wife's church. He told Darrel this preacher had been praying for him for years and years. He wanted to go there and make a public commitment when Robbie, his daughter Julie, and Grant were there. He said Robbie and Julie were out of town visiting Robbie's only sister. They would be back the following week.

He told Darrel he had seen a change in me spiritually and he knew it was wonderful for me. He said that made him know how real God was and how He changed people's lives. He knew it was time for him and Grant to turn around and live for God like they were supposed to. He confessed to Brother Darrel this had been going on for generations in his family and he was putting a stop to it as far as his family was concerned. He said Robbie, Julie, and all her family were saved, but none of the men he was related to by blood were saved.

Brother Darrel told me he told Franklin he could accept Jesus today and still go and make a public commitment like he planned. Franklin wanted to wait against Brother Darrel's pleading and Brother Darrel had to let it go. They shook hands and Franklin took him to see Grant.

Brother Darrel said Grant and him talked and Grant listened and talked about how he felt about the revival in Harlem. He told me that Grant was almost persuaded, but would not make a commitment (Acts 26:28). He told me he pleaded with Grant and told him that tomorrow might be too late. Grant listened and thought about it, but he didn't do anything. Darrel finally realized he had to go on. Grant was teetering the entire time, but just wouldn't make a decision. He said he wanted to go to his wife's church and talk with her minister.

Same story, the wife's preacher had been praying for him and he wanted to go there with his wife. That was fine if it wasn't too late and if the Holy Spirit was on them and if they did make a commitment. They might die, and never feel the Holy Spirit on them again, or they might get back in their busy little world and it might never happen. They shook hands and Grant took him in to see Justin.

Brother Darrel said Justin was very uncomfortable and after he talked to him he told Darrel about the men in his family. He told him all of them for generations had been very successful, hard-working professionals. They were very well thought of in the community they lived and played an important role in its development and well-being. They were all very happy and life was smooth and good to them. In other words, what more could he possibly ask for in this life?

Brother Darrel told him it was the decision he made in this life that determined where he would spend eternity. Justin said he believed God was a good God and would not send someone to hell who was a person of good works (Eph. 2:9). He said he didn't have to make a decision because God had blessed him and must be taking care of him as good as his life was.

Brother Darrel showed him Ephesians 2:8–9 and told him you could not be saved by good works, only grace. He said Justin got very uncomfortable with him after reading that. He told Justin not making a decision was making a decision. He said Justin looked at his watch and said he had to be at the airport in one hour to pick up his cousin. He shook his hand and thanked him for coming to talk to him.

Brother Darrel left the office and went to talk to Nick at his deli. Angelina was there and was thrilled to see him and she knew why he was there. He said Nick came running out and was carrying a load of food. He apologized and said thirteen people were waiting on late lunches already. He said he didn't have time to talk to him today, maybe another time, and ran out of the deli. Brother Darrel said Angelina just sat down and cried. He said he felt so sorry for her. He told her we were all praying for Nick, but he had to stop running from God. Angelina told him he had been running all of his life. She said Satan had a fire under him and he would end up in the fire if he kept running from God. She couldn't understand why he didn't see it. She told him all their children were saved and so concerned for their father. He had had many opportunities and had run from them all. Brother Darrel prayed with her and told her someone would be back next week.

Brother Darrel said he then went over to Herring's Business Equipment and met with Mr. Herring. He introduced himself and he said Mr. Herring put his hand up like a stop sign and said, "You are not one of those religious fanatics my ex-wife sent are you?" Brother Darrel told him that he came as a request from Carl and that he had been on our prayer list. Mr. Herring told Brother Darrel he did not care to waste his time or Brother Darrel's time. He said he was a very busy man and turned and walked away.

I told Brother Darrel I appreciated what all he had done and he said it was a privilege for him because he always did what the Lord wanted him to do. He said there wasn't anything more important than witnessing to people. He just had to shake the dust off his feet and go on (Mark 6:11). He said the next day he contacted Honey over at Tilly's and talked to her and Eric about having PALS started in the back of Tilly's. I told him I had called her several weeks ago and told her about PALS and they wanted to have the classes there and have Sharon and Kimberly come in too. He said Sharon and Kimberly were set for two meetings there today and tomorrow. I was so excited!

He said they spent Thursday night in my apartment and were coming back to Amber Lake Monday morning. He laughed and said all of them had left my apartment Thursday afternoon and he passed Sharon and Kimberly coming back into Amber Lake. Honey and Eric were real excited about PALS. They told him they were both saved, and that the Lord had given them such peace over Kent's death and wanted them to go about His work.

Honey knew several widows who were having problems with grief, and she knew Kimberly could help them. She told him many ladies who were obsessed with their weight and Sharon could help them. Brother Darrel said Honey and Eric were two special people and she had passed out all the church cards I had sent her. I told Darrel I had given her at least fifty.

Honey and Eric wanted to go back up to church Sunday with Sharon and Kimberly to Harlem. They were going Sunday morning, staying in Harlem, and Sylvia and some other ladies were having a big dinner after church. Carol and Faune were going up there too. Honey told me she and Eric were really looking forward to seeing them. They were staying for the revival Sunday night.

All this just thrilled me. Everything that was taking place was amazing! All of our lives had changed in less than a year. I felt like something even more amazing was getting ready to happen. The Holy Spirit was pouring it on all of us in all realms of our lives! People were being saved left and right. Some people were running left and right too.

"I've got some more good news for you," Brother Darrel said.

"What is it?" I asked.

"Well, the last person I saw that day was Mike down at the cab station. I went in and introduced myself. We remembered each other from your wedding. We talked and when I asked him if he knew Jesus he told me he knew who He was and what He came to do. I asked him if he wanted to accept Him as his Lord and Saviour. He began to weep and several other taxi drivers saw this and they began to pay attention to what was happening. He repented of his sins and repeated the sinner's prayer after me and it was quite a moving moment for all of us in there," he admitted.

I felt tears filling my eyes and then Brother Darrel continued, "When we finished I started talking to the other men who had gathered around and two of them accepted Jesus too. It was quite an evening!" Brother Darrel announced.

"Oh, I can't believe it! Thank you, Jesus!" I exclaimed. I was so happy! "Three souls for heaven!" I told Darrel.

"Yes, that is right!" Brother Darrel laughed. I was so elated I could barely be still. I was walking back and forth with the phone. I told Brother Darrel, "See, what if you had given up after the first few stops? You shook the dust off your feet and just kept going and three people were saved!"

Brother Darrel was going back to the revival tonight in Springfield and he and Judy were both taking carloads. We laughed about that. I told him Carl and I would be going and would try to bring some people. I thanked him and he said there was nothing more rewarding than being able to lead the lost to Christ. I could agree with that, although I had never done it. That made me think again. I had never personally lead anyone to Christ, and that began to weigh heavy on me. What a rewarding experience that must be!

Carl and I worked around the house the next morning. We sat and watched the puppies a little while. We told the boys to come down and see them. They walked down the road with Harold. They all sat around and watched them. Carl went on and told them he was going to give them the one they wanted. They were beside themselves. Harold wanted to pay for one and Carl told him he wanted to give them one. They were always there to help Carl take care of the dogs or whatever he needed. He said the boys meant a lot to him and he loved seeing them happy.

Carl asked them if they wanted to go to revival and Glenn told Carl he had two friends that wanted to go. Carl said he would be glad to take them if they wanted to go. David had two friends that wanted to go and I agreed to take them. That was fine with Harold. We told them to call their friends and we would both go around and pick them up and take them for pizza before the meeting. They headed on back home and thanked us for the puppy they would get. They were so excited. They couldn't stop smiling and talking about it.

We picked up everyone and headed for Springfield. We ate at a pizza buffet and all the boys were having a ball. We went on to church and I knew some of these boys wouldn't know what to think of the service. Several of them didn't even go to church. The young people loved going and they wanted to know what it was like to experience a touch from the Holy Spirit. Well, there was nothing like it. Of course, there is nothing like what God can do anyway!

One of David's friends and one of Glenn's friends went up and accepted Christ. Hallelujah! We were full of joy all the way home and they were excited! This was thrilling for us, and they were excited knowing they were saved. Those boys said they didn't know church could be so much fun. They had no idea. One of them said it was way better than playing video games. I was glad to hear that!

On Sunday morning Carl and I talked about all the revival excitement while we ate breakfast. We were right in the middle of seeing the Holy Spirit moving and we were so on fire. We were seeing people coming out of wheelchairs. We were seeing sad faces changed to happy faces. People were coming in there heavy laden and leaving with huge weights taken off their shoulders. All things are possible through God . . . all things (Matt. 19:26).

We went to church and there was excitement there. Eleven more people were baptized that morning. There were going to be five baptisms that evening! Relatives of some of our church members couldn't be there in the morning, but they could be there at night. Thirty-one people were being baptized in Springfield that morning. It was unreal and awesome at the same time.

Brother Darrel and Judy were so caught up in the movement of God they had insurmountable energy and power. You could feel it through the church. There were thirty minutes of testimonies that were personal and written ones that were sent in. Eight testimonies were from the city. Three of them were called in.

Mike was one of them. He told Brother Darrel his restless spirit had been settled and he was totally at peace. The whole world looked different to him now. He said he had gathered his whole family together Saturday night so he could tell them about accepting Jesus. They all met at his mother's. He took his girlfriend along, and none of them had any idea what he was going to say.

He said he stood in front of all of them and wept and told them what happened and he said all of them hugged him and wept with joy. He said his one nephew was not saved, but upon seeing Mike's testimony, he told them he wanted to know Jesus too. His nephew's father, Mike's brother, lead him to Christ right there in front of all of them.

Mike and his nephew were going up in front of their church this morning. They were going to be baptized tonight because that was what they wanted to do. He said it was so emotional for all of them they went through a tissue box and had to bring out several roles of toilet paper to dry their tears on. He said after they all dried their tears they started preparing a feast for Sunday dinner like it was Christmas. He said everyone in their family was saved now.

Brother Darrel began to weep and all of us did too. He was the one who lead Mike to the Lord. Who knows what happened to the other men Darrel lead to Christ at the taxi company that night!

After the service many of us went to Grinder's Mill. It was beautiful outside with everything in bloom. Susan and Casey said they would be at Lakeside this week. Casey, Gary, and Jesse had to do the churchyard this week. Susan was preparing for several meetings she and Casey had later in the week. Brother Darrel and Judy said they were busy at the church and the lunch crowd was growing too.

Judy said people were coming in from the surrounding little towns now. Cassie and Joy and their families were excited about all that was happening in Amber Lake too. They really enjoyed hearing about the lunches, It is Done Ministries, and Your Loss Is His Gain. A lot was taking place at Amber Lake. Cassie and Joy were going to clean up in the church early in the week so they could devote the rest of the week to helping Judy.

They were having to start cooking at eight in the morning now. Nancy's Cafe was still packed, so Amber Lake was drawing quite a lunch crowd. Judy said she had finally left the bank and Leanne took over her job full-time. She was trying to get Wayne, Reggie, and herself over to the lunches or church, but to no avail.

I asked Judy where April was today. She said she was on a mission trip in Honduras. I was so surprised she was down there. Judy said, "She went with some people from her college and they all couldn't wait to go. It was a medical team that went and she is helping with the toddlers while families see the doctor."

"She loves doing that and she will be gone ten days," Judy said. "She told us she knows God wants her to go in the mission field and this is her second mission trip. This is her first one in a foreign country. She said it is hot and dusty there and there is no electricity. Some of the ladies at church made her long, full skirts to wear. She has to have her legs covered and then she can wear T-shirts and such. They do not wear shorts, slacks, or skirts that show their legs," Judy informed me.

"We gathered a bunch of supplies for her to take to the people this week. We went to a wholesale outlet and bought combs, toothpaste, toothbrushes and such. We don't realize how lucky we are in this country! Everyone should go to a country like that once just to see how blessed we are here!" Judy proclaimed. All of us at the table agreed with that!

We all had a wonderful fellowship and departed for the afternoon. Carl and I got back home and there was a message from Carol. I called her and she said a meeting with Anderson, Inc., had been moved up from Thursday to Tuesday and we had to prepare for it. "Is that the one we were going to work on every day right up until Thursday morning?" I asked.

"Yes! Can you believe it?" Carol replied.

"Good grief!" I burst out. Carl got up from his recliner and was standing there looking at me with the Sunday paper in his hand. I started laughing and told her about Carl.

She laughed and said, "Tell Carl not to stand there, just go get your bags packed!" I started laughing too.

She said Franklin, Grant, and Justin were in the office today. "I had gone up to Pine Mountain yesterday and Franklin called me about Anderson and I left Glenn up there and came back. Glenn called me a few minutes ago and he and Russ just found out their song they wrote last November, 'I'll Meet You in the Clouds,' has been released and will be playing on the radio next week!"

"You are kidding!" I shrieked. "Isn't that great?" Carol laughed. She was so excited.

"They are about to have another one ready to cut. They'll be sitting out on Russ's front porch in those rockers, playing their guitars, and writing this week. This week worked out good, because we will be working so late I wouldn't get to see him anyway," Carol said.

"I hope it is not windy. They will dehydrate since they drink out of their paperweights," I said as we both laughed, remembering how they sit their coffee cups or glasses on top of their stacks of papers out on the porch. We both talked about how beautiful it would be looking all over the countryside from up there. "What song are they working on now? I asked.

"'You Better Be Ready,'" she said. "Great title and great message. If the rapture doesn't come, then death will and we don't know which one will come first!" I professed.

I told her I would drive straight in from Amber Lake in the morning. "You didn't have to call Sam did you?" I asked.

"No, thank heavens! Franklin said we could handle it. Sam is not coming back until Wednesday. He and Jamie are getting everything lined up for the wedding and that takes a lot of planning!" Carol said.

"Yeah, he told me they would be very busy every day in order to get everything done. Jamie is shopping for her dress Monday and he is picking out the tuxes and all. He said they were going shopping for his ring Tuesday. He has to drive all the way back here Tuesday night from Mount Sandy," I said. We talked a while about Anderson, Inc., and I told her I would see her first thing in the morning.

I told Carl I had to leave in the morning since the major meeting we were working on was moved up two days. We had to meet over at Mr. Randall's office at ten o'clock Tuesday morning. Carl couldn't think which building that was. I told him it was that tall, beautiful building with all the smoked glass in it.

"Good grief, you and I can't even remember the names of the buildings anymore. We used to know every building, street, restaurant, you name it!" I laughed.

"Yep, we must be getting old!" Carl laughed.

"Anyway, four partners of Anderson, Inc., are flying in their company jet and taking a helicopter to the top of the glass building for the meeting. We had better have our act together!" I stated.

I called Jan to see how they were doing. She said the kids had just gotten out of school and were having a ball. She said she had gotten real brave and was going to wallpaper her bedroom. She was tired of looking at the same walls and saw some beautiful wallpaper and bought it. "I have never put up wallpaper before, so I had one of my friends show me how," she laughed. She said the girls were busy and every morning they were getting ready to go somewhere or babysit for someone. She said Ray and Michael were working on the garden in the morning before it got too hot. They really enjoyed that.

Carl called Alvin this afternoon to check on all of them. He said everyone was fine and the three brothers were going down to Nashville this week together. Don and John had written several songs and they were going to a studio to record them and see how they sounded. He told Carl he needed to fly in as soon as possible to practice and get ready to record. After he hung up I called Mom and Dad and then Sis, Brian, and Thomas. Sis told me they were about to call me and had some fantastic news. Brian and Thomas got on the phone and told me they had been saved at their church service this morning. Now all my family was saved! Praise God!

By the time Carl and I talked to everyone and I got my things packed it was time to eat dinner. Carl cooked a couple of steaks and we ate out in the gazebo again. May was a beautiful time of the year. The year was just going so fast! Carl said he would come out here in the mornings and bring his iced tea and lay back in his lounge and have devotion time. He said it was really peaceful that time of day.

"I see Harold and the boys go by in the boat about that time. They are out of school now and they go fishing in the morning. Mary is cooking pies and cakes galore now that they are home during the day. I'll have to walk over there and sample them everyday I guess!" Carl laughed. "Trish told me over lunch she is working on her fall line of makeup already and has the huge worktable upstairs covered up. She is picking out colors, textures and such," I added.

"She sure has a beautiful room to work in, overlooking that lake and the woods both," I said.

We went over to Lakeside that evening. Millie and Nancy were there. It was great seeing them. Nancy said Adon and Ian were working at her cafe full-time during the summer. April would be once she got back from Honduras. I asked her where Max was and she said there was no way she could get him to church. She said Roger, Wayne, Jack, Reggie, Leanne, and Max drove up to Clifton Cape early this morning to play golf all day.

Millie said she was over at the cemetery in the mornings this whole week. She was putting flower arrangements on the graves because of

Memorial Day and all. She had many orders, and she was very busy getting them ready.

We had a wonderful service and seven people were baptized that morning and five more people gave their hearts to Jesus that night. Two of them were over sixty years old and one was over seventy. You talk about tears. I didn't know what was going on in the world, but it was something. Sin was running more rampant by the day, yet people were being saved by the masses. If you weren't saved the way the Holy Spirit was moving, you were determined you weren't going to be in that number. The Bible says "narrow is the path and few are the number," so I figured there must be a lot of people that are going to be left behind or going to hell (Matt. 7:14).

Carl and I got back and watched the puppies for a while and then decided to turn in fairly early since I had to head out of here about 6:00 A.M. We sat down and looked at all of our wedding pictures again. I told Carl he needed to get all of our shells in the garage and have the sand hosed out and then let them dry. I had bought a huge glass jar to put them all in. I wanted to sit them in the den beside some of the pictures from our honeymoon.

We put our wedding pictures up and went back to the bedroom. Carl stretched out on the bed and told me he had not been feeling well lately. He asked me to press down on his left side. I did that and my heart jumped a beat as I felt a huge lump in there.

"Carl, how long has that been there?" I shouted.

"Oh, for almost two months, but it has gotten larger in the last few weeks," he sheepishly admitted.

"Why on earth haven't you seen a doctor?" I scolded.

"Well, I thought maybe I had gotten a hernia or that it would go away," he said.

"You see a doctor first thing tomorrow morning!" I demanded. I was almost shaking.

Carl fell asleep. I couldn't go to sleep. I laid there thinking about that horrible lump. Surely, God didn't arrange everything so wonderful in our life for something horrible to happen. My mind was entertaining all kinds of awful thoughts. I got up and wiped my tears away. I remembered where He said in the Bible not to worry or fear (Ps. 23:4 and 27:1, Rom. 8:15). I had to turn it over to Him and leave it there. What good would worrying do? Worry and fear were the devil's playground.

Not only that, look at all the healing Scriptures and look at all the miracles I had seen in the last week. There were people that gave testimonies about malignant tumors disappearing. All of a sudden I heard in my mind "maybe they were faking it and lying to you" (John 10:10). I knew that was from Satan! God wouldn't put those thoughts in my mind!

I went in the den and got down on my knees in front of the window that overlooked the woods. I guess that was my own prayer spot. I asked God to heal Carl and let him be a testimony. I praised Him for all His promises and I knew the truth would set me free (John 8:32). I bound up Satan from our minds and bodies in the name of Jesus. I cast my cares on Him just like the Bible says and left them with Him to handle (Ps. 55:22). I knew I couldn't and didn't need to. I went back to bed and got a good night's sleep.

I left early in the morning and kissed Carl goodbye. I told him I loved him and he said "Me too," and rolled over and went back to sleep. I laughed to myself. I got in my car and took off for the city. All the way there I remembered the signs and wonders of God I had seen in those revivals. God put me in remembrance of all the healings I had seen. This is what Casey and Susan taught! Praise God, I had believers all around me. People that believed all things were possible—all things (Matt. 19:26).

I knew with great conviction that no doctor, cancer, or any disease has the last word. Doctors might tell you what is there and cancer is real, but Jesus paid for our healing as well as everything else. He didn't miss anything on the cross! He died for it all. When it is your time to die, you will die. We are not to decide or determine that, only He is. It is not for us to determine why or when someone is to die (Heb. 9:27).

I got in my office and Carol came in. She had a great time up in Harlem yesterday. I told her I better call my apartment before Sharon and Kimberly left. Carol went out to get ready for our nine o'clock meeting. I called at my apartment and Sharon answered. We talked and she told me about the weekend. They were at Tilly's for two days with Honey and Eric. She said a total of ninety-two women showed up and twenty-seven of them were lead to Christ. "Wow!" I exclaimed.

Sharon said it wouldn't have done any good to put makeup on them, they would have cried it off anyway. They were going back in two weeks. She said she and Honey, Eric, Kimberly, Faune, and Carol had a great time up in Harlem. I thought that was great. She said she and Kimberly were leaving in about an hour. They were going to catch up on speeches, paperwork, and phone calls at the office. The only break they would take would be to go to Lakeside for lunch.

I told her about Carl and for them to pray for him. She said they would and not to worry or fear anything. I told her I loved them as well as all my friends at Lakeside and how important they were to me. She said they loved Carl and I both and to just keep doing what the Lord wanted me to do. I told her I would and we said bye and hung up.

Carol came by and off we went to the boardroom. Franklin introduced us to Kelly, Franklin's niece. She came in from Baltimore and was Franklin's sister's daughter. She had been in a consulting firm for a number of years and was very well adept to the business, which was typical of this family. She had quite a record of being a top-notch partner in the firm she was with.

Franklin said she would be working with us for awhile. He had already told Carol, Sam, and I if she liked it here he would make it well worth it for her to stay in Manhattan. Franklin loved family, and it thrilled him when Justin had joined us. Now, it looked like Kelly might. I know one thing, Franklin would want her to prove herself as a solid partner first, niece or no niece. There was plenty of room for her here and great opportunities! We all introduced ourselves to her and shook her hand and welcomed her. She was all business, but that was all right. Justin and her were two peas in a pod and were very close.

We dove into our meeting and worked until one o'clock. Everyone left the boardroom with their lunches after Nick delivered them and went back to their offices. I went to see Grant and thanked him for seeing Brother Darrel. He smiled and shook his head and whispered, "I was almost persuaded," and the phone rang and it was for him (Acts 26:28). He waved bye and had to take the call.

I went to Justin's office and he was in there eating lunch with Kelly. I told him I didn't want to interrupt, but I wanted to thank him for seeing Brother Darrel. He looked at me and forced a slight smile and said, "You're welcome," just to be courteous and then turned as to continue talking with Kelly. I knew she would ask Justin what all that was about.

I went on to Franklin's office and decided to turn back and see if Grant was off the phone. I heard Kelly tell Justin, "Doesn't she know this is a business and not a church! You need a religious fanatic around here like you need a hole in the head!" she affirmed.

"Well, Franklin likes her, but she is leaving anyway. You catch on and show Franklin you can handle the load and she can go home as far as I'm concerned," Justin informed Kelly.

I had stopped dead in my tracks. I immediately turned and quietly headed back to Franklin's office. I couldn't believe my ears and was a little bit upset with both of them. The Lord suddenly put me in remembrance of when I did that. I know I had thought the same thing about "religious" people just like Kelly, but at least I didn't say it! Then suddenly I heard the Lord speak in my spirit, "I know you didn't say it, but I heard you think it."

"Oh my! Oh, Lord!" Then I knew what I had known all along . . . but now I really knew that I knew. The Lord knows our every thought and there is no fooling Him, for He knows our heart (Luke 9:47 and 11:17)!

Now I was going to see Franklin. Was Franklin going to think like Justin and Kelly? Should I go and see Franklin or not? Then the Lord spoke to me again, "Just go about my work. Their thoughts are not your concern." Oh, my Lord, thank you for your guidance. Thank you, Lord!

I knocked on Franklin's door and he said, "Come in." When he saw it was me he smiled and told me to take a seat. I did and then I told him I appreciated him spending some time with Brother Darrel. He told me he was going to his wife's church this Sunday.

"Maybe you shouldn't wait until Sunday," popped out of my mouth before I knew it. He looked at me and grinned and said he wasn't planning on anything happening to him before Sunday. "No one ever does," popped out of my mouth. He looked at me and he knew I was concerned for him. I proceeded to tell him what I saw when I stood at Kent's casket. I told him I didn't want that to happen to him and tears began to fall.

"Oh, you big baby," he kidded me and jumped up from his chair and came over and put his arm around me. He took his fine linen hanky out of his back pocket and came toward me and said, "Here, blow, and guess what? You can keep the hanky," and we both started laughing. I dried my tears on his hanky and held it in my hand.

"Franklin, you have to listen to me," I whimpered.

"I'll call Robbie's pastor right now. You're right. None of us ever know. I know without a shadow of a doubt what I want and need to do," he said.

"Then let me lead you to Christ right now," I announced. Franklin looked at me. He knew I meant business.

"I appreciate what you are saying, but I want to be in Robbie's church when I do this," he informed me.

We both looked at each other a minute. "All right then. I am right here if you change your mind. Remember today is the day of salvation!" I proclaimed and smiled, closing the door behind me.

I hurried and dried my tears with his hanky and delicately tucked it in my suit pocket. I sure didn't want anyone seeing me leaving Franklin's office crying. I sure didn't know I would cry! I don't know what came over me! I took the elevator down and out the front door. Maybe I just needed to go outside a minute. I stepped out on the sidewalk and looked down towards Nick's. There was Kimberly in there! I walked down there to make sure it was her, thinking my red eyes were playing tricks on me.

"Kimberly, what are you doing? I thought you and Sharon were at Amber Lake!" I exclaimed while I hugged her.

"Well, Sharon left this morning. The Lord told me to stay here and see Nick and he named several others I needed to see today. It was out of the clear blue, but you know I always do what the Lord tells me to do. So honey, here I am!" she laughed. Angelina was standing behind the counter listening to her, just smiling like hope for her lost husband had arrived again.

Kimberly said she was waiting for Nick to return so she could talk to him. She said Sylvia had planned on taking her back to Amber Lake tonight, but Sylvia's daughter had to use her car at the last minute to go out of town.

I told Kimberly to take my car and Sylvia could bring it back tomorrow. "Sylvia has to be at church in the morning though," Kimberly stated.

"Just let Sylvia bring it back to my apartment garage when she is done. I won't need it tomorrow anyway."

"Oh honey, me driving around in that gold Jag, what are people going to think!" she laughed.

"You are a King's kid!" I told her. We both laughed and I handed her my car keys. Kimberly said Sylvia would park it in my garage before noon tomorrow, since she had to be at work by then. Sylvia worked about five minutes from my apartment. I told her bye and she thanked me and I told her I would be praying for Nick.

Carol and I ate dinner together in my office. She got her radio and turned to the gospel station and we were hoping we would hear, "I'll Meet You In the Clouds," but we didn't. I told her about Carl and that lump in his side. I called him while she was sitting there. She wanted to know what the doctor said too. He said the doctor sent him for X rays and an ultrasound this morning. They would have something back by tomorrow afternoon. I sighed and knew the doctor wanted to see what this was as soon as possible.

"Where did you have your tests done, sweetie?" I asked.

"At Highland Center in Springfield," he said. He said he was not worried about it and was going to go to bed early. He had been in town all day long and was tired. I kidded him and asked him what he would do if he was back in the city again. He said he didn't want to think about it.

He said Don had called him and John, Alvin, and Don were practicing the new songs and everything was going smoothly. They wanted Carl to come in, practice with them, and be ready to record in a week or so. Carl said it would be good to be singing southern gospel again. After all, it had been over twenty years since they had sung together professionally! Carl said all the brothers wished they had not waited so long to get back together and sing for the Lord. They all had great voices the Lord had gifted them with and they needed to be about His work. Their songs would be a testimony to those who heard them. They would be in the studio again tomorrow.

Carl said he would be in the gazebo in the morning having his devotion time, then go back to the doctor in the afternoon. We talked for a while and I told him I missed him and he said, "Me too." I told him I loved him and he said "Me too." Carol was over there looking at me and I could read her lips saying "Me too," almost exactly when Carl would say it. Yep, she knew Carl all right! She was concerned like I was about this lump, but we both knew God could handle anything.

We all worked until eight o'clock. We had to be here at seven in the morning to finalize everything. Things had come together well. We would leave a little after nine in the morning and walk over there and get ready to brief. It was only two blocks away.

We all said goodnight and left. I walked out on the street and looked down towards Nick's. I saw Angelina in there and thought I would walk down to see her. I went down and asked her if Kimberly was able to talk to Nick. She started crying and said Nick came back, loaded up with another order, ran out while saying he appreciated it but he would have to see her another time.

"Where is he now?" I asked.

"He is across the street. He's delivering eight people a late dinner over at Nytel, Inc.," she whimpered. I told her to start praying. I went over to the building and pressed the button for the elevator. When it opened Nick came out.

"Diane, what are you doing here?" Nick asked in amazement.

"I'm here to see you," I answered.

"To see me?" he said.

"Yes, you and I need to talk," I said as I motioned for Nick to come over to the side of the elevators. I started telling him about me and where I was about a year ago and all that had happened. I told him how important it was to come to know Jesus in his heart. I told him how Kent ran from the Lord and I told him what Kimberly and I saw when we stood by his casket. I told him he was running and he was running into the fire if he didn't come to know Jesus.

He looked at me and I asked him if he was ready to know Jesus. His eyes filled with tears and he said, "Yes, I am ready."

"Hallelujah!" I shouted. I knew the sinner's prayer and asked him to repeat after me in a prayer and I took both his hands and we closed our eyes and we prayed together and both of us shed tears.

After we had prayed I hugged him and told him whatever happened, he would be in heaven for eternity. He wept and we sighed a sigh of relief at the same time. I told him he needed to go tell Angelina. She loved him very much and was so very concerned about his salvation.

We left the building and I waited to catch a taxi while he walked across the street. Angelina was looking at him through the glass front of their deli. I saw him start talking to her about the time a taxi pulled up for me and I saw her jump and put her arms around him and hug him. They were still hugging as I drove away. What an awesome God we serve!

I got to my apartment and as always I had a thank-you note from whoever stayed there. I saved them and kept them in my top dresser drawer in my bedroom. Some nights when I got home I would look at them and it made me feel good about doing something to help lead people to Christ. Now I knew how fantastic it was to have that opportunity. Just fantastic! Oh, Lord, if I leave here tonight, praise you for letting me have this experience.

I called Carl and told him what happened with Nick. "Well, that is wonderful!" he said. He was already in the bed. I told him to call me the minute he got in from the doctor. "It may not be the exact minute," he said. I laughed to myself.

"I miss you and I love you," I said.

"Me too," he replied.

"Until I see you at home," and I sent a kiss through the phone and said bye and hung up.

The next morning was a beautiful day! We were all in the office at seven o'clock. Franklin called me in his office and I went on down there. When I entered he told me to take a seat.

"I called Robbie's pastor and I am going to church service tomorrow night and give my profession of faith then. All of my family have made plans to be there," he told me.

"Franklin, that is great. Now if nothing happens all day today, all night tonight, and all day tomorrow, you'll be just fine," I said.

We both looked at each other again. "Well, that is definitely what I am going to do. I just thought you would like to know," he stated.

"I want to know you will be in heaven for all eternity, Franklin," I told him. We stood there again looking at each other.

"Well, that is definitely where I want to be too," he said.

He looked down at my blazer and noticed his fine linen hanky from yesterday about to fall from my pocket. I forgot I had put it there and had grabbed the same blazer this morning. Franklin smiled softly and looked at me and said, "Don't worry, you won't have to wipe away anymore tears."

"We better get busy while we are still down here in the concrete jungle for this important meeting. As you well know, if we land this client, it will be the largest account in the history of this company!" he smiled. I smiled back at him and he patted me on the shoulder and whispered, "And I know we can land it. After all, we are the best. I'll see you in the boardroom at eight o'clock."

"OK, Franklin. Thank you," I said as I turned and walked back to my office. Carol and I walked in the boardroom together. Justin and Kelly barely looked up long enough to acknowledge us. Grant was friendlier, but both Justin and Kelly were his first cousins and he tended to favor their opinions and objectives. They were certainly all business! I felt sorry for Carol if she was to be the only one left here. Of course, Sam was coming back and Franklin was still in charge and that was good!

We rounded everything up and Franklin said we better get going. "Pack up your briefcases and we'll hit the street," Franklin announced. We all got on the elevator and out to the street we went. Franklin and Grant, then Carol and I behind them, and Justin and Kelly behind us. Six of us heading to the meeting, briefcases in hand marching down the busy streets of Manhattan. We came around the corner and were walking down the street beside the glass building.

Suddenly, a car with no driver came full speed around the curve, hit a light pole, and another came from across the street with no driver! Franklin turned madly and yelled, "Get out of the way!" Justin and Kelly were standing back there in shock.

Franklin and Grant only saw Carol and Diane's briefcases lying together on the sidewalk and one tear-stained fine linen hanky. He looked frantically for Diane and Carol when suddenly there was a huge crash from on top of the building.

There was a helicopter on fire, coming over the side! It burst into flames knocking glass out as it came down. People were screaming and running everywhere! Franklin and Grant ran to the front door of the building dodging two more cars without drivers. They watched in horror as falling glass impaled Kelly's body, going straight through her. Justin ran and was hit by a car and thrown on top of the hood of another car. He tried to get up when the remains of the fiery helicopter came crashing down on top of him and the surrounding cars. Franklin screamed, "My God, what is happening!" and pushed Grant into the building to avoid three more driverless cars coming across the sidewalk. One careened into the building shattering glass throughout the grand entrance! People were running everywhere screaming and yelling! It was total chaos!

Franklin and Grant ran into the hallway, breathless and in great wonderment and shock as to what happened. Franklin had just seen his niece and nephew brutally killed! "Grant, did you see what happened to Diane and Carol? Where did they go?" he wailed between deep breaths as he leaned against the wall.

"I don't know! It was like they just disappeared from the earth!" he cried.

The Hour that Followed

THERE WERE MULTITUDES OF DEATHS AND FRANTIC, BEWILDERED
people. Many were screaming for loved ones, friends and family who
disappeared in the twinkling of an eye (1 Cor. 15:52). Many people
were in shock, staggering about like the insane. This had happened all
over the world. It was a horrible time to be alive and it would only get
worse (Matt. 24:21–22).

Franklin had made it back to the hallway to call his office. Faune
was left to answer the phones instead of attending the meeting this
morning. He called and the line was busy. On the other end, there was
just a dangling phone. Franklin tried to call his wife and there was no
answer. He tried to call his daughter and there was no answer. Grant
called his wife—no answer. All of them were gone.

At Herring's Business Equipment, the store was in shambles as a
driverless car had gone through the front window. Mr. Herring lay
behind the cash register with a bullet through his heart. The cash
register was open above him and all the cash was gone. Just a few coins
and dollar bills lay across his dead body, dropped by the looters who
killed and robbed him.

At Diane's apartment building, there was a half-eaten blueberry
bagel with cream cheese left lying on the sidewalk by the ornate front
doors. Guess who Gilbert met with cream cheese on both sides of his
face, smiling and laughing?

Over at Peggy's Piddl'n, in the kitchen, a tray of freshly cooked bagels lay on the floor. In the case there was one plain bagel and one whole-wheat missing in the perfect arrangement. The back door to the case was still open and there was a blueberry bagel laying right outside the case on the floor with one big bite taken out of it.

On 34th Street in Manhattan, there was a taxi sitting in the front of a building with no driver to be found. The window was down and the radio was playing, "I'll Meet You In the Clouds." Car number sixty-eight wouldn't report back in today.

At Nick's Deli, cold cuts lay all over the counter and Styrofoam containers were open and ready to be filled. A half-written order was lying on the counter.

At Tilly's, an armful of clothes from a new shipment lay in the middle of the floor in the back. A lady that was trying on clothes was yelling, "Honey, what is all that noise out there! Was there a wreck? Honey? Eric? Honey!"

At the Baptist Church in Harlem, there was a gold Jag that had crossed over the sidewalk, gone up on the front steps and was sitting at the front doors of the church. No driver was present.

In a Nashville, Tennessee, recording studio, a technician yelled, "Alvin? John? Don? Hey, guys! Why did ya'll drop your head phones on the floor? Hey, where ya'll at? Come on now, this ain't funny no more?"

In Rockvale, Tennessee, at Ray and Jan's home, a rake was lying in the garden. A water hose ran wide open at garden's edge, making a huge mud hole. The shower upstairs was running, but no one was in it. The receiver was lying on the floor in the girls' room. A strip of wall-paper suddenly stopped halfway down a wall. Jan didn't have to worry about that bedroom anymore. Imagine how she loved the bedroom she had in her mansion now (John 14:2)!

On the front porch of Russ's chalet on Pine Mountain a guitar lay on the porch in front of one of the rockers. Another guitar lay in front of the other rocker with a spilled glass of iced tea beside it. Papers beside that rocker blew in the wind and off the balcony. Notes and words to "You Better Be Ready" were lifted up page by page and danced in the summer breeze.

In Honduras, there was an empty dirt playground outside a makeshift medical clinic filled with toddlers and one beautiful young lady seconds ago. A hand puppet lay in the dust along with a few old toys and dolls—broken and worn. Now they walk streets of pure gold where nothing is broken or worn.

In Clear Lake at Lady Chandler's estate, no one answered the door. In the memorial gardens the graves of Elliston and Lady Chandler were open and empty.

At Wilson's Jewelry at Mount Sandy, a lady helping a young couple pick out the groom's wedding ring wondered where they went. She thought maybe they stole the ring and ran out while she turned her back for a moment. The ring was on the counter. How could they have left that fast she wondered! "I just turned around and they were gone. They were such a happy couple and well, they just disappeared!" she told the owner. He looked at her, rather stunned and at that moment a ball of flames shot up from the town square. A small plane had crashed, and a car careened into their front door . . . no pilot, no driver, only complete havoc!

"Where is Charmaine?" the assistant manager at Thornton's Bed and Breakfast asked the cashier. "She was just back here folding linens and now she is gone. I mean gone, like disappeared!" she stated. Suddenly, several people stood up in horror as two empty boats on Silver Lake collided and blew up in flames. Charmaine was up at the Master's table, running her hand over the finest linen tablecloth she had ever seen or even imagined.

At Amber Lake Bank, Wayne was lying out on the sidewalk with a car over him, barely alive, yelling for help. Reggie was trying to get help, but there wasn't any! Leanne just sat at her desk and cried. She was talking to the two tellers when they suddenly disappeared in front of her eyes.

At Amber Lake City Hall, Roger and Jack were running about frantically. What had happened to their wonderful town? A huge truck had run into the gazebo, knocking down one end of it, while driverless cars crashed into store fronts and other cars.

Roger and Jack ran in Nancy's Cafe and there was a dishcloth left in the middle of one half-cleaned table. A cart holding dishes gathered from the tables had rolled into the wall. The kitchen was in flames and beyond control. No Nancy, Adon, or Ian. Ronnie Macon was standing outside the cafe in shock. He said Nancy was back there cooking when a car hit the front of her cafe. He told Roger that Peter Yantz and him yelled for her, but she never answered, or came out. They ran back there and Nancy was not there.

Roger and Jack ran into Millie's Florist. No Millie. Roger said he knew she would be at the cemetery. They ran to the cemetery. Many graves were open and the remains were gone. In front of Nancy's parents' graves were the decorations Millie had carried over to put on their headstones. Her parents' graves were burst open and empty. Roger was running around the cemetery yelling for Millie.

Jack picked up the different decorations. They were ones he knew his mother was working on. He picked up the one she showed him yesterday that she had made for his grandparents' graves and held it to his face and whispered, "Oh, Mom," and wept. Millie got to see her parents and loved ones burst out of their graves in their perfect bodies. That must have been something!

Over at Amber Lake Cemetery, people were flocking out to the river by the cross and they were on their knees praying and crying. It was a sight of total remorse!

At Amber Lake Real Estate, Max had just gotten back in town. He was out showing property when the couple he was talking to just disappeared! He made it back but had to cut around wrecked cars and cars turned over in ditches and along fence rows. Most of them had no drivers in them, but there were more injured people than Amber Lake's ambulance could handle! Nancy's was up in flames by now and there was no one in the fire station. Max ran down the street, dodging wrecked cars and some people staggering around in shock. He saw Reggie trying to get the car off of Wayne.

Wayne was dead now and Reggie finally sat on the ground beside his dead uncle, stared into space, rocked back and forth . . . whispering John 3:16.

The podium at Your Loss Is His Gain had papers on it, but no one standing behind it. In front of the podium was Kimberly's desk and a receiver lying in her chair.

Out in the churchyard at Lakeside Church Jesse was standing in amazement. He was cleaning the lake bank when he looked up and saw Gary's pushmower coming down the bank by itself! It went straight into the lake. He ran up to find Gary and ask him what on earth he was doing. As he went to find Gary he saw Casey's weedeater lying on the ground running. No one was in the churchyard. He ran to the church and across the parking lot. There was Ralph's car with the back door open and a sack of groceries lying in the parking lot. The sack was ripped from an obvious fall and milk was leaking out of the bag. Ralph was gone.

He ran in the back of the church and the vacuum cleaner was running and had stopped against the altar. He ran in the back where Susan studied and the window was open and the breeze was blowing the pages of her Bible to and fro. Susan was gone. He ran to Darrel's study. His Bible lay open on his desk and notes had been written. His ink pen was on the floor. Darrel was gone.

He heard noises in the kitchen. He ran in there hoping he would find them. All he found was a mixer running, smoke coming out of the oven, and water running out of the sink and all over the floor. He ran and turned off the oven and the water. He turned and saw where a handful of silverware had been dropped beside the table. He fell to his knees and wept.

At the Goodfellow home, there was a cake mix made from scratch sitting in a bowl with a raw egg on the top. No one was there to mix it. Upstairs there was a tray of eye shadows on the floor. Harold's fishing boat had run up on a bank with the motor still running. Five life jackets and fishing rods lay askew in the boat with lines dangling outside the boat.

At Carl's home, out in the gazebo there was a Bible lying on the chair and half a glass of iced tea beside it. Yes, Diane got to see Carl when she got home today. They were spared the terrible news about Carl's tests results. Of course, if the world as Carl and Diane knew it had gone on, they would have known to turn to Jesus in their time of need and healing. Now, she could only praise His precious name as she met Him in the clouds. She shouted, "You saved me, you spared me, you had mercy on me, and you prepared this mansion for me!" So in awe of Him, the King of Kings, she whispered, "I want to thank you, Jesus! I love you!" and of course, Carl said "Me too!"

CONCLUSION

⟶————————⟵

THE TIMES THAT FOLLOWED ON EARTH WERE OF GREAT TRIBULATION.
God poured out His wrath like one has never seen before (Rev. 9:6). The
church was absent from the earth, as it had been raptured (1 Thess. 1:10).
The anti-Christ appeared and people around the world believed he was the
one who would save them and they put their hope and trust in him.

Unfortunately, many bowed down to Satan himself as he tricked
and deceived the world (2 John 7:11). There was pain, anguish, and
suffering like there had never been.

There were many that did not take the mark of the beast, claiming
their profession in Christ during this time. They came in remembrance
of knowing who the true Saviour was by what they had heard, were
taught, or were witnessed to about. They lead others who would listen
to them. They could have escaped all this torment if they had accepted
Jesus before the Rapture. They died brutal deaths, but it was worth
being received into heaven and living there for eternity (Rev. 20:4).

Those who took the mark of the beast sealed their destiny of eternity
in hell (Rev. 19:20–21). God gives us our own free will. God does not
send anyone to hell. We decide whether we go to heaven or hell. We
make that decision and to not make a decision at all, is making a decision!

God provided Jesus, who died for all of our sins, so that when we
accept Him in our hearts as our personal Lord and Saviour, we shall be
saved! Today is the day of salvation . . . today!

A SINNER'S PRAYER

Dear Heavenly Father,

I know Jesus died on the cross for my sins. I am a sinner and ask for forgiveness and repent of my sins.

I confess with my mouth Jesus as my personal Lord and Saviour and believe in my heart that God raised Him from the dead and that I am saved. For whoever calls upon the name of the Lord shall be saved.

Thank You, Lord for saving me!

Signed _____

Date _____

MINISTRY CREDITS

For information on *Your Loss Is His Gain*, please contact:
Sharon Wilson
125C Hibiscus Street
Ashland City, TN 37015

For information on *It Is Done Ministries, Inc.* please contact:
It Is Done Ministries
Casey and Susan Dunn
425 Page Road, #G-1
Nashville, TN 37205

For CDs and audio tapes of *The Frost Brothers Quartet*,
please contact:
Don Frost
1-888-645-5357

For information on *Prepare and Lead Study (PALS)*,
please contact:
Pastor Darrel G. Whaley
Kingdom Ministries Worship Center
675 E. Jefferson Pike
Murfreesboro, TN 37130
(615) 895-3913

For information on *Jesus Is Lord Ministries*, please contact:
Jesus Is Lord Ministries
Charles Thompson, Evangelist
P.O. Box 719
Heber Springs, AR 72543-0719
(501) 362-7244

ABOUT THE AUTHOR

DIANE FROST KNEW SHE HAD A TALENT FOR WRITING SINCE SHE
was in grade school. She had not used her talent much; however, she
did write a true story about the death of her infant daughter, Tina
Carlene, and *Tina Is Ten Today* was published in *Home Life* magazine
in December 1991. In 1996 God told her to write *Be Ready!* God
wrote the book through her and now He has asked her to write
another book. It will be completely different than *Be Ready!* but it
will be just as enjoyable and suspenseful. She knows that already, but
only when she sits down to write it will God unravel the mystery this
one is to be.

The Father Who dwells in me does the work. (John 14:10 NKJV)

She was saved at the age of thirty-three and has gone through many
growth spurts on her walk with God. She has prayed for God to lead
her to do what He wants her to do with her life. What an exciting
journey it has been and it is more exciting every day! She lives in
Tennessee with her husband, Carl, and their four sons. Their daughter
and son-in-law are attending seminary to become missionaries.